PIPING HOT
AND OTHER STORIES

Piping Hot
and Other Stories

BY EMILE ZOLA

"I see thee in the hemisphere advanced
and made a constellation there!"
From Ben Jonson's "Mr. William Shakespeare"

Shakespeare House
575 Madison Avenue   New York 22

CONTENTS

PIPING HOT

IN the Rue Neuve-Saint-Augustin, a block in the traffic stopped the cab which was bringing Octave and his three trunks from the Gare de Lyon.

The cabman leant back towards him. "It's the Passage Choiseul you mean, don't you?

"No, no; the Rue de Choiseul. A new house, I think."

So the cab had only to turn the corner, the house in question, a big four-storeyed one, being the second one in the street. Octave, who had got out on to the pavement, measured it and studied it with a mechanical glance, from the silk warehouse on the ground floor to the sunken windows on the fourth floor, which opened on to a narrow terrace.

A stout, fair gentleman, who was coming out of the vestibule, stopped short when he saw Octave.

"Hullo! you here?" he cried. "I did not expect you until to-morrow."

"Well, you see," replied the young man, "I left Plassans a day sooner than I at first intended. Is the room not ready?"

"Oh, yes! I took it a fortnight ago, and had it furnished just as you told me to do. Wait a moment, and I'll take you up there."

And, despite Octave's entreaties, he turned back. The cabman had brought in the three trunks. In the hall-porter's room a dignified-looking man, with a long, clean-shaven face like a diplomatist, stood gravely reading the *Moniteur*. However, he condescended to concern himself about this luggage that was being deposited at his door, and, coming forward, he asked his tenant, the architect of the third floor, as he called him:

"Is this the person, Monsieur Campardon?"

"Yes, Monsieur Gourd, this is Monsieur Octave Mouret, for whom I took the room on the fourth floor. He will sleep there and take his meals with us. Monsieur Mouret is a friend of my wife's relations, and I beg you to show him every attention."

The room was like a little parlour, bright with mirrors, rosewood furniture, and a red-flowered carpet.

Through the half-open door, one caught a glimpse of the bedroom, and of the pink hangings of the bed. Madame Gourd, a very stout person with yellow ribbons in her hair, reclined, with clasped hands, in an arm-chair. She was doing nothing.

"Well, let us go up," said the architect.

About the vestibule and staircase there was a certain gaudy splendour. But what most impressed Octave on entering was the hot-house temperature, a sort of warm breath puffed, as it were, by some mouth into his face.

"Hullo!" said he, "the staircase is heated."

"Of course," replied Campardon; "all self-respecting landlords go to that expense, now-a-days. The house is a very fine one—very fine."

He looked about him as though testing the solidity of the walls with his architect's eyes.

"My dear fellow, the house, as you will see, is a thoroughly comfortable one, and only lived in by thoroughly respectable people."

Then, as they slowly went up, he mentioned the names of the various tenants. He first of all said a word or two about Monsieur Auguste Vabre. He was the landlord's eldest son; that spring he had taken the silk warehouse on the ground floor, and occupied the whole of the *entresol* himself. Then the landlord's other son, Théophile Vabre, and his wife, lived on the first-floor back, and in the floor overlooking the street lived the landlord himself, formerly a Versailles notary, but now lodging with his son-in-law, a counsellor at the Court of Appeal.

Two steps higher up he turned sharp round and added:

"Water and gas on every floor."

Then, as he went past the second floor without mentioning the occupants, Octave asked:

"And who lives there?" pointing to the door of the principal suite.

"Oh, there!" said he. "People one never sees, and never knows. The house could well do without such as they. However, there are spots to be found everywhere, I suppose."

He sniffed disdainfully.

"The gentleman writes books, I believe."

But, on reaching the third floor, his complacent smile came back. The apartments facing the court-yard were subdivided.

Madame Juzeur lived there, a little woman who had seen much misfortune, and a very distinguished gentleman, who had hired a room, to which he came on business once a week. While explaining matters thus, Campardon opened the door of the opposite flat.

"This is where I live," he said. "Wait a minute; I must get your key. We'll go up to your room first, and afterwards you shall see my wife."

In those two minutes that he was left alone, Octave felt penetrated, as it were, by the grave silence of the staircase.

"You will have excellent neighbours," said Campardon, as he reappeared with the key; "the Josserands on the front floor —quite a family; the father's cashier at the St. Joseph glassworks, with two marriageable daughters. Next to you are the Pichons; he's a clerk. They're not exactly rolling in money, but are thoroughly well-bred. Everything has to be let, hasn't it? Even a house of this sort."

Little by little the staircase had filled him with awe; he was quite fluttered at the thought of living in such a thoroughly well-appointed house, as the architect had termed it. As he was following the latter along the passage to his room, through a half-opened door he caught sight of a young woman standing beside a cradle. Hearing a sound, she looked up. She was fair, with light, expressionless eyes; and all that he got was this marked look, for the young woman, blushing, suddenly pushed the door to with the bashful manner of someone taken by surprise.

Campardon, turning round, repeated:

"Water and gas on every floor, my dear boy."

Then he pointed out a door opening on to the servants' staircase—their rooms were overhead. Then, stopping at the end of the passage, he said:

"Here we are at last."

The room was large, and square-shaped, the design of the wall-paper being blue flowers on a grey ground. It was simply furnished.

"This will suit me perfectly," cried Octave, delighted.

"I thought it would," said Campardon.

And as Octave shook him by the hand and thanked him, he added in a more serious tone:

"Only, my good fellow, there must be no rows here, and, above all things, no women 'Pon my honour! if you were to bring a woman here, there would be a regular revolution."

"Don't be alarmed," muttered the young man, somewhat uneasy.

"No, let me tell you, for it is I who would be compromised You see what the house is. All middle-class people, and so awfully moral. Between ourselves, I think they rather overdo it. Ah, well! Monsieur Gourd would at once fetch Monsieur Vabre, and we should both be in a nice mess. So, my dear chap, for my own peace of mind's sake, I ask you, do respect the house."

Overcome by so much virtue, Octave declared on oath that this he would do. Then Campardon, looking around him warily and lowering his voice, as if fearful of being overheard, added, with shining eyes:

"Elsewhere, it's nobody's business, eh? Paris is so big; there's plenty of room. I myself am an artist at heart, and personally I don't care a damn about such things."

A porter brought up the luggage. When everything had been put straight, the architect took a fatherly interest in the details of Octave's toilet. Then, rising, he said:

"Now let us go down and see my wife."

On the third floor the maid-servant, a slim, dark coquettish-looking girl, said that madame was engaged. In order to put his young friend at ease, Campardon showed him over the flat. First of all, there was the big white and gold drawing-room profusely ornamented with sham mouldings This was placed between a little green parlour, which had been turned into a study, and the bedroom, into which they could not go, but the architect described its narrow shape and the mauve wall-paper. When he took him into the dining-room, all in imitation wood, with its strange combination of beading and panels, Octave, enchanted exclaimed:

"It's very handsome!"

"Yes, it's effective," said the architect, slowly.

He led Octave through the ante-room again, with its ground-glass windows To the left, overlooking the courtyard, there was another bedroom, where his daughter Angèle slept; all its whiteness, on this November afternoon, made it seem mournful as a tomb. Then, at the end of the passage, there was the kitchen, which he insisted on showing to Octave, saying that he must see everything.

"You've seen everything now. The rooms are the same on each floor. Mine costs me two thousand five hundred francs; on the third floor, too! Rents are going up every day. Monsieur Vabre must make about twenty-two thousand francs a year out of his house.

He spoke of his age—forty-two—of the emptiness of existence, and hinted at a melancholy which in nowise assorted with his robust health. Under his flowing hair and beard, trimmed à la Henri IV., there was the flat skull and square jaw of a middle-class man of limited intelligence and animal appetites. When younger, he had been hilarious to the point of boredom.

Octave's eyes fell on a number of the *Gazette de France*, which was lying among some plans. Then Campardon, becoming more and more embarrassed, rang for the maid, to know if madame was at length disengaged. Yes, the doctor was going, and madame would come directly.

"Is Madame Campardon not well?" asked the young man.

"No, she is as usual," said the architect, with a touch of annoyance in his voice.

"Oh, what's the matter with her?"

More confused than ever, he answered evasively: "Women, you know, have always got something the matter with them. She's been like that for thirteen years—ever since her confinement. In other respects she is flourishing. You'll even find that she has grown stouter."

Octave forbore to question further. Just then, Lisa came back, bringing a card, and the architect, apologising, hurried into the drawing-room, begging the young man to talk to his wife meanwhile. As the door quickly opened and shut, in the centre of the spacious white and gold apartment Octave caught sight of the black spot of a cassock.

At the same moment Madame Campardon came in from the ante-room. He did not recognise her. Years ago, when, as a lad, he knew her at Plassans, at the house of her father, M. Domergue, a director of bridges and roads, she was thin and plain, and for all her twenty years, as puny as a girl that has just reached puberty. Now, he found her plump, with clear complexion, and as composed as a nun; soft-eyed, dimpled, and sleek as a fat tabby cat.

"Why, you're quite a man now," she said, gaily, holding out both hands. "How you've grown since our last journey!"

And she surveyed him—tall, brown, comely young fellow that he was, with his carefully trimmed beard and moustache. When he told her his age, twenty-two, she would not believe it—declaring that he looked at least twenty-five. He—whom the very presence of a woman, even of the lowest maid-servant, enraptured—laughed a silvery laugh as he delightedly watched her with eyes the colour of old gold and soft as velvet.

"Yes," he repeated, gently, "I've grown, I've grown. Do you remember when your cousin, Gasparine, used to buy me marbles?"

Then he told her news about her own people. Monsieur and Madame Domergue were living quite happily and quietly in their own house; all that they complained of was that they were so much alone, and they bore Campardon a grudge for having thus carried off their little Rose when he had come down to Plassans on business. The young fellow then tried to make his cousin Gasparine the subject of conversation, and so satisfy his roguish curiosity of long standing, respecting a mystery that for him had never been solved—the architect's sudden passion for Gasparine, a tall, handsome girl without a penny, and his hasty marriage with Rose, a thin damsel who had as dowry thirty thousand francs, and the whole scene of tears and recriminations, followed by the flight of the forsaken one to her dressmaker aunt in Paris. But Madame Campardon, though her calm face flushed slightly, appeared not to understand. He could get no details from her.

Madame Campardon, who seemingly could not stand for any length of time without fatigue, was sitting in a high easy-chair, her limbs extended beneath her tea-gown, and he, taking a low chair looked up at her with his wonted air of adoration—with his big shoulders, there was something feminine about him, something taking to women, that touched them and made them instantly take him to their heart. Thus, in ten minutes' time they were both chatting like two old friends.

"Well, here I am, your boarder," said he, stroking his beard with a shapely hand, the nails of which were carefully trimmed.

8

' We're sure to get on famously together, you'll see. It was awfully nice of you to think of the little urchin of Plassans, and to trouble about everything directly I asked you."

"No, no, don't thank me," she protested. "I am far too lazy; I never stir. It was Achille who arranged everything. After all, when your mother told us that you wanted to board with some family, that was quite enough for us to make you welcome. You won't be among strangers now, and it will be company for us."

Then he told her of his own affairs. After getting his bachelor's diploma, to please his family, he had just spent three years in Marseilles, in a large calico print warehouse which had a factory near Plassans. He had a passion for trade, for the trade in women's luxuries, in which there was something of the pleasure of seduction, of slow possession achieved by gilded words and flattering looks. And with the laugh of a conqueror, he told her how he had made the five thousand francs, without which he would never have risked coming to Paris, natural prudence underlying his flighty good-nature.

"I've travelled for two years," he went on, "and that's enough. Now there's Paris for me to conquer. I must look out for something at once."

"Why, didn't Achille tell you?" she exclaimed. "He's got a berth for you, and close by, too."

He thanked her, as much astonished as if he were in fairy-land, and asked, jokingly, if he would find a wife with a hundred thousand francs a year in his room that evening, when the door was pushed open by a plain, lanky girl of fourteen with straw-coloured hair, who uttered a slight cry of alarm.

"Come in, and don't be shy," said Madame Campardon. "This is Monsieur Octave Mouret, of whom you have heard us speak."

Then, turning to Octave, she said:

"My daughter, Angèle. On our last journey we did not take her with us; she was so delicate. But she's getting stouter now."

Angèle, with the awkwardness of girls at this ungraceful age, took up her stand behind her mother and stared at the smiling young man. Almost immediately Campardon came back, looking excited, and he coul' not keep from hurriedly telling his wife of the good luck that had befallen him. The Abbé

9

Mauduit, vicar of Saint-Roch, had come about some work—merely repairs, but it might lead to far more important things. Then, vexed at having talked of this before Octave, still trembling with excitement, he struck both hands together, and said:

"Well, well, what are we going to do?"

"Why, you were going out," said Octave. "Don't let me disturb you."

"Achille," murmured Madame Campardon, "that situation at the Hédouins'?"

"Why, of course," exclaimed the architect, "I had forgotten that. My dear fellow, it's a berth of head assistant at a large haberdasher's. I know somebody there who has put in a word for you. They expect you. As it's not four o'clock yet, would you like me to take you round there?"

Octave hesitated, and, in his mania for being well-dressed, felt nervous about the sit of his neck-tie. However, when Madame Campardon assured him that he looked very neat, he decided to go. With a languid gesture, she offered her forehead to her husband, who kissed her with effusive tenderness, as he repeated:

"Ta-ta, pussy; good-bye, my pet."

"Remember, we dine at seven," said she, as she accompanied them across the drawing-room to get their hats.

When they got downstairs Campardon turned up the Rue Neuve-Saint-Augustin. He was silent, preoccupied, like a man who is waiting to broach a subject.

"Do you remember Mademoiselle Gasparine?" he asked, at length. "She is forewoman at the Hédouins'. You will see her."

Octave thought this a good chance of satisfying his curiosity.

"Oh," said he, "does she live with you?"

"No, no!" exclaimed the architect hastily, and as if stung at the suggestion.

Then, as Octave seemed surprised at his emphatic denial, he added, in a gentler tone of embarrassment:

"No, my wife and she never meet now. In families, you know—— I've met her myself, and I couldn't very well refuse to shake hands, could I? More especially as the poor girl's badly off. So that now they get news of each other through me. In old quarrels of this sort one must leave it to time to heal the wounds"

10

Octave determined to question him plainly about his marriage, when the architect suddenly cut matters short by saying: "Here we are!"

It was a linendraper's shop, facing the narrow, three-cornered Place Gaillon. On a signboard, just above the shop, were the words in faded gilt lettering, "The Ladies' Paradise: Established 1822," while the shop-windows bore the name of the firm, in red: "Deleuze, Hédouin and Co."

"In style it's not quite up to date, but it's a sound, straightforward concern," explained Campardon, rapidly. "Monsieur Hédouin, at one time a clerk, married the daughter of the elder Deleuze, who died two years ago, so that the business is now managed by the young couple—old Deleuze and another partner, I think, both keep out of it. You'll see Madame Hédouin. Ah, she's got a head on her shoulders! Let's go in."

Monsieur Hédouin just then happened to be away at Lille, buying linen, so Madame Hédouin received them. She was standing, with a pen behind her ear, giving orders to two shopmen, who were putting pieces of stuff in order on the shelves. He thought her so tall and attractive-looking, with her regular features and neatly-plaited hair, black dress, turn-down collar, and man's tie. As she gravely smiled at him, Octave, not generally bashful, could hardly stammer out a reply. In a few words everything was settled.

"Well," said she, in her quiet way and her professional grace of manner, "as you're at liberty, perhaps you might like to look over the premises."

Calling a clerk, she entrusted Octave to his care, and then, after politely replying to Campardon that Mademoiselle Gasparine was out, she turned her back and went on with her work, giving orders in the same gentle, firm voice.

"Not there, Alexandre. Put the silks up at the top. Look out! those are not of the same make."

After some hesitation, Campardon said he would call again and fetch him back to dinner. So for two hours the young man explored the warehouse. Several times he met Madame Hédouin tripping busily along the narrowest of the passages without ever catching her dress in anything. She seemed to be the life and soul of the place, the least sign of whose white hands all the assistants obeyed. Octave was rather hurt that she did not take more notice of him. About a quarter to seven, just as he was coming up from the basement for the last time, he was told that Campardon was on the first floor, with Mademoiselle Gasparine. That was the hosiery department, which this young lady superintended. But, at the top of the winding staircase, Octave stopped short behind a pyramid of calico, bales, symmetrically arranged, as he heard the architect talking in the most familiar way to Gasparine.

"I'll swear I haven't," he cried, forgetting himself so far as to raise his voice.

There was a pause.

"How is she now?" asked the young woman.

"Oh, good Lord! she's always the same. One day better; one day worse. She knows that it's all over now, and that she'll never be right again."

Then Gasparine, with pity in her voice, continued:

"It's you, my poor friend, who are to be pitied. However, as you have been able to manage things otherwise, do tell her how sorry I am to hear that she is still so poorly——"

Without letting her finish the sentence, Campardon caught her by the shoulders and kissed her roughly on the lips in the gas-heated air growing ever more vitiated under the low ceiling. She returned his kiss, murmuring:

"To-morrow morning, then, at six, if you can manage it. I'll stop in bed. Knock three times."

Octave, astounded, but beginning to understand, coughed first and then came forward. Another surprise awaited him. Gasparine, his cousin, had become shrivelled, lean and angular, with projecting jaws and coarse hair. All that she had kept in this cadaverous face of hers were her great, splendid eyes. Her envious brow and sensuous, stubborn mouth distressed him as much as Rose had charmed him by her tardy development into an indolent blonde.

Gasparine, if not effusive, was polite. She remembered Plassans, and she talked to the young man of old times. As Campardon and he took their leave she shook them by the hand. Downstairs Madame Hédouin simply said to Octave:

"Well, then, we shall see you to-morrow."

When he got into the street, deafened by cabs and hustled by passers-by, the young fellow could not help observing that the lady was certainly very handsome, if not particularly affable. In the Rue Neuve-Saint-Augustin, just before turning into the Rue de Choiseul, Campardon bowed as he passed one of these shops.

A young lady, slim and elegant, wearing a silk mantle, stood at the door, holding a little boy of three close to her so that he might not get knocked down. She was talking familiarly to an old, bareheaded woman, evidently the shopkeeper. It was too dark for Octave to distinguish her features, but, in the flickering gaslight, she seemed to him to be pretty, and he only caught sight of two bright eyes, fixed for a moment upon him like two flames.

"That is Madame Valérie, wife of Monsieur Théophile Vabre, the landlord's youngest son, you know—the people on the first floor," said Campardon, after they had gone a little further. "She's a most charming person—born in that very shop, one of the best paying linen-drapers' of the neighbourhood, which her parents, Monsieur and Madame Louhette, still manage, just to have something to do. They've made some coin ther , you bet!"

Thus chatting, they reached the top of the stairs. Dinner was waiting for them. Madame Campardon had put on a grey silk gown, and had dressed her hair most coquettishly, paying great attention to her toilette. Campardon kissed her on the neck, with all the emotion of a dutiful husband.

"Good evening, love; good evening my pet."

After dinner, they stayed in the drawing-room until midnight. It was a sort of orgy to celebrate Octave's arrival. Madame Campardon seemed dreadfully tired; ere long she subsided on the sofa.

"Are you in pain, love?" asked her husband.

"No," she replied, under her breath. "It's always the same thing."

Then, looking at him, she said, softly:

"You saw her at the Hédouins'?"

"Yes; she asked me how you were."

Tears came into Rose's eyes.

"She's always well, she is!"

"There, there," said Campardon, as he lightly kissed her hair, forgetting that they were not alone. "You'll make yourself

13

worse again. Don't you know that I love you all the same, my poor darling?"

Octave, who had discreetly moved to the window, and pretended to be looking into the street, once more proceeded to scrutinise Madame Campardon's features, for his curiosity was roused, and he wondered what could be the matter with her. But she wore her usual look, half doleful, half good-tempered, as she curled herself up on the sofa, like a woman who submits resignedly to her share of caresses.

At length Octave bade them good-night. Candlestick in hand, he was still on the landing when he heard the rustle of silk dresses as they brushed the stairs. He politely stood back to let them pass. Evidently these were the ladies on the fourth floor, Madame Josserand and her two daughters coming home from a party. As they went by, the mother, a stout, arrogant-looking dame, stared full in his face; the elder of the daughters stepped aside with a petulant air, while her sister, heedless, looked up at him and smiled in the bright light of the candle. She was charmingly pretty, with tiny features, fair skin, and shining auburn hair, and there was about her a certain intrepid grace, the easy charm of a young bride, as she came back from some ball, in an elaborate gown covered with bows and lace, such as girls never wear. Their trains disappeared at the top of the stairs, and a door closed behind them. Octave was quite amused by the merry twinkle in her eyes.

Slowly he went upstairs in his turn. Only one gas-jet was alight; the staircase, in this heavy heated air, seemed fast asleep. Not a whisper was audible; it was a silence as of well-mannered people holding their breath.

However, Octave found it hard to get to sleep. He tossed about feverishly, his brain filled with all the new faces he had seen. What on earth made the Campardons so civil to him? Did they think of giving him their daughter later on? Perhaps the husband had taken him in as a boarder just to amuse his wife and cheer her up. Poor woman! what could the extraordinary complaint be from which she was suffering? Then his ideas grew more confused; phantoms passed before him; little Madame Pichon, his neighbour, with her vacuous look; handsome Madame Hédouin, calm and self-possessed, in her black dress; the fiery eyes of Madame Valérie, and the merry smile of

14

Mademoiselle Josserand. How he had grown during just these few hours spent in Paris! This had always been his dream, that ladies would take him by the hand, and help him on in his business. Again and again the faces came back, blending themselves with wearisome iteration. He knew not which to choose, as he strove to let his voice be tender and his gestures seductive. Then, all at once, tired out, exasperated, he gave rein to the brutal impulse within him, to his ferocious disdain of womankind, which his air of amorous devotion masked.

"Are they ever going to let me go to sleep?" he exclaimed aloud, throwing himself violently on his back. "I'll take the first one on that wants it, and give it to them all at once if they like. To sleep! to sleep!"

W HEN Madame Josserand, preceded by her daughters, left Madame Dambreville's party in the Rue de Rivoli, fourth floor at the corner of the Rue de l'Oratoire, she slammed the street door in a sudden outburst of wrath that she had been suppressing for the last two hours. Her younger daughter Berthe had again just missed getting a husband.

"Well, what are you standing there for?" she angrily asked the girls, who had stopped under the arcade and were watching the cabs go by. "Walk on, do; for you needn't imagine that we're going to have a cab and spend another two francs!"

And when Hortense, the elder, grumbled:

"H'm! pleasant, walking in all this mud! It will do for my shoes, that's one thing!"

"Walk on, I say," rejoined the mother, in a fury. "When your shoes are done for, you'll have to stop in bed, that's all! A lot of good it is, taking you out!"

The mother grew more exasperated as she thought of many similar home-comings extending over the last three winters, hampered by their smart gowns, in all the black mud of the streets, a butt for the wit of belated loafers. No, she had certainly had enough of this, of this carting about of her daughters to all the four corners of Paris, without ever daring to enjoy the luxury of a cab, for fear of having to curtail the morrow's dinner by a dish!

"So she's a match-maker, is she?" she went on out loud, as she thought of Madame Dambreville, talking to herself by way of solace, not even addressing her daughters, who had gone along the Rue Saint-Honoré. "Fine matches she makes! A lot of pert hussies that come from goodness knows where! Oh, if one weren't obliged to go through it all! That was her last success, I suppose—that bride which she trotted out just to show us that she isn't always a failure! A fine specimen, too, and no mistake! A wretched child, forsooth, that, after making a slight mistake, had to be sent back to a convent for six months to get another coating of whitewash!"

As the girls crossed the Place du Palais Royal, a shower came on. This was the last straw. Slipping and splashing about, they stopped and again cast glances at the empty cabs that rolled by.

"On you go!" cried the mother, ruthlessly. "We are too near home now; it is not worth forty sous And your brother Léon, who wouldn't come away with us for fear of having to pay for the cab! If he can get what he wants at that woman's so much the better. But I can safely say it isn't at all decent. A frump, past fifty, who only invites young people to her house! An elderly impropriety that some exalted personage, by the bribe of a head-clerkship, made that idiot Dambreville marry!"

Hortense and Berthe plodded along in the rain, one in front of the other, without appearing to listen. When their mother let herself go like this, oblivious of all the strict rules laid down for their own superfine education, it was tacitly agreed that they were to be deaf. But on reaching the dark, low Rue de l'Echelle, Berthe rebelled.

"There!" she cried. "There goes my heel. I can't stir another step!"

Madame Josserand waxed furious.

"Walk on at once! Do I complain? Do you think it's fit for me to be traipsing about the streets at this time of night, and in such weather, too? It would be different if you had a father like that of other people. Oh, no; my lord must stay at home and take his ease! It always falls to me to take you about to parties; he'll never be bothered to do so! I assure you that I've had just about enough of it. Your father shall take you out in future, if he likes; you may go to the devil before I drag you about any more to places where I only get put out! A fellow that completely deceived me as to his capabilities, and from whom I have never got the least pleasure! Good Lord! If ever I were to marry again, it wouldn't be a man of *that* sort!"

The girls stopped grumbling. They well knew this eternal chapter in the history of their mother's blighted hopes. With their lace mantillas sticking to their faces, and their ball-shoes soaked through, they hurried along the Rue Sainte-Anne. In the Rue de Choiseul, at the very door of her own house, Madame Josserand had to undergo yet another humiliation, for the Duveyriers' carriage splashed her all over as it drove up.

Fagged and furious, both mother and girls got back some

17

of their grace and deportment when they had to pass Octave on
the stairs. But, directly their door was shut, they rushed helter
skelter through the dark drawing-room, bumping against the
furniture, till they got to the dining-room, where Monsieur
Josserand was writing by the feeble light of a little lamp.

'Another failure!' cried Madame Josserand, as she flopped
into a chair.

And she roughly tore the lace covering from her head, flung
off her fur cloak, and appeared in a gaudy red dress, trimmed
with black satin, and cut very low. She looked enormous,
though her shoulders were still comely, and resembled the shining flanks of a mare. Her square face, with its big nose and
flabby cheeks, expressed all the tragic fury of a queen checking
her desire to lapse into the language of Billingsgate.

"Ah!" said Monsieur Josserand, simply, bewildered by this
boisterous entrance.

His eyelids blinked uneasily. It was positively overwhelming
when his wife displayed that mammoth bosom; it seemed as if
he felt its weight crushing the back of his neck. Dressed in a
seedy frock-coat that he was wearing out at home, his countenance washed out and dingy with thirty years of office routine, he
looked up at her with his large lack-lustre eyes. Pushing back his
grey locks behind his ears, he was too disconcerted to speak, and
attempted to go on writing.

"But you don't seem to understand!" continued Madame
Josserand, in a harsh voice. "I tell you, there goes another
marriage that hasn't come off—the fourth!"

"Yes, yes, I know—the fourth," he murmured. "It's annoying, very."

And to avoid his wife's appalling nudity he turned towards
his daughters with a kindly smile. They also took off their lace
and their cloaks; the elder was in blue, the younger in pink, and
their dresses, too daring in cut and over trimmed, had something tempting about them. Hortense had a sallow complexion;
her nose spoilt her; it was like her mother's, and gave her an
air of stubborn disdain. She was only just twenty-three, but
looked twenty-eight. Berthe, however, who was two years
younger, had kept all her childish grace, with similar features,
only more delicate, and a skin of dazzling whiteness, to be
menaced only by the coarse family mask when she had got to

fifty or thereabouts.

"What's the good of staring at us?" cried Madame Josserand. "For God's sake put your writing away; it gets on my nerves!"

"But, my dear, I've got these wrappers to do!" said he, gently.

"Oh, yes, I know your wrappers—three francs a thousand! Perhaps, you think that with those three francs you'll be able to marry your daughters!"

By the faint light of the little lamp one, indeed, could see that the table was strewn with large sheets of coarse paper, printed wrappers on which Monsieur Josserand wrote addresses for a well-known publisher who had several periodicals. As with his cashier's salary he could not make ends meet, he spent whole nights at this unprofitable sort of work, doing it on the quiet, afraid that anyone should find out how poor they were.

"Three francs are three francs," he rejoined in his slow, tired voice. "With those three francs you'll be able to add bows to your gown, and get a cake for your guests on Tuesdays."

He regretted the remark directly he had made it, for he felt that with Madame Josserand it had gone straight home, and had touched her pride in its most sensitive part. Her shoulders grew purple; she seemed just about to burst forth with some vindictive reply, but, by a majestic effort, she only stammered:

"Good gracious me! Well, I never!" And she looked at her daughters, shrugging those awful shoulders, as if in masterful scorn of her husband, and as much as to say: "There! you hear the idiot, don't you?"

The girls nodded. Seeing himself vanquished, he regretfully laid down his pen and took up a copy of the *Temps,* which he brought home with him every evening from the office.

"Is Saturnin asleep?" asked Madame Josserand, drily, referring to her younger son.

"Yes, *long* ago; and I told Adèle she could go to bed, too. I suppose you saw Léon at the Dambrevilles'?"

"Of course. Why, he sleeps there!" she rapped out, in a sudden paroxysm of spite that she could not check.

The father, surprised, ingenuously asked:

"Do you think he does?"

Hortense and Berthe became deaf, smiling slightly; they pretended to be examining their shoes, which were in a pitiable state. By way of a diversion, Madame Josserand tried to pick another quarrel with her husband. She begged him to take away his newspaper every morning, and not to leave it lying about all day long, as he had done last night, for instance. That particular copy just happened to contain details of a scandalous trial, which his daughters might easily have read. His utter want of moral principle was evident from such negligence as that.

"So it's bedtime, is it?" yawned Hortense. "I'm hungry."

"What about me?" said Berthe. "I'm simply starving."

"What's that?" cried Madame Josserand. "Hungry? Didn't you get some *brioche* when you were there? What a couple of ninnies! Hungry, forsooth: I took good care to eat something."

But the girls persisted in saying that they were dying of hunger, so their mother at last went with them into the kitchen to see if there was anything left. Their father furtively set to work upon his wrappers again. He was well aware that without those wrappers of his all the petty household luxuries would have disappeared, and thus it was that, in spite of gibes and bickerings, he doggedly kept at this secret drudgery until daybreak, quite pleased, poor man, at the thought that just one more scrap of lace might bring about a wealthy marriage. Though household expenses were being cut down, and still funds proved insufficient to pay for dresses and those Tuesday receptions. he resigned himself to this quill-driving like a martyr, dressed in tatters, while his wife and daughters went tearing about to parties with flowers in their hair.

Monsieur Josserand continued writing. He hoped that his wife would be satisfied at crushing him with a look as she went past on her way to bed. But she again sank into a chair facing him, and gazed at him without speaking. This gaze he felt, and it made him so uneasy that his pen sputtered on the flimsy wrapper-paper.

He never attempted to exculpate himself. Afraid to go on with his work, he began to toy with his penholder. There was a lull.

"To-morrow morning," said Madame Josserand, "I shall be obliged if you will call on the Campardons and remind them as politely as you can that we expect them in the evening. The

20

young man, their friend, arrived this afternoon. Ask them to bring him, too. Remember, I wish him to come."

"What young man?"

"A young man; it would take far too long to explain the whole thing to you. I have found out everything about him. I am obliged to try all I can since you leave your two daughters on my hands like a bundle of rubbish, caring no more about getting them married than about the Grand Turk."

At this thought her anger revived.

"You see, I keep myself in, but, upon my word, it's more than anyone can stand. Don't answer, sir; don't answer, or I shall positively explode!"

He forbore to answer, and she exploded all the same.

"The long and the short of it is, I won't put up with it. I warn you that one of these fine days I shall go off and leave you with your two empty-headed daughters. Do you think I was born to lead such a beggarly life as this?"

"I draw eight thousand francs a year," murmured the hireling; "it's a very good berth."

"A good berth, indeed! After more than thirty years' service. They grind you down, and you're delighted. Do you know what I should have done, if it had been me? I should have seen to it that the business filled my pocket twenty times over. That was easy enough; I saw it when I married you, and I have never stopped urging you to do so ever since. But it wanted initiative, intelligence; it meant not going to sleep like a blockhead on the office stool!"

"With eight thousand francs one can do a good deal," he went on. "You're always grumbling. But you ought not to have attempted to do things on a scale above our means. It's all your mania for entertaining and for paying visits, for having an 'at home' day with tea and cakes——"

"It's vou who'll look foolish if your daughters become old maids!"

"Why, it's you who scare away all the likely men with your fine dresses and ridiculous parties! I look foolish? God blast you!"

In all his life Monsieur Josserand had never gone so far. His wife, gasping, stuttered: "I ridiculous—I!" when the door opened. Hortense and Berthe came back in petticoats and dressing-jackets, with their hair down and wearing slippers.

"Oh, the cold in our room!" said Berthe, shivering. "It freezes the very food in your mouth. Here, at least, there has been a fire this evening."

And they both drew up their chairs and sat close to the stove, which still retained some heat. Hortense held the rabbit bone between her finger-tips, and adroitly picked it. Berthe dipped bits of bread in her tumbler of syrup. But their parents were so excited that they hardly noticed them enter, but went on:

"Ridiculous, did you say, sir, ridiculous? I will be so no longer. Hang me if ever I wear out another pair of gloves in trying to get them husbands! Now it's your turn; and I hope you'll not prove more ridiculous than myself!"

"I daresay, madam; after you've trotted them about and compromised them everywhere! Whether you get them married or whether you don't, I don't care a hang!"

"And I care less still, Monsieur Josserand! So little do I care, that if you aggravate me much more I'll send them flying into the street. And you can go, too, if you like; the door is open. Lord! what a good riddance of bad rubbish that would be!"

The girls listened tranquilly. They were used to such lively discussions. They went on eating, with dressing-jackets unbuttoned and showing their shoulders, and they let their bare skin gently chafe against the lukewarm earthen sides of the stove. They looked charming in this undress, charming with their youth and healthy appetites, and their large eyes heavy with sleep.

"It's silly of you to quarrel like this," said Hortense, at length, with her mouth full. "Mamma will ruin her temper, and papa will be ill at the office all to-morrow. It seems to me that we are big enough to get husbands for ourselves."

This speech created a diversion. The father, utterly worn out, pretended to go on with his wrappers, while the mother, who was pacing up and down the room like a lioness that has got loose, came and stood in front of Hortense.

"If you're alluding to yourself," she cried, "you are a precious fool! That Verdier of yours will never marry you!"

"That's my look-out," replied Hortense, bluntly.

After having disdainfully refused five or six suitors—a clerk,

22

a tailor's son, and other young men of no prospects, as she thought, she pitched upon a lawyer, over forty, whom she had met at the Dambrevilles'. She thought him very clever, and found to make a large fortune by his talents. The worst of it was that, for fifteen years, Verdier had been living with a mistress, who in their neighborhood, even passed as his wife. This Hortense knew, but did not appear to be much troubled thereat.

"My child," said the father, looking up from his work, "I have begged you to give up all idea of such a marriage. You know what the situation is."

She stopped sucking her bone and impatiently rejoined:

"Well, what of it? Verdier's promised me to give her up. She's only a fool."

"You've no right to talk like that, Hortense. And if the fellow gives *you* up, too, one day, and goes back to the very woman you made him leave?"

"That's my look-out," said the girl, drily.

Berthe listened, as she knew of the whole matter, and discussed each new development of it with her sister every day. Like her father, she sided with the poor woman, who, after fifteen years of housekeeping, was to be turned into the street. But Madame Josserand struck in:

"Oh, do leave off! Wretched women of that sort always drift back at last to the gutter whence they came. It's Verdier, though, who will never have the strength of mind to leave her. He's hoaxing you nicely, my dear. If I were you I wouldn't wait another second for him, but I'd try and find somebody else."

The girl's voice grew harsher still, and two livid spots appeared on her cheeks.

"You know what I am, mamma. I want him, and him I will have. I shall never marry anybody else, if I have to wait for him a hundred years!"

The mother shrugged her shoulders.

"And yet you call other people fools!"

Hortense rose, trembling with anger.

"Now then, don't pitch into me!" she cried. "I've done eating my rabbit, and I'd rather go to bed. Since you can't manage to get us husbands, you must let us try and find them ourselves in whatever way we choose!"

23

And she went out, slamming the door behind her.

Madame Josserand turned majestically towards her husband with the profound remark:

"There, sir; that's how you have brought them up."

Stopping short in front of Berthe, she shook her finger at her, and said:

"As for you, if you behave like your sister, you'll have me to deal with."

Then she resumed her march, talking meanwhile to herself, jumping from one idea to another, contradicting herself with the complacent effrontery of a woman who is always right.

"I did what I ought to have done, and if need were I'd do it again. In life it's only the most timid who go to the wall. Money is money, and if you haven't got any you'd better shut up shop at once. For my part, whenever I had twenty sous I always pretended I had forty, for the great thing is to command envy, not pity. It is no good having a fine education if one has shabby clothes, for then people only look down on you. It mayn't be right; but, anyhow, it is so. I'd rather wear dirty petticoats than a cotton gown. Eat potatoes if you like, but put a chicken on the table if you ask people to dinner. It's only *fools* who would deny that."

She looked hard at her husband, for whom these last remarks were intended. But, utterly exhausted, he declined to enter the lists a second time, and was cowardly enough to say:

"Ah, too true! money is everything nowadays."

"You hear that," said Madame Josserand, approaching her daughter. "Go straight ahead and try and do us credit. How was it you managed to let this marriage slip through your fingers?"

Berthe felt that now it was her turn.

"I don't know, mamma," she faltered.

"An assistant manager," continued her mother, "not yet thirty, and with magnificent prospects. Money coming in every month—a regular income; there's nothing like it. I am sure you were up to some nonsense, as before."

"No, I'm sure I wasn't, mamma. I expect he found out that I hadn't got a farthing."

Madame Josserand's voice rose.

"And what about the dowry that your uncle is going to give

you? Everyone knows about that. No, it must have been something else, he hedged off too abruptly. After dancing with him you went into the parlour, and——"

Berthe became confused.

"Yes, mamma, and, as we were alone, he tried to do all sorts of horrid things—caught me by the waist and kissed me. And I was frightened, and—I pushed him up against the table."

Her mother, boiling over with rage, interrupted her.

"Pushed him up against the table! Oh, the vixen! She pushed him up against the table, did she?"

"Well, mamma, he caught hold of me."

"What's that? Caught hold of you? As if that mattered. A lot of good it is to send simpletons like you to school! Whatever did they teach you there, eh?"

Blushes covered the girl's cheeks and shoulders, while, in her virginal confusion, tears came into her eyes.

"I could not help it. He looked so wicked; I didn't know what to do."

"Didn't know what to do? She didn't know what to do! Haven't I told you a hundred times not to be so absurdly timid? You've got to live in society. When a man takes liberties, it means that he's in love with you, and there is always a way of prettily keeping him in his place. Just for a kiss behind the door! Why, I'd be ashamed to mention such a thing, I should. And you go pushing people up against the table and spoiling all your chances of getting married?"

Then, assuming a learned air, she went on:

"I give it up in despair; you're really so silly, my child. I should have to coach you in everything, and that would be a bore. As you have no fortune, do try and understand that you've got to catch men by some other means. One ought to be amiable, give tender glances, let your hand go sometimes, and submit to a little playfulness without appearing to do so; in short, one should fish for a husband. Now, you needn't think it improves your eyes to cry like a great baby."

Berthe was sobbing violently.

"Look here, you exasperate me—do leave off crying! Monsieur Josserand, just tell your daughter not to disfigure herself by crying like that. If she loses her looks, that will really be too much."

"My child," said her father, "be good and listen to your mother's advice. You mustn't spoil your looks, my pet."

"And what annoys me is, that when she likes she can be agreeable enough," continued Madame Josserand: "Come, dry your eyes and look at me as if I was a gentleman making love to you. You must smile and let your fan drop, so that, as he picks it up his fingers just touch yours. No, no, that's not the way! With your head stuck up in the air like that, you look like a man with the pip. Throw back your head and show your neck; it's pretty enough to be looked at."

"Like this, mamma?"

"Yes, that's better. And don't be so stiff; keep your waist lissom. Men don't care about deal boards. And, above all, if they go a little bit too far, don't behave like a noodle. When a man goes too far, he's done for, my dear!"

The drawing-room clock struck two, and, excited as she was by sitting up so late, and as her desire for an immediate marriage grew frenzied, the mother, in her abstraction, began thinking aloud as she twisted her daughter about like a Dutch doll. Berthe, heavy at heart, submitted in a tame, spiritless fashion; fear and confusion half choked her. Suddenly, in the middle of a merry laugh that her mother was forcing her to attempt, she burst into tears, exclaiming:

"No, no, it's no use; I can't do it!"

For a moment Madame Josserand remained speechless with astonishment. Ever since leaving the Dambrevilles' party her hand had been itching; there were slaps in the air. All at once she boxed Berthe's ears with all her might.

"There, take that! You're positively too annoying, you great booby. Upon my word, I don't blame the men!"

As Berthe felt her way across the ante-room she found her brother Saturnin, barefooted, was up, listening. Saturnin was a big hulking fellow of twenty-five, wild-eyed, and who had remained childish after an attack of brain fever. Without being actually insane, he occasionally frightened the household by fits of blind fury whenever anybody annoyed him. Berthe alone was able to subdue him by a look. When she was still a little girl he had nursed her throughout a long illness, obedient as a dog to all her little caprices; and, ever since he had saved her life, he adored her with a deep, passionate devotion.

26

"Has she been beating you again?" he asked, in a deep, tender voice.

Surprised at meeting him. Berthe cried to send him back to his room.

"Go to bed . it has nothing to do with you "

"Yes it has. I won't let her beat you. She shouted so that she woke me up. She'd better not do it again, or else I'll give it her"

Then she caught hold of his wrists, and talked to him as if he were a disobedient animal. He was at once subdued, and whimpered like a little boy:

"It hurts you dreadfully, doesn't it? Where is the place? Let me kiss it."

And when he had found her cheek in the dark, he kissed it, wetting it with his tears, as he repeated:

"Now it's well again; now it's well again."

A S SOON as the fish had been served (some dubiously fresh skate, with black butter, which that muddling Adèle had swamped in vinegar), Hortense and Berthe, seated on either side of the uncle Bachelard, kept urging him to drink, filling his glass up in turns, and repeating:

"Now, then, uncle, drink away; it's your fête day, you know! Here's your health, uncle!"

They had conspired together to make him give them twenty francs. Every year their thoughtful mother placed them thus, on either side of her brother, leaving him to their tender mercies. But it was up-hill work, needing all the cupidity of two girls spurred thereto by visions of Louis Quinze shoes and five-button gloves. In order to get him to give them the twenty francs, they had to make him perfectly drunk. In his own family circle he was furiously avaricious, though elsewhere he would squander in drunken debauchery the eighty thousand francs which he made by his commission agency. Fortunately, that evening he had arrived half-screwed, having spent the afternoon with a lady in the Faubourg Montmartre, a dyer, who used to get vermouth for him from Marseilles.

"Your health, my duckies!" he replied in his big, raucous voice, whenever he emptied his glass.

Covered with jewellery, and with a rose in his buttonhole, he filled the centre of the table—the type of a huge, boozing, brawling tradesman who has wallowed in all sorts of vices. There was a lurid brilliancy about the false teeth in his furrowed, evil face; his great red nose poised thereon like a beacon below his snow-white, close-cropped hair; while now and again his eyelids dropped involuntarily over his rheumy eyes. Gueulin, son of his wife's sister, declared that his uncle had never been sober during the whole ten years that he was a widower.

"Narcisse, may I give you some skate? It is excellent," said Madame Josserand, smiling at her brother's drunken condition, though inwardly somewhat disgusted.

She sat opposite him, with little Gueulin on her left, and

on her right, Hector Trublot—a young man to whom she was obliged to show some attention. She usually took advantage of this family dinner to pay back certain invitations which had to be returned; and so it came about that Madame Juzeur, a lady living in the house, was also present, and sat next to Monsieur Josserand. As the uncle behaved outrageously at table, and it was only the thoughts of his fortune which helped to temper their disgust, she only asked her intimate acquaintances to meet him, or else such people as she deemed it useless to hoodwink any longer. For instance, at one time she had thought of young Trublot as a son-in-law, who was then in a money-changer's office, expecting that his wealthy father would buy him a share in the business. But as Trublot displayed a calm disdain for marriage, she took no further trouble about him, even putting him beside Saturnin, who had never yet learnt how to eat decently. Berthe, who always had to sit next to her big brother, was charged to keep him in order with a look whenever his fingers found their way too frequently into the sauce.

After the fish came a pasty, when the damsels thought the moment ripe for their preliminary attack.

"Do drink, uncle dear!" said Hortense. "It is your saint's day; now aren't you going to give us something on your saint's day?"

"Oh! so it is," added Berthe, with an innocent air. "One always gives something on one's saint's day; so you must give us twenty francs."

Directly there was any mention of money, Bachelard pretended to be more tipsy still. That was his usual trick. His eyelids drooped, and he became absolutely drivelling.

"Eh, what's that?" he stuttered.

"Twenty francs. You know very well what twenty francs are; it's no use pretending that you don't," said Berthe. "Give us twenty francs; and then we'll love you—oh, ever so much!"

They flung their arms about his neck, called him the most endearing names, and kissed his inflamed face, without showing any disgust for the revolting odour of low debauchery which he exhaled. Monsieur Josserand, upset by this nauseous smell—a mixture of absinthe, tobacco and musk—was shocked to see his daughters' virginal charms in such close contact with this lecherous old blackguard.

"Do leave him alone!" he cried.

"What for?" asked Madame Josserand, as she gave her husband a terrible look. "They are only having a game. And if Narcisse likes to give them twenty francs, he has a perfect right to do so!"

"Monsieur Bachelard is so good to them," murmured little Madame Juzeur, complacently.

Struggling thus, the uncle became more and more idiotic, as he slobbered out:

"It'sh funny thing, but, 'pon by soul! don't know (*hic*)— don't, really!"

Hortense and Berthe exchanged glances and then let him go. No doubt, he had not had enough to drink. So they filled up his glass anew, laughing like whores who mean to pick a man's pocket. Their bare arms, delightfully plump and fresh, kept passing every moment under their uncle's luminous proboscis.

Then they had a sudden scare. Saturnin, whom Berthe was no longer watching, being so busy with her uncle, had begun playing with his food, making a revolting mess with it on his plate. To his mother, the poor lad was a source of exasperation, for she was both afraid and ashamed of him. How to rid herself of him she knew not, her pride forbidding her to make a common workman of him after she had sacrificed him in favour of his sisters, by taking him away from a school where his slothful intelligence was all too long in becoming roused. All these years that he had lounged about the house, helpless and stupid, had been years of terror for her, especially when she had to let him appear in society. This was as gall and wormwood to her pride.

"Saturnin!" she cried.

But Saturnin grinned again with delight at the nasty mess on his plate. He had no respect for his mother, but frankly treated her as a lying old hag, with the strange intuition of idiots who think aloud. Matters were, indeed, becoming unpleasant, and he would have thrown the plate at her head if Berthe, recalled to her duty, had not fixed him with a look. He tried to resist; then his eyes dropped, and he leant back in his chair, gloomy and depressed, as if in a trance, until dinner was over.

Then, losing all restraint, Hortense and Berthe flung themselves upon their uncle anew. Checked at first by their good breeding, this desire for the twenty francs suddenly got the better of them, and in their wild excitement they flung manners to the winds. The one, with both her hands, searched his waistcoat pockets, while the other thrust her fist into the pockets of his frock-coat. Assailed in this way, uncle Bachelard still struggled with his persecutors, but laughter overcame him, a laughter broken by drunken hiccups.

" 'Pon m'honour, not got a sou. Leave off, do; you're tickling me!"

"Look in his trousers!" cried Gueulin.

So Berthe, grown resolute, thrust her hand into one of his breeches pockets. The girls trembled with excitement as they grew rougher and rougher, and they could almost have boxed their uncle's ears. Then Berthe uttered a cry of victory; from the depths of his pocket she drew forth a handful of money, which she scattered on a plate, and there, among copper and silver, was a gold twenty-franc piece.

"I've got it!" she cried, as, with disordered hair and flushed cheeks, she tossed the coin into the air and caught it.

All the guests clapped their hands; they thought it a great joke. There was a buzz of merriment, and it was the success of the dinner. Madame Josserand smiled a smile of motherly solicitude as she watched her dear daughters. The old man, collecting his money, remarked sententiously that if one wanted twenty francs one ought to earn them. And the two girls, exhausted by content, sat panting on either side of him, their lips still quivering with the excitement of the fray.

A bell rang. They had sat a good while over dinner, and guests were now beginning to arrive. Monsieur, who had decided to laugh, like his wife, at what had occurred, would willingly have had them sing a little Béranger at table, but she silenced him; that sort of entertainment was too much for her poetic taste. She hurried on the dessert, the more so because her brother Bachelard, vexed at having to make this present of twenty francs, was becoming quarrelsome, complaining that Léon, his nephew, had not even deigned to trouble about wishing him many happy returns. Léon had only been invited to the soirée. Then, as they rose from table, Adèle said that the architect from the floor above and a young gentleman were in the drawing-room.

"Ah, yes! that young man," whispered Madame Juzeur, as she took Monsieur Josserand's arm. "So you invited him? I saw him to-day in the hall-porter's room. He is a very nice-looking young fellow."

Madame Josserand took Trublot's arm, and then Saturnin, who alone remained at table, and whom all the fuss about the twenty francs had not roused from his torpor, with eyes rolling, upset his chair in a sudden paroxysm of fury, crying:

"I won't have it, by God! I won't!"

This was just what his mother feared. She motioned to Monsieur Josserand to go on with Madame Juzeur, while she disengaged her arm from that of Trublot, who, acting on the hint, disappeared. But, apparently, he made some mistake, for he slipped off towards the kitchen, in the wake of Adèle. Bachelard and Gueulin ignoring the "crack-pot," as they called him, stood chuckling and nudging each other in a corner.

"He was quite queer all the evening; I feared something like this might occur," muttered Madame Josserand, in great alarm. "Berthe, quick, quick!"

But Berthe was shewing her booty to Hortense. Saturnin had caught up a knife, and kept repeating: "By God, I won't have it. I'll rip their bellies up, I will!"

"Berthe!" shrieked her mother, in despair.

And as the girl came rushing up, she had only just time to prevent her brother from going straight to the drawing-room, knife in hand.

She angrily shook him, while he, insanely logical, tried to explain.

"Leave it to me; they've got to have it. It will be all right, I tell you. I'm sick of their beastly goings on. They all want to sell us."

"Stuff and nonsense!" cried Berthe. "Why, what's the matter with you? What are you jawing about?

Confused and trembling with vague fury, he stared at her, as he stammered out:

"They've been trying again to get you married. They never shall. Do you hear? I won't let anybody harm you!"

His sister could not help laughing. How had he got hold of the notion that they were going to marry her? He nodded his head, declaring that he knew it, that he was certain of it. And when his mother interposed to soothe him, he gripped the knife so fiercely that she shrank back, appalled. It alarmed her, too, to think that others had witnessed the scene; and she hurriedly told Berthe to take him away and lock him into his room, while Saturnin meanwhile kept gradually raising his voice as he became more and more excited.

"I won't have them marry you to anybody. I won't have them hurt you. If they do, I'll rip their bellies up!"

Then Berthe put her hands on his shoulders and looked him straight in the face.

"I'll tell you what," said she; "you just be quiet, or else I won't love you any more."

He staggered back, his face wore a gentler, despairing look, and his eyes filled with tears.

"You won't love me any more? You won't love me any more? Oh, don't say that! Oh, say that you'll love me still; say that you'll always love me, and never love anybody else!"

She caught him by the wrist and led him out, docile as a child.

In the drawing-room Madame Josserand, with exaggerated cordiality, addressed Campardon as her dear neighbour. Why had not Madame Campardon given her the great pleasure of her company? When the architect replied that his wife was always ailing, she grew more gushing still, and declared that she would have been delighted to welcome her in a dressing-gown and slippers. But her smile had lighted on Octave, who was talking to Monsieur Josserand; all her gushing speeches were meant to reach him over Campardon's shoulder. When her husband introduced the young man to her, she displayed such effusive cordiality that Octave was actually disconcerted.

Guests now arrived—stout mothers with lean daughters; fathers and uncles only just roused from their day of somnolence at the office, driving before them their flocks of marriageable daughters. Two lamps, covered with pink paper shades, threw a subdued light over the room, hiding up the shabby yellow velvet of the furniture, the dingy piano, and the three dirty prints of Swiss scenery, which formed black patches against the bare, chilly panels of white and gold.

At last Berthe came back. She hurriedly approached her mother.

"Well, I have had a nice job," she whispered. "He wouldn't go to bed. I double-locked the door, but I'm afraid he'll break everything in his room."

Madame Josserand tugged her daughter's frock furiously. At that moment Octave, close by, turned his head.

"My daughter Berthe, Monsieur Mouret," she said, in her most gracious manner, as she introduced her to him. "Monsieur Octave Mouret, my love."

She gave her daughter a look. The latter well knew the significance of that look—an order, as it were, to commence action, a supplementary lesson to those of the previous night. She at once obeyed, with the complacent indifference of a girl who no longer cares to pick and choose a suitor. She went through her part quite prettily, with the easy grace of a Parisienne, already a trifle bored, but completely at home with all subjects, speaking enthusiastically of the South, where she had never been. Used as he was to the starched manner of the provincial virgin, Octave was charmed by this voluble little lady, who chattered away as if she were his comrade.

Just then Trublot, who, ever since dinner, had disappeared, suddenly slipped in through the dining-room door, when Berthe, observing him, asked, thoughtlessly, where he had been. He did not answer, which embarrassed her somewhat, and, to get out of her awkward position, she introduced the two young men to each other. Her mother, meanwhile, never took her eyes off her, assuming the attitude of a commander-in-chief, and directing the progress of the campaign from her arm-chair. When satisfied that the first engagement had been thoroughly effective, she made a sign to her daughter, and whispered:

"Wait until the Vabres come before you play. And mind you play loud enough."

Octave, finding himself alone with Trublot, began to question him.

"Charming, isn't she?"

"Yes, not half bad."

"The young lady in blue is her elder sister, isn't she? She is not so pretty."

"Rather not. Why, look how much thinner she is."

Trublot, who, short-sighted as he was, could really distinguish nothing, had the build of a strapping male, stubborn in his tastes. He had come back contented, chewing little black things, which Octave, to his surprise, perceived were coffee-berries.

"I say," he asked, bluntly, "in the South the women are plump, I reckon?"

Octave smiled, and immediately he and Trublot were on the best of terms. Their similarity of ideas brought them into touch. Lolling back on the sofa, they proceeded to exchange confidences. The one talked of his manageress at "The Ladies' Paradise"—Madame Hédouin, a damned fine woman, but too frigid. The other said that he was employed as correspondent from nine to five at Monsieur Desmarquay's, the money-changer's, where there was a most awfully fine slavey. Just then the door opened, and three people came in.

"Those are the Vabres," whispered Trublot, as he leant forward to his new friend. "Auguste, the tall one, with a face like a diseased sheep, is the landlord's eldest son. He is thirty-three, and suffers continually from splitting headaches, which affect his eyesight, and at one time hindered him from learning Latin—a bad-tempered fellow, who's gone into trade. The other, Théophile, that sandy-haired abortion with a weedy-looking beard, that little old man of twenty-eight, a victim to coughs and toothache, first tried all sorts of trades, and then he married the young woman walking in front, Madame Valérie."

"I've seen her before," interrupted Octave. "She is the daughter of a neighboring haberdasher, isn't she? But how deceptive those little veils are. At first sight I thought her pretty, but she's only striking-looking, with her dried-up, leaden complexion."

"Yes, there's another woman that's not my style at all," replied Trublot, sententiously. "She's got splendid eyes; some fellows are satisfied with that. But, my word, what a plate-rack!"

Madame Josserand had risen to shake hands with Valérie.

"What?" cried she, "Monsieur Vabre hasn't come with you? And Monsieur and Madame Duveyrier have not honoured us by their presence either, though they promised to come. It's really most unfortunate!"

The young wife made excuses for her father-in-law on the score of his age, though he really preferred to stay at home and work in the evening. As for her brother-in-law and sister-in-law, they had charged her to offer their excuses, as they had been invited to an official reception which they were obliged to attend. Madame Josserand bit her lips. She had never missed one of the Saturdays of those stuck-up first-floor people, who thought it *infra dig.* to come up to the fourth floor for her Tuesdays. Certainly, her modest tea-party was not equal to their concerts with grand orchestra. But, wait a bit! When her daughters were both married, and she had got two sons-in-law and their relatives to fill her drawing-room, she would have choral entertainments, too.

"Get ready to begin," she whispered in Berthe's ear.

"Hush, hush!" murmured several obliging voices. Berthe had opened the piano.

"Well, you know," explained Madame Josserand, "it's quite an unpretentious sort of piece—a simple little rêverie. You are fond of music, Monsieur Mouret, I dare say. Won't you come closer to the piano? My daughter plays this rather well—only an amateur, you know; but she plays with feeling—a great deal of feeling."

"You're in for it!" said Trublot, under his breath. "That's the sonata dodge."

Octave was obliged to rise, and he remained standing near the piano. To see the bland attentions which Madame Josserand lavished upon him, one would have thought that she was making Berthe play simply and solely for him.

"'The Banks of the Oise'," she went on. "It's really very pretty. Now, my love, begin; and don't be nervous. I'm sure Monsieur Octave will make allowances."

The girl attacked the piece without the least sign of nervousness; albeit her mother never took her eyes off her, with the air of a sergeant ready to punish with a slap the least technical blunder. What mortified her was that the instrument, cracked and wheezy after fifteen years of daily scale-playing, had not the sonorous quality of tone possessed by the Duveyriers' grand-piano. Moreover, as she thought, her daughter never would play loud enough.

Then came a catastrophe. The bell rang outside, and a gentleman entered carelessly.

"Oh, Doctor!" said Madame Josserand, in a vexed tone.

Doctor Juillerat bowed his excuses, and remained stationary.

At this moment Berthe, in die-away fashion, dwelt lingeringly upon a certain tender phrase, which her listeners greeted with a buzz of approval. "Charming!" "Delightful!" Madame Juzeur assumed a languishing attitude, as though someone were tickling her. Hortense, who stood by her sister, was turning over the pages, insensible to the surging torrent of notes, her ear alert to catch the sound of the door-bell; and when the doctor came in, her gesture of disappointment was so marked that she tore one of the leaves. Then suddenly the piano trembled beneath Berthe's frail fingers, that beat upon it like hammers. The dream had come to an end in a deafening crash of furious harmonies.

There was a moment's hesitation. The hearers roused themselves. Had it really finished? Then came a shower of compliments. "Quite too lovely!" "Talent of a very superior kind."

"Mademoiselle is really an artist of the first rank," said Octave, interrupted in his observations. "No one has ever given me such pleasure before."

Once more a confused sound of voices filled the room. Berthe coolly accepted all the praise bestowed upon her performance, and did not leave the piano, waiting for her mother to relieve her from this boredom. The latter was just telling Octave of the astonishing dash with which her daughter played "The Reapers," a brilliant galop, when a dull, far-off sound of knocking created some commotion among the guests.

Every minute the noise grew louder, as if someone were endeavouring to break open a door. The guests were silent, and exchanged questioning glances.

"What can that be?" Valérie ventured to enquire. "There was a sound of knocking like that just now as the music ended."

Madame Josserand turned quite pale. She had recognised Saturnin's lusty blows from the shoulder. Wretched lunatic that he was. She seemed to see him rushing into the room among her guests. If he went on thumping like that, there was another marriage knocked on the head!

"It's the kitchen door that keeps banging," said she, with a forced smile. "Adèle never will shut it. Just go and see, Berthe."

Her daughter had also understood, and, rising she disappeared. The knocking at once ceased, but she did not immediately return. Uncle Bachelard, who had scandalously disturbed the performance of "The Banks of the Oise" by making loud remarks, succeeded in disconcerting his sister by shouting out to Gueulin that he was bored to death, and was going to get himself some grog. They both returned to the dining-room, slamming the door after them.

"Dear old Narcisse—such an original!" said Madame Josserand to Valérie and Madame Juzeur, as she sat down between them. "He's so bothered about business! You know, he made nearly a hundred thousand francs this year!"

Free at last, Octave hastened to rejoin Trublot, lolling drowsily on the sofa. Near them a group surrounded Doctor Juillerat, the old physician of the neighborhood, a man of mediocre ability, but who, by degrees, had got a thriving practice, having attended all the mothers in their confinements, and prescribed remedies for all their daughters' ills. He made a special study of diseases of women, so that in the evening he was besieged by husbands eager to obtain advice gratis in some corner of the room.

"By-the-bye," said Octave to Trublot, "as you seem to know everything, do tell me what is the matter with Madame Campardon. Whenever her ill-health is mentioned I notice that everyone assumes a rueful visage."

"Why, my dear fellow," replied the young man, "she has got——"

And he whispered in Octave's ear. At first his listener smiled, then he made a long face of deep astonishment.

"Is it possible?" said he.

Whereupon Trublot declared upon his word of honour that it was so. He knew another lady who had the same thing.

"Besides," added he, "after a confinement it sometimes happens that——"

And he began to whisper again. Octave, convinced, felt sad. For a moment he had imagined all sorts of things—a regular romance; the architect attracted elsewhere, and urging him to provide amusement for his wife! At any rate, he could feel sure that her honour was safe. The young men pressed closer against each other in the excitement of disclosing all these feminine secrets, forgetful that they might be overheard.

"Mamma, tea is ready," said Berthe, as he and Adèle opened the folding doors.

Then, as peoples slowly passed into the dining-room, she went up to her mother and whispered:

"I've had about enough of it. He wants me to stop and tell him stories or else he says he'll smash up everything."

Meanwhile the uncle slumbered in a corner. They did not wake him; they even politely pretended not to see him. One lady spoke of the fatigues of business. Berthe was most attentive, handing round sandwiches, carrying cups of tea, asking the men if they would like any more sugar. But she could not attend to everybody, and Madame Josserand kept looking for Hortense, whom she suddenly descried in the centre of the empty drawing-room talking to a gentleman whose back alone was visible.

"Yes, yes," she blurted out, in a sudden fit of wrath, "he's come at last!"

The guest began to whisper. It was that Verdier, who had been living with a woman for fifteen years, while waiting to marry Hortense. Everybody knew the story, and girls exchanged significant glances; but for propriety's sake they forbore to speak of it, and merely bit their lips. When Octave had been enlightened, he watched the gentleman's back with interest. Trublot knew the woman, a good soul as ever was; a reformed prostitute, as well-conducted now, said he, as the best of wives, looking after her chap and keeping all his shirts in order. He was full of brotherly sympathy for her. Whilst thus watched from the dining-room, Hortense was scolding Verdier for being so late, rebuking him after the manner of a peevish boarding-school miss.

"You are looking at her again," said Trublot to Octave, whose eyes were riveted on Valérie.

"So I am," he replied, somewhat confused. "A funny thing, but just now she looks quite pretty. I say, do you think one might risk it?"

Trublot puffed out his cheeks.

"She's hot enough, but you never know. Strange you should fancy her. Anyway, it's better than marrying the little girl."

"What little girl?" cried Octave, forgetting himself. "Why, do you think I am going to let myself be landed? Not I. My good fellow, we don't go in for marrying at Marseilles."

Madame Josserand, close by, overheard that last phrase. It stabbed her like a knife. Another fruitless campaign, another wasted soirée. The blow was such that she had to lean against a chair as she ruefully surveyed the table, swept clean of all refreshments, on which there only now remained the burnt top of the *brioche*. She no longer counted her defeats; but this, in truth, should be the last. And she swore a hideous oath that never again would she feed folk who simple came there to stuff themselves. And, in her exasperation, she looked around the room to see what man there was at whom she could hurl her daughter, when she spied Auguste leaning against the wall, resigned, having had no refreshment.

Just then Berthe, all smiles, was moving towards Octave with a cup of tea in her hand. She was carrying on the war in obedience of her mother's instructions. The latter seized her roughly by the arm, and whispered to her as if she were some refractory animal. Then she said out loud, in her most gracious manner:

"Take the cup to Monsieur Vabre, who has been waiting a whole hour."

Then came another whisper and another war-like look.

"Make yourself agreeable, or you'll have me to deal with!"

Out of politeness, some of the guests went and sat down again for a moment in the drawing-room. They had got their food, and now it was time to go. When they looked for Verdier he had already left, and the girls in their merriment could only take away with them the blurred impression of his back. Without waiting for Octave, Campardon went away with the doctor, whom he still kept on the staircase to ask him if there was really no hope. During tea one of the lamps had gone out, exhaling an odour of rancid oil; the other lamp, with its burnt wick, gave such a lugubrious light that the Vabres rose of their own accord, despite the profuse attentions with which Madame Josserand overwhelmed them. Octave, preceding them, had reached the ante-room, where a surprise was in store for him. Trublot, who was looking for his hat, suddenly disappeared. He could only have made his exit by the passage leading to the kitchen.

"Why, what's become of him? Does he make use of the servants' staircase?" murmured the young man.

However, he thought no more about the matter. Valérie was there, looking for her China crape fichu. The two brothers, Théophile and Auguste, without heeding her, were going downstairs. Having found the fichu, the young man presented it to her with the air of rapture with which he served pretty customers at "The Ladies' Paradise." She looked at him, and he felt certain that her eyes, as they met his, shot forth amorous flames.

"You are too kind, sir," said she, simply.

Madame Juzeur, who was the last to leave, wrapped them both with a smile at once tender and discreet. And when Octave, greatly excited, had got back to his cold bedroom, he glanced at himself in the glass, and determined, by Jove, to have a try for it!

Berthe, who had gone out to set Saturnin at liberty, brought him back with her. She was trying to soothe him, as, with a haggard look of mistrust in his eyes, he feverishly hunted about in the corners of the room like a dog that has been long shut up.

"How silly he is!" said Berthe, 'he thinks that I have just been married, and he is looking for the husband! My dear boy, you may well look! Didn't I tell you that it had all come to nothing. You know very well that it never *does* come to anything!"

Then Madame Josserand burst forth:

"Ah, but it shan't come to nothing this time, that I swear!— even though I have to hook him on to you myself! It's he that shall pay for all the others. Yes, yes, Monsieur Josserand, you may stare, as if you didn't understand. The wedding shall come off; and, if you don't approve of it, you can stay away. So, Berthe, you've only got to pick him up, do you hear?"

Saturnin apparently did not understand. He looked under the table. The girl pointed to him, but Madame Josserand made a sign as if to say that they would get rid of him. And Berthe murmured:

"So it's settled, is it, that it's to be Monsieur Vabre? It's all the same to me. But I do think you might have managed to save me just one sandwich!"

Chapter Four

NEXT day Octave began to grow interested in Valérie.
He watched her ways, and found out the time when
he was likely to meet her on the staircase, managing
to go up frequently to his room, either when lunch-
ing at the Campardons' or when he got away under some
pretext from "The Ladies' Paradise." He soon noticed that
every day, about two o'clock, when taking her child to the
Tuilieries gardens, the young woman went down the Rue
Gaillon. Accordingly, he used to stand at the door and wait for
her, greeting her, like a comely shopman, with a gallant smile.
Every time they met, Valérie politely bowed, but never stopped,
though he noticed that her dark glance was full of the fire of
passion, and he found encouragement in her unhealthy complexion and the supple undulation of her hips.

He had already made his plan—the bold one of a seducer
used to the chivalrous conquest of shop-girl virtue. It was
merely a question of luring Valérie into his room on the fourth
floor; the staircase was always quiet and lonely, and up there
nobody would ever catch them. He laughed inwardly as he
thought of the architect's moral advice; for having a woman
who lived in the house was not the same as bringing one into it.

There was one thing, however, which made him uneasy. The
Pichons' kitchen was separated from their kitchen by the passage, and this constantly obliged them to leave their door open.
At nine in the morning Pichon went off to his office, whence he
did not return until five o'clock. Every other night of the week
he went out after dinner, from eight to twelve, to do some
book-keeping. Moreover, as soon as she heard Octave's step, the
young woman, shy and reserved, would push the door to, and
he only got a back view of her as she fled, with her light hair
tied up into a scanty knot. By such discreet glimpses he had
only caught hitherto a corner of the room, the furniture, sad-
looking and clean; the linen of a dull whiteness, as seen through
an invisible window; the corner of a cot, at the back of the
inner room—in fact, all the monotonous solitude of a woman
who busies herself from morn till night with the petty cares

ot a clerk's household. But not a sound was heard there; the child seemed as silent and apathetic as its mother. Sometimes one could just hear her humming some tune for hours together in a feeble voice. Octave, however, was none the less furious with the scornful jade, as he called her. Perhaps she was playing the spy. In any case, Valérie could never come up to his room if the Pichons' door was always being opened in this way.

He had just begun to think that matters were going right. One Sunday, in the husband's absence, he had managed to be on the first-floor landing just as Valérie, in her dressing-gown, was leaving her sister-in-law's to return to her own apartments. She was obliged to speak to him, and they had just exchanged a few polite remarks. Next time he hoped that she might ask him in. With a woman of her temperament the rest would follow as a matter of course.

During dinner that evening at the Campardons', the talk turned upon Valérie, when Octave tried to draw them out. But as Angèle was listening, and looking slyly at Lisa, who gravely handed round the roast mutton, the parents at first were lavish of their praise. Besides, the architect was for ever upholding the respectability of the house, with the conceited assurance of a tenant who appeared to derive therefrom a certificate of his own moral probity.

During dessert Octave, seated between husband and wife, got to know more than he had asked. They forgot Angèle's presence, talked with hints, with winks that, as it were, underlined the double meaning of their words; and if these failed them, they whispered to him, confidentially, by turns. In short, Théophile was an impotent idiot, who deserved to be what his wife had made him. As for Valérie, she was not worth much; she would have behaved just as badly even if her husband had been able to satisfy her, being so carried away by her natural impulses. Moreover, everybody knew that, two months after marriage, in despair at finding that she could never have a child by her husband, and fearing to lose her share of old Vabre's fortune if Théophile happened to die, she had her little Camille got for her by a brawny young butcher's assistant of the Rue Sainte-Anne.

Finally, Campardon whispered in Octave's ear:

"In short, you know, my dear fellow, an hysterical woman!"

And he put into the word all the gross indecency of the middle classes, together with the loose-lipped grin of the father of a family, whose imagination, suddenly let loose, battens upon pictures of lascivious orgies.

Then came other details. It would be impossible to find a woman better brought up than she, or who had stricter principles. And how happy her husband was! Their little home was so neat, so pretty; each adored the other, and they never had the least word!

"Besides, if they misbehaved themselves, they would not be allowed to remain in the house," said the architect, gravely, forgetting his disclosures anent Valérie. "We only want decent folk here. 'Pon my honour! I would give notice the same day that my daughter ran the risk of meeting disreputable people on the stairs."

That very evening he had made secret arrangements to take cousin Gasparine to the Opéra-Comique. So he at once went to fetch his hat, saying something about a business engagement, which might detain him until very late. However, Rose must have known something about this, for Octave heard her whisper, in her resigned, motherly way, as Campardon stooped to kiss her with his usual effusive tenderness:

"I hope you'll enjoy yourself—and don't catch cold coming out."

Next morning Octave had an idea. It was to make Madame Pichon's acquaintance by doing her some trifling neighbourly service; and in this way, if she ever caught Valérie, she would keep her eyes shut. That very day an opportunity presented itself. Madame used to take out her little Lilitte, aged eighteen months, in a wicker perambulator, a proceeding which roused the righteous wrath of Monsieur Gourd, who never would allow the vehicle to be taken up by the main staircase, so that Madame Pichon had to pull it up by the servants' stairway. Moreover, as the door of her apartment was too narrow, she had to take off the wheels every time, which was quite a long business. It so happened that on this particular day, as Octave was coming home, he found Marie with her gloves on, trying all she could to unscrew the wheels. When she felt him standing close behind her, waiting until the passage was clear, her hands trembled, and she quite lost her head.

"But why do you take all that trouble, madam?" asked he, at length. "It would be far simpler to put the perambulator at the end of the passage, behind my door."

She did not reply, but remained in a squatting position, excessive timidity preventing her from rising, and under the flaps of her bonnet he noticed that her neck and ears were suffused by a burning blush. Then he insisted:

"I assure you, madam, that it will not inconvenience me in the least."

Without further delay, he lifted the perambulator and carried it off in his easy, unaffected way. She had to follow him, but felt so confused, so amazed at this startling adventure in her hum-drum every-day existence, that she watched his action, unable to do more than stammer out a few disjointed phrases:

"Dear me, sir, it's giving you too much trouble. I am so confused—you'll be putting yourself to such inconvenience. My husband will be so pleased——"

And she went in, half-ashamed, this time tightly fastening the door after her. Octave thought she must be stupid. The perambulator was very much in his way, for it prevented him from opening his door, and he had to get through it sideways. But he seemed to have won his neighbour's goodwill, the more so because Monsieur Gourd, owing to Campardon's influence, had graciously consented to sanction this obstruction at the end of this out-of-the-way passage.

Every Sunday Marie's parents, Monsieur and Madame Vuillaume, used to come and spend the day with her. On the following Sunday, as Octave was going out, he perceived the whole family just about to have their coffee, and was discreetly hurrying past, when the young wife hastily whispered something to her husband. The latter at once rose, saying:

"Pray excuse me, sir. I am always out, and have not yet had an opportunity of thanking you; but I am anxious to be able to tell you how pleased I was——"

Octave, protesting, was at last obliged to go in, and, though he had already had some, was obliged to accept a cup of coffee, and the place of honour between Monsieur and Madame Vuillaume. Facing him on the opposite side of the round table, Marie had one of her sudden blushing fits, which for no apparent reason sent all the blood from her heart to her face. He noticed how she never seemed at her ease, and agreed with Trublot that she was certainly not his ideal; she looked so puny, so washed-out, with her flat bosom and scanty hair, though her features were delicate, even pretty. When she had somewhat regained her composure, she began giggling, as she enthusiastic-ally discussed the perambulator incident.

After this experience, Octave on Sundays would always hurry past the Pichons' door, especially if he heard the rasping voices of the Vuillaumes. Besides, he was wholly bent upon the conquest of Valérie. Despite the burning glances, of which he believed himself to be the object, she displayed an unaccount-able reserve; this was her coquetry, so he thought. One day, too, he met her by chance in the Tuileries gardens, when she began to talk calmly about the storm of the previous night; and this sufficed to convince him that she had a deuced amount of nerve. And he was always up and down the staircase, watching his opportunity to pay her a visit, being determined to come straight to the point.

Every time that he now passed, Marie, blushing, smiled at him. They nodded to each other in neighbourly fashion. One morning, about lunch-time, as he was bringing her a letter that Monsieur Gourd had entrusted to him so as to avoid the long journey up to the fourth floor, he found her in great perplexity. She had just placed Lilitte on the round table in her chemise and was trying to dress her.

"What is the matter?" asked the young man.

"Oh, it's this child!" she replied. "I was so silly as to un-dress her because she was fretful. And I don't know how to get on; I don't indeed!"

He looked at her in astonishment. She kept turning the child's petticoat over and over, trying to find the hocks and eyes. Then she added:

"You see, her father always helps me to dress her of a morn-ing, before he starts. I never have to see to it all by myself. It's such a bother, it worries me so!"

The little girl, tired of being in her chemise, and frightened at seeing Octave, struggled and turned over on the table.

"Take care," cried he; "she will fall."

A catastrophe seemed imminent. Marie looked at though she dared not touch the naked limbs of her child. She gazed at her in a sort of original surprise, amazed at having been able to produce such a thing. Besides the fear of harming the child, there was in her awkwardness a certain vague repugnance to its living flesh. However, helped by Octave, who soothed Lilitte, she was able to dress her again.

"How will you manage when you have a dozen?" he asked, laughingly.

"But we are never going to have any more!" she replied, in a frightened tone.

Then he chaffed her, telling her it was a mistake to be so sure; it was so easy to make a little baby!

"No, no," she obstinately repeated. "You heard what mamma said the other day. She told Jules that she would not allow it. You don't know what she is; there would be endless squabbles if another were to come."

Octave was amused at the calm way in which she discussed this question. Though he kept drawing her out, he could not succeed in embarrassing her. Moreover, she just did as her husband wished. She was fond of children, of course, and if he wanted any more, she would not say no. And under all this complacent submission to her mother's orders, one could note the indifference of a woman whose maternal instinct had not yet been roused. Lilitte had to be looked after in the same way that her home required attention—a mere duty that must be done. When she had washed up the crockery, and had taken the child for a walk, she continued to live her old life as a girl —a somnolent, empty existence, lulled by vague expectations of a joy that never came. When Octave observed that she must find it very dull to be always alone, she seemed surprised. Oh, no, she was never dull! the days slipped by somehow without her knowing, as she went to bed, how she had employed her time. Then on Sundays she sometimes went out with her husband, sometimes her parents came, or else she had a book to read. If reading had not given her a headache, she would have read from morning till night, now that she was allowed to read every sort of book.

"The annoying thing is," she continued, "that they have got nothing at the lending library in the Passage Choiseul. For instance, I wanted to read 'André' again, just because it made me cry so when I first read it. Well, that's the very volume that has been stolen; and my father won't lend me his copy because Lilitte might tear out the pictures."

"Well, my friend Campardon has got all George Sand's works," said Octave. "I'll ask him to lend me 'André' for you."

She blushed again, and her eyes sparkled. It was really too kind of him! And when he left her she stood there, in front of Lilitte, her arms a-flop, without an idea in her head, in the same position that she was wont to remain for whole afternoons together. She hated sewing, but used to do crochet; always the same little scrap of wool, which was left lying about the room.

The following day, which was Sunday, Octave brought her the book. Pichon had been obliged to go out, to leave a card on one of his superiors. Finding her in walking dress, as she had just come back from an errand close by, Octave, just for curiosity's sake, asked her if she had been to Mass, thinking that possibly she was very religious. She said no. Before her marriage her mother used to take her to church regularly. And for six months after her marriage she used to go from sheer force of habit, being always afraid of getting there too late. Then, she hardly knew why, after missing two or three times, she left off going altogether. Her husband could not bear priests, and her mother now never mentioned the subject. Octave's question, however, was a disturbing one, as if it had roused within her emotions long since buried beneath the indolent apathy of her actual existence.

"I must go to Saint-Roch one of these days," said she. "When you stop doing something you've been accustomed to, you always feel the miss of it."

And over the pallid features of this girl, begotten out of due season by elderly parents, there came an expression of sickly regret, of longing for some other existence, dreamed of long since in shadowland. She could hide nothing; everything revealed itself in her face, with her skin as tender, as transparent as that of some chlorotic patient. Then she impulsively caught hold of Octave's hand.

"Oh, I must thank you so much for bringing me this book! Come in to-morrow, after lunch. I will give it back to you, and tell you what effect it had upon me. That will be amusing, won't it?"

There was something droll about the woman, thought Octave, as he came away. He had begun to feel interested in her, and he thought of speaking to Pichon, so as to get him to wake her up a bit, for there was no doubt that the little woman only wanted rousing. It so happened that he met Pichon the very next day as he was going out, and he walked some part of the way with him, though he himself risked being a quarter of an hour late at "The Ladies' Paradise." Pichon, however, appeared to be even less wide-awake than his wife, full of incipient manias, and entirely overcome by a dread of dirtying his boots, as it was rainy weather. He walked along on tiptoe, talking incessantly about his sub-director. As Octave's motive in this matter was a purely brotherly one, he left him at last in the Rue Saint-Honoré, after advising him to take Marie as often as possible to the theatre.

"Whatever for?" asked Pichon, in amazement.

"Because it does women good. It makes them nicer."

"Do you really think so?"

He promised to think about it, and crossed the street, looking about in terror lest the cabs should splash him, this being his one and only torment in life.

At lunch-time Octave knocked at the Pichons' door to fetch the book. Marie, with her elbows on the table, was reading, her hands thrust through her dishevelled hair. She had just been eating an egg, cooked in a tin pan, which now lay on the untidy table devoid of a cloth. Lilitte, neglected, was asleep on the floor, her nose touching the fragments of a plate which, doubtless, she had smashed.

"Well?" said Octave, enquiringly.

Marie did not immediately reply. She was still in her dressing-gown, which, being buttonless, displayed her neck and breasts in all the disorder of a woman who has just got out of bed.

"I've only read about a hundred pages," she said, at last. "My parents were here yesterday."

Then she talked in a dreary, mournful way. When younger she had longed to live in the depths of the forest, and was for ever dreaming that she would meet a huntsman there sounding his horn. Approaching, he knelt down before her. All this happened in a coppice far, far away, where roses bloomed as in a park. Then, all at once, they were married, and lived on there, wandering about together eternally. She, in her perfect happiness, desired nothing more; while he, tender, submissive, as a slave, remained ever at her feet.

"I had a chat with your husband this morning," said Octave. "You don't go out enough, and I have persuaded him to take you to the theatre."

But she shook her head, pale and trembling. There was a silence. The narrow, chilly dining-room once more appeared to her, and the dull, decorous figure of Jules suddenly blotted out the huntsman of her romance, the distant sound of whose horn still rang in her ears. At times she would listen; perhaps he was coming. Her husband had never taken her feet in his hands and kissed them, nor had he ever knelt down to tell her that he adored her. Nevertheless, she was very fond of him, but it amazed her that love did not possess more sweetness.

"The parts that touch me in novels," she said, coming back to the book, "are the parts where lovers tell each other of their love."

Octave at last sat down. He wanted to treat the matter as a joke, caring little for such sentimental stuff.

"I hate a lot of speechifying," he said. "If two people adore each other, the best thing is for them to prove it there and then."

But apparently she did not understand, as she looked at him with lack-lustre eyes. Stretching out his hand, he just touched hers, and leant close to her to look at a passage in the book, so closely that his breath warmed her bare shoulder. But she remained impassive, cold as a corpse. Then he got up to go, full of a contempt touched with pity. As he was leaving, she said:

"I read very slowly; I shall not have finished it until to-morrow. That's when it will be amusing; so do come in in the evening."

It is true Octave had no designs upon the woman; and yet, somehow, he was angry with her. He had felt a curious sort of attachment for this young couple, who exasperated him, just because they were content to lead such a stupid life. And he half resolved to do them a service, in spite of themselves. He would take them out to dinner, make them drunk, and then amuse himself by pushing them into each other's arms. When a good-natured fit like this came over him, he, who was loth to

lend anyone ten francs, delighted to squander money in bringing lovers together and in giving them joy.

However, this coldness on the part of little Madame Pichon
recalled Octave to Valérie, the ardent. She surely would not
want her neck to be breathed upon twice. He had made advance
in her favour. One day, as she was going upstairs in front of
him, he had ventured to compliment her upon her leg without
her showing any signs of displeasure.

At length the long-watched-for opportunity came. It was
the evening that Marie had made him promise to come and talk
about the novel, as they would be alone, for her husband was
not coming home until very late. But the young fellow would
have preferred to go out; the bare thought of this literary treat
appalled him. However, about ten o'clock he thought he would
try it on, when, on the first-floor landing, he met Valérie's
maid, who, with a scared look, said:

"Madame is in hysterics, master is out, and everyone opposite
has gone to the theatre. Do, please, come in, as I am all alone,
and I don't know what to do."

Valérie was in her bedroom, stretched out in an armchair, her
limbs rigid. The maid had unlaced her stays where her breasts
protruded. The attack was over almost directly. She opened her
eyes, seemed surprised to see Octave there, and behaved just as
if he were the doctor.

"I must ask you to excuse me, sir," she murmured, in a choking voice. "This girl only came yesterday, and she lost her
head."

Her perfect composure in taking off her stays and in button-
ing up her dress, disconcerted the young man. He remained
standing, resolved not to go like this, yet not daring to sit down.
She had sent away her maid, the sight of whom seemed to irri-
tate her, and she went to the window to breathe the cool night
air, which she inhaled in long, nervous gasps, with her mouth
wide open. After a pause, they began to talk. She first had these
attacks when she was fourteen, and Doctor Juillerat was tired
of prescribing for her; sometimes she had them in her arms,
and sometimes in her loins. However, she was getting used to
them; as well suffer from them as from anything else, for nobody had perfect health, you know. And as she talked thus,
her limbs placid, almost lifeless, the sight of her roused his

51

sensual appetites, and he thought her tempting, in all her disorder, with her leaden complexion and her drawn features, as if by the exhaustion of a long night of love. Behind the dark tresses of her hair, that fell all about her shoulders, he thought he beheld the puny, beardless face of her husband. Then, with outstretched arms, he roughly caught her round the waist, as he would have clipped some harlot.

"Well, what is it?" she asked, in surprise.

Now, in her turn, she looked at him, her eyes so cold, her body so impassive, that he felt frozen, and awkwardly his hands dropped. The absurdity of his gesture did not escape him. Then, stifling a last nervous yawn, she slowly murmured:

"Ah, my dear sir, if you only knew!"

And she shrugged her shoulders, showing no sign of anger, but merely of overwhelming contempt and weariness of the male. Octave thought she was about to have him turned out when he saw her go towards the bell-rope, trailing her petticoats as she went. But she only wanted some tea, and this she ordered to be very weak and very hot.

Utterly nonplussed, he muttered some excuse and made for the door, while she lay back in her armchair, like some chilly woman in absolute need of sleep.

As he went upstairs, Octave stopped on each landing. So she did not care for that, then? He had just seen how indifferent she was, without desire and without resentment, as disobliging as his employer, Madame Hédouin. Why, then, did Campardon say that she was hysterical? How absurd to hoax him with such a nonsensical tale! But for the architect's lie he would never have risked such an adventure. The result of it quite bewildered him, and his ideas as to hysteria became confused as he thought of the various tales about Valérie that were afloat. Trublot's remark came back to his mind: one never knew what to expect from this sort of crazy women with eyes like burning coals.

On reaching his own floor Octave, vexed with womankind in general, walked as noiselessly as possible. But the Pichons' door opened, and he was obliged to resign himself to his fate. Marie stood waiting for him in the little, ill-lighted room. She had drawn the cot close to the table, and Lilitte lay asleep in the yellow circle of light made by the lamp. The same plates which had done duty at lunch-time must have been used for dinner, for

52

the closed book lay close to a dirty plate filled with the remains of some radishes.

"Have you finished it?" asked Octave, surprised at her silence.

She looked like one intoxicated, her cheeks puffy, as if just awaking from some heavy sleep.

"Yes, yes!" she exclaimed with difficulty. "Oh, I have spent the whole day poring over it! When one is absorbed like that, one hardly knows where one is. Oh, my neck *does* ache!"

So fagged was she that she could speak no more about the novel; the emotions, the confused dreams that it had aroused in her mind, almost overwhelmed her. Still ringing in her ears she heard the faint clarion notes of her ideal huntsman, wafted to her across the dim blue landscape of her dreams. Then she suddenly said that she had been that morning to the nine o'clock Mass at Saint-Roch. She had wept much; in religion lay the one substitute for all other things.

"Oh, I am better now!" she said, as, sighing deeply, she stood still in front of Octave.

There was a pause. She smiled at him with her light-blue eyes. Never had she seemed to him so utterly useless, with her scanty hair and muddy complexion. Then, as she continued to gaze at him, her face grew very pale, and she tottered forward, so that he had to hold out his hands to save her from falling.

"My God! my God!" she sobbed out.

He looked at her in embarrassment.

"You ought to take a little *tilleul*. This comes of reading too much."

"Yes, it upset me when, on closing the book, I found myself alone. How good you are, Monsieur Mouret! Without you, I should have come to some harm."

Meanwhile, he looked about for a chair on which to place her.

"Would you like me to light a fire?"

"No, thank you; it would make your hands dirty; I have noticed that you always wear gloves."

The idea brought back that choking sensation at her throat, and, as she suddenly sank down, half swooning, she clumsily launched a kiss into the air, vaguely, as if in her dream. It just touched Octave's ear.

Such a kiss amazed him. The young woman's lips were cold as ice. Then, as she fell forward upon his breast, yielding up her whole body, he felt a sudden desire burn within him, and he was for carrying her into the room beyond. But this abrupt advance roused Marie from her swoon; her womanly instincts revolted. Struggling, she called upon her mother, forgetting her husband, who would soon come home, and her daughter, asleep at her side.

"No, no, not that! no, it is wrong."

But he kept saying, in his excitement:

"Nobody will ever know; I shall never tell."

"No, no, Monsieur Octave! You will spoil all the happiness that is mine in knowing you. I am sure it won't do us any good, and I had dreamed of—oh, such things!"

Then, without another word, he felt that he must have his revenge upon womankind, saying coarsely to himself, "You've got to have it." As she would not go into the bedroom with him, he brutally thrust her backwards across the table. She gave in, and he enjoyed her there, midway between the dirty plate and the novel, which, when the table shook, fell on to the floor. The door had not even been shut; the solemn silence of the staircase pervaded all. Lilitte lay sleeping peacefully in her cot.

When Marie and Octave got up, she with her rumpled petticoats, neither had a word to say. Mechanically she went and looked at her daughter, took up the plate, and then laid it down again. He, too, was dumb, feeling equally ill at ease, for this had happened so unexpectedly. He recollected, too, how he had formed the brotherly plan of making husband and wife fall round each other's necks. Impelled to break this insufferable silence, he at length muttered:

"Why, you didn't shut the door!"

She looked out on to the landing, and stammered:

"No more I did. It was open."

She seemed to walk with difficulty, and on her face there was a look of disgust. The young man began to reflect that there was nothing particularly amusing in an adventure of this sort with a helpless, lonely woman. She had not even had any pleasure from it.

"Oh, look! the book has tumbled down!" she continued, as she picked the volume up. One of the corners of the binding was crushed and bent. This brought them together again; it was a relief. Speech came back to them. Marie appeared much distressed.

"It wasn't my fault. You see, I had put a paper cover on it, for fear it should get soiled. We must have knocked it off the table by mistake."

"It was there, then?" asked Octave. "I never noticed it. It doesn't matter a bit to me; but Campardon thinks such a lot of his books."

Each kept handing the book to the other, and trying to bend the corner straight. Their fingers touched, yet neither felt a thrill. As they thought of the consequences, they were both dismayed at the accident which had befallen the beautiful volume of George Sand.

"It was bound to end badly," said Marie, with tears in her eyes.

Octave felt obliged to console her. He would invent some story or other. Campardon wouldn't eat him. And, as they were about to separate, the feeling of uneasiness returned. One kind word, at least, they would like to have said to each other, but somehow it stuck in their throats. Fortunately, just then a step was heard; it was the husband coming upstairs. Silently Octave put his arms about her again, and kissed her in his turn upon the mouth. And again she complacently submitted, her lips icy cold as before. When he had noiselessly got back to his room, he remarked to himself, as he took off his coat, that apparently she didn't like that either. Then what on earth was it that she wanted? And why did she go tumbling into fellows' arms? Women were certainly queer folk.

Next day, after lunch at the Campardons', as Octave was again explaining how by his clumsiness he had damaged the book, Marie came in. She was going to take Lilitte to the Tuileries gardens, and had called to ask if they would let Angèle go with her. She smiled at Octave with perfect self-possession, and glanced innocently at the book lying on a chair.

"Why, of course," said Madame Campardon, "I shall be delighted. Angèle, go and put on your hat. With you she's quite safe."

Looking like modesty personified in her simple dark stuff dress, Marie spoke about her husband, who had come home late last night and had caught cold. She also mentioned the price of meat; soon people would not be able to afford any at all. Then, after she had left, taking Angèle with her, they all leant out of the window to see them start. There was Marie leisurely pushing Lilitte's perambulator along with her gloved hands, while Angèle, who knew that she was being watched, walked beside her, with downcast eyes.

"Doesn't she look nice!" exclaimed Madame Campardon. "So ladylike, so respectable!"

Then, slapping Octave on the back, her husband said:

"In a family, education is everything, my dear boy—everything!"

Chapter Five

AT the Duveyriers' that evening there was a reception and a concert. Octave had been invited for the first time, and about ten o'clock he was just finishing dressing. He was in a serious, half-irritable mood. How was it that his affair with Valérie had not come off—a woman so well connected as she was? And Berthe Josserand, ought he not to have reflected before refusing her? Just as he was tying his white tie, the thought of Marie Pichon became positively unbearable to him. Five months in Paris, and only a paltry adventure like that! He felt ashamed of himself, being well aware of the hollowness and the vanity of such a connection. And as he drew on his gloves, he vowed that he would no longer waste his time in such a way. Now that at last he had got into society, he resolved to act, for opportunities were certainly not lacking.

Marie was looking out for him at the end of the passage. As Pichon was not there, he had to go in for a moment.

"How smart you are!" she whispered.

They had never been invited to the Duveyriers'; accordingly she felt for these first-floor people excessive awe. But she was jealous of no one; for this she had neither the strength nor the will.

"I shall wait for you," she said, holding up her forehead. "Don't stay too late; and you must tell me how you enjoyed yourself."

Octave was constrained to kiss her hair. Though a relationship had been established between them which depended upon his inclination, it was not really an intimate one. At last he went downstairs, and she, leaning over the banisters, followed him with her eyes.

At the same moment quite a drama was being enacted at the Josserands'. According to the mother, this evening party at the Duveyriers' was to decide the match between her daughter Berthe and Auguste Vabre. Despite sundry vigorous onslaughts during the past fortnight, the latter still hesitated, evidently exercised by doubts as to the dowry. With a view to striking a

57

decisive blow, Madame Josserand had written to her brother announcing the projected marriage, and reminding him of his promises, hoping that his reply might furnish her with something which she could use to advantage. And, at nine o'clock, as the whole family stood round the dining-room stove, in full dress and ready to go downstairs. Monsieur Gourd brought up a letter from uncle Bachelard, which had been left lying under Madame Gourd's snuff-box ever since the last delivery.

"Ah, at last!" cried Madame Josserand, as she tore open the envelope.

The girls and their father anxiously watched her as she read. Adèle, who had been obliged to dress the ladies, was moving about in her clumsy fashion as she cleared away the dinner-service. Madame Josserand turned very pale.

"Not a word!" she stuttered, "not a single clear sentence! He says that he will see later on, at the time of the marriage. And he sends his best love to us all! The wretched old humbug!"

Monsieur Josserand, in evening clothes, sank backwards into a chair. Hortense and Berthe, whose legs ached, sat down as well; the one in blue, the other in pink; those eternal frocks of theirs that they had furbished up yet once again.

"Bachelard is an impostor; I have always said so," murmured the father. "He'll never part with a sou."

Standing there in her flaming red gown, Madame Josserand read the letter over agin. Then she burst forth:

"Oh, you men! Take him, for instance. One would think he was an idiot, to judge by the life he leads. But, no, not a bit of it! He may look like a fool, but he's wide-awake enough directly you mention money. Oh, you men!"

Then she turned towards her daughters, to whom this lesson was addressed.

"Look here, it's got to this, that I positively wonder why you girls are so mad to get married! Ah, if you'd been worried to death by it, as I have! A fellow who doesn't love you for yourself, nor brings you a fortune without haggling over it! A millionaire uncle, who, after living upon you for twenty years, declines even to give his niece a dowry! A husband who is incompetent—do you hear me, sir, incompetent!"

Monsieur Josserand bowed.

Adèle, not even listening, had just cleared away the things. Madame Josserand swerved round furiously at her.

"What are you listening here for? Go back to the kitchen at once!"

Then came her peroration.

"In short, everything for these vile men, and nothing for us —not even a crust if we're starving! Depend upon it, the only thing they're fit for is to be taken in! So just mark my words!"

Hortense and Berthe nodded as though profoundly impressed by the truth of such counsel. Their mother had long since convinced them of the absolute inferiority of man, a creature whose sole mission in life was to marry and to pay. There was a long silence in that fusty dining-room that smelt of the stale food which Adèle had omitted to remove. Sitting about in their finery the Josserands forgot the Duveyriers' concert as they meditated upon life's perpetual deceptions. From the adjoining room came the sound of Saturnin's snoring, whom they had sent to bed early.

At last Berthe spoke.

"So there's an end of that! Had we better go and take our things off?"

In an instant Madame Josserand's energy came back. What! take their things off! And why, pray? Was their family not a respectable one, or an alliance with them not as good as with other people? The marriage should come off all the same; she would die rather. And she hastily gave to each their parts. The girls were told to make themselves particularly agreeable to Auguste, and not to let go of him until he had taken the plunge. The father was entrusted with the task of conquering the sympathies of old Vabre and Duveyrier, by always agreeing with everything they said, if this proceeding were not too great a strain upon his intellect. As for herself, she would tackle the women, and knew well how to win them all over to her side of the game. Then, collecting her thoughts, and glancing round the dining-room once more, as if to make sure that no weapon had been overlooked, she assumed the terrible mien of a warrior leading forth his daughters to be massacred, as in a loud voice she cried:

"Let us go down!"

The Duveyriers' rooms were already crowded as they entered. The huge grand piano filled one side of the panelled drawing-room; the ladies were seated before it in rows, as if at a theatre, a dense black background being formed by the men in evening dress, which extended to the dining-room and parlour beyond. The chandelier and six bracket-lamps lighted up the white and gold apartment to a pitch of brilliancy that was positively dazzling, exhibiting in all their crudeness of tone the red silk hangings and furniture. The heat was great; and, as they regularly rose and fell, fans dispersed the pungent aroma of corsets and of naked busts.

Just at that moment Madame Duveyrier was about to sit down at the piano. With a gesture, Madame Josserand smilingly besought her hostess not to trouble herself. Leaving her daughters among the men, she took a chair between Valérie and Madame Juzeur. Monsieur Josserand found his way to the parlour, where Monsieur Vabre, the landlord, was asleep in his customary corner of the sofa. Here, too, in a group, were Campardon, Théophile and Auguste Vabre, Doctor Juillerat, and the Abbé Mauduit; while Trublot and Octave had just fled together from the music to the far corner of the dining-room. Near them, behind the sea of black coats, stood Duveyrier, tall and thin, watching his wife at the piano, and waiting for silence. At his button-hole, in a neat little rosette, he wore the ribbon of the Légion d'Honneur.

Then they both began talking about women, without paying further heed to her performance. On seeing Valérie, Octave felt rather embarrassed. How should he behave? Speak to her, or pretend not to see her? Trublot put on an air of fine disdain; not a woman among the lot that took his fancy; and, in reply to his companion's protest that there was surely somebody to suit his taste, he sagely remarked:

"Well, pick and choose, and then you'll soon see when they get up. Eh? Not that one at the back there, with feathers; nor yet the blonde person in mauve; nor that elderly female, although she, at least, is plump. I tell you, it is absurd to look for anything of that sort in society. Lots of airs and graces, but no fun!"

Octave smiled. He had his position to make in the world; he could not afford merely to follow his taste, like Trublot, whose father was so rich. Those long rows of women set him thinking, and he asked himself which of them all he would have chosen for his fortune or his pleasure if it had been allowed him to take one of them away. Suddenly, as he was appraising them all, he exclaimed, in surprise:

"Hullo! there's my employer's wife! Does she come here?"

"Yes; didn't you know that?" rejoined Trublot. "In spite of the difference in their ages, Madame Hédouin and Madame Duveyrier are old school friends, inseparables, who went by the name of the Polar Bears, as they were always twenty degrees below zero. Another pair of figure-heads for you! I pity Duveyrier, if he's no other hot-water bottle than that to warm his feet in winter!"

Octave, however, had grown serious. He now, for the first time, saw Madame Hédouin in an evening gown, cut low, showing her neck and arms, her dark hair being plaited across her forehead, and in this heated glare she seemed the realisation of his desires. A superb woman—healthy, handsome, who could but prove a benefit to a man. A thousand schemes absorbed him, when a loud noise of clapping roused him from his dream.

Everyone was congratulating Clotilde. Rushing forward, Madame Josserand seized her by both hands, as the men went on talking, and the women plied their fans with greater vigour. Duveyrier then ventured to retreat to the parlour, whither Trublot and Octave followed him. Hemmed in by petticoats, the former whispered:

"Look there, on your right! The hooking process has begun."

It was Madame Josserand inciting Berthe to the conquest of young Vabre, who imprudently had gone up to them to pay his respects. That evening his headache was better, and he only felt a slight touch of neuralgia in the left eye; but he dreaded the end of the party, as there was going to be singing—the very worst thing for him.

"Berthe, tell Monsieur Auguste about the remedy which you copied for him out of that book—a sovereign cure for headache!"

And, having started them, Madame Josserand left them standing near the window.

"By Jove! they've got to chemistry," whispered Trublot.

Just then there was a faint murmur in the drawing-room, which brought Trublot and Octave back to the door. They saw a lady of about fifty coming in. She was powerfully built, still handsome, and was accompanied by a serious-looking, carefully-dressed young man.

The newcomers were Madame Dambreville and Léon Josserand. She had agreed to get him a wife, but meanwhile had reserved him for her own personal use, and now, as their honeymoon was at the full, they advertised their *liaison* in every middle-class drawing-room. There was much whispering among mothers with marriageable daughters.

"I say, have you seen Julie?" asked Trublot suddenly, in a mysterious voice.

As Octave looked at him in amazement, he added:

"My dear fellow, she is stunning. Go and have a look at her. Just pretend that you want to go to the rear, and then slip through into the kitchen. She is simply stunning."

It was the Duveyriers cook to whom he alluded.

With a complacent air of self-sacrifice, Hortense stood by to help her sister, echoing her laughter and pushing her up against the young man, while air from the open window behind them lightly stirred the large red-silk curtains.

The two were now by themselves, breathing the cool outdoor air, while Hortense played sentry, leaning against the curtain and mechanically twisting the loop. No one was looking at them now; Madame Josserand and Madame Dambreville even had given up watching them, after exchanging significant glances. Hortense had unhooked the loop by a movement which might have been unintentional, and the curtain as it fell had completely hidden Auguste and Berthe. They were there behind it, leaning against the window-bar; not a single movement betrayed their presence.

All at once a voice was heard to exclaim:

"Don't. You're hurting me!"

Everyone looked round towards the window. Madame Dambreville, anxious to make herself useful, was kind enough to pull the curtain aside. And the whole room beheld Auguste, looking very confused, and Berthe, very red, as they still leant against the window-bar.

"What is it, my precious?" asked Madame Josserand, eagerly.

"Nothing, mamma. Monsieur Auguste knocked my arm in

opening the window, I was so hot."

And she blushed deeper still. There was some covert tittering and grimacing among the audience. Madame Duveyrier, who for a while had been trying to keep her brother out of Berthe's way, turned quite pale. The girl had certainly been too greatly compromised; an engagement was inevitable.

"Well so he's hooked!" said Trublot on rejoining Octave.

Berthe, who had now completely regained her composure, was laughing again; while Hortense surveyed Auguste with the sullen air of a girl who has got her diploma: In this their conquest, one could detect the mother's tuition—the result of her lessons regarding undisguised contempt for man. All the male guests now invaded the drawing-room, mixing with the ladies, and talking in a loud voice. Annoyed at the scene in which Berthe had figured, Monsieur Josserand drew nearer to his wife. It irked him to hear her thanking Madame Dambreville for all her lavish attentions to Léon, in whom, there was no doubt, she had wrought a most beneficial change. She pretended to talk in a low voice to Madame Juzeur, intending Valérie and Clotilde, who stood by to overhear her.

"Yes, you know, her uncle only wrote to me to-day; Berthe is to have fifty thousand francs. That's not much, certainly; but still, it's a lump sum, in hard cash, you know!"

This lie absolutely disgusted her husband. He could not help lightly touching her on the shoulder. She looked up at him; so resolute was the expression on her face that his eyes fell.

At the same moment, Trublot, on the sofa, was leaning over and whispering to Octave.

"By the way," he asked, "would you like me to get you an invitation from a lady at whose house one has some fun?"

And, as his companion wished to know what kind of lady, he added, as he pointed to Duveyrier:

"His mistress."

"Never!" exclaimed Octave, in amazement.

Trublot slowly opened and shut his eyes. It was so. When one had married a wife who was not obliging, who appeared disgusted at the idea of having babies, and who thrashed the piano until all the dogs of the neighbourhood fell sick, why, one went elsewhere about town to find consolation.

"Well, that's a nice state of affairs!" said Octave to himself, whose respect for the house had received another shock.

Then, seeing that Madame Hédouin was going to the cloak-room, and wishing to get there before her, he followed Trublot, who was also about to leave. Octave's idea was to see her safely home. She declined his escort, as it was barely midnight and she lived so close by. Then, as a rose fell from the bouquet at her bosom, he picked it up with an injured air and made a show of keeping it as a souvenir. For a moment her handsome brows contracted. Then she said, in her calm, self-possessed way:

"Kindly open the door for me, Monsieur Octave—thank you."

When she had gone downstairs, Octave, in his embarrassment, looked about for Trublot. But, as before at the Josserands', Trublot had just disappeared. He must have slipped away by the servant's staircase.

About one o'clock the Josserands, in their turn, went home. On a chair in the hall, Adèle had placed a candlestick and matches. None of them spoke as they came upstairs, but on reaching the dining-room, which they had erst quitted in such a despairing mood, they yielded to a sudden burst of mad merriment, wildly seizing each other's hands as they danced a sort of savage dance all round the table. The staid father, even, yielded to the infection; the mother cut elephantine capers, and the girls uttered little inarticulate cries, while the candles on the table flung their huge dancing shadows along the wall.

"Well, at last that's settled!" exclaimed Madame Josserand, as she sank breathlessly into a chair.

But in a sudden paroxysm of maternal tenderness, she at once got up again, and running to Berthe, kissed her effusively on both cheeks.

"I am pleased, very pleased, with you, my darling. You have just rewarded me for all my exertions. My sweet child! my sweet child! so it really is true this time."

Her voice was broken by emotion, sudden and heartfelt, as in her flame-coloured gown she collapsed at the very moment of victory, prostrated by the fatigues of her terrible campaign of three winters. Berthe was obliged to protest that she was not unwell, for her mother thought that she was looking pale, and paid her all sorts of little attentions. She even insisted upon making her a cup of linden-tea. When Berthe had gone to bed, her mother, barefoot, went softly to her bedside, as in the far-off days of her childhood.

Meanwhile, with his head on the pillow, Monsieur Josserand awaited his wife's return. She blew out the light, and got across him to her side, nearest the wall. Then he again felt ill at ease, and the same qualms of conscience assailed him as he thought of the promise of a dowry of fifty thousand francs. And he ventured to express his scruples out loud. Why promise when one did not know if one could keep one's word? It was not honourable.

"Not honourable, indeed!" cried Madame Josserand, out of the darkness, as her voice again assumed its usual ferocity of tone. "I'll tell you what is not honourable, sir, and that is to let your daughters turn into old maids; yes, old maids, which was probably your intention. Why, good gracious me! we've lots of time to look about us; we must talk the matter over, and get her uncle to make up his mind. Moreover, *my* family, I would have you know, sir, have always acted honourably."

Chapter Six

*T*HE next day, which was Sunday, Octave lay for an extra hour drowsing in the warm sheets. He awoke in the mood of lazy good-humour which accompanies the mental clearness that morning brings. Why should he be in any hurry? He was quite comfortable at "The Ladies' Paradise"; he was shaking off his provincial airs, and he felt absolutely certain that one day Madame Hédouin would become his, when she would make his fortune. The matter, however, required prudence, a long series of gallant tactics, the thoughts of which appealed pleasurably to his voluptuous sense for the female. As he dropped off to sleep again, making plans, and giving himself six months in which to succeed, the vision of Marie Pichon served to soothe his impatience. A woman of that sort was very handy; he had only to stretch out his arm if he wanted her, and she did not cost him a sou. While waiting for the other one, surely no better arrangement than this was possible. As, in this drowsy way, he reflected upon her cheapness and utility, he became quite tender-hearted towards her, and, in her good-nature, she seemed charming to him, and he resolved to treat her henceforth with greater kindness.

"Nine o'clock, by Jove!" said he, as the clock, striking, thoroughly roused him. "I suppose I must get up."

A fine rain was falling, so he determined not to go out all day. He would accept an invitation to dine with the Pichons, an invitation which for a long while he had always refused, owing to his dread of the Vuillaumes. That would please Marie; and he would find some opportunity of kissing her behind the door. As she liked books, he even thought of taking her a whole parcelful as a surprise—some that he had left in one of his trunks in the loft. When he had dressed, he went downstairs to Monsieur Gourd to get the key to the loft, which was used in common by the different tenants for storing their superfluous and cumbersome articles.

Cosily ensconced in an easy-chair, Madame Gourd was drinking her coffee out of a silver cup before a wood fire, which brightened the whole room by its blaze. She didn't know where the key was—at the back of the chest of drawers, perhaps. And, while dipping her pieces of toast in the coffee, she kept her eyes fixed upon the door of the servants' staircase at the other end of the courtyard, which looked bleaker and more gloomy on this rainy morning.

"Look out! there she is!" grunted Madame Gourd, as a woman came through the door in question.

Monsieur Gourd at once stood in front of his lodge to block the woman's way. She advanced at a slower pace, looking uneasy.

"We've been watching for her all the morning, Monsieur Mouret," said Gourd, under his breath. "We saw her pass yesterday evening. She's come from that carpenter upstairs—the only working-man we have got in the house, thank God! And if the landlord would only listen to me, he'd keep the room (it's only a servants' attic) empty. For the sake of a hundred and thirty francs a year, it's really not worth while having filthy goings-on in your house——"

Interrupting himself, he roughly asked the woman:

"Where have you come from?"

"Why, from upstairs, of course," she replied, as she went on without stopping.

Then he burst out:

"We're not going to have any women here; do you understand? The man who brings you here has been told as much already. If you come back here to sleep, I'll fetch a policeman, and we'll soon see if you shall play any of your dirty games in a decent house."

"Oh, what a bother you are!" said the woman. "It's my home, and I shall come back to it when I like."

And she went off, pursued by the righteous wrath of Monsieur Gourd, who talked of going upstairs to fetch the landlord. Did you ever hear of such a thing? A creature like that among respectable folk, in a house where not the faintest immorality would be tolerated! It would seem as if this carpenter's garret were the cesspool, so to speak, of the house—a sink of iniquity, the surveillance of which was revolting to all his delicate instinct and a source of trouble to him o' nights.

"And the key, where is it?" Octave ventured to repeat.

But the hall-porter, furious that a lodger should have seen his authority set at naught, fell to badgering poor Mother Péron again, in his desire to show how he could command obedience. Did she mean to defy him? She had just splashed his door again with her broom. If he paid her out of his own pocket, it was because he did not want to soil his hands, and yet he had always had to clean up after her! He'd see her damned before he would give her another job just for charity's sake. She might starve first.

Worn out by such work, which was too hard for her, the old woman, without answering, went on scrubbing with her skinny arms, keeping back her tears for very awe of this alarming personage in smoking-cap and slippers.

"Now I remember, my dear," cried Madame Gourd, from the arm-chair in which she spent the whole day, warming her fat body, "I hid the key under some shirts, so that the maid-servants should not always be messing about in the lumber-room. Pray let Monsieur Mouret have it."

"A nice set, too, those maid-servants!" muttered Monsieur Gourd, whose long life as a servant had led him to loathe his fellow-menials. "Here is the key, sir, but please let me have it back again, for one can't leave a single place open anywhere, or the maids go there to misconduct themselves."

Not wishing to cross the wet courtyard, Octave ascended the front stairs, only going up by the back stairs when he got to the fourth floor, as the door communicating with this was close to his room. At the top was a long passage, with two turnings at right angles; it was painted in light yellow, with a darker dado of ochre, and, as in hospital corridors, the doors of the servants' rooms, also yellow, were ranged along at regular intervals. It was as cold as ice under the zinc roofing, bare and cleanly, with a sort of stale smell, like the smell of pauper lodging-houses.

The lumber-room looked out on to the courtyard at the extreme end of the left wing. But Octave, who had not been up there since the day of his arrival, went along the left-hand passage, when suddenly a sight which met his view through one of the half-open doors caused him to stop short in sheer amazement. A gentleman in his shirt sleeves stood before a small looking-glass, tying his white tie.

"What, you here?" he exclaimed.

It was Trublot. At first he seemed like one petrified. No one ever came up there at that hour. Octave, who had entered, looked first at him and then at the room, with its narrow iron bedstead and washhand-stand, where a little ball of woman's hair was floating on the dirty water in the basin. Seeing a black dress-coat still hanging up beside the aprons, he could not help exclaiming:

"So you sleep with the cook?"

"No, I don't," answered Trublot, with a wild look in his eyes.

Then, aware of the folly of telling such a lie, he began to laugh complacently.

"Well, she is rare good fun, my dear fellow; most awfully smart, I assure you."

Whenever he dined out, he used to slip out of the drawing-room and go and pinch the cooks over their ovens, and when one of them let him have her key he managed to leave before midnight, and would go and wait patiently for her in her room, sitting on her trunk in his evening clothes and white cravat. The next morning, about ten o'clock, he would leave by the front stairs, and passed the hall-porter's as if he had been calling upon one of the tenants at an early hour. As long as he kept office hours his father was satisfied. Besides, he had to be at the Bourse now every day from twelve to three. On Sundays he sometimes spent the whole day in some servant's bed, quite happy, with his nose buried under her pillow.

"You, too, who some day will be so rich!" said Octave, with a look of disgust.

Then Trublot learnedly remarked:

"My dear boy, you don't know what it is, so you can't judge."

And he spoke up for Julie, a tall Burgundian woman of forty, her big face all pock-pitted, but whose body in formation was superb. One might strip all the other women in the house; they were all sticks; not one of them would come up to her knee. Then, too, she was a well-to-do girl; and, to prove this, he opened drawers and showed a bonnet, some jewellery, and some lace-trimmed skirts, all of which had doubtless been stolen from Madame Duveyrier. Octave, in fact, now noticed a certain coquettishness about the room—some gilt cardboard

boxes on the drawers, a chintz curtain hanging over the petticoats, and other things which testified to the cook trying to
play the fine lady.

"With this one," repeated Trublot, "I don't mind admitting
that I do. If all the others were only like her!"

Just then there was a noise on the back stairs; it was Adèle
coming up to clean her ears, as Madame Josserand, furious, had
forbidden her to touch the meat until she had washed them
thoroughly with soap and water. Trublot, peeping out, recognised her.

"Shut the door, quick!" he cried, anxiously. "Hush! Not a
word!"

Listening attentively, he heard Adèle's heavy footstep along
the passage.

"So you sleep with her too, then?" asked Octave, astonished
to see him turn so pale, and guessing that he was afraid of a
scene.

This time, however, Trublot's cowardice made him answer:

"No, hang it all, not with that filth-bag! My good fellow,
what do you take me for?"

He sat down at the edge of the bed waiting to finish dressing
himself, while begging Octave not to move. So they both remained perfectly quiet, as Adèle, the beastly, kept scrubbing
her ears, an operation which lasted a good ten minutes. They
heard the whirlpool in the basin.

When Adèle had gone down again, his bold air returned as
he finished dressing with the help of Julie's combs and poma-
tum. When Octave mentioned the lumber-room, he insisted
on showing him where it was, as he knew every hole and
corner of that place.

"Don't lock the door again, there's a good fellow, just to
oblige me," said Trublot, when he had helped Octave to get out
the books, "You see, when the lumber-room is open, one can
hide in there and wait."

Octave was opening the hall-door when Valérie came back.
He politely stood aside to let her pass.

"Are you quite well, madame?"

"Yes, thank you, monsieur."

She was out of breath, and as she went upstairs he looked at
her muddy boots, and thought about the lunch alluded to by

the servants—the lunch with her head down and her legs in the air. No doubt she had walked home, not having been able to get a cab. A warm, stale smell came from her damp petticoats. Fatigue and utter physical languor made her catch hold of the banisters every now and then.

"What an awful day, madame, isn't it?"

"Awful, and so close, too!"

She had reached the first floor, when they exchanged bows. At a glance he saw how haggard was her face, how heavy her eyelids were with sleep, and how her towzled hair showed underneath the hastily-tied bonnet. And, as he went along upstairs, his thoughts vexed, angered him. Why, then, would she not do that with him? He was not sillier nor uglier than anybody else.

On passing Madame Juzeur's on the third floor, he felt a sort of curiosity as to that discreet little woman with eyes like periwinkles. He rang the bell, when Madame Juzeur answered the door herself.

"Oh, my dear sir, how good of you! Do come in!"

There was a certain stuffiness about the apartments. Carpets, curtains everywhere; chairs as soft as eider-down, and the atmosphere as warm and heavy as that of a chest lined with old rainbow-coloured satin. In the drawing-room, which with its double curtains had the solemn stillness of a sacristy, Octave was asked to take a seat on a broad, low sofa.

Then, without waiting further, he stooped down and kissed her fingers, which were small and delicate as those of a little girl.

"Oh, Monsieur Octave, at my age! You can't think what you're doing!" exclaimed Madame Juzeur, with a pretty air of surprise, though not at all annoyed.

She was thirty-two, and gave out that she was quite an old woman. As usual, she spoke of her troubles. Gracious goodness! after ten days' married life the cruel man had gone and left her one morning and had never returned—nobody knew why.

"You can well understand," she said, looking up to the ceiling, "that after such a shock as that, it is all over for any woman."

Octave had kept hold of her warm little hand, which seemed

to melt into his own, and he kept lightly kissing it on the finger-tips. She looked down at him vaguely, tenderly, and then, in a maternal way, she exclaimed:

"Oh, you child!"

Believing himself to be encouraged, he tried to put his arm round her waist and pull her on to the sofa, but she gently slipped away from him, laughing as if she thought he were only joking.

"No, leave me alone, and don't touch me if you wish us to remain good friends."

"Then you don't want it?" he asked, in a low voice.

"Want what? I don't know what you mean. Oh, you may have my hand as much as you like."

He caught hold of her hand again. But this time he opened it, kissing the palm. With half-shut eyes, she treated the process as a joke, opening her fingers as a cat puts out its claws so as to be tickled inside its paw. She would not let him go farther than the wrist. The first day a sacred line was drawn there where naughty things began.

About five o'clock that evening Octave felt it a positive relief to make himself at home with the Pichons, while waiting for dinner.

When she saw him put down the parcel of books which he had fetched for her that morning, Marie grew crimson with pleasure.

"How good of you, Monsieur Octave!" she kept repeating. "Thank you so much. How nice of you to come so early. Will you have a glass of sugar and water, with some cognac in it? That will give you an appetite."

Just to please her, he accepted. There was something pleasant about everyone; even about Pichon and the Vuillaumes, who gossiped on in their doddering Sunday fashion. Every now and then Marie ran to the kitchen, where she was cooking a shoulder of mutton, and Octave, jokingly, followed her thither, and catching her round the waist, in front of the oven, kissed the back of her neck. Without a cry, without a start, she turned round and kissed him on the mouth with her icy lips. To the young man their coldness seemed delicious.

At ten o'clock punctually the Vuillaume: rose to go. Pichon put on his hat. Every Sunday he went with them as far as their 'bus. It was a habit which, out of deference, he had observed ever since his marriage, and the Vuillaumes would have been much hurt if he had now tried to discontinue it. They all three set out for the Rue Richelieu, and walked slowly up it, scrutinising the Batignolles omnibuses, which were always full. Pichon thus was often obliged to go as far as Montmartre, for it would never have done for him to leave the Vuillaumes before putting them into their 'bus. As they walked very slowly, it took him nearly two hours to go there and back.

There was much friendly shaking of hands on the landing. As Octave went back with Marie to the room, he said:

"It is raining. Jules won't get back before midnight."

As Lilitte had been put to bed early, he at once made Marie sit on his knee, drinking the remainder of the coffee with her out of the same cup, like a husband who is glad that his guests have gone and that he is all to himself after the excitement of a little family gathering, and able to kiss his wife at his ease, when the door is shut. A drowsy warmth pervaded the poky little room, and a faint odour of vanilla from the dish of frosted eggs which they had eaten. As he was lightly kissing the young woman under the chin, someone knocked at the door. Marie did not even start up in fear. It was young Josserand, the half-witted lad. Whenever he could escape from the apartment opposite, he used to come across and chat to her, as her gentleness had an attraction for him; and they both got on very well together as they exchanged inconsequent remarks at intervals of ten minutes.

Octave, greatly annoyed, remained silent.

"They've got some people there to-night," stammered Saturnin. "I don't care a hang if they won't have me at table. I've taken the lock off and got out that way. That will make them swear."

"But they will wonder what has become of you. You ought to go back," said Marie, who observed Octave's impatience.

Then the idiot grinned with delight as, in his faltering way, he told her all that had happened at home. His visit each time seemed to be in order to relieve his memory.

"Papa has been working all night again, and mamma boxed Berthe's ears. I say, when one gets married, does it hurt?"

Then, as Marie did not answer, he excitedly continued:

"I won't go away into the country, that I won't! If they do but touch her, I'll strangle them; that is easy enough, at night-time, while they are asleep. The palm of her hand is as smooth as note-paper; but the other is a beast of a girl."

Then he began again, and got more muddled, as he could not express what he had come to say. Marie at last persuaded him to go back to his parents without his even having noticed her companion.

Fearing another interruption, Octave wanted to take the young woman across to his own room; but, blushing violently, she refused. Not understanding such bashfulness, he continued assuring her that they would be certain to hear Jules coming upstairs, and there would be plenty of time for her to get back to her room. Then, as he was pulling her along, she became quite angry, as indignant as a woman to whom violence is offered.

"No, not in your room; never! It would be too dreadful. Let us stop here." And she rushed away to the back of her apartment.

Octave was still on the landing, amazed at such unexpected resistance, when he heard a loud noise of wrangling in the courtyard below. Things were evidently all wrong today; it would have been better if he had gone to bed. A noise of this sort was so unusual at that hour, that at last he opened a window so as to listen. Monsieur Gourd was shouting out:

"I tell you, you shall not pass! The landlord has been sent for. He will come down himself and kick you out!"

"Kick me out? What's that for?" said a gruff voice. "Don't I pay my rent? Go on, Amélie, and if the gentleman touches you, he'll know it!"

It was the carpenter from upstairs, who was returning with the woman they had sent off that morning. Octave leant out to look; but in the black courtyard he only saw great moving shadows thrown by the dim gaslight in the hall.

"Monsieur Vabre! Monsieur Vabre!" cried the porter, as the carpenter pushed him aside. "Quick, quick! she's coming in!"

Despite her bad legs, Madame Gourd had gone up to fetch the landlord, who, just then, was at work upon his great task. He was coming down. Octave heard him furiously reiterating:

"It is scandalous, disgraceful! I won't allow such a thing

in my house!" Then, addressing the workman, who at first seemed somewhat abashed, 'Send that woman away at once! At once, do you hear? We don't want any women brought in here."

"But she's my wife!" replied the carpenter, with a scared look. "She's in service, and only comes once a month, when her people let her have a day off. That's the plain truth about it. It's not your place to prevent me from sleeping with my wife, I should think!"

Then both porter and landlord lost their heads.

"I give you notice to quit," stuttered old Vabre, "and, meanwhile, I forbid you to make a brothel of my premises! Gourd, turn that person into the street, No, sir, none of your nonsense with me. If a man is married, he ought to say so. Hold your tongue, and let me have no more of your insolence!"

The carpenter, good-natured fellow as he was, and who, no doubt, had had a little too much wine, burst out laughing.

"It's a damned funny thing, all the same. Well, Amélie, as the gentleman objects, you had better go back to your employer's. We'll make our baby some other time. We wanted to make a baby, that's all we wanted. I'll take your notice with pleasure, old boy! Don't think I want to stop in your dirty show. Nice goings-on there are, too; some fine dirt about the place! He won't have women brought into the house—oh, no! but he lets well-dressed hussies stop on every floor, who, behind their doors, lead the life of a bitch. Oh, you bloody toffs!"

Octave shut the window. Then, just as he was returning to Marie, some one lightly brushed past him in the passage.

"Hullo! you again!" he said, recognising Trublot.

For a moment the latter was speechless; then he sought to explain his presence.

"Yes; I've been dining with the Josserands, and I was going up to——"

Octave was disgusted.

"To that slut, Adèle, I suppose? And you swore you didn't!"

Then, brazening it out in his usual way, Trublot said, with an enthusiastic air:

"I assure you, my dear fellow, it's a rare sport! She's got a skin—you've no idea!" Then he abused the workman, who, with his damned nonsense about women, had almost caused him to be caught coming up the back stairs. He had been obliged to come round by the front staircase. Then, as he hurried away, he added: "Remember, it's next Thursday that I am going to take you to Duveyrier's mistress. We will dine together first."

The house regained its holy calm which, coming from each chaste bedchamber, seemed to pervade it. Octave had rejoined Marie in her bedroom, sitting beside her on the conjugal couch while she was arranging the pillows.

As upstairs the only chair had a basin on it and an old pair of slippers, Trublot sat down on Adèle's narrow bed and waited for her there in his evening dress. When he recognised Julie's step as she came up to bed, he held his breath, being perpetually terrified of women's quarrels. At last Adèle appeared. She was angry, and, seizing his arm, said:

"I say, why do you treat me like that when I am waiting at table?"

"What do you mean?"

"Well, you never so much as look at me, and you never say 'if you please,' when you want some bread. This evening, as I was handing the veal around, you looked as if you had never had anything to say to me. I've just had about enough of it. The whole house torments me, and it's a little bit too much if you side with the rest!"

She undressed herself in a great fury, and, flinging herself down on the old bed, which cracked again, she turned her back upon him. He had to eat humble pie.

Meanwhile, in the next room, the carpenter, still full of wine, was talking to himself at the top of his voice, so that the whole corridor could hear him.

"Well, that's a rum thing, ain't it; when they won't let you sleep with your own lawful wife? You won't have any women in the house, won't you, you silly old bugger! Go and stick your snout at this moment under all the bed-clothes, and you'll pretty soon see."

Chapter Seven

*I*N order to induce Uncle Bachelard to give Berthe a dowry, for the past fortnight the Josserands had asked him to dinner almost every evening, in spite of his revolting habits.

When they told him about the marriage, all he did was to pat his niece on the cheek and say:

"What! so you're going to get married? That's nice, isn't it, my girlie?"

The thing must be settled somehow, for time was short. So Madame Josserand determined to put matters plainly before him.

"As we are now by ourselves," she continued, "let us make the most of it. You just go away, dears, as we have to talk with your uncle. Berthe, do look after Saturnin, and see that he doesn't take the lock off the door again."

Ever since they had been busy about his sister's marriage, keeping it a secret, Saturnin wandered about the house with wild eyes, suspicious that something was going on; he imagined all sorts of awful things, to the utter consternation of his family.

"I am only afraid of one thing," continued she, as she resolutely planted herself in front of her brother; "and that is, that he may break it off if the dowry is not forthcoming on the day the contract is to be signed. One can easily understand that; he wants money, you know."

Just then she heard the sound of laboured breathing close behind her, and she turned round. It was Saturnin, who had thrust his head round the door, glaring at her with wolfish eyes. They were all panic-stricken, for he had stolen a spit from the kitchen, to spit the geese, so he said. Uncle Bachelard, who had felt very uncomfortable at the turn their conversation was taking, profited by the general scare.

"Don't disturb yourselves," he called out from the anteroom. "I'm off; I have got a midnight appointment with one of my clients, who has come over expressly from Brazil."

Next day all three—mother, father, and daughter—paid an official visit to the uncle's premises, on the ground floor and the basement of an enormous house in the Rue d'Enghien. The entrance was blocked by large vans. In the covered courtyard numerous packers were nailing up cases, and through open doorways one caught sight of piles of goods, dried vegetables, and remnants of silk, stationery, and tallow, all accumulated in executing the thousands of commissions given by customers, and by buying in advance when prices were low. Bachelard was there, with his big red nose, his eyes still inflamed by last night's debauch, but with his intellect clear, as his business tact and good-luck came back to him directly he sat down to his account-books.

"Hullo! is that you?" he said, utterly bored at the sight of them. He took them into a little office, whence he could over-look his men from a window.

"I have brought Berthe to see you," exclaimed Madame Josserand. "She knows how much she is indebted to you."

Then, after kissing her uncle, when the girl, obedient to a wink from her mother, had gone off to look at the goods in the courtyard, Madame Josserand resolutely broached the subject.

"Look here, Narcisse, this is just how we are situated. Relying upon your kindheartedness and your promises, I have engaged to give a dowry of fifty thousand francs. If I don't do so, the match will be broken off, and, now that things have gone so far, this would be a disgrace. You cannot possibly leave us in such an awkward position."

A film came over Bachelard's eyes, and he stammered out, as if quite drunk:

"Eh? What's that? You should never promise; bad thing to promise."

Then he pleaded poverty. For instance, he had bought a whole lot of horse-hair, thinking that the price of it would go up. Not a bit of it; the price had fallen lower still, and he had been obliged to get rid of it at a loss. Rushing to his books, he opened his ledger, and insisted on showing them the invoices. It was simply ruin.

"Rubbish!" exclaimed Monsieur Josserand, at last, losing all patience. "I know all about your business, and that you're coining money. You would be lolling in wealth if you did not squander it as you do. Mind, I don't ask you for anything for myself. It was Eléonore who determined to take such a step.

But allow me to tell you, Bachelard, that you have been fooling us. For fifteen years, every Saturday, when I went through your books for you, you always promised that——"

The uncle interrupted him, violently slapping his chest.

"*I* promise? Nothing of the sort. No, no! let me do as I like, and then you'll see. I don't like to be asked; it annoys, it upsets me. One day you'll see what I shall do."

Even Madame Josserand herself could wring nothing further from him. Shaking them by the hand, he brushed away a casual tear, spoke of his kindheartedness and of his affection for the family, and begged them to tease him no further, as, by God! they would never have cause to repent it. He knew his duty, and would do it to the uttermost. Later on Berthe would find out how much her uncle was attached to her.

"And what about the dotal insurance?" he asked, resuming his natural voice. "Those fifty thousand francs for which you had insured the girl's life?"

Madame Josserand shrugged her shoulders.

"That was all done for fourteen years ago. We've told you twenty times that when the fourth premium became due we were unable to pay the two thousand francs."

"That doesn't matter," he murmured, with a wink. "You must talk about this insurance to the family, and take your time about paying the dowry money. One never pays a dowry."

Monsieur Josserand rose in disgust.

"So that's all you have to tell us, is it?"

Pretending not to understand, the uncle insisted that such a thing was always done.

"One never pays, I tell you. You pay something on account, and then the interest. Why, look at Monsieur Vabre himself! Did my father ever pay you Eléonore's dowry? Of course not. Each one sticks to his money, you bet."

"In short, you advise me to do a blackguardly thing!" cried Monsieur Josserand. "It would be a lie! I should be committing forgery if I produced the life policy of that insurance——"

Madame Josserand cut him short. At this suggestion of her brother's she became grave. It was surprising that she had never thought of this before.

"Good gracious me! how touchy we are, to be sure! Narcisse never told you to commit forgery!"

"Of course I didn't," muttered Bachelard. "There's no need to show any papers."

"The point is to gain time," she continued. "Promise the dowry, and we must manage to give it later on."

Then the worthy man's conscientious scruples drove him to speak. No, he refused; not again would he venture to approach the brink of such a precipice. They were always taking advantage of his easy-going nature, so getting him gradually to consent to things which afterwards made him quite ill, so greatly did he take them to heart. Since he had no dowry to give, it was impossible for him to promise one. Bachelard whistled and drummed on the window-pane, as if to show his utter contempt for such scruples. Madame Josserand listened, while her face grew livid with pent-up fury that suddenly burst forth:

"Very well, monsieur, since that is so, the marriage shall take place. It is my daughter's last chance. I would rather cut off my right hand than let it slip. So much the worse for the others. When you're driven to it, why you're capable of anything at last."

"Then, madame, I presume you would commit murder in order to get your daughter married?"

She drew herself up to her full height.

"So I would!" she retorted, angrily.

Then she smiled. Bachelard was obliged to quell the tempest. What was the use of wrangling? It was far better to come to some amicable arrangement. Thus, worn out and trembling from the effects of the quarrel, Monsieur Josserand agreed to talk matters over with Duveyrier, on whom, according to Madame Josserand, everything depended. In order to get hold of the counsellor when he was in a good humour, Bachelard proposed to let his brother-in-law meet him at a house where he could refuse nothing.

"It is merely to be an interview," said Josserand, still protesting. "I will enter into no engagement, that I swear."

"Of course not, of course not," said Bachelard, "Eléonore does not want you to do anything dishonourable."

Then Berthe came back. She had spied some boxes of preserved fruits, and by dint of much kissing and coaxing she tried to get her uncle to give her one. But he again became afflicted by his stammer. He couldn't possibly do so; they were all counted, and had to be sent off to St. Petersburg that very night. He gradually got them out into the street, while his sister, at the sight of these huge warehouses packed to the roof with every sort of merchandise conceivable, lingered behind, mortified to think that such a fortune should have been made by a man totally devoid of principle, and comparing it bitterly with her husband's impotent honesty.

"Well, then, to-morrow night, about nine o'clock, at the Café de Mulhouse," said Bachelard, as he shook Monsieur Josserand's hand when they got into the street.

It so happened that the next day, Octave and Trublot, who had dined together before going to see Clarisse, Duveyrier's mistress, went into the Café de Mulhouse so as not to call too early, though she lived a good way off, in the Rue de la Cerisaie. It was hardly eight o'clock. On entering, they heard a loud noise of quarreling at the further end of the room. There they saw Bachelard, drunk already, enormous in size, with flaming cheeks, who was having a row with a little pale-faced, testy gentleman.

"You've been spitting in my beer again," roared he, in a voice of thunder. "I won't stand it, sir!"

"Hold your damned row, will you, or I'll punch your head!" said the little man, standing on tip-toe.

Then Bachelard raised his voice to an exasperating pitch, without ceding an inch. "Just you dare, sir! just you dare!"

And when the other man knocked his hat off, which he always wore cocked on one side of his head, he repeated, with fresh energy:

"Just you dare, sir! just you dare!"

Then, picking up his hat, he sat down majestically, and called out to the waiter:

"Alfred, change this beer!"

Octave and Trublot, greatly astonished, had noticed Gueulin sitting beside his uncle, with his back to the wall, smoking away with utter indifference. They asked him what was the reason of the quarrel.

"Don't know," he replied, watching the cigar-smoke curling upwards. "There's always some row or other. A rare one for getting his head punched! He never gives in!"

Bachelard shook hands with the new-comers. He adored

81

young fellows. He was delighted to hear that they were going to see Clarisse. So was he; Gueulin was coming too; only he had to keep an appointment here first with Monsieur Josserand, his brother-in-law.

"If you're very good," quoth he, suddenly, "I'll let you see something."

And, after paying, he took them out.

Octave reminded him of his appointment with Monsieur Josserand. That did not matter; they would come back for him. Before leaving the room, Bachelard looked around furtively and then stole the lumps of sugar left by a customer at an adjoining table.

"Follow me," said he, when they got out. "It's close by."

He walked along, gravely meditating, without a word, and stopped before a door in the Rue Saint-Marc. The three young men were about to follow him, when suddenly he seemed to hesitate.

"No, let's go back. I don't think I will."

But they cried out at this. Why was he trying to humbug them in this way?

"Well, Gueulin mustn't come up, nor you either, Monsieur Trublot. You don't behave nicely; you'd only laugh and jeer. Come on, Monsieur Octave, you're a steady sort of fellow."

He made Octave go upstairs in front of him, while the other two laughed, and from the pavement begged to be kindly remembered to the ladies. On reaching the fourth floor he knocked, and an old woman opened the door.

"Oh! it's you, is it, Monsieur Narcisse? Fifi did not expect you this evening."

She was a fat old party, and her face was white and calm as that of a sister-of-mercy. In the narrow dining-room which they entered, a tall, fair girl, pretty and simple-looking, was embroidering an altar-cloth.

"Good-day, uncle," said she, as rising, she put out her forehead to Bachelard's thick, tremulous lips.

As the latter introduced Monsieur Octave Mouret, a distinguished young friend of his, the two women dropped him an old-fashioned curtsey, and they sat down at a table, lighted by a petroleum lamp. It was like some calm provincial interior; two regular lives lost to the outside world, supported by next to nothing. As the room looked on to an inner courtyard, even the sound of traffic was inaudible.

While Bachelard, with paternal solicitude, questioned the girl as to her employments and interests since the previous evening, her aunt, Mademoiselle Menu, confided their whole history to Octave, with the frank simplicity of an honest woman who has nothing to conceal.

"Yes, sir, I come from Villeneuve, near Lille. I am well known at Mardienne Brothers', in the Rue Saint-Sulpice, where I worked as embroideress for thirty years. Then, when a cousin of mine left me a house in the country, I was lucky enough to let it for life, at a thousand francs a year, to some people who hoped that they would bury me the next day, and who have been finely punished for their wicked thought, for I'm still alive, in spite of my seventy-five years."

She laughed, showing teeth as white as those of a girl.

"I was unable to work, she went on, "for my eyesight was gone, when my niece Fanny needed looking after. Her father, Captain Menu, died without leaving a farthing, and not a single relative to help her, sir. So I had to take the girl away from school, and I have taught her embroidery—poor sort of trade, it's true, but either that or nothing; it's always the women who have to die of starvation. Luckily, she met Monsieur Narcisse, so now I can die happy."

And with hands across her stomach, like some old seamstress who had sworn never to touch a needle again, she enveloped Bachelard and Fifi in a humid glance. Just then the old man was saying to the child:

"Now, did you really think about me? And what did you think, then?"

Fifi raised her clear eyes, without ceasing to go on with her embroidery.

"Why, that you were a good friend, and that I loved you very much."

She hardly looked at Octave, as if indifferent to the charm of such a comely young fellow. However, he smiled at her struck by her grace, and not knowing quite what to think; while the spinster aunt, staled by a chastity that had cost her nothing, continued in an undertone:

"I could have married her to somebody, eh? A workman

would beat her; a clerk would only make her bear him heaps of children. It's better that she should behave nicely to Monsieur Narcisse, who seems such a good, kind gentleman."

Then, raising her voice:

"Well, Monsieur Narcisse, it isn't my fault if you're not satisfied with her. I always tell her, 'Make yourself pleasant— be grateful.' It's only natural that I should be glad to know that she is well looked after. When one has no relatives, it is so difficult to find a home for a young girl."

Then Octave gave himself up to the quiet enjoyment of this pleasant little home. The heavy air of the apartment was charged with an odour of ripe fruit. Only Fifi's needle, as it pricked the silk, made a slight noise at regular intervals, like the ticking of a cuckoo-clock, which might have regulated Bachelard's idyllic amours. The old spinster, however, was probity personified; she lived on her income of a thousand francs and never touched a farthing of Fifi's money, who spent it just as she pleased. The only things she ever allowed her to pay for occasionally were roast chestnuts and white wine, when she emptied the money-box where she collected the pence given her as good-conduct medals by her kind friend.

"My little duck," said Bachelard, as he rose to go, " we have got some business on hand. I shall look in tomorrow. Be a good girl."

He kissed her on the forehead. Then, looking affectionately at her, he said to Octave:

"You may give her a kiss, too. She is but a child."

The young man's lips touched her cool skin. She smiled; she was so modest. It seemed as if he were one of the family; he had never met worthier folk. Bachelard was going away, when he suddenly came back, crying out:

"Oh, I forgot! Here's a little present for you!"

And, emptying his pocket, he gave Fifi the sugar which he had just stolen at the café. She thanked him heartily, and blushed with pleasure as she crunched one of the lumps. Then, growing bolder, she said:

"You have not any four-sou pieces, have you?"

Bachelard searched his pockets, but in vain. Octave happened to have one, which the girl accepted as a souvenir. She did not go to the door with them, no doubt for propriety's sake; and they could hear the click of her needle as she at once sat down to her altar-cloth, while Mademoiselle Menu showed them out in her good-natured, old-fashioned way.

"Well, that's worth seeing, eh?" said Bachelard, stopping short on the stairs. "You know that doesn't cost me five louis a month. I've had about enough of those hussies tha fleece one. 'Pon my word! I wanted something with a heart."

Then, as Octave laughed, his misgivings came back.

"You're a steady chap, now; you won't take advantage of my good nature. Not a word, mind, to Gueulin; swear it, on your honour! I am waiting till he is worthy to be shown such an angel. Say what you like, virtue is a good thing; it refreshes one. I myself have always believed in the ideal!"

His old toper's voice trembled; tears filled his flabby eyelids. Down below, Trublot began chaffing him, and pretended he would take the number of the house, while Gueulin shrugged his shoulders and asked Octave, to his astonishment, what he thought of the little thing. When maudlin after a carouse, Bachelard could never resist taking people to see these ladies, feeling vain at displaying such a treasure, yet fearful lest someone should rob him of it. Then, next day, he would forget all about it, and go back to the Rue Saint-Marc with his wonted air of mystery.

"Everybody knows Fifi," said Gueulin, quietly.

Bachelard, meanwhile, was looking for a cab, when Octave exclaimed:

"What about Josserand, who is waiting for you at the café?"

The other two had forgotten all about him. Extremely annoyed at wasting his evening like this, Monsieur Josserand stood fidgeting at the door of the café, not going inside, as he never took any refreshment out-of-doors. At last they started for the Rue de la Cerisaie. But they were obliged to have two cabs, the commission agent and the cashier going in one, and the three young men in another.

At the bottom of the Rue Montmartre, a block in the traffic stopped the cab. The young men, having let down the windows, could hear Bachelard abusing the driver in a furious voice. Then, as they moved on again, Gueulin gave his listeners certain details about Clarisse. Her name was Clarisse Bocquet, the daughter of a man who once kept a small toy-shop, but now went about to fairs with his wife and a troop of brats in tatters. One evening, when it was thawing, Duveyrier had met her just as one of her gallants had kicked her out-of-doors. Probably this buxom wench corresponded to the long-sought ideal, for the next day he was landed, weeping as he kissed her on the eyelids, overcome by a tender yearning to cultivate just one little blue flower of romance, apart from all his grosser sexual desires. Clarisse had consented to live in the Rue de la Cerisaie, so as not to show him up; but she led him a rare dance, had made him buy her twenty-five thousand francs' worth of furniture, sponging on him to her heart's content, together with several artistes from pure, and—intolerable!"

The cab stopped. They alighted in front of a dark, silent house in the Rue de la Cerisaie. But they had to wait a good ten minutes for the other cab, Bachelard having taken his driver to have some grog, after their quarrel in the Rue Montmartre. On the stairs, assuming his respectable-tradesman air, Bachelard, when questioned once more by Josserand as to this friend of Duveyrier's, merely said:

"A woman of the world—very nice girl. She won't eat you."

The door was opened by a little rosy-faced maid, who, smiling half-tenderly, half-familiarly, helped the gentlemen off with their coats. Trublot stopped behind in the ante-room with her for a moment, whispering something in her ear which set her giggling as if she were being tickled. Bachelard had already pushed open the drawing-room door, and he at once introduced Monsieur Josserand. The latter felt momentarily ill at ease; Clarisse seemed quite plain; he could not imagine why Duveyrier preferred her to his own wife, one of the most beautiful women in society—this queer sort of person, very dark, very thin, and with a fluffy head like a poodle's. However, Clarisse had charm. She chatted like a true Parisian, with her frothy, borrowed wit, and her droll ways, acquired by constant contact with men; though, if need be, she could put on her fine lady airs when it suited her.

"Monsieur, I am charmed. All Alphonse's friends are mine as well. Pray make yourself quite at home."

Duveyrier received Monsieur Josserand most cordially, acting on a hint given to him in a letter of Bachelard's. Octave was surprised at his youthful appearance. He was no longer the severe-looking, restless individual of the Rue de Choiseul, who never looked as if he were at home in his own drawing-room. The unsightly blotches on his face had become pink; his wizened eyes sparkled with childish glee as Clarisse was telling a group of guests how he sometimes paid her a flying visit during some short adjournment of the Court, having only just time to jump into a cab, kiss her, and drive back again. Then he complained of being overworked—four sittings a week, from eleven to five; always the same tangled skein of roguery to be unravelled; it positively shrivelled up all feeling.

"Among all that," said he, laughing, "one really wants a few roses. I feel the better for it afterwards."

Octave, who at once shook her by the hand as if she were his comrade, listened and looked about him. The room, with its staring carpet, red satin furniture and hangings, was very much like the drawing-room in the Rue de Choiseul, and, as if to complete this resemblance, several of the counsellor's friends whom Octave had seen on the night of the concert were here also, forming the same groups. But people smoked and talked loudly; everybody seemed bright and merry in the brilliant candle-light. Two gentlemen, with outstretched legs, took up the whole of a divan; another, seated crosswise on a chair, was warming his back at the fire. There was a pleasant, free-and-easy air about everyone—a freedom, however, which did not go any farther. Clarisse never invited any women to these parties—for propriety's sake, she averred. When her guests remarked that ladies were missing from her drawing-room, she would laughingly rejoin:

"Well, and what about me? Don't you think I am enough?"

Thoroughly middle-class in her ideas, she had made a fairly comfortable little home for Alphonse, her passion being for the respectable, the proper, during all the heights and declensions of her career. When she received company she declined to be addressed as "thou"; but when her guests had gone, and the doors were closed, all Alphonse's friends enjoyed her favours in succession, clean-shaven actors and painters with bushy beards. It was an ingrained habit this, the need of enjoying herself a bit behind her keeper's back. Only two out of all her friends had not been willing to comply—

Gueulin, who dreaded consequences, and Trublot, whose heart lay elsewhere.

The little maid was just then handing round some glasses of punch in her engaging way. Octave took one, and whispered in Trublot's ear:

"The maid is better-looking than the mistress."

"Of course; she always is," replied Trublot, shrugging his shoulders with an air of disdainful conviction.

Clarisse came up and talked to them for a moment. She tripped about hither and thither, from one to the other, joking, laughing, gesticulating. As each new-comer lighted his cigar, the room soon became filled with smoke.

"Oh, you horrid men!" she archly exclaimed, as she went to open a window.

Bachelard, without loss of time, made Monsieur Josserand take a seat in the recess of this window, so that, as he said, they might get a breath of air. Then, by a masterly manœuvre, he brought up Duveyrier and at once plunged *in medias res*. So the two families were about to be united by a close tie; he felt extremely gratified. Then he enquired what day had been fixed for signing the contract, and this gave him the chance to broach the subject.

"We had meant to call on you to-morrow, Josserand and I, to settle everything, being well aware that Monsieur Auguste can do nothing without you. It is with reference to the payment of the dowry, and really, as we seem so comfortable here——"

Seized by fresh qualms of conscience, Monsieur Josserand looked out in the gloomy depths of the Rue de la Cerisaie, with its deserted streets and sombre façades. He was sorry that he had come. They were again going to take advantage of his weakness to involve him in some disgraceful matter which he would live to regret. In a sudden fit of repugnance, he interrupted Bachelard.

"Some other time; this is hardly the place."

"Why not?" exclaimed Duveyrier, most courteously. "We are more comfortable here than anywhere else. You were saying, sir, that——"

"We are going to give Berthe fifty thousand francs. Only, these fifty thousand francs are represented by a dotal insur-

ance at twenty years' date, which Josserand took out for his
daughter when she was four years old. It will be three years,
therefore, before she can draw the money."

"Allow me," interrupted Josserand, amazed.

"No, just let me finish what I was saying; Monsieur Duveyrier understands perfectly. We do not wish the young couple
to wait three years for money which they may need at once,
and so we engage to pay the dowry in instalments of ten thousand francs every six monthe, on the condition that we repay
ourselves later with the insurance money."

There was silence. Monsieur Josserand, chilled and confused,
looked out again into the dark street. The counsellor appeared
to be thinking the matter over for a moment. Perhaps he
scented something fishy about it, and felt delighted at letting
the Vabres be tricked, whom he detested in the person of his
wife.

"It all seems to me a most reasonable arrangement. It is
we who ought to thank you. A dowry is seldom paid in full."

"Of course not," affirmed Bachelard, energetically. "Such a
thing is never done!"

And the three shook hands, after making an appointment
to meet at the notary's on the following Thursday.

When Monsieur Josserand came back into the light, he
looked so pale that they asked him if he felt unwell. This
was, in fact, the case, and he withdrew, not caring to wait
for Bachelard, who had just gone into the dining room,
where the traditional tea nad been replaced by champagne.

Meanwhile, Gueulin, sprawling on a sofa near the window,
muttered:

"Oh, that old wretch of an uncle!"

He had overheard a phrase about the insurance money, and
chuckled as he told Octave and Trublot the actual truth of
the matter. The policy had been taken out at his office; there
was not a farthing due; the Vabres were being utterly hoaxed.
Then as the other two, holding their sides, roared at this
splendid joke, he added, with absurd vehemence:

"I want a hundred francs. If uncle doesn't give me a hundred francs, I'll split!"

Louder grew the buzz of voices, as the champagne gradually upset the decorum upon which Clarisse delighted to in-

sist. Her parties always became rather rowdy before they ended. Even she herself had occasional lapses. Trublot pointed her out to Octave. She was standing behind a door with her arms round the neck of a strapping young fellow with the build of a peasant, a stone-cutter from the South, whom his native town desired to transform into an artist. Duveyrier pushed open the door, however, when she quickly removed her arms and introduced him to the young man—Monsieur Payan, a sculptor of charming talent. Duveyrier was delighted, and promised to get him some work.

On Thursday the marriage-contract was signed before the notary, Maître Rénaudin, Rue de Grammont. Just as they were starting, there had been another furious row at the Josserands', as the father, in a moment of supreme revolt, had told his wife that she was responsible for the lie to which they wanted him to subscribe.

However, at the notary's, the reading of the contract, drawn up from notes furnished by Duveyrier, somewhat soothed Monsieur Josserand. There was no mention of an insurance; moreover, the first instalment of ten thousand francs was only to fall due six months after the marriage. This, as any rate, left them breathing-time. Auguste, who listened most attentively, showed some signs of impatience. He looked at smiling Berthe, at the Josserands, at Duveyrier, and at last ventured to speak of the insurance, a guarantee which he thought it only reasonable should be mentioned. Then they all appeared astonished. What was the good of that? The thing was understood; and they quickly signed the paper, while Maître Rénaudin, a most obliging young man, said not a word, but handed the ladies a pen. It was not till they had got outside that Madame Duveyrier ventured to express her surprise. Not a syllable had been uttered about any insurance. The dowry, so they understood, was to have been paid by uncle Bachelard.

But Madame Josserand naïvely remarked that her brother's name had never even been mentioned by her in connection with so paltry a sum. It was the whole of his fortune that he would eventually leave to Berthe.

That same evening a cab came to take away Saturnin.

His mother had declared that it was too dangerous to let him be present at the ceremony. It would never do, at a wedding, to turn loose among the guests a lunatic who talked of spitting people; and Monsieur Josserand, half broken-hearted, had been obliged to get the poor lad into the Moulineaux Asylum, kept by Doctor Chassagne. The cab was brought up to the porch at dusk. Saturnin came down, holding Berthe's hand, and thinking he was going into the country with her. But when he had got into the cab, he struggled furiously, breaking the windows and shaking his blood-stained fists. Monsieur Josserand went upstairs in tears, overcome by this departure in the gloom; his ears yet rang with the wretched boy's shrieks, mingled with the cracking of the whip and the galloping of the horse.

During dinner, as tears again rose to his eyes at the sight of Saturnin's empty place, his wife, not understanding, impatiently exclaimed:

"Come, that's enough, isn't it, sir? Are you going to your daughter's wedding with that funereal face? Listen! By all that I count most sacred, by my father's grave, I swear to you that her uncle will pay the first ten thousand francs. He swore solemnly to me that he would, as we were leaving the notary's!"

Monsieur Josserand did not even answer. He spent the night in addressing wrappers. By the chill daybreak he finished his second thousand, and had earned six francs. Several times he raised his head, listening, as usual, if Saturnin moved in his room close by. Then, at the thought of Berthe, he worked with fresh ardour. Poor child! she would have liked a wedding-dress of white *moiré*. Never mind; six francs would enable her to have more flowers in her bridal bouquet.

Chapter Eight

TWO days later, about seven o'clock, as Octave got to the Campardons' in time for dinner, he found Rose by herself, dressed in a cream-coloured silk dressing-gown trimmed with white lace.

"Do you expect anybody?" he asked.

"Oh, no!" she said, looking somewhat confused. "We will have dinner directly Achille comes in."

Latterly the architect had been much worried, and never came back to meals at the proper time, but at last he appeared, looking flushed and scared, abusing the business that had delayed him. Then every night he went off somewhere, making all sorts of excuses, appointments at *cafés*, social gatherings and the like. Thus Octave often kept Rose company until eleven o'clock, for he had begun to see that the husband, in taking him as a boarder, only wanted him as a companion for his wife. She used gently to complain as she expressed her fears. Oh, yes, she let Achille do just as he liked, only she always felt anxious if he was not home by midnight!

"Don't you think he looks rather sad lately?" she asked, in her tenderly timorous way.

No, Octave had not remarked it. "I rather think he seems worried. The restorations at Saint-Roch are probably causing him a deal of bother."

But she shook her head, and made no further remark. Then she showed her kindly interest in Octave by asking him how he had spent his day, affectionately, as if she were his mother or his sister. During the whole time—nearly nine months—that he had been their boarder, she treated him thus, as if he were one of the family.

At last Campardon appeared.

"Good evening, my pet! good evening, my darling!" said he, fondly kissing her like an affectionate husband. "Another idiot again kept me standing a whole hour in the street!"

Octave, moving away, heard them exchange a few words under their breath.

"Is she coming?"

"No; where's the use? Whatever you do, don't worry about it."

"You swore that she would come?"

"Well, there, she *is* coming. Are you pleased? I only did it for your sake."

During dessert, a ring at the bell made Madame Campardon start.

"It is madame's cousin," said Lisa, on returning, in the injured tone of a domestic to whom one has neglected to communicate some family secret.

It was, in fact, Gasparine. She wore a plain black stuff dress, with her thin face and jaded shop-girl air. Snug in her cream-coloured dressing-gown, Rose, looking plump and fresh, got up to greet her, with tears in her eyes.

"Oh, my dear," she murmured, "this *is* nice of you! We will let bygones be bygones, won't we?"

Then, embracing her, she kissed her twice, effusively. Octave was about to withdraw discreetly, but they insisted upon his remaining; he was one of the family. So he amused himself by watching the whole scene. Campardon, at first greatly disconcerted, avoided looking at the women, but fussed about in search of a cigar; while Lisa, as she roughly removed the dinner-service, exchanged glances with the astonished Angèle.

At length the architect addressed his daughter: "This is your cousin of whom you have heard us speak. Go and give her a kiss."

Angèle kissed her in her sulky way, feeling uncomfortable beneath the scrutiny of Gasparine's governess eyes, as she said how old she was and what she was learning. Then, as they went out into the drawing-room, she slunk behind Lisa, who, banging the door, remarked, without any fear of being overheard:

"Things are coming to a pretty pitch!"

Next day, feeling interested, Octave tried to sound Gasparine at the shop, as they were sorting a consignment of linen goods. But she gave him curt answers, and he felt that she was hostile to him, being vexed that he was a witness of the reconciliation of the previous evening. Moreover, she did not like him; even in their business relations she showed towards him a kind of spite. For a long while past she had seen through the game he was pursuing with regard to the mistress, and for his assiduous courtship she had only black looks and a contemptuous curl of the lip. This caused him occasional uneasiness. As long as this lanky devil of a girl put out her bony fingers to part them, he had the impression, at once firm and unpleasant, that Madame Hédouin would never become his.

Octave, however, had given himself six months. Four had hardly passed, and he was growing impatient. Every morning he asked himself whether he should not hasten matters somewhat, since he saw such slight advance towards gaining the affection of this woman, always so icy and so gentle. However, she showed real esteem for him, taken by his large ideas, by his dreams of huge modern warehouses, unloading millions of bales of merchandise in the streets of Paris. Often, when her husband was not there, as she and the young man opened the letters of a morning, she detained him and consulted him, glad of his advice. Thus a sort of commercial intimacy was established between the two. Their hands met amid piles of invoices; as they counted rows of figures, each felt the other's warm breath touching their cheeks in moments of excitement over the cash-box after unusually lucky receipts. Of such moments he even sought to take advantage, his plan now being to touch her affections through her tradeswoman instinct, and to conquer her on some day of weakness when excited by the good news of some unlooked-for sale. So he kept waiting for some surprising stroke of luck, that thus should deliver her up to him. However, whenever she did not keep him talking business to her, she at once resumed her quiet tone of authority, politely ordering him to do this or that, just as she would the other shopmen. In fact, she superintended the whole establishment, coldly beautiful, with a man's little cravat round her classic neck, and girt in her demure, tightly-fitting bodice of eternal black.

About this time, as Monsieur Hédouin became ill, he went to take a course of the waters at Vichy, much to Octave's undisguised delight. Though as cold as marble, Madame Hédouin, during this term of widowhood, would, as he thought, relent. But vainly did he watch for a single shiver, a single languorous symptom of desire. Never had she seemed so active, her head so clear, her eye so bright.

However, the young fellow did not despair. At times he thought he had reached the goal of his desire, and was already mapping out his life for the day, so close at hand, when he would be the lover of his employer's wife. He had kept Marie on merely as an aid to his patience; nevertheless, though obliging and cheap, she might eventually prove troublesome with her fidelity of the whipped-cur species. And, while always going to her on nights when he was dull, he bethought himself of some method of breaking off their intimacy. To do this abruptly seemed inexpedient. One holiday morning, when bound for the bed of his neighbor's wife, while his neighbour was taking an early constitutional, the idea possessed him of giving Marie up to her Jules, and of letting them fall into one another's arms, so amorous, that, with conscience clear, he could retire. A kind action, after all; so touching, indeed, that it left him quit of all remorse in the matter. Nevertheless, he waited, not wishing to be without female consolation of some kind.

At the Campardons' another complication gave Octave matter for reflection. He felt that the moment was coming for him to get his meals elsewhere. For three weeks Gasparine had been making herself thoroughly at home there; her authority, day by day, increased. First she began by coming every evening, then she made her appearance at lunch, and, in spite of her work at the shop, she began to undertake everything, whether it was Angèle's education, or the purchase of provisions for the house. Rose never ceased saying to Campardon: "Ah, if Gasparine only lived with us!" Yet every time the architect, conscientiously scrupulous, blushed, as he shame-facedly replied:

"No, no; that would never do! Besides, where could she sleep?"

And he explained that he should have to give up his study to Gasparine as a bedroom, he moving his table and plans into the drawing-room. Certainly, it would not inconvenience him at all, and one day, perhaps, he would agree to the alteration, for he did not want a drawing-room, and his study was too small for all the work that he now had in hand. Yet, Gasparine, after all, had better stay where she was. It was no good living in such hugger-mugger style.

About that time he was obliged to go to Evreux for a couple of days. The work for the archbishop worried him. He had acceded to the wishes of monseigneur, though no credit had been opened for the purpose, to construct new kitchens and heating apparatus; the expenses for this seemed likely to be very heavy, far too heavy to include in the cost of repairs. Besides this, the pulpit, for which there was a grant of three thousand francs, would cost ten, at the very least. For safety's sake, he desired to come to some arrangement with the archbishop.

Rose did not expect him home before Sunday night; but he arrived in the middle of luncn, and his sudden appearance quite scared them. Gasparine was at table, sitting between Octave and Angèle. They pretended to be perfectly at their ease, but there was evidently something mysterious in the air. Lisa had just shut the drawing-room door, obedient to a despairing gesture of her mistress, while Gasparine kicked certain pieces of paper out of sight which lay about here and there. When he talked of changing his things, they stopped him.

"Do wait a moment. Have some coffee, as you lunched at Evreux."

Then, as he noticed how embarrassed Rose was, she flung her arms round his neck.

"Don't scold me, dear. If you had not come until this evening you would have found everything straight."

She tremblingly opened the folding-doors, and took him into the drawing-room and the study. A mahogany bedstead, brought in that morning from a furniture dealer's, stood in the place of his drawing-table, which had been moved into the middle of the next room. But nothing had been put straight yet; portfolios were jumbled up with some of Gasparine's clothes, while the Virgin of the Bleeding Heart was leaning against the wall, propped up by a new wash-hand basin.

"It was to be a surprise!" murmured Madame Campardon, as, with swelling heart, she hid her face in the folds of her spouse's waistcoat.

Much moved, he looked at her in silence, while he avoided meeting Octave's eyes.

Then Gasparine, in her dry voice, asked:

"Will it put you out, cousin? Rose pestered me so to have

it done. But, if you think I shall be in your way, of course
I can go."

"No, cousin!" cried the architect, at last; "whatever Rose
does is right."

Then, as his wife burst out sobbing on his breast, he said:

"There, there, darling; it's silly to cry. I am very pleased.
You want to have your cousin with you; very well, so you
shall. It won't disturb me in the least. Now, don't cry any
more! See, I'll kiss you like I love you—oh, such a lot!"

And he devoured her with kisses. Then Rose, who, at a
word, became dissolved in tears, smiling again directly afterwards, took comfort while she wept. She, in her turn, kissed
him on his beard, saying gently:

"You were rather hard upon her. Give her a kiss, too."

Campardon embraced Gasparine. Angèle was called, who
looked on from the dining-room with mouth and eyes agape;
she, too, had to kiss the cousin. Octave stood aloof, having
come to the conclusion that in this family they were really
getting rather too affectionate. He had noticed with surprise
Lisa's respectful manner and smiling attentiveness towards
Gasparine. A sharp girl, evidently, that strumpet with the
blue eyelids!

About five o'clock, as he was regretting that he did not
know where to find Trublot, he suddenly thought he would
invite himself to dinner at the Pichons', so as not to spend
th evening by himself. No sooner had he got to their rooms,
however, than he found himself in the midst of a deplorable
family scene. The Vuillaumes were there, indignant and
trembling.

"It is disgraceful, sir!" said the mother, standing erect as
she apostrophised her son-in-law, prone upon a chair. "You
gave your word of honour."

"And you," added the father, making his trembling daughter retreat in terror to the sideboard—"don't make any excuses; you're just as much to blame. I suppose you both want
to starve, eh?"

Madame Vuillaume had put on her bonnet and shawl again,
saying solemnly:

"Good-bye! we, at least, will not encourage your concupis-
cence by our presence. Since you no longer pay the least atten-

tion to our wishes, we have nothing more to do here. Good-bye!"

And as Jules, from force of habit, rose to accompany them, she added:

"Never mind; we are quite able to get a 'bus without you. Go on, Monsieur Vuillaume. Let them eat their dinner, and much good may it do them, for they won't always have one!"

Octave, astonished, stood aside to let them pass. When they had gone, he looked at Jules, prostrate in his chair, and Marie standing by the sideboard, pale as death. Both were speechless.

"What is the matter?" he asked.

But, without answering him, the young woman dolefully began to scold her husband.

"I told you how it would be. You ought to have waited until you could break the matter to them gently. There was no hurry about it; nothing can be noticed so far."

"Why, what is it?" asked Octave, again.

Then, not even looking away, she blurted out, in her emotion:

"I am in the family-way."

"Oh! they're a damned nuisance!" cried Jules, indignantly, as he rose from his chair. "I thought it right to tell them straight off about this bother. Do they think it amuses me? Not a bit of it. I am far more let in than ever they are, more especially as it's through no fault of mine. We can't think where the likes of that came from, can we, Marie?"

"No, indeed!" said the young woman.

Octave made a calculation. She was five months gone—from the end of December to the end of May. His calculation was correct; it quite affected him. Then he preferred to doubt; but, as his emotion became deeper, he felt a longing to do the Pichons a kindness of some sort. Jules went on grumbling. They would look after the child, of course they would; but, all the same, it had far better have stopped where it was. Marie, usually so quiet, got into a temper, too, siding with her mother, who never forgave disobedience. A quarrel seemed imminent, each blaming the other for the youngster's appearance, when Octave gaily interposed:

"Come, come, it's no use quarrelling, now that it's on the way. I vote we don't dine here; it's too dismal by half. I'll take you both to a restaurant. Will you come?"

Marie blushed. Dining at a restaurant was her delight. But she mentioned her little girl, who always prevented her from getting out to enjoy herself. However, they settled that this time Lilitte should come too. They had a most pleasant evening.

"Well," thought he, as he slipped in between the sheets, "it's cost me fifty francs, but I owed them every bit as much as that. My own wish, after all, is that her husband may make her happy, poor little woman!"

And quite overcome by a sense of his good-nature, before going to sleep he resolved to make his grand attempt the very next evening.

Every Monday, after dinner, Octave helped Madame Hédouin to check the orders of the week. For this purpose they both withdrew to a little parlour at the back, a narrow room which only contained a safe, a bureau, two chairs, and a sofa. It so happened that on this particular Monday the Duveyriers were going to take Madame Hédouin to the Opéra-Comique. Accordingly, she sent for the young man about three o'clock. In spite of the bright sunshine, they had to burn the gas, as the room was only faintly lighted by windows overlooking the dismal inner courtyard. He bolted the door, and, noticing her surprised look, he said, gently:

"Now nobody can come and disturb us."

She nodded assent, and they commenced work. The summer novelties were going splendidly; business was always increasing. That week, in particular, the sale of little woollen goods had looked so promising that she heaved a sigh.

He had got as far as figures, counting up the probable cost with the passionate air of a page making a romantic declaration of long-hidden love. Suddenly, she found herself in his arms. He thrust her on to the sofa, believing that now at last she would succumb.

"Dear, dear! so that was why, was it?" she said, sadly, as she shook him off as if he were some tiresome child.

"Well, yes; for I'm in love with you!" he exclaimed. "Don't repulse me. With you, I might do such great things——"

So he went on to the end of his grand speech, which somehow rang false. She did not interrupt him, but stood turning over the leaves of the ledger. Then, when he had done, she replied:

"I know all that; I've heard it all before. But I thought that you, Monsieur Octave, had more sense than the others. I am really very sorry, for I had counted upon you. However, all young men are unreasonable. A house like this needs a deal of order, and you begin by wanting things which would unsettle us from morning to night. I am not a woman here; there's far too much for me to do. Come, now, how is it that you, with all your intelligence, could not see that I would never do such a thing as that: first, because it is silly; secondly, because it is useless; and thirdly, because, luckily for me, I don't care the least bit about it!"

He would like to have seen her full of wrath and of indignation, overflowing with exalted sentiments. Her calm voice, her quiet way of reasoning like a practical, self-possessed woman, disconcerted him. He felt that he was becoming ridiculous.

"Pity me, madam," he stammered. "You see how miserable I am!"

"Nonsense! you're not miserable at all. Anyhow, you'll soon get over it. Listen! there's somebody knocking; you'd far better go and open the door."

Accordingly, he was obliged to draw back the bolt. It was Mademoiselle Gasparine, who wanted to know about some chemises. She had been surprised to find the door bolted. But she knew Madame Hédouin too well, and as she saw her, frigid and erect, confronting Octave, who looked thoroughly ill at ease, there was in her smile something that seemed to mock him. It exasperated him, and he vaguely ascribed his failure to her.

"Madame," said he, suddenly, when Gasparine had gone, "I leave your employ this evening."

Madame Hédouin looked at him in surprise.

"What for? I did not dismiss you. Oh, that won't make any difference! I am not afraid."

This last speech drove him frantic. He would leave that very moment, refusing to endure his martyrdom an instant longer.

"Very well, Monsieur Octave," she continued, in her calm

way. "I will settle with you directly. All the same, the firm will be sorry to lose you, for you were a good assistant."

That evening, at half-past six, as he went into the Campardons' flat without ringing, he suddenly caught the architect and Gasparine kissing in the ante-room. She had only just got home from the shop, and had not even shut the door. They both looked rather foolish. "My wife—er—is combing her hair," stammered the architect, merely to make a remark of some sort. "You go in and see her."

Octave, feeling as uncomfortable as they did, hastily knocked at the door of Rose's bedroom, which he was wont to enter in his capacity of relative. He certainly could not continue to board there any longer, now that he caught them kissing like this, behind the door.

"Come in!" cried Rose. "Oh! it's you, Octave? That won't matter."

She had not yet put on her dressing-gown, and her soft, milk-white shoulders and arms were bare. Carefully scrutinising herself in the mirror, she was twisting her golden hair into tiny curls. Every day she sat for hours thus, busied with minute details of her toilet, thinking of nothing but the pores of her skin, of beautifying her person. Then, when her adornment was achieved, she would recline at full length in an easy-chair, luxurious and lovely, like some idol devoid of sex.

"You're making yourself a great swell again to-night, I see," said Octave, smiling.

"Well, there! it's my only amusement," she replied. "It's something to do. I never cared about housekeeping, you know; and now that Gasparine is here—these little curls suit me, eh? It's a sort of consolation to be nicely dressed, and to feel that I look pretty."

As dinner was not ready, he told her how he had left "The Ladies' Paradise." He invented a story about some other situation which he had long been looking out for, and this gave him a pretext for his intention of taking his meals elsewhere. She was surprised at his leaving a firm like that, where he had such good prospects. But she was far too busy at her looking-glass to listen carefully.

Octave was about to go upstairs to bed, when a desire to

get some fresh air led him out-of-doors. It was barely ten o'clock; he would take a stroll as far as the Palais Royal. Now he was single again, with no woman whatever in tow. Neither Valérie nor Madame Hédouin would have anything to say to his courtship, and he had been in too great a hurry to give up Marie to Jules—Marie, his only conquest, and whom he had been at no pains to win. He endeavored to laugh at it all, but at heart he felt sad, bitterly recollecting his successes at Marseilles. In the repeated failure of all his attempts at seductions, he saw an evil omen, an actual blow aimed at his good-fortune. The atmosphere about him seemed so chilly with no petticoats hovering near. Even the lachrymose Madame Campardon had let him go without a tear. Surely a terrible revenge, this. Was Paris going to deny him her favours, after all? No sooner had he got into the street than he heard a woman's voice calling him. It was Berthe, standing at the door of the silk shop. A man was just putting up the shutters.

"Oh, Monsieur Mouret!" she asked, "is it true that you have left 'The Ladies' Paradise'?"

He was surprised to find that people already knew it in the neighbourhood. Berthe called her husband. He had meant to have a talk next day with Monsieur Mouret; well, he might just as well do so at once. And there and then Auguste, in his sulky way, offered the young man a post in his employ. Taken aback, Octave hesitated, and was on the point of refusing, as he reflected upon the insignificance of such an establishment. But when he saw Berthe's pretty face and welcoming smile, the same bright glance that twice had met him, once on the day of his arrival, and again on her wedding-day, he said, with decision:

"All right; I'll come."

Chapter Nine

OCTAVE now found himself brought into closer contact with the Duveyriers. As often as Madame Duveyrier came through the shop on her way home she would stop and talk to Berthe for a moment; and the first time she saw the young man behind one of the counters, she good-humouredly scolded him for not keeping his promise of long standing to come and see her one evening and try his voice. She was going to give another performance of the *Benediction of the Poniards* at one of her first Saturday parties in the ensuing winter, with two more tenors this time—something thoroughly complete.

"If it is not inconvenient," said Berthe one day to Octave, "could you go upstairs after dinner to my sister-in-law? She expects you."

The attitude she maintained towards him was that of a mistress who desires to be studiously polite.

"Well, the fact is," said he, "I thought of putting these shelves in order this evening."

"Never mind about them," she rejoined; "there are plenty of people to do that. You can have the evening off."

About nine o'clock Octave found Madame Duveyrier waiting for him in her large white and gold drawing-room. Everything was ready, the piano open, the candles lit. A lamp, placed on a small table near the instrument, lighted half the room, the other half remaining only in shadow. Seeing that she was alone, Octave thought it behoved him to ask after Monsieur Duveyrier. He was in excellent health, she said; his colleagues had entrusted him with the drawing up of a report concerning a most serious matter, and he had just gone out to obtain certain information respecting it.

"You know, it is the affair of the Rue de Provence," she said, naïvely.

"Oh! he has to deal with that, has he?" exclaimed Octave.

It was a scandal that had become the talk of all Paris—a story of wholesale traffic in children, little girls procured for personages of exalted station. Clotilde continued:

103

"Yes, it gives him a great deal to do. For the past fortnight, every evening has been taken up with it."

He looked at her, knowing from Trublot that Bachelard had invited Duveyrier to dinner that evening, and they were afterwards to make a night of it at Clarisse's. She seemed quite serious, however, and talked gravely about her husband, relating, in her eminently respectable way, various singular stories as to the why and wherefore of the counsellor's perpetual absence from the conjugal hearth.

"He has charge of so many human souls," said Octave, somewhat out of countenance by her frank gaze.

"Madame! madame!"

Starting up, she saw Clémence, her maid.

"Well, what is it?"

"Oh, madame, Monsieur Vabre has fallen forward on his writing-desk, and he doesn't stir! We are all so frightened!"

Then, without exactly grasping the maid's meaning, she rose from the piano in astonishment, and went out with Clémence. Octave, who did not venture to follow her, remained walking up and down the drawing-room. Then, after some moments of awkward hesitation, as he heard the sound of hurrying footsteps and anxious voices, he determined to see what was the matter. Crossing the next room, which was quite dark, he reached Monsieur Vabre's room. All the servants had hastened thither—Julie, in her kitchen apron; Clémence and Hippolyte, their minds still full of a game of dominoes from which they had just got up. And there they all stood in bewilderment round the old man; while Clotilde, stooping down, shouted in his ear and implored him to speak. But still he never moved, his face buried in his catalogue-tickets. His forehead had struck the inkstand. There was a splash of ink over his left eye, which was trickling slowly down towards his lips.

"He is in a fit," said Octave. "It won't do to leave him there. We must put him on to the bed."

Madame Duveyrier, however, grew terribly excited. Her callous nature was gradually stirred to its depths. She kept repeating:

"Do you think it is? Do you think it is? Goodness gracious! Oh, my poor dear father!"

Hippolyte, the footman, was in no hurry to move. He felt

a kind of repugnance to touch the old man, vaguely afraid that he might die in his arms. Octave was obliged to call upon him for assistance. Between them, they aid him down on the bed.

"Bring some warm water," said the young may to Julie. "We must wash his face."

Clotilde now became incensed against her husband. Ought he ever to have been away? If anything happened, what would become of her? It was as if done on purpose; he was never at home when wanted, and the Lord knew that was not very often! Octave, interrupting, advised her to send for Doctor Juillerat. No one had thought of that before. Hippolyte started off at once, glad to get away.

"Leaving me all alone like this!" Clotilde went on. "I don't know, myself, but there must be all sorts of things to settle. Oh, my poor dear father!"

"Would you like me to inform the other members of your family?" said Octave. "I can fetch your two brothers. It might be as well."

Clotilde stood before him, saying resolutely, in an undertone.

"Go and fetch him."

And as he seemed surprised, she, as it were, with a shrug disposed of the tale about drawing up a report of the Rue de Provence affair—one of those perpetual fictions with which she had to supply the outside world. In her emotion, she kept nothing back.

"You know, Rue de la Cerisaie. All our friends know where it is."

Octave bent down as Julie was wiping Monsieur Vabre's eye with the corner of a towel; the ink had dried on to the skin, leaving a livid mark. Madame Duveyrier advised her not to rub so hard, and then she turned back to Octave, who had already got to the door.

"Not a word to anyone," she murmured. "It is useless to upset the whole house. Take a cab, knock at the door, and be sure and bring him back with you."

When Octave had gone she sank into a chair near the sick man's pillow. He had not recovered consciousness; his long-drawn, painful breathing alone broke the lugubrious silence of the chamber. Then, as the doctor did not come, and seeing herself alone with two terrified maidservants, she burst into tears, sobbing violently in a paroxysm of grief.

It was at the Café Anglais that Bachelard had invited Monsieur Duveyrier to dine, though one hardly knew why. Perhaps it was for the pleasure of having a distinguished magistrate as his guest, and of showing him that tradespeople knew how to spend their money. He had asked Trublot and Gueulin as well—four men and no women; women don't know how to appreciate a good dinner. They prevent one from enjoying the truffles, and ruin one's digestion.

"I'm thoroughly disillusioned!" declared uncle Bachelard. "There's nothing like virtue, after all." (Duveyrier nodded in sign of assent.) "And I've bid good-bye to fun of that sort. At one time I used to go it pretty hot, I confess. Why, in the Rue Godot-de-Mauroy, I know them every blessed one —fair girls, dark ones, and red-haired ones, who occasionally have got good limbs; not often, though. Then there are those dirty holes at Montmartre—furnished lodgings, you know; filthy little streets in my part of the world, where one can pick up the most amazing creatures, with such extraordinary tricks——"

"Oh—bitches!" broke in Trublot, in his contemptuous manner. "What utter rot! You don't catch me at that sort of game; with them you never get your money's worth."

By bawdy talk of this kind Duveyrier was deliciously tickled. He drank his *Kümmel* in sips, his stiff magistrate's features distorted now and again by little sensual thrills.

"For my part," said he, "I cannot stand vice; it disgusts me. In order to love a woman, you must respect her, mustn't you? It would be quite impossible for me to have anything to do with one of those unfortunates, unless, of course, she appeared ashamed of her way of living, and had been rescued from it with a view to making her become a decent woman. Love could not have a more noble mission than that. In short, a respectable mistress—you understand? In that case I do not say that I should be able to resist."

"But I've had no end of respectable mistresses," cried Bachelard. "They are a damned sight worse than the others, and such sluts, too! Bitches that behind your back go on the loose,

106

and then pox you up to your eyes! My last one, for instance—a most respectable-looking little lady that I met at a church-door. I took a milliner's shop for her at Ternes, just to give her a position, you know. However, she never had a single customer. Well, sir, would you believe it?—she used to have the whole street in to sleep with her!"

Gueulin chuckled, his red hair growing more bristly than usual, while the hot air brought beads of perspiration to his brow. Sucking his cigar, he mumbled:

"And the other one, that tall girl at Passy, who had a sweet meat-shop? And the other one in a room yonder, with her outfits for orphans? And the captain's widow, do you remember, who used to show the mark of a sword-cut on her belly? They all of them, every one, made a fool of you, uncle! It does not matter my telling you now, does it? Well, one evening I had to be on my guard against the lady with the sword-mark on her belly. She wanted me to ——; but I was not such a fool! You never know how far women like that may lead you." screwed up his great eyelids and winked hideously.

"My boy, you may have them all if you like. I've got some-
Bachelard seemed vexed. Recovering himself, however, he thing better than that."

And he refused to explain himself, delighted to have roused the others' curiosity. Yet he burned to be indiscreet, to let them guess his treasure.

"A little girl," said he at last; "but the real thing, upon my honour!"

"Impossible!" cried Trublot. "They no longer make such articles."

"Respectably connected?" asked Duveyrier.

"Most respectable as regards family," affirmed Bachelard. "Imagine something stupidly chaste—a mere chance—I just had her like that. I firmly believe she doesn't think she's been jammed!"

Gueulin listened in astonishment. Then, with a sceptical gesture, he muttered:

"Ah, yes! I know."

"Eh? What? You know?" said Bachelard, angrily. "You know nothing whatever, my boy; no more does anybody else. She Bibi's property; she is not to be looked at, not to be touched—a case of 'Hands off!'"

Then, turning to Duveyrier, he said:

"You, sir, being kindhearted, can quite understand my feelings. It has a softening influence, somehow, to go and see her; it almost makes one feel young again. Anyhow, there I've got a nice quiet little nook where I can rest after all the old whoreshop business. Ah, and if you knew how sweet and clean she is, such a soft white skin, with proper little bubbies and thighs on her—not a bit scraggy, but round and firm as a peach!"

The counsellor's red blotches glowed again as, in a wave, the blood rushed to his face. Trublot and Gueulin looked at Bachelard, feeling half inclined to hit him as he sat leering there, with his row of glittering false teeth, and saliva dribbling down from either side of his mouth. What! this old carcass of an uncle, this worn-out debauchee, this wreck, whose flaming nose alone kept its place between his blubbered, flabby cheeks—so he had got, stored up discreetly, out of ken, some flower of innocence, some soft budding body, whose virginal flesh he tainted with the stench of his stale fornications, masking his lechery by a false air of drunken benevolence!

Meanwhile, growing tender, he continued the subject, as he licked the edge of his liqueur glass:

"After all, my one dream is to make the dear child happy! But, you know, her belly has begun to swell; I shall soon be a papa! 'Pon my honour! if I could come across some steady young chap I'd give her to him—marry her to him, mind you! nothing else."

The house in the Rue de la Cerisaie seemed fast asleep amid the solitude and silence of the street. Duveyrier was surprised at not seeing any lights in the third-floor windows. Trublot gravely observed that no doubt Clarisse had gone to bed to wait for them. Or, perhaps, added Gueulin, she was playing a game of bésique in the kitchen with her maid. They knocked. The gas on the stairs burnt with the straight, motionless flame of a lamp in some chapel. Not a sound, not a whisper. But, as the four men passed the hall-porter, he rushed out of his room, saying:

"Sir, sir, the key!"

Duveyrier stopped short on the first step.

"Is madame not at home, then?" he asked.

"No, sir. And wait a moment; you will want a light."

As he handed him the candlestick, the porter, despite the look of exaggerated respect on his pallid face, could not repress a brutal grin. Neither the uncle nor the two young men said a word. So, in silence, with backs bent, they filed up the stairs, the ceaseless beat of their footsteps echoing along the gloomy passages. Duveyrier, trying to understand it all, led the way, moving his limbs mechanically, like one that walks in a dream, while the candle that he held in his trembling hand flung the four shadows of this weird procession on the wall, like a march of broken marionettes.

On the third-floor he suddenly grew faint and could not find the key-hole. So Trublot was obliging enough to open the door for him. The key, as it turned in the lock, made a hollow, reverberating sound, as if beneath the vaulted roof of some cathedral.

"By Jove!" muttered he, "the place does not look much as if anybody lived in it!"

"Sounds pretty empty," said Bachelard.

"Like a regular little family vault," added Gueulin.

They entered. Duveyrier went first, holding the candle aloft. The ante-room was empty; even the hat-pegs had vanished. The drawing-room was empty; so, too, was the parlour; not a single piece of furniture, not a curtain at one of the windows, not even a brass rod. Petrified, Duveyrier glanced down at his feet and then looked up at the ceiling, and then went round examining the walls as if to discover the hole through which everything had disappeared.

"When did you see her last?" asked Bachelard.

"Yesterday, sir," exclaimed Duveyrier.

"Hullo! here she is, coming back!" said Gueulin, straining his ears to listen.

Some one, indeed, was walking in the hall; and a voice cried: "Hullo here, what's up? Is everybody dead?" And then Octave appeared. These empty rooms and open doors astonished him. But his amazement increased as, in the centre of the bare drawing-room, he saw the four men—one on the floor, and three standing—in the dim light of a single candle, which the counsellor carried like a church taper. A few words sufficed to explain all to him.

"By the way, it was your wife who sent me to fetch you. Your father-in-law is dying."

Meanwhile, as they drove along, Octave briefly described Monsieur Vabre's seizure to his companion, without concealing the fact that Madame Duveyrier knew the address in the Rue de la Cerisaie.

After a pause, the counsellor asked, in a doleful voice:

"Do you think that she will forgive me?"

Octave was silent. The cab went rumbling along, as every now and then a ray of light from some gas-lamp shot across its gloom. Just as they arrived, Duveyrier, full of anguish, asked another question.

"The best thing I can do at present is to make it up with my wife; don't you think so?"

"Perhaps that would be the wisest plan," said Octave, obliged to make some sort of reply.

Upstairs, in the drawing-room, Madame Duveyrier came forward to meet them. She had been crying a good deal; her eyes shone beneath their reddened lids. The counsellor, greatly embarrassed, held out his arms and embraced her, murmuring:

"My poor Clotilde!"

Surprised at such unwonted effusiveness, she shrank back. Octave had kept behind; but he heard the husband say, in a low voice:

"Forgive me! Let us forget our quarrels on this sad occasion. You see, I have come back to you and for always. Oh, I have been well punished!"

When Duveyrier had gone into the adjoining room, she approached Octave, who, in order to keep in countenance, was standing by the piano.

Madame Duveyrier looked at the young man for a moment without speaking, tormented by an anxiety which led her to throw off her habitual reserve.

"Was he there?" she asked, briefly.

"Yes, madame."

"Then, what is it? What is the matter with him?"

"That person has left him, madame, taking all the furniture with her. I found him in the bare walls with only a candle!"

Clotilde made a gesture of despair. She understood. Her

110

handsome face wore an expression of discouragement and of disgust. It was not enough that she had lost her father, but the mischance must needs serve as a pretext to bring about a reconciliation between herself and her husband! She knew him well; he would always be on top of her, now that there was nothing elsewhere to protect her, and, with her respect for all duties, she trembled at the thought that she could not refuse to submit to the abominable nuisance. For a moment she looked at the piano. Great tears filled her eyes as she said, simply:

"Thank you, sir."

Chapter Ten

ONSIEUR VABRE'S funeral did not take
place for two days. Notwithstanding, on the
circulars announcing his death, Duveyrier
caused the words to be printed, "Provided
with the Holy Sacraments of the Church." The shop being
closed, Octave was free, and felt delighted at getting such
a holiday, as for a long while he had wanted to rearrange
his room, move the furniture, and put his books together
in a little bookcase that he had picked up second-hand. He
had risen earlier than usual, and had just finished his altera-
tions about eight o'clock, on the morning of the funeral,
when Marie knocked at the door. She had brought him a
bundle of books.

"As you don't come and fetch them," said she, "I've got
to take the trouble to return them myself."

But, blushing, she refused to come in, shocked at the idea
of being in a young man's room. Their intimacy, however,
had completely ceased in the most natural manner possible,
as he had no longer run after her. But she was as affectionate
as ever, always greeting him with a smile when they met.

"You're giving me another one of Balzac's," said she, looking over the fresh batch of books that he was lending her.
"No, take it back; his tales are too much like real life!"

As she held the volume out to him, he caught hold of her
wrist and tried to pull her into the room. She amused him with
all her curiosity about death; she suddenly seemed to him
droll, full of life, desirable. But she understood his meaning,
and blushed scarlet. Then, freeing herself from his grasp, she
ran away, saying:

"Thank you, Monsieur Mouret; we shall meet by-and-by,
at the funeral."

Louise, the little maid at Madame Juzeur's, let Octave in.
She took him into the drawing-room, looked at him for a
moment, grinning sheepishly, and at last said that her mistress was dressing. Madame Juzeur, however, at once made
her appearance, wearing black, and in this mourning she

112

seemed gentler, more refined, than ever.

"I was sure that you would come this morning," she sighed, languidly. "All night long I kept dreaming about you. Quite impossible to sleep, you know, with that corpse in the house!"

And she confessed that she had got up three times in the night to look under the furniture.

"Why, you ought to have called me, said the young man, gallantly. "Two in a bed are never afraid."

She affected a charming air of shame.

"Be quiet; it's naughty!"

And she held her hand over his lips. Of course, he was obliged to kiss it. Then she spread out her fingers, laughing as if she were being tickled. Excited by this game, he sought to push matters further. He caught her in his arms and pressed her close to his breast without her offering any resistance. Then he whispered:

"Come, now, why won't you?"

"Oh, in any case, not to-day!"

"Why not to-day?"

"What, with that dead body downstairs? No, no, it's impossible!"

He tightened his embrace, and she yielded. Their warm breaths mingled.

"When will you, then? To-morrow?"

"Never."

"But you're quite free; your husband behaved so badly that you owe him nothing."

He sought to force her consent. But in her supple way she slipped from him. Then putting her arms round him, she held him tightly so that he could not move, and murmured caressingly:

"Anything you like except that! Do you understand me! Not that, never, never! I would rather die! It's an idea of mine, that's all. I've sworn to Heaven I wouldn't, but you need not know anything about that. So you're just as selfish, it seems, as other men, who are never satisfied as long as one refuses them anything. Yet I am very fond of you. Anything you like, only not that, my sweetheart!"

She allowed him to caress her in the warmest, most secret way, only repulsing him by a sudden movement of nervous vigour when he sought to perform the one forbidden act. Her obstinacy had in it a sort of Jesuitical reserve, a fear of the confessional, a certitude of pardon for petty sins, while so gross a one might cause overmuch trouble with her spiritual pastor. Then there were other unavowed sentiments, a blending of honour and of self-esteem, the coquetry of always having an advantage over men by never satisfying them, together with a shrewd personal enjoyment of getting kisses in abundance from everybody without the final, humiliating touch of the male rod. This she thought better, and stubbornly persisted in it. Not a man could flatter himself that he had had her since her husband's cowardly desertion. She was an honest woman, that she was!

No, sir, not one! Ah, I can hold my head up, I can! How many unfortunate women in my position would have gone wrong!"

She gently moved him aside and rose from the sofa.

"Let me alone. That corpse downstairs worries me dreadfully. The whole house seems to smell of it!"

Meanwhile, the time drew near for the funeral. She wished to get to the church before they started, so as not to see all the funeral trappings. But, on going to the door with him, she suddenly remembered telling him about her liqueur from the West Indies. So she made him come back, and brought the bottle and two glasses herself. It was creamy and very sweet, with a scent of flowers. When she had drunk it, a sort of girlish greediness gave a look of languid rapture to her face. She could have lived on sugar; sweets scented with vanilla and with rose troubled her senses as greatly as the touch of a lover.

"That will keep us up," said she.

And, when in the ante-room he kissed her on the mouth, she shut her eyes. Their sugary lips seemed to melt like bon-bons.

At the Père-la-Chaise Cemetery, while the coffin was being lowered into the grave, Trublot, still arm-in-arm with Octave, saw him smile once more at Madame Juzeur.

"Ah, yes!" muttered he; "that's the little woman who's awfully unhappy. 'Anything-you-like-except-that!' "

Octave started. What? Had Trublot tried it on, too? Then, with a gesture of disdain, the latter explained that he had not, but a friend of his had. Lots of other fellows, too, who went

114

in for that sort of rot.

"Excuse me," he added; "now that the old boy has been stowed away, I must go and see Duveyrier about something that I had to do for him."

The relatives, silent and doleful, were now departing. Then Trublot, detaining Duveyrier, told him that he had seen Clarisse's maid, but he could not find out the address, as the maid had left the day before Clarisse moved, after a wild row. Thus the last ray of hope vanished, and Duveyrier, burying his face in his handkerchief, rejoined the other mourners.

That evening quarrelling began. The family had made a disastrous discovery. With that sceptical carelessness that notaries sometimes display, Monsieur Vabre had left no will. Cupboards and drawers were all searched in vain, the worst of it being that not a stiver of all the hoped-for six or seven hundred thousand francs was forthcoming, neither in the shape of money, title-deeds, nor shares. All that they found was the sum of seven hundred and thirty-four francs in ten-sou pieces —the hidden store of a drivelling dotard. Moreover, there were undeniable traces—a note-book filled with figures and letters from stockbrokers—which convinced his relatives, livid with rage, of the old man's secret vice—an ungovernable passion for gambling, an inept, furious craving for dabbling in stocks and shares, which he hid behind his innocent mania for compiling his masterpiece of statistical research. Everything had been sacrificed; his Versailles savings, his house-rents; even the moneys squeezed out of his children. During recent years, indeed, he had even mortgaged the house for a hundred and fifty thousand francs, at three different periods. The family, dumbfounded, stood round the wonderful safe in which they believed the fortune was locked up. All that it contained, however, was a lot of odds and ends—scraps picked up about the house, old bits of iron and glass, tags of ribbon, and broken toys stolen long since when Gustave was a baby.

Then came violent abuse. They called the old man a swindler; it was scandalous to fool away his money in this way, like a sly rogue who cares not a straw for anybody, but who acts out his infamous comedy so as to get people to pet and coddle him. The Duveyriers seemed grieved beyond measure that they had boarded him for twelve years, without ever once asking him for the eighty thousand francs of Clotilde's dowry, only ten thousand of which they had received. Never mind; that was always ten thousand francs, as Théophile angrily remarked. he had not yet got a penny of the fifty thousand francs promised at the time of his marriage. Auguste, however, complained more bitterly, reproaching his brother with having, at any rate, been able for three months to pocket the interest on that sum, whereas he would never see a farthing of the fifty thousand francs specified in his contract. Then Berthe, spurred on by her mother, made various cutting remarks, and appeared to be highly indignant at having become connected with a dishonest family, while Valérie, bewailing the rent which she had continued paying for so long through fear of being disinherited, was at a loss to comprehend it all, regretting the money as though it had been used to promote debauchery.

For a whole fortnight these matters were excitedly discussed by the whole house. Finally it appeared that all that remained was the building, valued at three hundred thousand francs. When the mortgage had been paid off, there would be about half that sum to divide between Monsieur Vabre's three children. Fifty thousand francs apiece! a meagre consolation, truly, but with which they must needs be content. Théophile and Auguste had already settled what to do with their shares. It was agreed that the building should be sold. In his wife's name Duveyrier undertook all arrangements. First of all, he persuaded the two brothers not to have a public auction; if they were willing, the sale could take place at his notary's, Maître Renaudin, a man for whose integrity he could answer. Then, acting on the notary's advice, he slyly hinted to them that it would be best to put up the house at a low figure, only a hundred and forty thousand francs to begin with. A very knowing dodge, this, which would bring crowds of people to the sale; the bids would mount rapidly, and they would realise far more than they expected. Full of happy confidence, Théophile and Auguste chuckled again. However, on the day of the sale, Maître Renaudin abruptly knocked the house down to Duveyrier for a hundred and forty thousand francs. There was not even enough to pay off the mortgage! This was the last straw.

Never were the details disclosed of the fearful scene which

took place at the Duveyriers' that same evening. The house's solemn walls muffled the shouts of the combatants. Théophile denounced his brother-in-law as a scoundrel, openly accusing him of having bribed the notary by promising to appoint him a justice of the peace. As for Auguste, he actually talked of the assize court, and declared that he would drag Maître Renaudin into it as well, whose roguery was the talk of the neighbourhood. But it never transpired how the good people, as rumour said, got at last to blows; their parting words on the threshold were overheard—words that amid the austere decorum of the staircase rang out with disagreeable force.

"Dirty blackguard!" cried Auguste. "You sentence people to penal servitude who have not done half as much!"

Théophile, coming last, kept the door opened as, half choked by fury and a fit of coughing, he yelled:

"Thief! thief! Yes, thief! You, too, Clotilde, do you hear? You're a thief!"

Then he slammed the door so violently that all the adjoining ones shook again. Monsieur Gourd, who was listening, grew alarmed. He glanced up enquiringly at the several floors, but all that he could see was Madame Juzeur's delicate profile. With back bent he returned on tiptoe to his room, at once reassuming his dignified mien. One could deny having heard any disturbance. Personally, he was delighted, and sided with the new landlord.

A few days afterwards there was a reconciliation between Auguste and his sister. It surprised everybody. Octave had been seen going to the Duveyriers'. The counsellor, ill at ease, had decided to charge no rent for the ground-floor shop for five years, thus shutting one of the inneritors' mouths. When Théophile heard this, accompanied by his wife, he went downstairs to his brother's and made another scene. So he, too, had sold himself, and had joined the gang of thieves! However, Madame Josserand happened to be in the shop at the time, and she soon extinguished him. She frankly advised Valérie not to sell herself any more than her daughter had done. And Valérie, forced to retreat, exclaimed:

"So we're the only ones who are to grin and bear it, are we? Damned if I'll pay any more rent. I've got a lease, and that gaol-bird will never dare to turn us out. And as for you, my little Berthe, one day we shall see what it will take to have you."

Once more there was a banging of doors. A deadly feud now existed between the two families. Octave, who had been of service, was present on this occasion, just as if he were one of the family. Berthe almost swooned in his arms, while August made sure that none of his customers had overheard. Even Madame Josserand put faith in the young man. On the Duveyriers, however, she was very severe.

"The rent is something," said she, "but I want those fifty thousand francs."

"Of course you do, if you pay yours," Berthe ventured to remark.

Her mother, seemingly, did not understand.

"I tell you, I want them, do you hear? Well, well, that old rip of a Vabre must be chuckling in his grave. I'm not going to let him boast of having made a fool of me, though. What scoundrels there are in this world, to be sure! Fancy promising money that one hasn't got! Wait a bit, my girl; they shall pay you, or else I'll go and dig him out of his grave just to spit in his face!"

Chapter Eleven

ONE morning, when Berthe was at her mother's, Adèle came in, looking very scared, to say that Monsieur Saturnin was there, with a man. Doctor Chassagne, the director of the Moulineaux Asylum, had repeatedly informed the Josserands that he could not keep their son, he not being a patient in whom the symptoms of insanity were sufficiently marked.

Having got to know about the papers making over the three thousand francs, which Berthe had cajoled her brother into signing, he feared being compromised in the matter, and suddenly sent Saturnin home.

The news was alarming to all. Madame Josserand, who feared she might be throttled, sought to reason with the attendant. But he curtly said:

"The director wished me to tell you that when a person is sane enough to give money to his parents, he is sane enough to live with them."

"But he is mad; he will murder us!"

"Not so mad that he can't sign his name, anyhow!" rejoined the man, as he went away.

However, Saturnin came in very quietly, with his hands in his pockets, just as if he were returning from a stroll in the Tuileries gardens. As to his stay in the asylum, he said not a word.

He embraced his father, who wept, and he gave hearty kisses to his mother and Hortense, who both trembled with fright. Then, as he saw Berthe, he became delighted, caressing her with the charming impulsiveness of a schoolboy. She at once took advantage of his tender mood to tell him of her marriage. He showed no signs of anger, and at first hardly seemed to understand, as if forgetful of his former fits of rage. But when she was about to go downstairs, he began to yell; married or not married, he did not care, so long as she stayed where he was, always with him, always close to him. Seeing how her terrified mother rushed away to lock herself in, Berthe thought of taking Saturnin to her own home. They would

119

make use of him in some way, in the basement of their shop, even if it were but to tie up parcels.

That same evening, Auguste, despite his evident repugnance, consented to his wife's wish. They had hardly been married three months, yet insensibly were becoming estranged. It was a collision of two individuals widely different from each other in temperament as in education—a husband glum, crotchety, and devoid of passion, and a wife reared in the hot-house of specious Parisian luxury, bent on getting all the enjoyment she could out of life, though for herself alone, like a selfish, spoilt child. Thus he was at a loss to understand her desire for gaiety and movement, her perpetual goings-out to shop, to take walks, or pay visits; her racing hither and thither to theatres, exhibitions or other places of amusement.

One evening, about eleven o'clock, Auguste kept continually going to the shop door and looking up and down the street with ever-increasing impatience. Berthe, whom her mother and sister had fetched at dinner-time, not letting her finish her dessert even, had not yet come back, though she had been gone more than three hours, and had promised to return before closing time.

"Ten minutes past eleven—damn it all!" exclaimed Auguste, who never swore, as a rule.

At that moment, however, the ladies came in. Berthe wore a charming costume of pink silk embroidered with white jet, while her sister, always in blue, and her mother, always in mauve, kept to their gaudy, elaborate gowns which every season they furbished up anew. Madame Josserand came first, large and imposing, to stop her son-in-law from making any complaints. These the three had foreseen when holding council together at the top of the street. She even condescended to explain their delay by saying that they had dawdled along, looking in at shop-windows. Auguste, however, grew very pale, and made no remonstrance, speaking in a dry tone of voice. Evidently, he was restraining himself until later on. For a moment, Madame Josserand, used as she was to family jars, felt disposed to intimidate him; then being obliged to withdraw, she was content to say:

"Good-night, my girl, and sleep well if you want to live long."

Instantly Auguste, not longer master of himself and oblivious of the presence of Octave and Saturnin, pulled a crumpled piece of paper out of his pocket, which he thrust into Berthe's face, as he stuttered:

"What—what—what is this?"

Berthe had not even taken off her bonnet. She grew very red.

"That?" she replied. "Why, it's a bill."

"Yes, it's a bill, and for false hair, too! For false hair, of all things; as if you hadn't got any on your head! But that's not the point. You've paid this bill; now, tell me, what did you pay it with?"

Becoming more and more embarrassed, Berthe at last rejoined:

"With my own money, of course!"

"Your own money! Why, you haven't got any. Somebody must have given you some, or else you took it from here. Yes; and, look here, I know everything. You've been running into debt. I'll put up with anything you like, but I won't have debts, do you hear? I won't have debts—never!"

Upstairs, Monsieur Josserand opened the door in great surprise, as Adèle had gone to bed. He was just getting ready to spend the night in addressing wrappers, in spite of the indisposition of which for some time he had complained. Thus, feeling embarrassed, and fearful of being found out, he took his son-in-law into the dining-room, alluding to some urgent work which he had to finish—a copy of the inventory of the Saint-Joseph Glass Works. But when Auguste roundly accused his daughter of running into debt, and told him of the quarrel occasioned by the incident of the false hair, the poor man trembled in every limb; he stammered incoherently, and tears filled his eyes. His daughter was in debt, and led a life of household bickering just like his own! All his own misfortunes had begun anew for his child! Another fear possessed him, and this was that his son-in-law would broach the subject of money, claim the dowry and denounce him as a swindler. No doubt the fellow knew everything, or he would never have knocked them up in this way at nearly midnight.

"My wife has gone to bed," he stuttered, in confusion. "It is no good waking her up, is it? Really, I am surprised to hear all this! My poor dear Berthe is not a naughty girl, that

I assure you! Do be indulgent towards her. I'll speak to her myself. As for ourselves, my dear Auguste, I don't think we have done anything to displease you——"

He looked at him enquiringly, feeling reassured; Auguste evidently knew nothing as yet. Then Madame Josserand appeared outside her bedroom door. She stood there in her night-dress, white and appalling. Infuriated though he was, Auguste recoiled. She must have been listening at the door, for she at once delivered a blow straight from the shoulder.

"I don't suppose you've come for your ten thousand francs, have you? The instalment is not due for two months and more. We will pay you in two months, sir. We are not in the habit of dying to avoid keeping *our* promises."

Her astounding assurance completely overpowered Monsieur Josserand. Having once begun, she went on making the most extraordinary statements, to the utter bewilderment of Auguste, whom she would not give time to speak.

"You are utterly wanting in common-sense, sir. When you've made Berthe ill, you'll have to send for the doctor, and then you'll have a chemist's bill to pay. I went away just now because I saw that you had determined to make a fool of yourself. Pray do so. Beat your wife, if you like; my mother's heart is easy, for God sees all, and punishment is never far behind!"

At last Auguste was able to explain his grievances. He complained once more of the perpetual gadding about, the expensive dresses and all the rest of it, having even the hardihood to condemn the way that Berthe had been brought up. Madame Josserand listened with an air of supreme contempt. Then, when he had finished, she said:

"All that you tell me, my good fellow, is so nonsensical that it does not deserve an answer. My conscience is my own; that is enough for me. A man like that, to whom I entrusted an angel! As I am only insulted, I shall have nothing more to do with your quarrels. Settle them as best you can!"

"But your daughter will end by deceiving me, madame!" cried Auguste, in a fresh burst of rage.

Madame Josserand, about to withdraw, turned round and looked him full in the face.

"Sir," said she, "you're doing all you possibly can to make her."

Then she went back to her room, majestic as some colossal triple-breasted Ceres robed in white.

Downstairs, in the shop, Berthe remained motionless for a moment, her face buried in her hands. One of the men, having put up the shutters, went below into the basement, and it was then that Octave thought he might approach the young woman. Ever since Auguste had gone, Saturnin kept making signs over his sister's head, inviting Octave to comfort her. Now, looking radiant, he redoubled his winks, and fearing that he was not understood, he emphasized his hints by blowing kisses with childish impulsiveness.

"What? Do you want me to kiss her?" Octave asked him, by signs.

The madman vigorously nodded assent. Then as he saw Octave smilingly approach Berthe, who had observed nothing, he sat on the floor behind a counter, out of sight, so as not to be in their way. The gas-jets still were burning—tall flames in the silent, empty shop. There was a sort of death-like peace, and a stuffy smell from all the bales of silk.

"Madame, let me beg you not to take it too much to heart," said Octave in his caressing voice.

In her furious spite, she blurted out everything. A man whom she thought had married her for love, but who very soon would leave her without a chemise to her back! Didn't she do her duty by him? Could he charge her with the least neglect? If he had not flown into a rage when she asked him to get her some false hair, she would never have been obliged to buy some with her own pocket-money. For the least thing there was always the same fuss; she could never express a wish or say that she wanted some trivial article of dress, without meeting with such sullen, ferocious opposition. Naturally, she had some self-pride; she now asked for nothing and preferred to go without necessaries, rather than humiliate herself to no purpose. For instance, the last fortnight she had been longing for some ornaments that she had seen, with her mother, in a jeweller's window in the Palais Royal.

"You know, three paste stars to put in the hair. A mere trifle —a hundred francs, I fancy. Well, it was no good my talking about them from morning till night; my husband wouldn't see it!"

Octave could never have hoped for a more favourable opportunity. He resolved to come straight to the point.

"Oh, yes, I remember! I often heard you speak about them. Well, madame, your parents have always shown me such kindness, and you yourself have been so extremely obliging towards me, that I thought I might venture to———"

Hereupon he drew from his pocket a long box containing the three stars which sparkled on cotton-wool. Berthe excitedly rose from her seat.

"But, sir, it's impossible for me to—I cannot, really—it was most wrong of you!"

With mock ingenuousness he invented various excuses. In the South such things were done every day. Besides, the ornaments were of no value at all. Her face became suffused with blushes; she ceased sobbing and looked with sparkling eyes at the contents of the cardboard box.

"Pray do me the favour, madame, just to show me that you are satisfied with my work."

"No, Monsieur Octave, really, you must not insist. I am sorry that you should have———"

At this moment, Saturnin came back and examined the jewellery with as much rapture as if they were holy relics. Soon his sharp ear detected Auguste's returning footsteps. He apprised Berthe of this by a slight click of his tongue. Just as her husband was about to enter she made up her mind.

"Well, look here" she hurriedly whispered, thrusting the box into her pocket, "I'll say that my sister Hortense made me a present of them."

Auguste ordered the gas to be turned out, and then went upstairs with his wife to bed, without saying a word about their quarrel, being secretly glad to find that Berthe had recovered her spirits as if nothing had ever taken place. The shop became wrapped in darkness, and, just as Octave was leaving also, he felt two hot hands squeezing his in the gloom. It was Saturnin, who slept in the basement.

"Friend, friend, friend!" reiterated the lunatic, in an outburst of wild affection.

Thwarted somewhat in his scheme, Octave by degrees began to conceive for Berthe a virile and vehement desire. If at first he had followed his usual plan of seduction, and his wish to make women a means of self-advancement, he now no longer regarded Berthe merely as his employer, whom to possess was tantamount to gaining control of the entire establishment. What he desired, above all, was to enjoy his little Parisienne, fascinating in all her luxury and grace, a dainty creature such as he had never tasted at Marseilles. He felt a sudden hunger for her tiny gloved hands, her tiny feet in their high-heeled boots, her soft bosom concealed by lace frippery, though maybe some of her underlinen was of doubtful cleanliness, its shabbiness being hidden by magnificent dresses. This sudden impetus of passion even served to sway his parsimonious temperament to such a degree that he began to squander in presents, and the like, all the five thousand francs which he had brought with him from the South, and which by financial speculations he had already contrived to double.

But that which annoyed him more than anything was that he had become timid by falling in love. He lacked his wonted decision, his haste to reach his goal, desiring now, on the other hand, a certain languid enjoyment from not being too abrupt in his manœuvres. Moreover, this passing weakness in so thoroughly practical a nature as his, led him to conclude that the conquest of Berthe would be a campaign fraught with great difficulties, needing much delay and exquisite diplomacy. His two failures, with Valérie and with Madame Hédouin, doubtless made him more fearful of yet another rebuff. But, beneath all his uneasiness and hesitation, there lurked a fear of the woman he adored, an absolute belief in Berthe's virtue, and all the blindness of a desperate love paralysed by desire.

Next day, Octave, pleased that he had prevailed upon Berthe to accept his present, thought that it would be expedient to stand well with her husband. Accordingly, when taking his meals with him—for Auguste always boarded his assistants so as to have them close at hand—he paid him the utmost attention, listened to him during dessert and loudly approved all that he said. He specially pretended to share his discontent with regard to Berthe, feigning to play the detective and report various little incidents to him from time to time.

Days passed; Octave was building his nest in the house—a downy nest, which he found snug and warm. The husband esteemed him; and Madame Josserand herself, though he avoided being too polite to her—even she looked encouragingly upon him. As for Berthe, she treated him with delightful familiarity. His great friend, however, was Saturnin, whose mute affection he watched steadily increasing—a devotion as of some faithful dog, which became more fervent as his desire for Berthe grew more ardent. Of everyone else the madman appeared grimly jealous; no man could go near his sister but he at once became restless, with teeth set, as if ready to bite. If, on the other hand, Octave bent over her unrestrainedly, making her laugh with the soft velvety laugh of a merry mistress, Saturnin would laugh for glee as well, while his face in part reflected their sensual delight. For this poor witless fellow, love was incarnate in this soft woman's flesh, that instinctively he felt belonged to him, while for the chosen lover he felt nothing but ecstatic gratitude. He would stop Octave in all sorts of corners, looking about him suspiciously; and then, if they chanced to be alone, he would talk about Berthe, always repeating the same tales in disjointed phrases.

"When she was little, she had tiny legs as big as that! She was so fat, so rosy, so merry! She used to crawl about on the floor then. Then whack! whack! whack! she used to kick me in the stomach. That's what I liked! Oh, I liked it awfully!"

In this way Octave got to know the entire history of Berthe's childhood, of her babyish accidents, her playthings, of her gradual growth as a charming uncontrolled animal. Saturnin's empty brain carefully treasured up facts of no importance, which he alone had remarked, such as the day she pricked herself and he sucked the blood; the morning he held her in his arms when she wanted to get on to the table. But he always harked back to the supreme episode, the episode of the girl's illness.

"Ah, if you had only seen her! At night-time I used to be all alone with her. They beat me in order to make me go to bed. But I used to creep back barefoot. All by myself. It made me cry, she was so white. I used to feel her to see if she were growing cold. Then they let me be, for I nursed her better than they did; I knew about her medicine, and she took what-

126

ever I gave her. Sometimes, when she complained very much, I laid her head on my breast. It was so nice being together. Then she got well, and I wanted to go back to her, but they beat me again!"

His eyes sparkled, he laughed and wept, just as if the whole thing had happened only the day before. From these broken phrases of his, the whole story of this strange attachment could be made clear; this devotion of a poor half-witted fellow, keeping watch at the little patient's bedside after all the doctors had given her up; devoted body and soul to his beloved sister, who lay there dying, and whom he nursed in her nakedness with all a mother's tenderness—all his affection and all his virile impulses stopping short there, being checked once and for all by this episode of suffering, from the shock of which he had never yet recovered. Ever since that time, despite the ingratitude which had followed such devotion, Berthe became his all in all, a mistress in whose presence he trembled; at once a daughter and a sister whom he had saved from death; his idol, whom he jealously adored. Moreover, her husband he pursued with the wild hatred of a thwarted lover, being lavish of his abuse when unbosoming himself to Octave.

"His eye is still bunged up! What a nuisance that headache of his is! Did you hear how he shuffled about yesterday? Look! there he is, gaping out of the window. Was there ever such a fool! Oh, you dirty brute, you dirty brute!"

Auguste could hardly move without angering him. Then he would make horrible proposals.

"If you like, we'll both of us bleed him like a pig!"

Octave sought to soothe him. Then, on his quiet days, Saturnin would go from Octave to Berthe, delighted to repeat what one had said about the other, running errands for them, and constituting himself a perpetual bond of tenderness. He would willingly have flung himself down as a carpet for their feet.

Berthe made no further allusion to the present. She appeared not to notice Octave's trembling attentions, treating him quite unconcernedly as a friend. Never before had he taken such pains with his dress, and he was for ever gazing languishingly at her, with his eyes the colour of old gold, whose velvety softness he considered irresistible. But she was solely grateful to

127

him for the lies that he told on her behalf when helping her to escape from the shop now and again. The two thus became accomplices, and he favoured her goings-out with her mother hoodwinking her husband if ever he showed the slightest suspicion. Her mania for such frivolous excursions at last made her absolutely reckless, and she relied entirely upon his tact and intelligence to screen her. Then, on her return, if she found him behind a pile of goods, she rewarded him with the hearty handshake of a comrade.

One day, however, she was greatly upset. She had just come back from a dog-show, when Octave beckoned her to follow him downstairs into the basement, where he gave her an invoice which had been presented during her absence—sixty-two francs for embroidered stockings. She turned quite pale, exclaiming:

"Good gracious! Did my husband see this?"

He hastened to reassure her, telling her what trouble he had had to smuggle the bill away from under Auguste's very nose. Then, in an embarrassed tone, he added:

"I paid it."

She at once pretended to feel in her pockets, and, finding nothing, merely said:

"I will pay you back. Oh, I am ever so much obliged to you, Monsieur Octave! I should simply have died if Auguste had seen that!"

And this time she took hold of both his hands, and for an instant pressed them in her own. But the sixty-two francs was never mentioned again. Hers was an ever-increasing desire for liberty and for pleasure—all that as a girl she had expected marriage would yield her, all that her mother had taught her to exact from man.

One Saturday a fearful quarrel occurred between the young couple, owing to a deficit of twenty sous in Rachel's housebook. As Berthe used to pay this account, Auguste always doled her out the requisite money to meet the household expenses of each week. That evening the Josserands were coming to dinner, and the kitchen was littered with provisions— a rabbit, a leg of mutton, and cauliflowers. Near the sink Saturnin squatted, blacking boots. The quarrel arose out of a long enquiry respecting the twenty-sou piece. What could have become of it? How could one lose twenty sous? Auguste wanted to check the bill, to see if it were added up correctly. Meanwhile Rachel, hard of face but willowy of figure, kept calmly putting her piece of mutton on the spit, with mouth shut and eyes for ever on the watch. At last Auguste disbursed the sum of fifty francs, and was going downstairs, when he suddenly came back, tormented by the thought of the lost coin.

"It will have to be found," said he. "Perhaps you may have borrowed it from Rachel and forgotten all about it."

Berthe at once became greatly annoyed. "So you accuse me of falsifying the accounts, do you? Thank you, I am obliged by the compliment."

This was the starting-point; high words soon followed. Auguste, despite his desire to pay dearly for peace, became aggressive, exasperated at the sight of the rabbit, the leg of mutton, and the cauliflowers—all that pile of provisions that his wife was going to stuff under her parents' noses. He looked through the house-book, exclaiming at every item. Good heavens! it was monstrous! she must be in league with the cook to make a profit on the marketing.

"What!" cried Berthe, beside herself with anger, "you accuse *me, me* of being in league with the cook? Why, it is you, sir, who pay her to spy upon me! Yes, I always feel her dogging me; I can't move a step but her eye is on me. Ah, she may look through the keyhole as much as she likes when I am changing my underlinen; I don't do anything I'm ashamed of, and I don't care a hang for all your detectives! Only don't carry your audacity to such a pitch that you actually accuse me of being in league with my cook!"

For a moment this unlooked-for onslaught completely dumb-founded Auguste. Without relinquishing her leg of mutton, Rachel turned round, and with hand on heart protested.

"Oh, madame, how can you believe such a thing? And about me, who respect madame so highly!"

"She's mad!" exclaimed Auguste, shrugging his shoulders. Don't trouble to make any excuse, my good girl She's mad!"

Suddenly a noise from behind startled him. It was Saturnin, who had hurled away one of the half-cleaned shoes and was coming to his sister's help. His face wore a furious expression, and his fists were clenched as, stammering, he declared that he would throttle the dirty beast if he dared to say she was mad again. Auguste, terror-stricken, rushed behind the filter, exclaiming:

"This is positively too much! I can no longer say a word to you but this fellow interferes! It's true I took him in, but on the condition that he behaved properly. He's another nice present from your mother! She was terrified of him, and so she saddled me with him, preferring to let me be murdered in her stead. I'm greatly obliged to her. Look, he's got hold of a knife. For God's sake, stop him!"

Disarming her brother, Berthe pacified him with a look, while Auguste, turning deadly pale, continued muttering incoherently. Always flourishing knives! So easy to get wounded. In the case of a madman one got no redress whatever. In short, it was not fair to keep a brother like that as a body-guard, ready to maim one's husband at any minute, paralysing him if he sought to give vent to his just indignation, and forcing him to swallow his wrath.

"Look here, sir! you are utterly wanting in tact!" cried Berthe, scornfully. "No gentleman discusses matters of this sort in the kitchen!"

She withdrew to her room, banging the door after her. Rachel went back to her spit, as if she had heard nothing of this altercation between her superiors. Like a maid who, though aware of all that went on, yet knew her place, she discreetly forbore to look at madame as she left the room; and when her master stamped about, she never moved a muscle. Very soon, however, Auguste rushed out after his wife, and then Rachel, impassive as before, put the rabbit on to boil.

"Pray understand, my dear," said Auguste, on joining Berthe in her bedroom, "it was not about you that I made that remark. I meant it for that girl who is robbing us. Those twenty sous will have to be found somehow."

Berthe shook with nervous exasperation as, pale and resolute, she glared at him.

"Look here! how much longer are you going to worry me about your twenty sous? It's not twenty sous I want—it's five hundred francs. Yes, five hundred francs to dress on. It's all very fine; you talk about money in the kitchen before the cook. Very well, then, I'm determined to talk about money, too! I've been keeping myself in for a long while; I want five hundred francs!"

"Five hundred francs?" said Auguste, at last. "I'd rather shut up shop at once."

She looked at him coldly.

"You refuse? Very well, then, I'll run into debt."

"What? More debts, you miserable creature?"

He roughly caught her by the arms and pushed her violently against the wall. Choking with passion, she uttered no cry, but rushed forward and flung the window open as if she meant to jump into the street. But she came back, and in her turn pushed him out of the room, stammering:

"Go away, or I shall do myself some injury!"

And she noisily bolted the door in his face. For a moment, hesitating, he stood still to listen. Then he hurried downstairs to the shop, scared afresh at the sight of Saturnin, whose eyes glittered in the gloom. The noise of their brief wrangle had brought him out of the kitchen.

Octave, downstairs, was selling some *foulard* to an old lady. He at once noticed Auguste's agitation, and furtively watched him restlessly pacing up and down in front of the counters.

As soon as the customer had gone, Auguste's feelings brimmed over.

"My dear fellow, she's going mad!" he said, without mentioning his wife. "She has locked herself in. Will you oblige me by going up and speaking to her? I really am afraid of some accident; upon my word, I am!"

Octave pretended to hesitate. It was such a delicate matter! However, out of pure devotion, he consented. Upstairs, he found Saturnin keeping guard outside Berthe's door. Hearing footsteps, the madman grunted menacingly. But on recognising Octave his face brightened.

"Oh, yes, you!" he murmured. "You are all right. She mustn't cry. Be nice to her and comfort her. And stop with her, you know. There's no fear of anybody coming. I'm here. If the servant tries to peep, I'll hit her."

And, sitting down, he mounted guard before the door. As

131

he had a boot in his hand, he began polishing it just to pass the time away.

Octave determined to knock. No answer, not a sound. Then he called out his name. The bolt was at once drawn back. Berthe, half opening the door, begged him to come in. Then she nervously bolted it again.

"I don't mind *you*," said she, "but I won't have *him!*"

She paced up and down in a whirlwind of fury, from the bed to the window, which was still open. She muttered disconnected phrases: he might entertain her parents himself, if he chose; yes, and explain her absence to them as well, for she wouldn't sit down to table—not she; she'd rather die first! No, she preferred to go to bed. In fact, she excitedly flung back the coverlet, shook up the pillows and turned down the sheets, being so far forgetful of Octave's presence as to begin unhooking her dress. Then she went off at a tangent to something else.

"Would you believe it? He beat me, yes, beat me! And merely because I was ashamed of always going about in rags and asked him for five hundred francs."

Standing midway in the room, Octave sought to find words that might conciliate her. She ought not to let the matter upset her like that. Everything would come all right. Then he timidly ventured to make an offer to help.

"If you are bothered about any bill, why not apply to your friends? I should be most happy. Merely a loan, you understand, and you can pay me back."

She looked at him. After a pause, she replied:

"No, it would never do. What would people think, Monsieur Octave?"

So firm was her refusal, that the question was no longer one of money. Her anger, however, seemed to have subsided. Breathing heavily, she bathed her face, and became very pale, very calm, looking somewhat languid with her large, resolute eyes. As he stood there before her he felt overcome by amorous bashfulness, stupid though he deemed such emotion to be. Never before had he loved with such ardour; the very vehemence of his desire gave an awkwardness to his charms as a comely shopman. All the while he was uttering vague commonplaces about the advisability of making it up as he was really debating in his own mind whether he should not take her in his arms. But the fear of another rebuff made him hesitate. She sat mute, watching him with her resolute air and slightly contracted brow.

"Well, well," he falteringly continued, "you must have patience. Your husband's not a bad sort of fellow. If you know how to manage him he'll let you have what you want."

Beneath hollow talk such as this, they felt the same thought seize them both. There they were, alone, free, secure from being surprised, the door bolted. Such safety as this and the tepid atmosphere of the room touched their senses. And yet he did not date; the feminine side of him, his womanly instinct, in that moment of passion so far refined him as to make of him the woman in their encounter. Then, as if mindful of her early lessons, she dropped her handkerchief.

"Oh, thanks, so much!" said she to the young man as he picked it up.

Their fingers touched; such momentary contact brought them closer to each other. Now she smiled fondly; her waist grew willow and supple, for she remembered that men hate boards. One must not behave like a ninny; one must submit to a little playfulness without seeming to do so, if one would land one's fish.

"It is getting quite dark," she said as she went to close the window.

He followed, and in the shadow of the curtains she allowed him to take her hand. She began to laugh louder—a silvery laugh that almost dazed him; importuning him with all her pretty gestures. Then, as he at length grew bold, she flung back her head, disclosing her ripe, soft bosom, all palpitating with merriment. Distract by such a vision, he kissed her under the chin.

"Oh, Monsieur Octave," said she, confusedly, making a feint of gracefully keeping him in his proper place.

Then, catching hold of her, he threw her backwards upon the bed, which she had just been opening; and, as his desire was slaked, all the brute force within him reappeared—his ferocious discain for the female under his gentle air of adoration. She submitted tacitly, without fruition. When she rose up, with limp wrists and her face drawn by a spasm of pain, all her contempt for the male was apparent in the black look which she flung at him. Then for a while came silence. One only heard Saturnin outside the door cleaning the husband's boots, and the regular beat of his brush.

Chapter Twelve

*I*T was precisely on a Tuesday evening that Octave caught Monsieur Gourd on the watch near his room. This redoubled his fears. For a whole week he had been vainly imploring Berthe to come upstairs to his room at night when everybody was asleep. Is this what Gourd supected? Octave went back to bed in grievous discontent, tortured alike by passion and by fear. His amour was growing troublesome; it was turning to an insane passion; and he angrily saw himself becoming guilty of every sort of sentimental absurdity. As it was, he could never meet Berthe in these same side-streets without buying for her whatever took her fancy in a shop-window. For instance, only the day before, in the Passage de la Madeleine, she looked so avidly at a little bonnet, that he went into the shop and bought it for her as a present—plain white chip, with just a wreath of roses — something delightfully simple, but — two hundred francs! A trifle stiff, that, so he thought.

Towards one o'clock he fell asleep, after feverishly tossing about for a long while between the sheets.

Then he was roused by a gentle tapping at his door.

"It is I," faintly whispered a woman's voice.

It was Berthe. Opening the door, he clasped her passionately to him in the dark. But she had not come upstairs for that. Having lit a candle, he saw that she was in a great state of mind about something. The day before, as he had not had enough money about him, he could not pay for the bonnet at the time, while she was so delighted that she actually gave her name; and accordingly they had just sent her in the bill. Then, trembling lest they might call on her husband for the amount in the morning, she had ventured to come upstairs, emboldened by the profound silence of the house and feeling certain that Rachel was asleep.

"To-morrow morning, without fail!" she said, cajolingly, while trying to escape. "It must be paid to-morrow morning!"

But he again wound his arms about her.

"Stay here, do!"

Half awake and shivering, he whispered the words close to her bosom as he drew her nearer to the warm bed. Half clad, she wore only a petticoat and a dressing-jacket; to his touch she seemed as if naked, with her hair already knotted up for the night, and her shoulders still warm from the *peignoir* she had flung round them on coming out.

"I promise to let you go in an hour. Do stay!"

She stayed. Slowly the clock chimed the hours in the voluptuous warmth of the room; and at each stroke he held her back, pleading so tenderly that all strength forsook her. She succumbed. Then, about four o'clock, as she at last was going, they both fell sound asleep in each other's arms. When they opened their eyes, broad daylight streamed through the window. It was nine o'clock. Berthe uttered a cry of despair.

"Gracious heavens! I'm lost!"

Then came a moment of confusion. She leaped out of bed, her eyes half closed with sleep and weariness, groping about vaguely, blindly, putting her clothes on upside down, amid stifled cries of terror. Himself equally desperate, Octave stood before the door, to stop her from going out in such a dress at such an hour. Was she mad? People might meet her on the stairs; it was far too dangerous. They must think out some plan by which she could get downstairs unobserved. But she obstinately persisted in trying to leave the room there and then, endeavouring to push past him as he barred the doorway. At last he bethought himself of the back staircase. Nothing could be more convenient, and she might hurry back to her own room through the kitchen. Only as Marie Pichon was always in the passage of a morning, Octave thought it best, for safety's sake, to go and engage her in conversation while Berthe made good her escape. He hurriedly put on his trousers and an overcoat.

"My goodness! What a time you are!" muttered Berthe, to whom the bedroom had become a veritable furnace.

Henceforth, however, the lovers' assignations became less frequent still. He, in his ardour, grew despairing, and followed her about into every nook and corner, entreating her to make some appointment, whenever and wherever she liked. She, on the other hand, with the indifference of a girl reared in a hothouse, took no pleasure in such guilty passion, except for

136

the secret outings, the presents, the forbidden enjoyments, and the hours of luxury spent in cabs, theatres and restaurants. All her early education now cropped up anew, her lust for money, for dress, for squandering; and she had soon grown tired of her lover, just as she had grown tired of her husband, deeming him all too exacting for what he gave her in return, and endeavouring, with calm unconsciousness, not to yield him his full, just measure of love. Then, exaggerating her fears, she kept constantly refusing him. Never again in his room; oh, no! she would die of fright! And to her apartment he could not possibly come, for they might be surprised. Then, as he begged her to let him take her to a hotel for an hour, she began to cry, saying that he really could not have much respect for her. However, the expenditure on her account went on, and her caprices only increased. After the bonnet, she conceived a desire for a fan of *point d'Alençon,* not counting the many little trifles that took her fancy here and there, in the shop-windows. Though as yet he did not dare say nay, his sense of thrift was once more roused as he saw all his savings frittered away in this fashion. Like the practical fellow he was, it at length seemed to him silly always to be paying, when all that he got from her in return was her foot under the table.

Auguste, however, did not embarrass them much. Ever since the bad state of affairs at Lyons, he had been racked more than ever by his neuralgic headaches. Berthe had felt a sudden thrill of delight as, on the first of the month, she saw him one evening put three hundred francs under the bedroom clock for her dress. And, despite the reduction in the sum demanded, as she had never hoped to get a farthing, she flung herself into his arms, all warm and palpitating with gratitude. On this occasion the husband had a night of endearments such as the lover never obtained.

As now September touched its close, and residents were about to return, Octave, in the midst of all his torment, conceived a mad idea. It so happened that Rachel, whose sister was to be married, had asked leave to stay away for a night during her master's absence at Lyons. The idea was that they should sleep together in the servants' room, where no one would ever dream of looking for them. Offended by such a proposal. Berthe at first appeared greatly disgusted; but, with tears in his eyes, he besought her to comply, and spoke of leaving Paris, where he suffered too much unhappiness. At last, bewildered and exhausted by all his arguments and entreaties, she at length consented, scarcely knowing what she did. All was then arranged. On Tuesday evening, after dinner, they had tea at the Josserands' to allay any suspicion. Trublot, Gueulin and uncle Bachelard were all there. Duveyrier even came in, very late, as he occasionally slept in town now, because of early business appointments, so he averred. With all these gentlemen Octave pretended to converse freely; and then, at the stroke of midnight, he slipped away and locked himself into Rachel's room, where Berthe was to join him an hour later, when everybody was asleep.

On getting back to Rachel's room Octave was once more disappointed. Berthe had not come. He now grew angry; she had simply fooled him, making such a promise in order to be quit of his entreaties. While thus he fumed and chafed, she was calmly sleeping, glad to lie alone and have the broad marriage-bed to herself. However, instead of going back to sleep in his own room, he stubbornly lay down in his clothes on the bed, meditating revenge at such an hour. This bare, cold servants'-room irritated him, with its dirty walls, its squalor, and its insufferable smell of an unwashed wench; he shrank from recognising to what depths his frenzied passion had lowered him in his craving to appease it. Far away in the distance he heard it strike three. Strapping maidservants snored away to the left of him; at times bare feet made the boards creak, and then the plashing as of a fountain resounded along the floor.

At daybreak Octave fell asleep. There was deep silence everywhere. The sun was shining in through the narrow window as the door being suddenly opened woke the young man. It was Berthe, who had just come up to see, driven to do so by an irresistible impulse. At first she had scouted the idea, and then had invented pretexts—the necessity of putting the room straight if, in his rage, he had left it in disorder. Nor had she ever expected to find him there. As she saw him rise from the little iron bedstead, pale and threatening, she was taken aback, and, with head lowered, listened to his furious scolding. He urged her to reply, to offer some sort of explanation. At last she murmured:

"At the last moment I could not; it was too revolting. I love you—on my oath, I do! but not here, not here!"

Then, as he approached her, she drew back, fearing that he might want to profit by the opportunity. This, indeed, he desired to do. It struck eight: all the servants had gone down, and Trublot also. Then, as he caught hold of her hands, saying that when one loves a person one doesn't mind anything, she complained of the smell of the room, and went to open the window. But he again drew her to him, and, bewildered by his persistence, she was about to give in when from the courtyard below there rose up a turbid wave of filthy talk.

"Oh, you sow! you slut! Shut up, do! Your beastly dishclout has fallen on my head again!"

Berthe, trembling, broke away from his embrace as she murmured:

"There! do you hear that? Oh, no, not here, I entreat you! I should feel too much ashamed of myself. Do you hear those girls? They make my very blood run cold. The other day they quite upset me. No, no! leave me alone, and I promise you that you shall have me next Tuesday in your own room."

Standing there motionless, the two lovers were forced to overhear everything.

Berthe again grew pale. Waiting thus, she was afraid to leave the room. She looked down in confusion, as if outraged in Octave's presence. Indignant with these servants, he felt that their talk was becoming too filthy and that to embrace her was impossible. His desire ebbed away, leaving him weary and extremely sad. Then Berthe trembled. Lisa had just mentioned her by name.

"Talking of high jinks, I know someone who seems to go it pretty hot! I say, Adèle, isn't it true that your Mademoiselle Berthe was up to all sorts of games when you used to wash her petticoats?"

"And now," said Victoire, "she gets her husband's clerk to turn her over, and shake out all the dust."

"Hush!" cried Hippolyte, gently.

"What for? Her pig of a cook isn't there to-day. Sly devil, she is, that looks as if she'd eat you if you mention her mistress! Perhaps Octave the good-looking gives it to her, too, when he gets her in a quiet corner. His governor must have engaged him just to make babies for him, the great booby!"

Then Berthe, evidently suffering unutterable anguish, looked at her lover, imploringly, as she stammered out:

"Good God! good God!"

"And, you know," said Hippolyte, "the young chap don't care a damn for his missus. He's only got hold of her to help him on in the world. At heart he's a regular miser, a fellow without any scruples whatever, who, while pretending to make love to women, wouldn't mind giving them a jolly good smack in the eye!"

Berthe, looking at Octave, saw him turn pale; so changed, so upset did his face seem that it frightened her.

"My word, they're a nice couple!" rejoined Lisa. "I wouldn't give much for her, either. Badly brought up, her heart as hard as a stone, caring for nothing but her own amusement, sleeping with chaps for money; yes, for money! I know the kind of woman, and I wouldn't mind betting that she doesn't even get any pleasure with a man!"

Berthe's eyes overflowed with tears. Octave remarked her confusion. It was as if they both had been beaten until the blood came—laid bare before each other, ruthlessly and without a chance of protest. Then the young woman, stifled by the stench of this open cesspool, sought to flee. He did not attempt to keep her; mutual self-disgust made their society excruciating; and they longed for the relief of no longer seeing each other.

"Then Tuesday next, you promise, in my room!"

"Yes, yes!"

Covered with confusion, she fled. He stayed behind, walking hither and thither, his hands twitching nervously as he rolled the bed linen up into a bundle. He no longer listened to the servants' gossip. Suddenly one phrase caught his ear.

"I tell you Monsieur Hédouin died last night. If only the good-looking Octave had foreseen that, he might have gone on keeping Madame Hédouin warm, for she's got the money-bags."

To hear news such as this in that sewer touched him to the core. So Monsieur Hédouin was dead! Profound regret took possession of him, as, thinking aloud, he could not forbear replying:

"Yes, by Jingo! I *was* a fool!"

Chapter Thirteen

EXT Tuesday Berthe did not keep her promise. She had, in fact, told Octave beforehand not to expect her, when they had ì hurried interview that same evening after closing time. She sobbed bitterly, for she had been to confession he day before, feeling the need of religious solace, and being still overcome by the Abbé Mauduit's dolorous counsel. Ever since her marriage she had given up going to church; but after the gross language with which the maids had bespattered her, she had become so sad, so forlorn, so sullied, that for an hour she went back to her childish beliefs, ardently yearning to be made pure and good. On her return, after the priest had wept with her, she grew quite horrified at her sin. Octave shrugged his shoulders, powerless and enraged.

Then, three days afterwards, she again promised to see him on the following Tuesday. Meeting him one day by appointment in the Passages des Panoramas, she had noticed some shawls of Chantilly lace, and of these she talked incessantly, her eyes full of desire. Thus, on the Monday morning, the young man told her, laughingly, with the view to tempering the brutality of such a bargain, that if she really kept her word she would find a little surprise waiting for her in his room. She guessed what he meant, and again began to cry. No, no; it was impossible for her to come now: he had spoilt all her pleasure in their projected meeting. She had talked about the shawl without thinking, and she did not want it now; in fact, she would throw it into the fire if he made her a present of it. Nevertheless, on the following day they arranged matters satisfactorily; at half-past twelve that night she was to knock three times very gently at his door.

That day, as Auguste was starting for Lyons, Berthe thought that he looked somewhat strange. She had caught him whispering with Rachel behind the kitchen-door; in addition to that, his face was all yellow, he trembled violently, and one of his eyes was closed up. But, as he complained of neuralgia, she thought he must be unwell, and assured him that the journey would do him good. No sooner had he gone than she went back to the kitchen, and, feeling uneasy, tried to sound Rachel, who, however, maintained her demeanour of discreet respect, being as stiff in manner as when she first came. Berthe, somehow, felt certain that she was dissatisfied, and she thought how extremely foolish she had been first to give the girl twenty francs and a dress, and then suddenly to stop all further gratuities, though she was obliged to do so, as she was always in want of a five-franc piece herself.

"My poor girl," said she, "I've not been over generous to you, have I? But that isn't my fault. I haven't forgotten you, and I mean to reward you some day."

Rachel coldly replied:

"Madame owes me nothing."

Then Berthe went to fetch two of her old chemises, just as a proof of her good intentions. But when the servant took them from her, she said they would do for kitchen-cloths.

"Much obliged, madame, but calico gives me pimples; I only wear linen."

However, so polite did she seem, that Berthe was reassured, and she spoke familiarly to the girl, telling her she was going to sleep out; asking her even to leave a lamp alight in case she came back. The front door was to be bolted, and she would go out by the back-stairs and take the key with her. Rachel took her instructions as calmly as if she had been told to cook some beef *à la mode* for the following day.

That evening, by a fine touch of diplomacy, as Berthe was dining with her parents, Octave accepted an invitation from the Campardons. He thought of staying there till ten o'clock, and then of going up to his room and of waiting as patiently as might be until half-past twelve.

During dessert, Campardon suddenly exclaimed:

"By the way, my dear fellow, I suppose you know that Duveyrier has found——" He was going to say Clarisse. But he recollected that Angèle was present, so with a side glance at his daughter, he added: "Has found his—relative, don't you know."

By biting his lip and winking, he at last made Octave understand, who at first quite failed to catch his meaning.

Shortly before ten o'clock, Octave professed to be so tired

that he was obliged to go up to bed. Despite Rose's tender attentions, he felt ill at ease in this worthy family, aware of Gasparine's ever-increasing hostility. He had done nothing, however, to provoke this. She merely hated him because he was a good-looking fellow, who, as she suspected, had all the women in the house; and this exasperated her, although she herself did not desire his embraces in the least. It was merely the thought of his enjoyment that instinctively roused her feminine wrath, now that her own comeliness had withered all too soon.

Directly he had left, the Campardons talked of going to bed. Every evening, before getting into bed, Rose spent a whole hour over her toilet, using face washes and scents, doing her hair, manipulating her eyes and mouth and ears; even putting a little patch under her chin. At night she replaced her sumptuous dressing-gowns by equally sumptuous nightcaps and chemises. On this particular evening she chose a night-dress and cap trimmed with Valenciennes lace. Gasparine had been helping her, holding basins for her, mopping up the water she had spilt, drying her with a face-towel, showing her various little attentions with far greater skill than Lisa.

"Ah! now I feel comfortable," said Rose, at last, lying full length in bed, while her cousin tucked in the sheets and raised the bolster.

She smiled contentedly as she lay there alone in the middle of the large bed. With her plump, soft body swathed in lace, she looked like some amorous siren about to welcome the lover of her choice. When she felt pretty, she could sleep better, so she said. Well, it was the only pleasure she had.

"Everything all right, eh?" asked Campardon, as he came in. "Well, good-night, my puss."

He pretended that he had got some work to do. He would have to sit up. Whereupon she was vexed, and begged him to have a rest; it was so foolish of him to fag himself to death in this way!

"Now, listen to me; you just go to bed! Gasparine, promise me you'll make him go to bed!"

Gasparine had just put a glass of sugar and water and one of Dickens's novels by the bed. She looked at Rose, without replying, and then, bending over her, whispered:

"You do look nice to-night!"

Then she kissed her on both cheeks, with arid lips and bitter mouth, with the subdued air of a poor, plain relation. Flushed, and suffering from frightful indigestion, Campardon surveyed his spouse as well. His moustache quivered slightly as, in his turn, he stooped to kiss her.

"Good night, my poppet!"

"Good night, my love! Now, mind you go to bed at once."

"Don't be afraid," said Gasparine; "if he's not in bed and asleep by eleven o'clock, I'll get up and turn the lamp out."

About eleven o'clock, after yawning over some plans for a Swiss cottage that a tailor in the Rue Rameau had taken into his head to have built, Campardon slowly undressed, thinking meanwhile of Rose lying there so smart and pretty. Then, after turning down his bed, because of the servants, he went and joined Gasparine in hers. It was most uncomfortable for them, as there was no elbow-room, and he in particular had to balance himself on the edge of the mattress, so that the next morning one of his thighs was quite stiff.

Just then, as Victoire, after washing up, had gone to bed, Lisa came in to see if mademoiselle were in want of anything. Angèle was waiting for her in bed; and then it was that, unknown to the parents, they played interminable games at cards on the counterpane. And as they played, their talk forever reverted to Gasparine, that dirty beast, whom the maid coarsely reviled before little Angèle. In this way they made up for their humble, hypocritical demeanour during the day; and Lisa took a certain base pleasure in corrupting Angèle thus, satisfying the girl's morbid curiosity now that she was on the verge of puberty. That night they were furious with Gasparine because for the last two days she had locked up the sugar with which the maid was wont to fill her pockets and afterwards empty them out on the child's bed. Nasty old cow! They couldn't even get a lump of sugar to munch when they went to sleep!

"And yet your papa gives her lots of sugar-stick!" said Lisa, with a sensual laugh.

"So he does," murmured Angèle, laughing too.

"What does your papa do to her? Just show me."

Then the child flung her arms round the maid's neck, hugging and kissing her vehemently, saying:

"Look, this is what he does, this is what he does!"

It struck midnight. Campardon and Gasparine were moaning in all the discomfort of their narrow bed, while Rose, supine in the centre of hers, stretched out her limbs and read Dickens till tears suffused her eyes. Deep silence covered all; the chaste night threw her pall over this eminently virtuous family.

On going upstairs, Octave found that the Pichons had company. Jules called to him, declaring that he must come in and have a glass of something with them. Monsieur and Madame Vuillaume were there; they had made their peace with Jules and Marie on the occasion of the latter's churching. Her confinement had taken place in September. They had even consented to come to dinner on Tuesday to celebrate the young woman's recovery. She had only been out the day before for the first time. Being desirous to appease her mother, whom the very sight of the baby, another girl, annoyed, Marie had put it out to nurse, not far from Paris. Lilitte was asleep with her head on the table, having imbibed a tumblerful of wine, which had upset her, her parents having forced her to drink to her little sister's health.

"Well, one can manage with two," said Madame Vuillaume, after clinking glasses with Octave. "Only no more of it, son-in-law, do you hear?"

The Pichons declared that they would obey. It wasn't likely that they'd be up to that game any more.

The Vuillaumes gave a nod of satisfaction. Since they had promised, they would forgive them. Then as it was just striking ten, they all embraced one another affectionately, and Jules put on his hat to see them into their omnibus. So touching, indeed, was this return to their old habits, that on the landing they kissed yet once again.

Having shut the door, she began to remove the glasses, which were still on the table. The small room, with its smoking lamp, was still quite warm from this little family festival. Lilitte still slumbered, her head resting on a corner of the oilcloth.

"I'm going to bed," said Octave.

"What! so early as this?" she replied. "You don't often

keep such respectable hours, I know. Perhaps you have got something to do early to-morrow morning, have you?"

"No, I haven't," said he. "I'm sleepy, that's all. But I can stop another ten minutes or so."

Then he remembered that Berthe would not be coming up till half-past twelve. There was plenty of time. Consumed as he had been for weeks past by this thought of having her in his arms for one whole night, it now no longer roused within him carnal thrills. The feverish impatience of that day, his torments of desire, as he counted every moment which brought him nearer and nearer to his long-coveted delight—all this now vanished, being dissipated by such wearisome delay.

"Will you have another little glass of cognac?" asked Marie.

"Well, I don't mind if I do."

He thought that it might stimulate his powers. As she took the glass from him he seized her hands and held them in his, she laughing meanwhile, unafraid. Pale as she was after physical suffering, he found her full of charm, and all his latent affection for her surged up again within him. As, one evening, he had given her back to her husband, after imprinting a parental kiss upon her brow, so now he felt impelled to re-possess her—a sudden, sharp desire, which extinguished all his longing for Berthe. That passion now seemed remote.

"Then you're not afraid to-day?" he asked, as he squeezed her hands tighter.

"No, as henceforth it is impossible. But we shall always be good friends."

Hereupon she let him perceive that she knew everything. Saturnin must have told her. Moreover, she always noticed on what nights Octave received a certain person in his room. Observing his pallor and confusion, she hurriedly assured him that she would never tell anyone. She was not displeased; on the contrary, she wished him every sort of happiness.

"Why, I'm married, you know," she said; "so I couldn't bear you any ill-will."

Taking her on his knee, he exclaimed:

"But it's you I love!"

He spoke the truth, for at that minute it was she that he loved, with deep, with overmastering passion. All his new intrigue, and the two months spent in hankering after another woman, had vanished. Once more he saw himself in the little flat, kissing Marie on the neck when Jules' back was turned, she being gentle and complacent as ever. That was real happiness. Why had he ever disdained it? It filled him with regret. He still desired Marie; if he no longer had her, he felt that he would be eternally unhappy.

"Leave me alone," she murmured, endeavouring to get away from him. "You're unreasonable, and you want to grieve me. Now that you are in love with somebody else, where's the good of teasing me?"

Thus did she try to offer resistance in her gentle, languid way, feeling actual disgust for what afforded her no sort of amusement. But he lost his head, and squeezed her more vigorously, kissing her breast through her coarse woollen bodice.

"It's you I love; can't you see that? I swear by all that's sacred that I'm not telling you a lie. Open my heart, and you'll see. Now, please, do be nice! Just this once, and then never, never again, if you don't want to. You really are too cruel; if you don't let me, I shall die!"

Then Marie became powerless, paralysed by the dominating force of this man's will. In her, good-nature, fear and folly were about equally blended. She moved away, as if anxious first of all to carry the sleeping Lilitte into the other room. But he held her fast, fearing that she would wake the child. Then she surrendered herself, in the same place where a year ago she had fallen into his arms like a woman that must obey. There was a sort of buzzing silence throughout the little apartment as the whole house lay merged in midnight peace. Suddenly the lamp grew dim, leaving them nearly in darkness, when Marie rose and just turned up the wick in time.

"You aren't cross with me?" asked Octave, still exhausted by pleasurable thrills such as he had never yet experienced.

She stopped winding up the lamp, and with her cold lips gave him one last kiss, as she said:

"No, because you enjoy it. But, all the same, it's not right, on account of that person. Doing that with me is no good whatever now."

Her eyes were wet with tears, and, though not annoyed, she seemed sad. After leaving her he felt dissatisfied with himself, and as if he should like to go straight to bed and to sleep.

He had gratified his passion, but it had left a disagreeable aftertaste; a touch of lechery that brought merely bitterness in its wake. The other woman was now coming, and he would have to wait for her; it was a thought that weighed terribly upon his mind, and he hoped that by some accident she might be prevented from coming. This, too, after hot nights of wild scheming to possess her, to harbour her, if for but one hour, in his room. Perhaps she would again fail to keep her word. He dared not venture to solace himself with such a hope.

It struck midnight. Tired as he was, Octave sat up and waited, dreading to hear the rustle of her skirts along the narrow passage. By half-past twelve he became positively anxious, and at one o'clock he thought he was safe, though there was a kind of vague irritation mixed with his relief, the vexation of a man who has been fooled by a woman. Then, just as, yawning vigorously, he was about to undress, there came three gentle knocks at the door. It was Berthe. Half cross, half flattered, he met her with outstretched arms, but she shrank aside trembling, and listened at the door, which she hastily closed behind her.

"What is it?" he asked, speaking low.

"I don't know," she stammered, "but I'm frightened. It's so dark on the staircase; I had an idea someone was following me. What nonsense all these adventures are, to be sure! I am certain that something horrid's going to happen."

On both, this speech had a chilling effect. They did not even kiss each other. However, she looked captivating in her white dressing-gown, and with all her golden hair twisted up into a coil at the back of her head. Gazing at her, she seemed to him far prettier than Marie; but he no longer desired to possess her; the whole thing was a bore. Being out of breath she sat down, and gave a sudden feigned start of annoyance at noticing a box on the table, which he felt positive contained the lace shawl about which she had talked for the last week.

"I shall go," said she, without moving from her chair.

"What's that for?"

"Do you suppose that I'm going to sell myself? You always manage to wound my feelings. Now, to-night, you've entirely spoilt all my pleasure. Whatever did you buy it for, after I told you not to do so?"

However, she got up and finally consented to look at it. So great was her disappointment on opening the box, that she could not forbear indignantly exclaiming:

"Why, it's not Chantilly, at all; it's llama!"

Growing less liberal as regarded present-giving, Octave this time had yielded to a niggardly impulse. He sought to explain to her that some llama was splendid—quite as handsome as Chantilly—and he extolled the beauties of the shawl just as if he were standing behind the counter, making her finger the lace, while assuring her that it would last for ever. But she shook her head disdainfully, saying:

"The fact is, this only cost one hundred francs, while the other would have come to three hundred."

Then, noticing that he turned pale, she sought to mend matters by adding:

"Of course, it's very kind of you, and I am much obliged. It's not what a gift costs, but the spirit in which it is given that makes it valuable."

Then she sat down again, and there came a pause. After a while he asked if she were not coming to bed. Of course she was; but she still felt so upset by her silly fright on the stairs. Then she disclosed her fears as to Rachel, telling how she had caught Auguste whispering with her behind the door. Yet it would have been so easy for them to bribe the girl by giving her a five-franc piece now and again. One had to get the five-franc pieces first, though; she never had a single one herself.

"Let's go to bed, eh?" said he, at last.

Mechanically, she began undressing herself.

Her petticoat-string had got into a knot, and she snapped it viciously. Then, sitting down on the bed to pull off her stockings, she exclaimed:

"How sorry I am for ever having been so weak! If one only could foresee things, how carefully one would reflect beforehand!"

She had now nothing on but her chemise; her legs and arms were naked—the nakedness of a soft, plump little woman. Her breasts, heaving in anger, peeped out of their covering of lace. He, who pretended to lie with his face to the wall, suddenly turned abruptly round, exclaiming:

"What's that? You're sorry you ever loved me?"

"Of course I am. A man like you, incapable of understanding a woman's feelings."

As they glared at each other their faces assumed a hard, loveless expression. She was resting one knee on the edge of the mattress, her breasts tense, her thigh bent, in the pretty attitude of a woman just getting into bed. But he had no eyes for her rosy flesh and the supple, fleeting outline of her back.

"Good God! If only it could all happen again!"

"You mean you'd have somebody else, I suppose?" he brutally ejaculated.

Lying beside him at full length under the bed-clothes, she was just about to reply in the same exasperated tone, when suddenly there came a knocking at the door. They started up, hardly knowing what it might mean; then they both remained motionless, as if frozen.

A faint voice was heard saying:

"Open the door! I can hear you, up to your filthy tricks! Open the door, or I'll smash it!"

It was Auguste's voice. Yet the lovers did not move; in their ears there was such a buzzing that they could think of nothing. They felt very cold lying there next to each other—as cold as corpses. At last Berthe jumped out of bed, instinctively feeling that she must escape from her paramour; while Auguste, outside, kept exclaiming:

"Open the door! Open the door, I say!"

Then there was a moment of terrible confusion—of unspeakable anguish. Berthe rushed about the room, distracted, trying to find some passage of escape, her face white through the fear of death. Octave's heart was in his mouth at each blow on the door, against which he leant mechanically, as if to strengthen it. The noise grew unbearable, the idiot would soon rouse the whole house; they would have to open. But when she perceived his intention, Berthe clung to his arms, imploring him in terror to desist. No, no; for mercy's sake! He would rush in upon them, armed with a knife or a pistol! Growing as pale as she, for her alarm affected him also, he hurriedly slipped on his trousers, while begging her in a low voice to get dressed. She sat there naked, doing nothing, being unable even to find her stockings. Meanwhile, Auguste grew ever more furious.

"Ah, so you won't open and you won't answer! Very well, you shall see!"

Ever since last quarter-day Octave had been asking the landlord to have two new screws fixed to the staple of his lock, as it had become loosened. All at once the wood cracked, the lock gave way, and Auguste, losing his balance, fell sprawling into the middle of the room.

"Blast it all!" he cried.

He had only got a key in his hand, which, grazed by his fall, was bleeding. Then he got up, livid with shame and fury at the thought of so absurd an entry. Waving his arms wildly about, he sought to spring upon Octave. But the latter, albeit embarrassed at being caught bare-foot with trousers buttoned awry, caught him by the wrists, and, being the stronger, held these as in a vise.

"Sir," cried he, "you are violating my domicile. It is disgraceful, it is ungentlemanlike!"

And he very nearly struck him. During their brief scuffle, Berthe rushed out over the shattered door in her chemise. In her husband's bloody fist she thought she saw a kitchen knife, and between her shoulders she seemed to feel the cold steel. As she fled along the dark passage she fancied she heard the sound of blows, though unable to tell by whom these were dealt or received. Voices, half unrecognisable, exclaimed: "Whenever you please, I am at your service!" "Very good; you shall hear from me."

She reached the back-stairs at a bound. But after rushing down two flights as if pursued by tongues of flame, she found her kitchen door locked, and that she had left the key upstairs in the pocket of her dressing-gown. Besides, there was no lamp, not the least light within; the maid had evidently betrayed them in this way. Without stopping to get her breath, she flew upstairs again and passed along the corridor leading to Octave's room, where the two men were still heard wrangling furiously.

They were still at it; perhaps, she would have time. And she ran down the front staircase, hoping that her husband had left the door of their flat ajar. She would lock herself into her bedroom and not open to anybody. But yet once more she found herself confronted with a closed door. Being thus naked and an outcast, she lost her head, and ushed from floor to floor like some poor hunted animal in search of a hiding-place. On no account dared she knock at her parents' door. For an instant she thought of taking refuge in the porter's lodge, but the shame of it made her turn back. Then, leaning over the banisters, she stopped to listen, her ears deafened by the beating of her heart in that great silence, and her eyes dazzled by lights that seemed to start up out of the inky darkness. The knife, that awful knife in Auguste's bloody fist! This is what terrified her. Its icy blade was about to be buried in her flesh! Suddenly, there was a noise. She fancied he was coming after her, and she shivered to the very marrow of her bones for fright.

It was a voice faintly whispering:

"Madame! madame!"

She looked over the banisters, but could see nothing.

"Madame, madame; it is I!"

And Marie appeared, in her night dress also. She had heard the disturbance, and had slipped out of bed, leaving Jules fast asleep, while she stopped to listen in her little dining-room in the dark.

"Come in. You're in distress, and I am your friend."

Then she gently comforted her, telling her all that had happened. The two men had not hurt each other. Octave, cursing horribly, had pushed the chest of drawers in front of his door, so shutting himself in; while the other had gone down carrying a bundle with him—some of her things that she had left, her shoes and stockings, which probably he had rolled up in her dressing-gown on seeing them lying about. Anyhow, the whole affair was over. Next day they would soon prevent their fighting a duel.

But Berthe stopped short on the threshold, still frightened and abashed at entering a stranger's house. Marie had to take her by the hand.

"See, you shall sleep here, on the sofa. I will lend you a shawl, and I'll go and see your mother. Dear, dear; what a dreadful thing! But when one's in love, one never stops to think of consequences!"

"Not much enjoyment, though, for either of us!" said Berthe, as she heaved a sigh of regret for all the emptiness and folly of her night. "I don't wonder he cursed and swore. If he's like me, he must have had more than enough of it!"

They were both going to speak about Octave, when suddenly they stopped, and, groping in the darkness, embraced each other, sobbing bitterly. Each clipped the other's naked limbs convulsively, passionately, crushing their breasts all wet with scalding tears. It was a sort of final collapse, an overmastering sorrow—the end of everything. No other word was spoken, but their tears kept falling, falling ceaselessly in the gloom; while, lapped in decency, the chaste house slumbered on.

Chapter Fourteen

UVEYRIER, like Bachelard, deemed a duel indispensable. He seemed much affected because of the shedding of blood, of which in fancy he saw a dark stream staining the staircase of his own house. But honour demanded it, and with honour no compromise was possible. Trublot took a broader view of the case; it was too silly, said he, to stake one's honour upon what, for courtesy's sake, he called a woman's frailty. With a faint movement of his eyelids, Auguste expressed his approval, being exasperated by the warlike fury of the other two, who certainly ought to have been wholly for reconciliation and peace.

"Well, what's going to be done?" he inquired.

"Look here, my lad," replied Bachelard, in familiar fashion, "if you like, we'll manage the whole thing nicely for you."

At this conclusion no one seemed surprised. Duveyrier nodded approvingly. Bachelard went on:

"I'll go with Monsieur Duveyrier and see the chap, and make the brute apologise, or my name isn't Bachelard. The mere sight of me will make him knuckle under, just because I am an outsider. I don't care a damn for anybody, I don't!"

Auguste, his head in a whirl, strove all he could to keep on his feet, until Duveyrier advised him to go to bed. It was the only cure for migraine.

"Just you go upstairs; we shan't want you any more. We'll let you know the result. My dear fellow, it's no good being upset about it— not a bit."

So upstairs to bed went the husband. At five o'clock the two others were still waiting for Octave. He, going out for no particular reason, except to get a little fresh air and forget the disagreeable adventures of the night, had walked past "The Ladies' Paradise." Madame Hédouin, in deep mourning, stood at the door, and he stopped to bid her good-day. On telling her that he had left the Vabres, she quietly asked him why he did not come back to her. Without thinking, the whole thing was settled there and then, in a moment.

He had hardly got to her room before Duveyrier and Bache-lard called. Astonished at seeing the latter, he at first sought to give the names of two of his friends. But, without replying, these worthies spoke of their age and read him a lecture upon his bad behaviour. Then as, in the course of conversation, he announced his intention of leaving the house as soon as possible, his two visitors both solemnly declared that this proof of his tact would suffice.

On the staircase they heard hideous cries, like those of an animal about to be slaughtered, which came from the bedroom. Saturnin, armed with his kitchen-knife, had noiselessly crept into the apartment, when, with eyes like gleaming coals, and frothing lips, he had leapt upon Auguste.

"Tell me where you ve hid her!" he cried. "Give her back to me, or else I'll bleed you like a pig!"

Startled thus from his painful slumber, Auguste attempted to escape. But the maniac, in the strength of his one fixed idea, had caught hold of him by the tail of his shirt, and, throwing him backwards, placed his neck at the edge of the bed, with a basin immediately underneath it, and held him there just as they hold brutes in a slaughter-house.

"Ah! I've got you this time. I'm going to bleed you; yes, bleed you like a pig!"

Luckily, the others came in time to release the victim. Saturnin had to be shut up, for he was raving mad. Two hours later, the commissary of police having been summoned, they took him once more to the Asile des Moulineaux, his family having consented to this. With chattering teeth poor Auguste remarked to Duveyrier, who had informed him of the arrangement made with Octave:

"No, I'd rather have fought a duel. One can't protect one's self from a maniac. What the deuce is he so anxious to bleed me for, the ruffian, after his sister has made a cuckold of me? Ah, I've had enough of it, my good fellow! upon my word, I have!"

Chapter Fifteen

ONTHS passed, and spring had come. In the house in the Rue de Choiseul everybody was talking of the approaching marriage of Octave and Madame Hédouin. Things, however, had not yet got so far as that. Octave had resumed his old post at "The Ladies' Paradise," and every day the business grew greater. Since her husband's death, Madame Hédouin had not been able to undertake the sole management of an ever-growing business. Old Deleuze, her uncle, was a martyr to rheumatism, and could attend to nothing; so that, naturally, Octave, young, active and full of ideas as to trading on a large scale, soon assumed a position of decided importance in the house. Still sore about his ridiculous love-affair with Berthe, he now no longer thought of making use of women; he even fought shy of them. The best thing, as he believed, would be for him quietly to become Madame Hédouin's partner, and then to pile up the dollars without delay. Recollecting, too, the absurd snub which she had given him, he treated her as if she were a man, which was exactly what she wanted.

Henceforth their relations became most intimate. They used to shut themselves up for hours together in the little back room. Here in former days, when he had determined to seduce her, he had followed a complete set of tactics, trying to profit by her excitement about business, breathing on the back of her neck as he mentioned certain figures to her, waiting for a time when takings were heavy to profit by her enthusiasm. Now he was merely good-tempered, with no end except business in view. He no longer felt wishful to enjoy her, although he still remembered her little thrill of excitement as she leaned against his breast when they waltzed together on the evening of Berthe's wedding. Perhaps she had been fond of him, after all? Anyhow, it was best to remain as they were; for, as she rightly observed, perfect order was necessary in a business like that, and it was foolish to want things which would only upset them from morning to night.

Seated, both of them, at the narrow desk, they often forgot

themselves after going through the books and settling the orders. Then it was that he reverted to his dreams of aggrandisement. He had sounded the owner of the next house, who was quite ready to sell. The umbrella-maker and the second-hand dealer must have notice given them to quit, and a special silk department must be opened. To this she gravely listened, not daring as yet to make the venture. But her liking for Octave's business capacity grew ever greater, for in his ideas she recognised her own; her aptitude for commerce, and the serious practical side of her character showed at is were beneath his urbane exterior of a polite shopman. Moreover, such zeal, such boldness were his—qualities lacking in herself, and which filled her with enthusiasm. It was imagination applied to trade, the only sort of imagination that ever troubled her. He was becoming her master.

Everyone in the house in the Rue de Choiseul declared that the match was made. Octave had given up his room there and had got lodgings in the Rue Neuve-Saint-Augustin, close to "The Ladies' Paradise." He no longer visited anyone, and never went to the Campardons' nor the Duveyriers' who were shocked at his scandalous intrigue. Even Monsieur Gourd, when he met him, pretended not to recognise him, to avoid having to bow. Only Marie and Madame Juzeur, if they met him of a morning in the neighborhood, stopped and chatted for a moment or two in some doorway.

Madame Juzeur, who eagerly questioned him as to his reported engagement to Madame Hédouin, wanted him to promise that he would come and see her and have a nice chat about it all. Marie was in despair at being again pregnant, and told him of Jules' amazement and of her parents' dreadful wrath. However, when the rumour of his marriage was confirmed, Octave was surprised to get a very low bow from Monsieur Gourd. Campardon, though he did not yet offer to make it up, nodded cordially to him across the street, while Duveyrier, when looking in one evening to buy some gloves, appeared very friendly. By degrees, the whole household seemed ready to forget and forgive.

Moreover, the inmates had one and all regained the beaten track of middle-class respectability. Behind the mahogany portals fresh founts of virtue played; the third-floor gentlemen came to work one night a week as usual; the other Madame Campardon passed by, inflexible in her integrity; the maids sported aprons of dazzling whiteness, while, in the tepid silence of the staircase all the pianos on all the floors flung out the self-same waltzes, making a music at once mystic and remote.

Yet the taint of adultery still lingered, imperceptible indeed to common folk, but disagreeable to those of fine moral sense. Auguste obstinately refused to take back his wife, and so long as Berthe lived with her parents, the scandal would not be effaced, material trace of it must remain. Yet not one of the tenants openly told the exact story, as it would have been so embarrassing for everybody. By common and, as it were involuntary consent, they agreed that the quarrel between Berthe and Auguste arose about the ten thousand francs—a mere squabble about money. It was so much more decent to say this; and one could allude to the matter before young ladies. Would the parents pay up, or would they not? The whole farce became so perfectly simple, for not a soul in the neighborhood was either amazed or indignant at the idea that money matters should provoke blows in a domestic circle. As a matter of fact, this polite arrangement did not affect the actual situation, and, though calm in the presence of mischance, the whole house had suffered a cruel shock to its dignity.

NANA'S MOTHER

NANA'S MOTHER.

(L'ASSOMMOIR.)

BY ÉMILE ZOLA.

AUTHOR OF

"THE ABBE'S TEMPTATION; OR, LA FAUTE DE L'ABBE MOURET,"
"HELENE; OR, UNE PAGE D'AMOUR."

TRANSLATED FROM THE FRENCH
BY JOHN STIRLING.

"L'Assommoir" is one of the greatest novels ever printed, having already attained a sale in France of over One Hundred Thousand Copies. It will also be found to be one of the most extraordinary works ever written, full of nature and of art, dramatic, narrative, and pictorial. In this translation, which has been toned down, with literary ability, combined with tact, delicacy and refinement, to suit the American reading public, vice is never made attractive, but as a picture of Paris life, springing from Intemperance, "L'Assommoir" is without a rival. Zola has attained a measure of success scarcely paralleled in our generation, and his themes and his style—his aims, methods, and performances provoke the widest attention and the liveliest discussions throughout the whole of Europe. The translator, John Stirling, has done his work in such an able and thorough manner, that it seems almost incredible it could have been written other than in English.

PHILADELPHIA:
T. B. PETERSON & BROTHERS;
306 CHESTNUT STREET.

-[CHAPTER 1]-

Gervaise

Gᴇʀᴠᴀɪsᴇ ʜᴀᴅ ᴡᴀɪᴛᴇᴅ and watched for Lantier until two in the morning. Then, chilled and shivering she turned from the window and threw herself across the bed, where she fell into a feverish doze with her cheeks wet with tears. For the last week when they came out of the *Veau à Deux Têtes* where they ate, he had sent her off to bed with the children, and had not appeared until late into the night, and always with a story that he had been looking for work.

This very night, while she was watching for his return, she fancied she saw him enter the ball room of the Grand-Balcon, whose ten windows blazing with lights illuminated, as with a sheet of fire, the black lines of the outer Boulevards. She caught a glimpse of Adèle, a pretty brunette who dined at their restaurant, and who was walking a few steps behind him, with her hands swinging as if she had just dropped his arm, rather than pass before the bright light of the globes over the door, in his company.

When Gervaise awoke about five o'clock, stiff and sore, she burst into wild sobs, for Lantier had not come in. For the first time he had slept out. She sat on the edge of the bed, half shrouded in the canopy of faded chintz that hung from the arrow fastened to the ceiling by a string. Slowly, with her eyes suffused with tears, she looked around this miserable *chambre garnie,* whose furniture consisted of a chestnut bureau of which one drawer was absent, three straw chairs and a greasy table, on which was a broken handled pitcher.

Another bedstead—an iron one—had been brought in for the children. This stood in front of the bureau and filled up two-thirds of the room.

A trunk belonging to Gervaise and Lantier stood in the corner wide open, showing its empty sides, while at the bottom a man's old hat lay among soiled shirts and hose. Along the walls, and on the backs of the chairs, hung a ragged shawl, a pair of muddy pantaloons and a dress or two—all too bad for the old clothes man to buy. In the middle of the mantel between two mismated tin candlesticks was a bundle of pawn tickets from the Mont-de-Piété. These tickets were of a delicate shade of rose.

The room was the best in the hotel—the first floor looking out on the Boulevard.

Meanwhile side by side on the same pillow, the two children lay calmly sleeping. Claude, who was eight years old was breathing calmly and regularly with his little hands outside of the coverings, while Etienne, only four, smiled with one arm under his brother's neck.

When their mother's eyes fell on them she had a new paroxysm of sobs, and pressed her handkerchief to her mouth to stifle them. Then with bare feet, not stopping to put on her slippers which had fallen off, she ran to the window, out of which she leaned as she had done half the night, and inspected the sidewalks as far as she could see.

The hotel was on the Boulevard de la Chapelle, at the left of the Barrière Poissonnièrs. It was a two story building, painted a deep red up to the first floor, and had disjointed weather-stained blinds.

Above a lantern with glass sides, was a sign between the two windows:

HOTEL BONCŒUR,

KEPT BY

MARSOULLIER.

in large yellow letters, partially obliterated by the dampness. Gervaise, who was prevented by the lantern from seeing as she desired, leaned out still further, with her handkerchief on her lips. She looked to the right toward the Boulevard de Rochechoumart, where groups of butchers stood with their bloody frocks before their establishments, and the fresh breeze brought in whiffs, a strong animal smell—the smell of slaughtered cattle. She looked to the left, following the ribbon-like avenue, past the Hospital de Lariboisière, then building. Slowly, from one end to the other of the horizon, did she follow the wall, from behind which in the night time, she had heard strange groans and cries, as if some fell murder were being perpetrated. She looked at it with horror, as if in some dark corner—dark with dampness and filth—she should distinguish Lantier,—Lantier lying dead with his throat cut.

When she gazed beyond this gray and interminable wall she saw a great light, a golden mist waving and shimmering with the dawn of a new Parisian day. But it was to the Barrière Poissonnièrs that her eyes persistently returned—watching dully the uninterrupted flow of men and cattle, wagons and sheep which came down from Montmartre and from la Chapelle. There were scattered flocks dashed like waves on the sidewalk by some sudden detention, and an endless succession of laborers going to their work with their tools over their shoulders and their loaves of bread under their arms.

Suddenly Gervaise thought she distinguished Lantier amid this crowd, and she leaned eagerly forward at the risk of falling from the window. With a fresh pang of disappointment she pressed her handkerchief to her lips to restrain her sobs.

A fresh, youthful voice caused her to turn around:

"Lantier has not come in then?"

"No, Monsieur Coupeau," she answered, trying to smile.

The speaker was a tinsmith who occupied a tiny room at the top of the house. His bag of tools was over his shoulder; he had seen the key in the door and entered with the familiarity of a friend.

"You know," he continued, "that I am working now-a-days at the Hospital. What a May this is! The air positively stings one this morning."

As he spoke he looked closely at Gervaise; he saw her eyes were red with tears, and then glancing at the bed, discovered that it had not been disturbed. He shook his head, and going toward the couch where the children lay with their rosy cherub faces, he said in a lower voice:

"You think your husband ought to have been with you, Madame. But don't be troubled, he is busy with politics. He went on like a mad man the other day when they were voting for Eugène Sue. Perhaps he passed the night with his friends abusing that reprobate, Bonaparte."

"No, no," she murmured, with an effort. "You think nothing of that kind. I know where Lantier is only too well. We have our sorrows like the rest of the world!"

Coupeau gave a knowing wink and departed, having offered to bring her some milk if she did not care to go out; she was a good woman, he told her, and might count on him any time when she was in trouble.

As soon as Gervaise was alone, she returned to the window.

At the two corners of La Rue des Poissonnièrs were two wine shops, where the shutters had just been taken down. Here some workmen lingered, crowding into the shop, spitting, coughing, and drinking glasses of brandy and water. Gervaise was watching the place on the left of the street, where she thought she had seen Lantier go in, when a stout woman, bareheaded, and wearing a large apron, called to her from the pavement,

"You are up early! Madame Lantier!"

"Ah! Is it you, Madame Boche! Yes, I am up early, for I have much to do to-day."

"Is that so? Well, things don't get done by themselves, that's sure!"

Madame Boche was the Concierge of the house wherein the restaurant *the Veau à Deux Têtes* occupied the rez de chaussée.

As she gabbled, she examined Gervaise with considerable curiosity, and seemed, in fact, to have come out under the window for that express purpose.

"Is Monsieur Lantier still asleep?" she asked suddenly.

"Yes, he is asleep," answered Gervaise, with flushing cheeks.

Madame saw the tears come to her eyes, and satisfied with her discovery was turning away, when she suddenly stopped and called out:

"You are going to the Lavatory this morning, are you not? All right then, I have some things to wash, and I will keep a place for you next to me, and we can have a little talk!"

Then as if moved by sudden compassion, she added:

"Poor child!—don't stay at that window any longer. You are purple with cold, and will surely make yourself sick!"

But Gervaise did not move. She remained in the same spot for two mortal hours, until the clock struck eight.

She was sitting on a chair, with her arms dropping drearily at her side, but not weeping, when Lantier quietly opened the door and walked in.

"You have come!" she cried, ready to throw herself on his neck.

"Yes, I have come," he answered, "and what of it? Don't begin any of your nonsense, now!"—and he pushed her aside. Then, with an angry gesture, he tossed his felt hat on the bureau.

He was a small, dark fellow, handsome and well made, with a delicate moustache, which he twisted in his fingers mechanically as he spoke. He wore an old coat, buttoned tightly at the waist.

Gervaise had dropped upon her chair again, and uttered disjointed phrases of lamentation.

"I have not closed my eyes—I thought you were killed! Where have you been all night? I feel as if I were going mad! Tell me, Auguste, where have you been?"

"Oh! I had business," he answered, with an indifferent shrug of his shoulders. "But you know I don't like to be watched and catechised. Just let me alone, will you?"

His wife began to sob. Their voices, and Lantier's noisy movements, as he pushed the chairs about, woke the children. They started up, half naked, with tumbled hair, and hearing their mother cry, they followed her example.

"Well, this is lovely music!" cried Lantier, furiously. "I warn you, if you don't all stop, that out of this door I go, and you won't see me again in a hurry! Will you hold your tongue? Good-bye, then; I'll go back where I came from."

He snatched up his hat, but Gervaise rushed toward him, crying: "No! no!"

And she soothed the children and stifled their cries with kisses, and laid them tenderly back in their bed, and they were soon happy, and merrily playing together. Meanwhile the father, not even taking off his boots, threw himself on the bed with a weary air. His face was white from exhaustion and a sleepless night; he did not close his eyes, but looked around the room.

"A nice looking place, this!" he muttered.

Then examining Gervaise, he said, half aloud and half to himself:

"So! you have given up washing yourself, it seems!"

Gervaise was only twenty-two. She was tall and slender, with delicate features, already worn by hardships and anxieties. With her hair uncombed and shoes down at heel, shivering in her white sack, on which was much dust and many stains from the furniture and wall where it had hung, she looked at least ten years older from the hours of suspense and tears she had passed.

Lantier's word startled her from her resignation and timidity.

"Are you not ashamed?" she said with considerable animation. "You know very well that I do all I can. It is not my fault that we came here. I should like to see you with two children, in a place where you can't get a drop of hot water. We ought as soon as we reached Paris to have settled ourselves at once in a home, that was what you promised."

"Pshaw," he muttered; "you had as much good as I had out of our savings. You ate the fatted calf with me—and it is not worth while to make a row about it now!"

She did not heed his words, but continued:

"There is no need of giving up either. I saw Madame Fauconnier, the laundress in La Rue Neuve. She will take me Monday. If you go in with your friend we shall be afloat again in six months. We must find some kind of a hole where we can live cheaply while we work. That is the thing to do now. Work! work!"

Lantier turned his face to the wall with a shrug of disgust which enraged his wife, who resumed:

"Yes, I know very well that you don't like to work. You would like to wear fine clothes and walk about the streets all day. You don't like my looks since you took all my dresses to the pawnbrokers. No, no, Auguste, I did not intend to speak to you about it, but I know very well where you spent the night. I saw you go into the Grand-Balcon with that street walker, Adèle. You have made a charming choice. She wears fine

170

clothes and is clean. Yes, and she has reason to be certainly, there is not a man in that restaurant who does not know her far better than an honest girl should be known!"

Lantier leaped from the bed. His eyes were as black as night and his face deadly pale.

"Yes," repeated his wife, "I mean what I say. Madame Boche will not keep her or her sister in the house any longer, because there are always a crowd of men hanging on the staircase."

Lantier lifted both fists, and then conquering a violent desire to beat her, he seized her in his arms, shook her violently.

A profound silence reigned in the room—they did not speak to each other. He seemed to be waiting for something. She, adopting an unconcerned air, seemed to be in haste.

She made up a bundle of soiled linen that had been thrown into a corner behind the trunk, and then he spoke:

"What are you doing? Are you going out?"

At first she did not reply. Then when he angrily repeated the question she answered:

"Certainly I am. I am going to wash all these things. The children cannot live in dirt."

He threw two or three handkerchiefs toward her, and after another long silence he said:

"Have you any money?"

She quickly rose to her feet and turned toward him, in her hand she held some of the soiled clothes.

"Money! Where should I get money unless I had stolen it? You know very well that day before yesterday you got three francs on my black skirt. We had breakfasted twice on that, and money goes fast. No, I have no money. I have four sous for the Lavatory. I cannot make money like other women we know."

He did not reply to this allusion, but rose from the bed, and passed in review the ragged garments hung around the room. He ended by taking down the pantaloons and the shawl and opening the bureau took out a sacque and two chemises. All these he made into a bundle, which he threw at Gervaise.

"Take them," he said, "and hurry back from the pawn-broker's."

"Would you not like me to take the children?" she asked.

171

"Heavens! if pawnbrokers would only make loans on children, what a good thing it would be!"

She went to the Mont-de-Piété, and when she returned, a half hour later, she laid a silver five-franc piece on the mantel-shelf, and placed the ticket with the others between the two candlesticks.

"This is what they gave me," she said, coldly. "I wanted six francs, but they would not give them. They always keep on the safe side there, and yet there is always a crowd."

Lantier did not at once take up the money. He had sent her to the Mont-de-Piété, that he might not leave her without food or money, but when he caught sight of part of a ham wrapped in paper on the table, with half a loaf of bread, he slipped the silver piece into his vest pocket.

"I did not dare go to the milk-woman," explained Gervaise, "because we owe her for eight days. But I shall be back early. You can get some bread and some chops, and have them ready. Don't forget the wine, too."

He made no reply. Peace seemed to be made, but when Gervaise went to the trunk to take out some of Lantier's clothing, he called out:

"No—let that alone."

"What do you mean?" she said, turning round in surprise. "You can't wear these things again until they are washed! Why shall I not take them?"

And she looked at him with some anxiety. He angrily tore the things from her hands and threw them back into the trunk.

"Confound you!" he muttered. "Will you never learn to obey? When I say a thing I mean it——"

"But why?" she repeated, turning very pale, and seized with a terrible suspicion. "You do not need these shirts—you are not going away. Why should I not take them?"

He hesitated a moment, uneasy under the earnest gaze she fixed upon him.

"Why? Why? Because," he said, "I am sick of hearing you say that you wash and mend for me. Attend to your own affairs, and I will attend to mine."

She entreated him—defended herself from the charge of ever having complained—but he shut the trunk with a loud bang, and then sat down upon it, repeating that he was master at least of his own clothing. Then, to escape from her eyes, he threw himself again on the bed, saying he was sleepy, and that she made his head ache, and finally slept, or pretended to do so.

Gervaise hesitated, she was tempted to give up her plan of going to the Lavatory, and thought she would sit down to her sewing. But at last she was reassured by Lantier's regular breathing, she took her soap and her ball of blueing, and going to the children, who were playing on the floor with some old corks, she said in a low voice:

"Be very good, and keep quiet. Papa is sleeping."

When she left the room there was not a sound except the stiffled laughter of the little ones. It was then after ten, and the sun was shining brightly in at the window.

The Lavatory, whither she went, was an immense shed, as it were, with a low ceiling—the beams and rafters unconcealed —and lighted by large windows, through which the daylight streamed. A light gray mist or stream pervaded the room, which was filled with a smell of soap suds and *eau de javelle* combined. Along the central aisle were tubs on either side, and two rows of women with their arms bare to the shoulders, and their skirts tucked up, stood showing their colored stockings and stout laced shoes.

"Here! this way, my dear," cried Madame Boche, and when the young woman had joined her at the very end where she stood, the Concierge, without stopping her furious rubbing, began to talk in a steady fashion.

"Yes, this is your place. I have kept it for you. I have not much to do. Boche is never hard on his linen, and you, too, do not seem to have much. Your package is quite small. We shall finish by noon, and then we can get something to eat. I used to give my clothes to a woman in La Rue Pelat, but bless my heart! she washed and pounded them all away; and I made up my mind to wash myself. It is clear gain, you see, and costs only the soap."

Gervaise opened her bundle and sorted the clothes, laying aside all the colored pieces, and when Madame Boche advised her to try a little soda, she shook her head.

Gervaise, with her sleeves rolled up, showing her pretty, fair

173

arms, was soaping a child's shirt. She rubbed it, and turned it, soaped and rubbed it again.

"You are a strong one, anyhow!" cried Madame Boche, astonished at the rapidity and strength of the woman. "Your arms are slender, but they are like iron."

Gervaise then took each piece separately, rinsed it, then rubbed it with soap and brushed it. That is to say, she held the cloth firmly with one hand, and with the other moved the short brush from her, pushing along a dirty foam which fell off into the water below.

As she brushed they talked.

"No, we are not married," said Gervaise. "I do not intend to lie about it. Lantier is not so nice that a woman need be very anxious to be his wife. If it were not for the children! I was fourteen and he was eighteen, when the first one was born. The other child did not come for four years. I was not happy at home. Papa Macquart, for the merest trifle, would beat me. I might have married, I suppose."

"He is not good to you, then?"

"He was very good to me once," answered Gervaise, "but since we came to Paris he has changed. His mother died last year, and left him about seventeen hundred francs. He wished to come to Paris, and as Father Macquart was in the habit of hitting me in the face without any warning, I said I would come too, which we did, with the two children. I meant to be a fine laundress, and he was to continue with his trade as a hatter. We might have been very happy. But you see, Lantier is extravagant; he likes expensive things, and thinks of his amusement before anything else. He is not good for much anyhow!

"We arrived at the Hôtel Montmartre. We had dinners and carriages, suppers and theatres, a watch for him, a silk dress for me—for he is not selfish when he has money. You can easily imagine therefore, at the end of two months, we were cleaned out. Then it was that we came to Hôtel Boncœur, and that this life began." She checked herself with a strange choking in the throat. Tears gathered in her eyes. She finished brushing her linen.

"I thought him somewhat dissipated," said Madame Boche, referring to Lantier without naming him.

Gervaise nodded in acquiescence.

"Yes," continued the Concierge, "I have seen many little things." But she started back, as Gervaise turned round with a pale face and quivering lips.

"Oh! I know nothing," she continued. "He likes to laugh, that is all, and those two girls who are with us, you know, Adèle and Virginie, like to laugh too, so they have their little jokes together, but that is all there is of it, I am sure."

The young woman, with the perspiration standing on her brow and her arms still dripping, looked her full in the face with earnest, inquiring eyes.

Then the Concierge became excited, and struck her breast, exclaiming:

"I tell you I know nothing whatever, nothing more than I tell you!"

Then she added in a gentle voice, "But he has honest eyes, my dear. He will marry you, child, I promise that he will marry you!"

Gervaise dried her forehead with her damp hand and shook her head. All this time Gervaise was going on with her task and had just completed the washing of her colored pieces, which she threw over a trestle to drip.

"You have nearly finished," said Madame Boche. "I am waiting to help you wring them."

"Oh! you are very good! It is not necessary though!" answered the young woman, as she swashed the garments through the clear water. "If I had sheets I would not refuse your offer, however."

Nevertheless she accepted the aid of the Concierge. They took up a brown woolen skirt badly faded, from which poured out a yellow stream as the two women wrung it together.

Suddenly Madame Boche cried out:

"Look! There comes Big Virginie! She is actually coming here to wash her rags tied up in a handkerchief."

Gervaise looked up quickly. Virginie was a woman about her own age—larger and taller than herself, a brunette, and pretty in spite of the elongated oval of her face. She wore an old black dress with flounces and a red ribbon at her throat. Her hair was carefully arranged and massed in a blue chenille net.

She hesitated a moment in the centre aisle and half shut her eyes, as if looking for something or somebody, but when she distinguished Gervaise she went toward her with a haughty, insolent air and supercilious smile, and finally established herself only a short distance from her.

"That is a new notion!" muttered Madame Boche, in a low voice. "She was never known before to rub out even a pair of cuffs. She is a lazy creature, I do assure you. She never sews the buttons on her boots. She is just like her sister, that minx of an Adèle, who stays away from the shop two days out of three. What is she rubbing now? A skirt, is it? It is dirty enough, I am sure!"

It was clear that Madame Boche wished to please Gervaise. The truth was she often took coffee with Adèle and Virginie, when the two sisters were in funds. Gervaise did not reply, but worked faster than before. She was now preparing her blueing water in a small tub standing on three legs. She dipped in her pieces, shook them about in the colored water, which was almost a lake in hue, and then wringing them, she shook them out, and threw them lightly over the high wooden bars.

While she did this she kept her back well turned on Big Virginie. But she felt that the girl was looking at her, and she heard an occasional derisive sniff. Virginie in fact, seemed to have come there to provoke her, and when Gervaise turned around the two women fixed their eyes on each other.

"Let her be," murmured Madame Boche. "She is not the one, now I tell you!"

At this moment, as Gervaise was shaking her last piece of linen, she heard laughing and talking at the door of the Lavatory.

All the women looked around, and Gervaise recognized Claude and Etienne. As soon as they saw her they ran toward her, splashing through the puddles, their untied shoes half off, and Claude, the eldest, dragging his little brother by the hand.

The women as they passed uttered kindly exclamations of pity, for the children were evidently frightened. They clutched their mother's skirts and buried their pretty blonde heads.

"Did papa send you?" asked Gervaise.

But as she stooped to tie Etienne's shoes, she saw on Claude's finger the key of her room, with its copper tag and number.

"Did you bring the key?" she exclaimed, in great surprise. "And why, pray?"

The child looked down on the key hanging on his finger, which he had apparently forgotten. This seemed to remind him of something, and he said, in a clear, shrill voice:

"Papa is gone!"

"He went to buy your breakfast, did he not? And he told you to come and look for me here, I suppose?"

Claude looked at his brother and hesitated. Then he exclaimed:

"Papa has gone, I say. He jumped from the bed, put his things in his trunk, and then he carried his trunk down stairs and put it on a carriage. We saw him—he has gone!"

Gervaise was kneeling, tying the boy's shoe. She rose slowly, with a very white face, and with her hands pressed to either temple, as if she were afraid of her head cracking open. She could say nothing but the same words over and over again:

"Great God! great God! great God!"

Madame Boche, in her turn, interrogated the child, eagerly; for she was charmed at finding herself an actor, as it were, in this drama.

"Tell us all about it, my dear. He locked the door, did he? and then he told you to bring the key here?" And then lowering her voice, she whispered in the child's ear.

"Was there a lady in the carriage?" she asked.

The child looked troubled for a moment, but speedily began his story again with a triumphant air.

"He jumped off the bed, put his things in the trunk, and he went away."

Then as Madame Boche made no attempt to detain him, he drew his brother to the faucet, where the two amused themselves in making the water run.

Gervaise could not weep. She felt as if she were stifling. She covered her face with her hands, and turned toward the wall. A sharp, nervous trembling shook her from head to foot. An occasional sobbing sigh, or rather gasp, escaped from her lips, while she pressed her clenched hands more tightly on her eyes, as if to increase the darkness of the abyss in which she felt herself to have fallen.

"Be reasonable, child! be quiet," whispered Madame Boche. "They are all looking at you. Is it possible you can care so much for any man? You love him still, although such a little while ago you pretended you did not care for him; and you cry as if your heart would break! O Lord! what fools we women are!"

Then in a maternal tone she added:

"And such a pretty little woman as you are, too. But now I may as well tell you the whole, I suppose? Well! then, you remember when I was talking to you from the sidewalk, and you were at your window? I knew then that it was Lantier who came in with Adèle. I did not see his face, but I knew his coat, and Boche watched and saw him come down stairs this morning. But he was with Adèle, you understand? There is another person who comes to see Virginie twice a week."

She stopped for a moment to take breath, and then went on in a lower tone still.

"Take care! she is laughing at you—the heartless little cat! I bet all her washing is a sham. She has seen her sister and Lantier well off, and then came here to find out how you would take it."

Gervaise took her hands down from her face, and looked around. When she saw Virginie talking and laughing with two or three women, a wild tempest of rage shook her from head to foot. She stooped, with her arms extended, as if feeling for something, and moved along slowly for a step or two, then snatched up a bucket of soap suds and threw it at Virginie.

"You Devil! be off with you!" cried Virginie, starting back.

All the women in the Lavatory hurried to the scene of action. They jumped up on the benches, and a circle of spectators was soon formed.

"Yes, she is a Devil!" repeated Virginie. "What has got into the fool?"

Gervaise stood motionless, her face convulsed and lips apart. The other continued:

"She got tired of the country, it seems, but she left one leg behind her, at all events."

The women laughed, and Big Virginie, elated at her success, went on in a louder and more triumphant tone:

"Come a little nearer, and I will soon settle you. You had better have remained in the country. It is lucky for you that your dirty soap suds only went on my feet, for I would have taken you over my knees and given you a good spanking, if one drop had gone in my face. What is the matter with her, anyway?" and Big Virginie addressed her audience. "Make her tell what I have done to her! Say! Fool—what harm have I ever done to you?"

"You had best not talk so much," answered Gervaise, almost inaudibly; "you know very well where my husband was seen yesterday. Now be quiet, or harm will come to you. I will strangle you—quick as a wink."

"Her husband, she says! Her husband! The lady's husband! As if a looking thing like that had a husband! Is it my fault if he has deserted her? Does she think I have stolen him? Anyway, he was much too good for her. But tell me, some of you, was his name on his collar? Madame has lost her—husband! She will pay a good reward, I am sure, to any one who will carry him back!"

The women all laughed. Gervaise, in a low, concentrated voice, repeated:

"You know very well—you know very well! your sister—yes, I will strangle your sister!"

"Oh! yes, I understand," answered Virginie, "strangle her if you choose. What do I care? and what are you staring at me for? Can't I wash my clothes in peace? Come, I am sick of this stuff! Let me alone!"

Big Virginie turned away, and after five or six angry blows with her beater, she began again:

"Yes, it is my sister, and the two adore each other. You should see them bill and coo together. He has left you, with these dirty-faced imps, and you left three others behind you with three fathers! It was your dear Lantier who told us all that. Ah! he had had quite enough of you—he said so!"

"Miserable fool!" cried Gervaise, white with anger.

She turned, and mechanically looked around on the floor, seeing nothing however, but the small tub of blueing water, she threw that in Virginie's face.

"She has spoiled my dress!" cried Virginie, whose shoulder

and one hand were dyed a deep blue. "You just wait a moment!" she added, as she in her turn snatched up a tub and dashed its contents at Gervaise. Then ensued a most formidable battle. The two women ran up and down the room in eager haste, looking for full tubs, which they quickly flung in the faces of each other, and each deluge was heralded and accompanied by a shout.

"Is that enough? Will that cool you off?" cried Gervaise.

And from Virginie:

"Take that! It is good to have a bath once in your life!"

Finally the tubs and pails were all empty, and the two women began to draw water from the faucets. They continued their mutual abuse, while the water was running, and presently it was Virginie who received a bucketful, in her face. The water ran down her back and over her skirts. She was stunned and bewildered, when suddenly there came another in her left ear, knocking her head nearly off her shoulders—her comb fell and with it her abundant hair.

Gervaise was attacked about her legs. Her shoes were filled with water, and she was drenched above her knees. Presently the two women were deluged from head to foot, their garments stuck to them, and they dripped like umbrellas which have been out in a heavy shower.

"What fun!" said one of the laundresses, as she looked on at a safe distance.

The whole Lavatory were immensely amused, and the women applauded as if at a theatre. The floor was covered an inch deep with water, through which the termagants splashed. Suddenly Virginie discovered a bucket of scalding water standing a little apart, she caught it and threw it upon Gervaise. There was an exclamation of horror from the lookers-on. Gervaise escaped with only one foot slightly burned; but exasperated by the pain, she threw a tub with all her strength at the legs of her opponent. Virginie fell to the ground.

"She has broken her leg!" cried one of the spectators.

"She deserved it," answered another, "for the tall one tried to scald her!"

"She was right, after all, if the blonde had taken away her man!"

Madame Boche rent the air with her exclamations, waving her arms frantically, high above her head. She had taken the precaution to place herself behind a rampart of tubs, with Claude and Etienne clinging to her skirts, weeping and sobbing in a paroxysm of terror and keeping up a cry of "Mamma! Mamma!" When she saw Virginie prostrate on the ground, she rushed to Gervaise and tried to pull her away.

But Gervaise pushed her aside, and the old woman again took refuge behind the tubs with the children. Virginie made a spring at the throat of her adversary, and actually tried to strangle her. Gervaise shook her off, and snatched at the long braid hanging from the girl's head, and pulled it as if she hoped to wrench it off, and the head with it.

The battle began again, this time silent and wordless, and literally tooth and nail. Their extended hands, with fingers stiffly crooked, caught wildly at all in their way, scratching and tearing. The red ribbon and the chenille net worn by the brunette were torn off, the waist of her dress was ripped from throat to belt, and showed the white skin on the shoulder.

Gervaise had lost a sleeve, and her chemise was torn to her waist. Strips of clothing lay in every direction. It was Gervaise who was first wounded. Three long scratches from her mouth to her throat bled profusely, and she fought with her eyes shut lest she should be blinded. As yet Virginie showed no wound. Suddenly Gervaise seized one of her ear-rings—pear-shaped, of yellow glass—she tore it out and brought blood.

"They will kill each other! Separate them," cried several voices.

The women gathered around the combatants; the spectators were divided into two parties—some exciting and encouraging Gervaise and Virginie as if they had been dogs fighting, while others more timid trembled, turned away their heads, and said they were faint and sick. A general battle threatened to take place, such was the excitement.

Both women lay on the ground. Suddenly Virginie struggled up to her knees. She had got possession of one of the beaters, which she brandished. Her voice was hoarse and low as she muttered:

"This will be as good for you, as for your dirty linen!"

Gervaise, in her turn, snatched another beater, which she held like a club. Her voice, also, was hoarse and low.

"I will beat your skin," she muttered, "as I would my coarse towels."

They knelt in front of each other in utter silence for at least a minute, with hair streaming, eyes glaring, and distended nostrils. They each drew a long breath.

Gervaise struck the first blow with her beater full on the shoulders of her adversary, and then threw herself over on the side to escape Virginie's weapon, which touched her on the hip.

Thus started they struck each other as laundresses strike their linen, in measured cadence.

The women about them ceased to laugh—many went away, saying they were faint. Those who remained watched the scene with a cruel light in their eyes. Madame Boche had taken Claude and Etienne to the other end of the room, whence came the dreary sound of their sobs which were heard through the dull blows of the beaters.

Suddenly Gervaise uttered a shriek. Virginie had struck her just above the elbow on her bare arm, and the flesh began to swell at once. She rushed at Virginie—her face was so terrible that the spectators thought she meant to kill her.

With almost superhuman strength, she seized Virginie by the waist, bent her forward with her face to the brick floor, and notwithstanding her struggles lifted her skirts and showed the white and naked skin. Then she brought her beater down as she had formerly done at Plassans under the trees on the river side, where her employer had washed the linen of the garrison.

Each blow of the beater fell on the soft flesh with a dull thud, leaving a scarlet mark.

The women were laughing again by this time, but soon the cry went up. "Enough! Enough!"

Gervaise did not even hear. She seemed entirely absorbed, as if she were fulfilling an appointed task, and she talked with strange, wild gayety.

They tore Virginie from her hands. The tall brunette, weeping and sobbing, scarlet with shame, rushed out of the room, leaving Gervaise mistress of the field; who calmly arranged her dress somewhat, and as her arm was stiff, begged Madame Boche to lift her bundle of linen on her shoulder.

While the old woman obeyed, she dilated on her emotions during the scene that had just taken place.

"You ought to go to a doctor and see if something is not broken. I heard a queer sound," she said.

But Gervaise did not seem to hear her, and paid no attention either, to the women who crowded around her with congratulations. She hastened to the door where her children awaited her.

"Two hours!" said the mistress of the establishment, already installed in her glass cabinet. "Two hours and two sous!"

Gervaise mechanically laid down the two sous, and then, limping painfully under the weight of the wet linen which was slung over her shoulder, and dripped as she moved—with her injured arm and bleeding cheek—she went away, dragging after her with her naked arm, the still sobbing and tear-stained Etienne and Claude.

-[*CHAPTER II*]-

Gervaise and Coupeau

THREE WEEKS LATER, about half past eleven one fine sunny morning, Gervaise and Coupeau, the tinworker, were eating some brandied fruit at the Assommoir.

Coupeau, who was smoking outside, had seen her as she crossed the street with her linen, and compelled her to enter. Her huge basket was on the floor, back of the little table where they sat.

Father Colombe's Tavern, known as the Assommoir, was on the corner of the Rue des Poissonnièrs and of the Boulevard de Rochechouart. The sign bore the one single word, in long, blue letters,

DISTILLATION.

And this word stretched from one end to the other. On either side of the door stood tall oleanders in small casks, their leaves covered thick with dust. The enormous counter with its rows of glasses, its fountain, and its pewter measures, was on the left of the door; and the huge room was ornamented by gigantic casks painted bright yellow, and highly varnished, hooped with shining copper. On high shelves were bottles of liquors, and jars of fruits; all sorts of flasks standing in order concealed the wall, and repeated their pale green or deep crimson tints in the great mirror behind the counter.

The great feature of the house however, was the distilling apparatus, which stood at the back of the room behind an oak railing, on which the tipsy workmen leaned, as they stupidly watched the still, with its long neck and serpentine tubes descending to subterranean regions—a very devil's kitchen.

At this early hour the Assommoir was nearly empty. A stout man in his shirt sleeves—Father Colombe himself—was serving a little girl not more than twelve years old, with four cents worth of liquor in a cup.

The sun streamed in at the door, and lay on the floor, which was black where the men had spat as they smoked. And from the counter—from the casks—from all the room—rose an alcoholic emanation which seemed to intoxicate the very particles of dust floating in the sunshine.

In the meantime, Coupeau rolled a new cigarette. He was very neat and clean, wearing a blouse and a little blue cloth cap, and showing his white teeth as he smiled.

The lower jaw was somewhat prominent, and the nose slightly flat; he had fine brown eyes, and the face of a happy child and good natured animal. His hair was thick and curly. His complexion was delicate still, for he was only twenty-six. Opposite him sat Gervaise in a black gown, leaning slightly forward, finishing her fruit, which she held by the stem.

They were near the street, at the first of the four tables arranged in front of the counter. When Coupeau had lighted his cigar, he placed both elbows on the table and looked at the woman without speaking. Her pretty face had that day, something of the delicate transparency of fine porcelain.

Then continuing something which they apparently had been previously discussing, he said in a low voice:

"Then you say no, do you? Absolutely no?"

"Of course. No it must be, Monsieur Coupeau," answered Gervaise, with a smile. "Surely you do not intend to begin that again here! You promised to be reasonable, too. Had I known, I should certainly have refused your treat."

He did not speak, but gazed at her more intently than before, with tender boldness. He looked at her soft eyes, and dewy lips, pale at the corners, but half parted, allowing one to see the rich crimson within.

She returned his look with a kind and affectionate smile. Finally she said:

"You should not think of such a thing. It is folly! I am an old woman. I have a boy eight years old. What should we do together?"

"Much as other people do, I suppose!" answered Coupeau, with a wink.

She shrugged her shoulders.

"You know nothing about it, Monsieur Coupeau, but I have had some experience. I have two mouths in the house, and they have excellent appetites. How am I to bring up my children if I trifle away my time? Then, too, my misfortune has taught me one great lesson, which is, that the less I have to do with men, the better!"

She then proceeded to explain all her reasons, calmly and without anger. It was easy to see that her words were the result of grave consideration.

Coupeau listened quietly, saying only at intervals:

"You are hurting my feelings. Yes, hurting my feelings ——"

"Yes, I see that," she answered, "and I am really very sorry for you. If I had any idea of leading a different life from that which I follow to-day, it might as well be with you as with another. You have the look of a good-natured man. But what is the use? I have now been with Madame Fauconnier for a fortnight. The children are going to school, and I am very happy, for I have plenty to do. Don't you see, therefore, that it is best for us to remain as we are?"

And she stooped to pick up her basket.

"You are keeping me here to talk," she said, "and they are waiting for me at my employers'. You will find some other woman, Monsieur Coupeau, far prettier than I, who will not have two children to bring up!"

He looked at the clock, and made her sit down again.

"Wait!" he cried. "It is still thirty-five minutes of eleven. I have twenty-five minutes still, and don't be afraid of my familiarity, for the table is between us! Do you dislike me so very much that you can't stay and talk with me for five minutes?"

She put down her basket, unwilling to seem disobliging, and they talked for some time in a friendly sort of way. She had breakfasted before she left home, and he had swallowed his soup in the greatest haste, and laid in wait for her as she came out. Gervaise, as she listened to him, watched from the windows —between the bottles of brandied fruit—the movement of the crowd in the street, which at this hour—that of the Parisian breakfast—was unusually lively. Workmen hurried into the Baker's, and coming out with a loaf under their arms, they went into the *Veau à Deux Têtes,* three doors higher up, to breakfast at six sous. Next the Baker's, was a shop where fried potatoes, and mussels with parsley, were sold. A constant succession of shop girls carried off paper parcels of fried potatoes and cups filed with mussels, and others bought bunches of radishes. When Gervaise leaned a little more toward the window, she saw still another shop, also crowded, from which issued a steady stream of children holding in their hands, wrapped in paper, a breaded cutlet, or a sausage, still warm.

A group formed around the door of the Assommoir.

"Say! Bibi-la-Grillade," asked a voice; "will you stand a drink all around?"

Five workmen went in, and the same voice said:

"Father Colombe, be honest now. Give us honest glasses, and no nutshells, if you please."

Presently three more workmen entered together, and finally a crowd of blouses passed in between the dusty oleanders.

"You have no business to ask such questions," said Gervaise to Coupeau; "of course I loved him. But after the manner in which he deserted me"—

They were speaking of Lantier. Gervaise had never seen him again; she supposed him to be living with Virginie's sister— with the friend who was about to start a manufactory for hats.

At first she thought of committing suicide, of drowning herself; but she had grown more reasonable, and had really begun to trust that things were all for the best. With Lantier she felt sure she never could have done justice to the children, so extravagant were his habits.

He might come, of course, and see Claude and Etienne. She would not show him the door; only so far as she herself was concerned, he had best not lay his finger on her. And she uttered these words in a tone of determination, like a woman whose plan of life is clearly defined; while Coupeau, who was by no means inclined to give her up lightly, teased and questioned her in regard to Lantier with none too much delicacy, it is true, but his teeth were so white and his face so merry that the woman could not take offence.

"Did you beat him?" he asked, finally. "Oh! you are none too amiable. You beat people sometimes, I have heard."

She laughed gayly.

Yes, it was true she had whipped that great Virginie. That day she could have strangled some one with a glad heart. And she laughed again, because Coupeau told her that Virginie, in her humiliation, had left the Quartier.

Gervaise's face, as she laughed, however, had a certain childish sweetness. She extended her slender, dimpled hands, declaring she would not hurt a fly. All she knew of blows was, that she had received a good many in her life. Then she began to talk of Plassans and of her youth. She had never been indiscreet, nor was she fond of men. When she had fallen in with Lantier she was only fourteen, and she regarded him as her husband. Her only fault, she declared, was that she was too amiable, and allowed people to impose on her, and that she got fond of people too easily; were she to love another man, she should wish and expect to live quietly and comfortably with him always, without any nonsense.

And when Coupeau slyly asked her if she called her dear children nonsense, she gave him a little slap and said that she, of course, was much like other women. But women were not like men, after all; they had their homes to take care of and keep clean; she was like her mother, who had been a slave to her brutal father for more than twenty years!

"My very lameness," she continued—

"Your lameness?" interrupted Coupeau, gallantly; "why, it is almost nothing. No one would ever notice it!"

She shook her head. She knew very well that it was very evident, and at forty it would be far worse; but she said softly, with a faint smile, "You have a strange taste, to fall in love with a lame woman!"

He, with his elbows on the table, still coaxed and entreated, but she continued to shake her head in the negative. She listened, with her eyes fixed on the street, seemingly fascinated by the surging crowd.

The bells of the various manufactories were ringing loudly, but the workmen did not hurry. They deliberately lighted their pipes, and then with rounded shoulders slouched along, dragging their feet after them.

Gervaise mechanically watched a group of three, one man much taller than the other two, who seemed to be hesitating as to what they should do next. Finally they came directly to the Assommoir.

"I know them," said Coupeau, "or rather I know the tall one. It is Mes-Bottes, a comrade of mine."

The Assommoir was now crowded with boisterous men. Two glasses rang with the energy with which they brought down their fists on the counter. They stood in rows, with their hands crossed over their stomachs, or folded behind their backs, waiting their turn to be served by Father Colombe.

"Hallo!" cried Mes-Bottes, giving Coupeau a rough slap on the shoulders, "how fine you have got to be with your cigarettes and your linen shirt bosom! Who is your friend that pays for all this? I should like to make her acquaintance."

"Don't be so silly!" returned Coupeau, angrily.

But the other gave a knowing wink.

"Ah! I understand— 'A word to the wise' "—and he turned round with a fearful lurch to look at Gervaise, who shuddered and recoiled. The tobacco smoke—the odor of humanity added to this air heavy with alcohol, was oppressive—and she choked a little and coughed.

"Ah! what an awful thing it is to drink!" she said in a whisper to her friend, to whom she then went on to say, how years before, she had drank anisette with her mother at Plassans, and how it had made her so very sick that ever since that day, she had never been able to endure even the smell of liquors.

Coupeau also failed to understand how a man could swallow glasses of brandy and water, one after the other. He always remained on the other side of the door, when they came in to swallow perdition like that.

His father, who was a tin worker like himself, had fallen one day from the roof of No. 25, in La Rue Coquenaud, and this recollection had made him very prudent ever since. As for himself, when he passed through that street and saw the place, he would sooner drink the water in the gutter, than swallow a drop at the wine shop. He concluded with the sentence:

"You see in my trade, a man needs a clear head and steady legs."

Gervaise had taken up her basket—she had not risen from her chair, however, but held it on her knees, with a dreary look in her eyes as if the words of the young mechanic had awakened in her mind strange thoughts of a possible future.

She answered in a low, hesitating tone, without any apparent connection:

"Heavens knows I am not ambitious. I do not ask for much in this world. My idea would be to live a quiet life, and always have enough to eat—a clean place to live in—with a comfortable bed, a table and a chair or two. Yes, I would like to bring my children up in that way, and see them good and industrious. I should not like to run the risk of being beaten—no, that would not please me at all!"

She hesitated, as if to find something else to say, and then resumed:

"Yes, and at the end I should wish to die in my bed in my own home!"

She pushed back her chair and rose. Coupeau argued with her vehemently, and then gave an uneasy glance at the clock. They did not, however, depart at once. She wished to look at the still, and stood for some minutes gazing with curiosity at the great copper machine. The tin worker, who had followed her, explained to her how the thing worked, pointing out with his finger the various parts of the machine, and showed the enormous retort whence fell the clear stream of alcohol. The still, with its intricate and endless coils of wire and pipes, had a dreary aspect. Not a breath escaped from it and hardly a sound was heard. It was like some night task performed in daylight, by a melancholy silent workman.

In the meantime Mes-Bottes, accompanied by his two comrades, had lounged to the oak railing, and leaned there until there was a corner of the counter free. He laughed a tipsy laugh as he stood with his eyes fixed on the machine.

"By thunder!" he muttered, "that is a jolly little thing!"

He went on to say that it held enough to keep their throats fresh for a week. As for himself, he should like to hold the end of that pipe between his teeth, and he should like to feel that liquor run down his throat, in a steady stream, until it reached his heels.

The still did its work slowly but surely. There was not a glimmer on its surface—no firelight reflected in its clean colored sides. The liquor dropped steadily, and suggested a persevering stream, which would gradually invade the room, spread over the streets and Boulevard, and finally deluge and inundate Paris itself.

Gervaise shuddered and drew back. She tried to smile, but her lips quivered as she murmured:

"It frightens me—that machine! It makes me feel cold to see that constant drip"——

Then returning to the idea which had struck her as the acme of human happiness, she said:

"Say, do you not think that would be very nice? To work and have plenty to eat—to have a little home all to one's self—to bring up children, and then die in one's bed?"

"And not be beaten," added Coupeau, gayly. "But I will promise never to beat you, Madame Gervaise, if you will agree to what I ask. I will promise also never to drink, because I love you too much! Come now, say yes."

He lowered his voice and spoke with his lips close to her throat, while she, holding her basket in front of her was making a path through the crowd of men.

But she did not say no or shake her head as she had done. She glanced up at him with a half tender smile, and seemed to rejoice in the assurance he gave that he did not drink.

It was clear that she would have said yes, if she had not sworn never to have anything more to do with men.

Finally they reached the door, and went out of the place, leaving it crowded to overflowing. The fumes of alcohol, and the tipsy voices of the men carousing, went out into the street with them.

Mes-Bottes was heard accusing Father Colombe of cheating, by not filling his glasses more than half full, and he proposed to his comrades to go in future to another place, where they could do much better and get more for their money.

"Ah!" said Gervaise, drawing a long breath when they stood on the sidewalk, "here one can breathe again. Good-bye, Monsieur Coupeau, and many thanks for your politeness. I must hasten now!"

She moved on, but he took her hand and held it fast.

"Go a little way with me. It will not be much further for you. I must stop at my sister's before I go back to the shop."

She yielded to his entreaties, and they walked slowly on together. He told her about his family. His mother, a tailoress, was the housekeeper. Twice she had been obliged to give up her work on account of trouble with her eyes. She was sixty-two on the third of the last month. He was her youngest child. One of his sisters, Madame Lerat, a widow, thirty-six years old, was a flower maker, and lived at Batignolles, in La Rue Des Moines. The other, who was thirty, had married a chain maker—a man by the name of Lorilleux. It was to their rooms that he was now going. They lived in that great house on the left. He ate his dinner every night with them; it was an economy for them all. But he wanted to tell them now, not to expect him that night, as he was invited to dine with a friend.

They by this time had turned into La Rue de la Goutte d'Or. He stopped and looked up.

"There is the house," he said, "and I was born only a few doors further off. It is an enormous place."

Gervaise looked up and down the façade. It was indeed enormous. The house was of five stories, with fifteen windows on each floor. The blinds were black, and with many of the slats broken, which gave an indescribable air of ruin and desolation to the place.

Gervaise looked at the entrance, an immense doorway which

191

rose to the height of the second story, and made a deep passage, at the end of which was a large courtyard.

"Come up," said Coupeau, "they won't eat you."

Gervaise preferred to wait for him in the street, but she consented to go as far as the room of the Concierge, which was within the porch, on the left.

"Are you looking for any one?" asked the Concierge, coming to her door considerably puzzled.

But the young woman explained that she was waiting for a friend, and then turned back toward the street. As Coupeau still delayed, she returned to the courtyard, finding in it a strange fascination.

The house did not strike her as especially ugly. At some of the windows were plants—a wall flower, blooming in a pot— a caged canary, who uttered an occasional warble—and several shaving mirrors caught the light and shone like stars.

A cabinet-maker sang, accompanied by the regular whistling sounds of his plane, while from the locksmith's quarters came a clatter of hammers struck in cadence.

At almost all the open windows the laughing, dirty faces of merry children were seen, and women sat, with their calm faces in profile, bending over their work. It was the quiet time— after the morning labors were over, and the men were gone to their work, and the house was comparatively quiet, disturbed only by the sounds of the various trades. The same refrain repeated hour after hour has a soothing effect, Gervaise thought.

To be sure, the courtyard was a little damp. Were she to live there, she should certainly prefer a room on the sunny side.

She went in several steps, and breathed that heavy odor of the homes of the poor—an odor of old dust, of rancid dirt and grease; but as the acridity of the smells from the dye-house predominated, she decided it to be far better than the Hôtel Boncœur.

She selected a window—a window in the corner on the left, where there was a small box planted with scarlet beans, whose slender tendrils were beginning to wind round a little arbor of strings.

"I have made you wait too long, I am afraid," said Coupeau, whom she suddenly heard at her side. "They make a great fuss when I do not dine there, and she did not like it to-day, especially as my sister had bought veal. You are looking at this house," he continued. "Think of it—it is always lit from top to bottom. There are a hundred lodgers in it. If I had any furniture I would have had a room in it long ago. It would be very nice here, wouldn't it?"

"Yes," murmured Gervaise, "very nice indeed. At Plassans there were not so many people in one whole street. Look up at that window on the fifth floor—the window, I mean, where those beans are growing. See how pretty that is!"

He, with his usual recklessness, declared he would hire that room for her, and they would live there together.

She turned away with a laugh, and begged him not to talk any more nonsense. The house might stand or fall—they would never have a room in it together.

But Coupeau, all the same, was not reproved when he held her hand longer than was necessary, in bidding her farewell, when they reached Madame Fauconnier's laundry.

For another month the kindly intercourse between Gervaise and Coupeau continued on much the same footing. He thought her wonderfully courageous—declared she was killing herself with hard work all day and sitting up half the night to sew for the children. She was not like the women he had known; she took life too seriously, by far!

She laughed and defended herself modestly. Unfortunately, she said, she had not always been discreet. She alluded to her first confinement when she was not more than fourteen—and to the bottles of anisette she had emptied with her mother—but she had learned much from experience, she said. He was mistaken, however, in thinking she was persevering and strong. She was, on the contrary, very weak, and too easily influenced, as she had discovered to her cost. Her dream had always been, to live in a respectable way, among respectable people; because bad company knocks the life out of a woman. She trembled when she thought of the future, and said she was like a sou thrown up in the air—falling, heads up or down, according to chance—on the muddy pavement. All she had seen, the bad example spread before her childish eyes, had given her valuable lessons. But Coupeau laughed at these gloomy notions and brought back her courage by attempting to put his arm around her waist. She slapped his hands, and he cried out that "for a weak woman, she managed to hurt a fellow considerably!"

As for himself, he was always as merry as a grig, and no fool, either. He parted his hair carefully on one side, wore pretty cravats and patent leather shoes on Sunday, and was as saucy as only a fine Parisian workman can be.

They were of mutual use to each other at the Hôtel Boncœur. Coupeau went for her milk, did many little errands for her, and carried home her linen to her customers, and often took the children out to walk. Gervaise, to return these courtesies, went up to the tiny room where he slept, and in his absence looked over his clothes, sewed on buttons and mended his garments. They grew to be very good and cordial friends. He was to her a constant source of amusement. She listened to the songs he sang, and to their slang and nonsense, which as yet had for her, much of the charm of novelty. But he began to grow uneasy, and his smiles were less frequent. He asked her whenever they met, the same question, "When shall it be?"

She answered invariably with a jest, but passed her days in a fire of indelicate allusions however, which did not bring a flush to her cheek. So long as he was not rough and brutal, she objected to nothing; but one day she was very angry when he, in trying to steal a kiss, tore out a lock of her hair.

About the last of June Coupeau became absolutely morose, and Gervaise was so much disturbed by certain glances he gave her, that she fairly barricaded her door at night. Finally one Tuesday evening, when he had sulked from the previous Sunday, he came to her door at eleven in the evening. At first she refused to open it; but his voice was so gentle, so sad even, that she pulled away the barrier she had pushed against the door for her better protection. When he came in, she was startled, and thought him ill, he was so deadly pale and his eyes were so bright. No, he was not ill, he said, but things could not go on like this; he could not sleep.

"Listen, Madame Gervaise," he exclaimed, with tears in his eyes and a strange choking sensation in his throat. "We must be married at once. That is all there is to be said about it."

Gervaise was astonished and very grave.

"Oh! Monsieur Coupeau, I never dreamed of this, as you know very well, and you must not take such a step lightly."

But he continued to insist—he was certainly fully determined. He had come down to her then, without waiting until morning, merely because he needed a good sleep. As soon as she said yes, he would leave her. But he should not go until he heard that word.

"I cannot say yes in such a hurry," remonstrated Gervaise. "I do not choose to run the risk of your telling me at some future day, that I led you into this. You are making a great mistake, I assure you. Suppose you should not see me for a week—you would forget me entirely. Men sometimes marry for a fancy, and in twenty-four hours would gladly take it all back. Sit down here and let us talk a little."

They sat in that dingy room, lighted only by one candle which they forgot to snuff, and discussed the expediency of their marriage until after midnight—speaking very low, lest they should disturb the children, who were asleep with their heads on the same pillow.

And Gervaise pointed them out to Coupeau. That was an odd sort of dowry to carry a man surely! How could she venture to go to him with such encumbrances? Then too, she was troubled about another thing. People would laugh at him. Her story was known—her lover had been seen, and there would be no end of talk if she should marry now.

To all these good and excellent reasons, Coupeau answered with a shrug of his shoulders. What did he care for talk and gossip? He never meddled with the affairs of others, why should they meddle with his?

Yes, she had children to be sure, and he would look out for them with her. He had never seen a woman in his life, who was so good and so courageous and patient. Besides, that had nothing to do with it! Had she been ugly and lazy, with a dozen dirty children, he would have wanted her, and only her.

"Yes," he continued, tapping her on the knee, "you are the woman I want, and none other. You have nothing to say against that, I suppose?"

Gervaise melted by degrees. Her resolution forsook her, and a weakness of her heart and her senses overwhelmed her in the face of this brutal passion. She ventured only a timid objection or two. Her hands lay loosely folded on her knees, while her face was very gentle and sweet.

Through the open window came the soft air of a fair June night—the candle flickered in the wind—from the street came the sobs of a child, the child of a drunken man, who was lying just in front of the door in the street. From a long distance the breeze brought the notes of a violin, playing at a restaurant for some late marriage festival—a delicate strain it was too, clear and sweet as musical glasses.

Coupeau, seeing that the young woman had exhausted all her arguments, snatched her hands and drew her toward him. She was in one of those moods which she so much distrusted, when she could refuse no one anything. But the young man did not understand this, and he contented himself with simply holding her hands closely in his.

"You say yes, do you not?" he asked.

"How you tease," she replied. "You wish it—well then, yes. Heaven grant that the day will not come when you will be sorry for it."

He started up, lifting her from her feet and kissed her loudly. He glanced at the children.

"Hush!" he said, "we must not wake the boys. Good night."

And he went out of the room. Gervaise, trembling from head to foot, sat for a full hour on the side of her bed without undressing. She was profoundly touched, and thought Coupeau very honest and very kind. The tipsy man in the street uttered a groan like that of a wild beast, and the notes of the violin had ceased.

The next evening, Coupeau urged Gervaise to go with him to call on his sister. But the young woman shrank with ardent fear from this visit to the Lorilleux. She saw perfectly well that her lover stood in dread of these people.

He was in no way dependent on this sister, who was not the eldest, either. Mother Coupeau would gladly give her consent, for she had never been known to contradict her son. In the family, however, the Lorilleux were supposed to earn ten francs per day, and this gave them great weight. Coupeau would never venture to marry unless they agreed to accept his wife.

"I have told them about you," he said. "Gervaise—Good Heavens! what a baby you are! Come there, to-night, with me; you will find my sister a little stiff, and Lorilleux is none too amiable. The truth is they are much vexed—because, you see, if I marry, I shall no longer dine with them—and that is their great economy. But that makes no odds; they won't put you out of doors. Do what I ask, for it is absolutely necessary."

These words frightened Gervaise nearly out of her wits. One Saturday evening, however, she consented. Coupeau came for her at half-past eight.

"They expect you," said Coupeau, as they walked along the street, "and they have become accustomed to the idea of seeing me married. They are really quite amiable to-night. Then, too, if you have never seen a gold chain made, you will be much amused in watching it. They have an order for Monday."

"And have they gold in these rooms?" asked Gervaise.

"I should say so! It is on the walls, on the floors—everywhere!"

By this time they had reached the door, and had entered the courtyard. The Lorilleux lived on the sixth floor—staircase B. Coupeau told her, with a laugh, to keep tight hold of the iron railing and not let it go.

On the fourth floor there was a great quarrel going on—blows and oaths; which did not prevent the neighbors opposite from playing cards with their door wide open for the benefit of the air. When Gervaise reached the fifth floor she was out of breath. Such innumerable stairs were a novelty to her. These winding railings made her dizzy. One family had taken possession of the landing—the father was washing plates in a small earthen pan, near the sink, while the mother was scrubbing the baby before putting it to sleep. Coupeau laughingly bade Gervaise keep up her courage: and at last they reached the top, and she looked around to see whence came the clear, shrill voice, which she had heard above all other sounds, ever since her foot touched the first stair. It was a little, old woman, who sang as she worked, and her work was dressing dolls at three cents apiece. Gervaise clung to the railing, all out of breath, and looked down into the depths below—the gas burner now looked like a star at the bottom of a deep well. The smells, the turbulent life of this great house seemed to rush over her in one tremendous gust. She gasped and turned pale.

"We have not got there yet," said Coupeau, "we have much further to go"; and he turned to the left, and then to the right again. The corridor stretched out before them, faintly lighted by an occasional gas burner—a succession of doors, like those of a prison or a convent, continued to appear—nearly all wide open, showing the sordid interiors. Finally they reached a corridor that was entirely dark.

"Here we are," said the tin-worker. "Isn't it a journey? Look out for three steps. Hold on to the wall."

And Gervaise moved cautiously for ten paces, or more. She counted the three steps, and then Coupeau pushed open a door, without knocking. A bright light streamed forth. They went in.

It was a long, narrow apartment, almost like a prolongation of the corridor; a woolen curtain, faded and spotted, drawn on one side, divided the room in two.

One compartment, the first—contained a bed, pushed under the corner of the Mansard roof—a stove, still warm from the cooking of the dinner; two chairs, a table and a wardrobe. To place this last piece of furniture where it stood, between the bed and the door, had necessitated sawing away a portion of the ceiling.

The second compartment was the workshop. At the back, a tiny forge, with bellows—on the right, a vice, screwed against the wall, under an étagère, where were iron tools piled up—on the left, in front of the window, was a small table, covered with pincers, magnifying glasses, tiny scales and shears—all dirty and greasy.

"We have come!" cried Coupeau, going as far as the woolen curtain.

But he was not answered immediately.

Gervaise, much agitated by the idea that she was entering a place filled with gold, stood behind her friend, and did not know whether to speak or retreat.

The bright light which came from a lamp, and also from a brasier of charcoal in the forge, added to her trouble. She saw Madame Lorilleux, a small, dark woman, agile and strong, drawing with all the vigor of her arms—assisted by a pair of pincers—a thread of black metal, which she passed through the holes of a draw-plate held by the vice. Before the desk or table in front of the window, sat Lorilleux, as short as his wife, but with broader shoulders. He was managing a tiny pair of pincers, and doing some work so delicate that it was almost imperceptible. It was he who first looked up, and lifted his head with its scanty, yellow hair. His face—the color of old wax—was long, and had an expression of physical suffering.

"Ah! it is you, is it? Well! well! But we are in a hurry, you understand. We have an order to fill. Don't come into the workroom. Remain in the chamber." And he returned to his work —his face was reflected in a ball filled with water, through which the lamp sent on his work, a circle of the brightest possible light.

"Find chairs for yourselves," cried Madame Lorilleux. "This is the lady, I suppose. Very well! Very well!"

She rolled up her wire, and carried it to the forge, and then she fanned the coals a little to quicken the heat.

Coupeau found two chairs, and made Gervaise seat herself near the curtain. The room was so narrow that he could not sit beside her, so he placed his chair a little behind, and leaned over her to give her the information he deemed desirable.

Gervaise, astonished by the strange reception given her by these people, and uncomfortable under their sidelong glances, had a buzzing in her ears, which prevented her from hearing what was said.

She thought the woman very old-looking for her thirty years, and also extremely untidy, with her hair tumbling over her shoulders and her dirty camisole.

The husband, not more than a year older, seemed to Gervaise really an old man, with thin, compressed lips and bowed figure. He was in his shirt sleeves, and his naked feet were thrust into slippers down at the heel.

She was infinitely astonished at the smallness of the atélier—at the blackened walls and at the terrible heat.

Tiny drops bedewed the waxed forehead of Lorilleux himself, while Madame Lorilleux threw off her sack, and stood in bare arms and chemise half slipped off.

"And the gold?" asked Gervaise softly.

Her eager eyes searched the corners, hoping to discover, amid all the dirt, something of the splendor of which she had dreamed.

But Coupeau laughed.

"Gold!" he said, "Look! here it is—and here—and here again, at your feet."

He pointed in succession to the fine thread with which his sister was busy, and at another package of wire hung against the wall near the vice; then falling down on his hands and knees, he gathered up from the floor, on the tip of his moistened finger, several tiny specks, which looked like needle points.

Gervaise cried out! "That surely was not gold! That black metal, which looked precisely like iron!"

Her lover laughed, and explained to her the details of the manufacture in which his brother-in-law was engaged.

All this time Lorilleux was watching Gervaise stealthily; and after a violent fit of coughing, he said with an air as if he were speaking to himself:

"I make columns"—

"Yes," said Coupeau, in an explanatory voice, "there are four different kind of chains, and his style is called a column."

Lorilleux uttered a little grunt of satisfaction, all the time at work, with the tiny pincers held between very dirty nails.

Gervaise returned to her chair entirely disenchanted. She thought it was all very ugly and uninteresting. She smiled in order to gratify the Lorilleux, but she was annoyed and troubled at the profound silence they preserved in regard to her marriage, on account of which she had called there that evening.

They began to talk, it was about the lodgers in the house. Madame Lorilleux asked her brother if he had not heard those Benard people quarrelling as he came up stairs. She said the husband always came home tipsy. Then she spoke of the Designer, who was overwhelmed with debts—always smoking and always quarrelling. The landlord was going to turn out the Coquets, who owed three quarters now, and who would put their furnace out on the landing, which was very dangerous. Mademoiselle Remanjon, as she was going down stairs with a bundle of dolls, was just in season to rescue one of the children from being burned alive.

Gervaise was beginning to find the place unendurable. The heat was suffocating—the door could not be opened, because the slightest draught gave Lorilleux a cold. As they ignored the marriage question utterly, she pulled her lover's sleeve to signify her wish to depart. He understood, and was himself annoyed at this affectation of silence.

"We are going," he said coldly. "We do not care to interrupt your work any longer."

He lingered a moment, hoping for a word or an allusion. Suddenly he decided to begin the subject himself.

"We rely on you, Lorilleux. You will be my wife's witness," he said.

The man lifted his head in affected surprise, while his wife stood still in the centre of the work-shop.

"Are you in earnest?" he murmured, and then continued as if soliloquizing, "it is hard to know when this confounded Cadet-Cassis is in earnest——"

"We have no advice to give," interrupted his wife. "It is a foolish notion, this marrying, and it never succeeds. Never—no—never."

She drawled out these last words, examining Gervaise from head to foot.

"My brother is free to do as he pleases, of course," she continued. "Of course his family would have liked——But then people always plan, and things turn out so different. Of course it is none of my business. Had he brought me the lowest of the low, I should have said, 'marry her, and let us live in peace!' He was very comfortable with us, nevertheless. He has considerable flesh on his bones, and does not look as if he had been starved. His soup was always ready to the minute. Tell me, Lorilleux, don't you think that my brother's friend looks like Thérèse—you know whom I mean—that woman opposite, who died of consumption?"

"She certainly does," answered the chain-maker, contemplatively.

"And you have two children, Madame? I said to my brother I could not understand how he could marry a woman with two children. You must not be angry if I think of his interests, it is only natural. You do not look very strong. Say, Lorilleux, don't you think that Madame looks delicate?"

This courteous pair made no allusion to her lameness, but Gervaise felt it to be in their minds. She sat stiff and still before them, her thin shawl, with its yellow palm leaves, wrapped closely about her, and answered in monosyllables as if before her judges. Coupeau, realizing her sufferings, cried out:

"This is all nonsense you are talking! What I want to know is, if the day will suit you, July 29th."

"One day is the same as another, to us," answered his sister, severely. "Lorilleux can do as he pleases in regard to being your witness. I only ask for peace."

Gervaise, in her embarrassment, had been pushing about with her feet some of the rubbish on the floor, then fearing she had done some harm, she stooped to ascertain. Lorilleux hastily approached her with a lamp, and looked at her fingers with evident suspicion.

"Take care," he said. "Those small bits of gold stick to the shoes sometimes, and are carried off without your knowing it."

This was a matter of some importance of course, for his employers weighed what they entrusted to him. He showed the hare's foot with which he brushed the particles of gold from the table, and the skin spread on his knees to receive them.

Madame Lorilleux did not take her eyes from the shoes of her guest.

"If Mademoiselle would be so kind," she murmured, with an amiable smile, "and would just look at her soles herself. There is no cause for offense, I am sure!"

Gervaise, indignant and scarlet, reseated herself and held up her shoes for examination. Coupeau opened the door with a gay good night, and she followed him into the corridor after a word or two of polite farewell.

‑{ CHAPTER III }‑

A Marriage of the People

GERVAISE DID NOT CARE for any great wedding. But Coupeau
objected. It would never do not to have some festivities—a little
drive and a supper perhaps, at a restaurant, he would ask for
nothing more. He vowed that no one should drink too much,
and finally obtained the young woman's consent and organized
a picnic at five francs per head, at the *Moulin d'Argent,* Boulevard de la Chapelle. He made out a list. Among others appeared
the names of two of his comrades, Bibi-la-Grillade and Mes-
Bottes. It was true that Mes-Bottes crooked his elbow, but he was
so deliciously funny that he was always invited to picnics.
Gervaise said she, in her turn would bring her employer,
Madame Fauconnier—all told there would be fifteen at the
table. That was quite enough.

The hour fixed for the party to assemble at the *Moulin
d'Argent,* was one o'clock sharp. From then they were to seek
an appetite on the Plaine St. Denis and return by rail. Saturday
morning, as he dressed, Coupeau thought with some anxiety of
his scanty funds, he supposed he ought to offer a glass of wine
and a slice of ham to his witnesses, while waiting for dinner;
unexpected expenses might arise—no—it was clear that twenty
sous were not enough. He consequently, after taking Claude and
Etienne to Madame Boche, who promised to appear with them
at dinner, ran to his brother-in-law and borrowed ten francs; he
did it with reluctance, and the words stuck in his throat, for
he half expected a refusal. Lorilleux grumbled and growled,
but finally lent the money. But Coupeau heard his sister mutter
under her breath, "that is a good beginning."

The civil marriage was fixed for half-past ten. The day was
clear, and the sun intensely hot. In order not to excite observation—the bridal pair, the mother and the four witnesses separated
—Gervaise walked in front, having the arm of Lorilleux,
while Monsieur Madinier gave his to Mamma Coupeau; on the
opposite sidewalk were Coupeau, Boche and Bibi-la-Grillade.

These three wore black frock-coats, and walked with their arms dangling from their rounded shoulders.

They reached the Mayor's office a half hour too early, and their turn was not reached until nearly eleven. They sat in the corner of the office, stiff and uneasy; pushing back their chairs a little, out of politeness, each time one of the clerks passed them, and when the magistrate appeared, they all rose respectfully. They were bidden to sit down again, which they did, and were the spectators of three marriages—the brides in white and the bridesmaids in pink and blue, quite fine and stylish.

When their own turn came Bibi-la-Grillade had disappeared, and Boche hunted him up in the Square, where he had gone to smoke a pipe. All the forms were so quickly completed that the party looked at each other in dismay, feeling as if they had been defrauded of half the ceremony. Gervaise listened with tears in her eyes, and the old lady wept audibly.

Then they turned to the Register and wrote their names in big, crooked letters—all but the newly-made husband, who, not being able to write, contented himself with making a cross.

Then the clerk handed the certificate to Coupeau. He, admonished by a touch of his wife's elbow, presented him with five sous.

It was quite a long walk from the Mayor's office to the church. The men stopped midway to take a glass of beer, and Gervaise and Mamma Coupeau drank some cassis with water. There was not a particle of shade, for the sun was directly above their heads. The Beadle awaited them in the empty church, he hurried them towards a small chapel, asking them indignantly, if they were not ashamed to mock at religion by coming so late. A Priest came towards them, with an ashen face, faint with hunger, preceded by a boy in a dirty surplice. He hurried through the service, babbling the Latin phrases, with side-long glances at the bridal party. The bride and bridegroom knelt before the altar in considerable embarrassment, not knowing when it was necessary to kneel and when to stand, and not always understanding the gestures made by the clerk.

When at last the signatures were again affixed to the Register in the vestry, and the party stood outside in the sunshine, they had a sensation as if they had been driven at full speed, and were glad to rest.

"I feel as if I had been at the dentist's. We had no time to cry out before it was all over!"

"Yes," muttered Lorilleux; "they take less than five minutes to do what can't be undone in all one's life! Poor Cadet-Cassis!"

Gervaise kissed her new mother with tears in her eyes, but with smiling lips. She answered the old woman gently:

"Do not be afraid. I will do my best to make him happy. If things turn out ill, it shall not be my fault."

The party went at once to the *Moulin d'Argent*.

The guests began to arrive. Madame Fauconnier, stout and handsome, was the first. Then came Mademoiselle Remanjon, in her scanty black dress, which seemed so entirely a part of herself, that it was doubtful if she laid it aside at night. The Gaudron household followed. The husband, enormously stout, looked as if his vest would burst at the least movement; and his wife, who was nearly as huge as himself, was dressed in a delicate shade of violet, which added to her apparent size.

"Ah!" cried Madame Lerat, as she entered; "we are going to have a tremendous shower!" and she bade them all look out the window to see how black the clouds were.

Madame Lerat, Coupeau's eldest sister, was a tall, thin, woman, very masculine in appearance. She brandished an umbrella as she kissed Gervaise.

"It will blow over," said Coupeau, with an air of confidence; "but I wish my sister would come, all the same."

Madame Lorilleux, in fact, was very late. Madame Lerat had called for her, but she had not then begun to dress; "and," said the widow, in her brother's ear: "you never saw anything like the temper she was in!"

They waited another half-hour. The sky was growing blacker and blacker. Clouds of dust were rising along the street, and down came the rain. And it was in the first shower, that Madame Lorilleux arrived—out of temper and out of breath —struggling with her umbrella, which she could not close.

"I had ten minds," she exclaimed, "to turn back. I wanted you to wait until next Saturday. I knew it would rain to-day—I was certain of it!"

She took no notice of Gervaise, who sat by the side of her mother-in-law. She called to Lorilleux, and with his aid carefully wiped every drop of rain from her dress with her handkerchief.

Meanwhile, the shower ceased abruptly, but the storm was evidently not over, for sharp flashes of lightning darted through the black clouds.

Suddenly the rain poured down again. The men stood in front of the door with their hands in their pockets, dismally contemplating the scene. The women crouched together with their hands over their eyes. They were in such terror they could not talk; when the thunder was heard further off, they all plucked up their spirits and became impatient, but a fine rain was falling that looked interminable.

"What are we to do?" cried Madame Lorilleux crossly.

Then Mademoiselle Remanjon timidly observed that the sun perhaps would soon be out, and they might yet go into the country; upon this there was one general shout of derision.

Something must be done, however, to get rid of the time until dinner. Bibi-la-Grillade proposed cards, Madame Lerat suggested story telling. To each proposition a thousand objections were offered. Finally when Lorilleux proposed that the party should visit the tomb of Abélard and Héloise his wife's indignation burst forth.

She had dressed in her best, only to be drenched in the rain and to spend the day in a wine shop it seemed! She had had enough of the whole thing and she should go home. Coupeau and Lorilleux held the door, she exclaiming violently:

"Let me go, I tell you I will go!"

Her husband having induced her to listen to reason, Coupeau went to Gervaise, who was calmly conversing with her mother-in-law and Madame Fauconnier.

"Have you nothing to propose?" he asked, not venturing to add any term of endearment.

"No," she said with a smile, "but I am ready to do anything you wish. I am very well suited as I am."

Her face was indeed as sunny as a morning in May. She spoke to every one kindly and sympathetically. During the storm she had sat with her eyes riveted on the clouds, as if by the light of those lurid flashes she was reading the solemn book of the Future.

Monsieur Madinier had proposed nothing, he stood leaning against the counter with a pompous air; he spat upon the ground, wiped his mouth with the back of his hand and rolled his eyes about.

"We could go to the Musée du Louvre, I suppose," and he smoothed his chin while awaiting the effect of this proposition.

"There are antiquities there, statues, pictures,—lots of things —it is very instructive. Have any of you been there?" he asked.

They all looked at each other. Gervaise had never even heard of the place, nor had Madame Fauconnier, nor Boche. Coupeau thought he had been there one Sunday but he was not sure, but Madame Lorilleux, on whom Madinier's air of importance had produced a profound impression, approved of the idea. The day was wasted anyway, therefore if a little instruction could be got it would be well to try it. As the rain was still falling they borrowed old umbrellas of every imaginable hue, from the establishment, and started forth for the Musée du Louvre.

There were twelve of them and they walked in couples. Madame Lorilleux with Madinier, to whom she grumbled all the way.

"We know nothing about her," she said, "not even where he picked her up. My husband has already lent them ten francs; and who ever heard of a bride without a single relation. She said she had a sister in Paris. Where is she to-day, I should like to know!"

She checked herself and pointed to Gervaise whose lameness was very perceptible as she descended the hill.

"Just look at her!" she murmured. "Wooden legs!"

This epithet was heard by Madame Fauconnier who took up the cudgels for Gervaise who, she said, was as neat as a pin and worked like a tiger.

Finally they reached the Louvre. Here Madinier politely asked permission to take the head of the party; the place was so large, he said, that it was a very easy thing to lose oneself; he knew the prettiest rooms and the things best worth seeing, because he had often been there.

The party entered the museum of Assyrian antiquities. They

shivered and walked about, examining the colossal statues—the gods in black marble—strange beasts and monstrosities, half cats and half women. This was not amusing.

But Madinier shouted to them from the stairs, "Come on! That is nothing! Much more interesting things up here, I assure you!"

With great respect and on the tips of their toes they entered the French gallery.

How many statues! How many pictures! They wished they had all the money they had cost.

They walked around the Salon. Gervaise asked the meaning of one of the pictures—the *Noces de Cana*—Coupeau stopped before *La Joconde* declaring that it was like one of his aunts.

Boche and Bibi-la-Grillade snickered and pushed each other at the sight of the nude female figures, and the Gaudrons, husband and wife, stood open-mouthed and deeply touched—before Murillo's "Virgin."

They heard the cry of the janitors resounding from room to room.

"Time to close the doors!"

They meekly followed one of them, and when they were outside, they uttered a sigh of relief as they put up their umbrellas once more, but one and all affected great pleasure at having been to the Louvre.

When they returned to the *Moulin d'Argent,* they found Madame Boche, with the two children, talking to Mamma Coupeau, near the table—already spread and waiting. When Gervaise saw Claude and Etienne, she took them both on her knees and kissed them lovingly.

"Have they been good?" she asked.

"I should think Coupeau would feel rather queer!" said Madame Lorilleux, as she looked on grimly.

Gervaise had been calm and smiling all day, but she had quietly watched her husband with the Lorilleux. She thought Coupeau was afraid of his sister—cowardly, in fact. The evening previous, he had said he did not care a sou for their opinion on any subject, and that they had the tongues of vipers; but now he was with them, he was like a whipped hound, hung on their words and anticipated their wishes. This troubled his wife, for it augured ill, she thought, for their future happiness.

The guests took their seats with a great clatter of chairs.

There was vermicelli soup, which was cold and greasy and which was eaten with noisy haste. There was, later, a rabbit stew in a deep dish, concerning which Coupeau made a delicate joke implying that the stew was a "gutter rabbit" and still alive, whereupon everybody laughed, Coupeau making a "mew" from deep in his throat. There were veal cutlets and string beans, and when two lean chickens on a bed of watercress were brought in, the men threw off their coats and ate in their shirt sleeves.

Loud chatter and the heavy odors of the banquet filled the room. Madame Boche accused her husband of holding Madame Lerat's hand under the table. Madinier talked politics. Lorilleux expanded on the agreeable coincidence of the Comte de Chambord's birthday with his own, September 29th.

The dessert was now on the table—a floating island flanked by two plates of cheese and two of fruit. The floating island was a great success. Mes-Bottes ate all the cheese and called for more bread. And then, as some of the custard was left in the dish, he pulled it toward him and ate it as if it had been soup.

"How extraordinary!" said Madinier, filled with admiration.

The men rose to light their pipes, and as they passed Mes-Bottes, asked him how he felt.

Bibi-la-Grillade lifted him from the floor, chair and all.

"Zounds!" he cried, "the fellow's weight has doubled!"

Coupeau declared his friend had only just begun his night's work, that he would eat bread until dawn. The waiters, pale with fright, disappeared. Boche went down stairs on a tour of inspection, and stated that the establishment was in a state of confusion, that the proprietor, in consternation, had sent out to all the bakers in the neighborhood; that the house, in fact, had an utterly ruined aspect.

"I should not like to take you to board," said Madame Gaudron.

"Let us have a punch," cried Mes-Bottes.

But Coupeau seeing his wife's troubled face, interfered, and said no one should drink anything more. They had all had enough.

This declaration met with the approval of some of the party, but the others sided with Mes-Bottes.

"Those who are thirsty are thirsty," he said. "No one need drink that does not wish to do so, I am sure," and he added, with a wink, "there will be all the more for those who do!"

Then Coupeau said they would settle the account, and his friend could do as he pleased afterward.

Alas! Mes-Bottes could produce only three francs; he had changed his five-franc piece, and the remainder had melted away somehow on the road from St. Denis. He handed over the three francs, and Coupeau, greatly indignant, borrowed the other two from his brother-in-law, who gave the money secretly, being afraid of his wife.

Monsieur Madinier had taken a plate. The ladies each laid down their five francs quietly and timidly, and then the men retreated to the other end of the room and counted up the amount, and each man added to his subscription five sous for the garçon.

But when Monsieur Madinier sent for the proprietor the little assembly was thrilled, at hearing him say that this was not all, there were "extras."

As this was received with exclamations of rage, he went into explanations. He had furnished twenty-five litres of wine instead of twenty as he agreed. The floating island was an addition, on seeing that the dessert was somewhat scanty, whereupon ensued a formidable quarrel. Coupeau declared he would not pay a sou of the extras.

"There is your money," he said, "take it, and never again will one of us step a foot under your roof!"

"I want six francs more," muttered the man.

The women gathered about in great indignation, not a centime would they give they declared.

Madame Fauconnier had had a wretched dinner—she said she could have had a better one at home for forty sous. Such arrangements always turned out badly, and Madame Gaudron declared aloud, that if people wanted their friends at their weddings they usually invited them out and out.

Gervaise took refuge with her mother-in-law in a distant window, feeling heartily ashamed of the whole scene.

Monsieur Madinier went down stairs with the man and low mutterings of the storm reached the party. At the end of a half hour he reappeared, having yielded to the extent of paying three francs, but no one was satisfied, and they all began a discussion in regard to the extras.

The evening was spoiled, as was Madame Lerat's dress; there was no end to the chapter of accidents.

"I know," cried Madame Lorilleux "that the garçon spilled gravy from the chickens down my back." She twisted and turned herself before the mirror until she succeeded in finding the spot.

"Yes, I knew it," she cried, "and he shall pay for it as true as I live. I wish I had remained at home!"

She left in a rage, and Lorilleux at her heels.

When Coupeau saw her go, he was in actual consternation, and Gervaise saw that it was best to make a move at once. Madame Boche had agreed to keep the children with her for a day or two.

Coupeau and his wife hurried out, in the hope of overtaking Madame Lorilleux, which they soon did, Lorilleux, with the kindly desire of making all smooth said.

"We will go to your door with you."

"Your door indeed!" cried his wife, and then pleasantly went on to express her surprise that they did not postpone their marriage until they had saved enough to buy a little furniture and move away from that hole, up under the roof.

"But I have given up that room," said her brother. "We shall have the one Gervaise occupies, it is larger."

Madame Lorilleux forgot herself; she wheeled around suddenly.

"What!" she exclaimed. "You are going to live in Wooden Legs' room?"

Gervaise turned pale. This name she now heard for the first time, and it was like a slap in the face. She heard much more in her sister-in-law's exclamation than met the ear. The room to which allusion was made, was the one where she had lived with Lantier for a whole month, where she had wept such bitter tears, but Coupeau did not understand that, he was only wounded by the name applied to his wife.

"It is hardly wise of you," he said sullenly, "to nickname people after that fashion, as perhaps you are not aware of what you are called in your Quartier. Cow's-Tail is not a very nice name, but they have given it to you on account of your hair. Why should we not keep that room? It is a very good one."

Madame Lorilleaux would not answer. Her dignity was sadly disturbed at being called Cow's-Tail.

They walked on in silence until they reached the Hôtel Bon-cœur; and just as Coupeau gave the two women a push toward each other, and bade them kiss and be friends, a man who wished to pass them on the right, gave a violent lurch to the left, and came between them.

"Look out!" cried Lorilleux, "it is Father Bazouge. He is pretty full tonight."

Gervaise, in great terror, flew toward the door. Father Bazouge was a man of fifty, his clothes were covered with mud, where he had fallen in the street.

"You need not be afraid," continued Lorilleux, "he will do you no harm. He is a neighbor of ours—the third room on the left in our corridor."

But Father Bazouge was talking to Gervaise. "I am not going to eat you, little one," he said. "I have drank too much, I know very well; but when the work is done, the machinery should be greased a little now and then."

Gervaise retreated further into the doorway, and with difficulty kept back a sob. She nervously entreated Coupeau to take the man away.

Bazouge staggered off, muttering as he did so:

"You won't mind it so much one of these days, my dear. I know something about women. They make a great fuss, but they get used to it all the same."

-[*CHAPTER IV*]-

A Happy Home

$\mathcal{F}$OUR YEARS OF hard and incessant toil followed this day. Gervaise and Coupeau were wise and prudent. They worked hard, and took a little relaxation on Sundays. The wife worked twelve hours of the twenty-four with Madame Fauconnier, and yet found time to keep her own home like waxwork. The husband was never known to be tipsy, but brought home his wages and smoked his pipe at his own window at night before going to bed. They were the bright and shining lights—the good example of the whole Quartier; and as they made jointly about nine francs per day, it was easy to see they were putting by money.

But in the first few months of their married life they were obliged to trim their sails closely, and had some trouble to make both ends meet. They took a great dislike to the Hôtel Bonceur. They longed for a home of their own, with their own furniture. They estimated the cost over and over again, and decided that for three hundred and fifty francs they could venture; but they had little hope of saving such a sum in less than two years, when a stroke of good luck befell them.

An old gentleman in Plassans sent for Claude, to place him at school. He was a very eccentric old gentleman, fond of pictures and art. Claude was a great expense to his mother and when Etienne alone was at home, they saved the three hundred and fifty francs in seven months. The day they purchased their furniture they took a long and happy walk together; for it was an important step they had taken—important not only in their own eyes, but in those of the people around them.

For two months they had been looking for an apartment. They wished, of all things, to take one in the old house where Madame Lorilleux lived, but there was not one single room to be rented, and they were compelled to relinquish the idea. Gervaise was reconciled to this more easily, since she did not care to be thrown in any closer contact with the Lorilleux. They looked further. It was essential that Gervaise should be near her friend and employer, Madame Fauconnier, and they finally succeeded in their search, and were indeed in wonderful luck for they obtained a large room, with a kitchen and tiny bed room, just opposite the establishment of the laundress. It was a small house, two stories, with one steep staircase, and was divided into two lodgings—the one on the right, the other on the left, while the lower floor was occupied by a carriage maker.

Gervaise was delighted. It seemed to her that she was once more in the country—no neighbors, no gossip, no interference; and from the place where she stood and ironed all day at Madame Fauconnier's she could see the windows of her own room.

They moved in the month of April. Gervaise was then near her confinement, but it was she who cleaned and put in order her new home.

It was, indeed, a fair and pleasant home.

"How much do you think we pay here?" Gervaise would ask of each new visitor.

And when too high an estimate was given, she was charmed.

"One hundred and fifty francs—not a penny more," she would exclaim. "Is it not wonderful?"

Her baby was born one afternoon. She would not allow her husband to be sent for, and when he came gayly into the room, he was welcomed by his pale wife, who whispered to him as he stooped over her:

"My dear, it is a girl."

"All right!" said the tin-worker, jesting to hide his real emotion. "I ordered a girl. You always do just what I want!"

He took up the child.

"Let us have a good look at you, young lady! The down on the top of your head is pretty black, I think. Now you must never squall, but be as good and reasonable always as your papa and mamma."

Gervaise, with a faint smile and sad eyes looked at her daughter. She shook her head. She would have preferred a boy, because boys run less risks in a place like Paris.

Madame Lorilleux, who was the baby's godmother, appeared on Saturday evening with a cap and baptism robe, which she had bought cheap, because they had lost their first freshness. The next day Lorilleux, as godfather, gave Gervaise six pounds of sugar. They flattered themselves they knew how to do things properly, and that evening, at the supper given by Coupeau, did not appear empty-handed. Lorilleux came with a couple of bottles of wine under each arm, and his wife brought a large custard which was a specialty of a certain restaurant.

Yes, they knew how to do things—these people—but they also liked to tell of what they did, and they told every one they saw in the next month, that they had spent twenty francs, which came to the ears of Gervaise, who was none too well pleased.

It was at this supper that Gervaise became acquainted with her neighbors on the other side of the house. These were Madame Goujet, a widow, and her son. Up to this time they had exchanged a good morning, when they met on the stairs, or in the street, but as Madame Goujet had rendered some small services on the first day of her illness, Gervaise invited them on the occasion of the baptism.

These people were from the *Departement du Nord*. The mother repaired laces, while the son, a blacksmith by trade, worked in a factory.

They had lived in their present apartment for five years. Beneath the peaceful calm of their lives lay a great sorrow. Goujet, the husband and father had killed a man in a fit of furious intoxication, and then while in prison, had choked himself with his pocket-handkerchief. His widow and child left Lille after this and came to Paris, with the weight of this tragedy on their hearts and heads, and faced the future with indomitable courage and sweet patience. Perhaps they were over proud and reserved, for they held themselves aloof from those about them. Madame Goujet always wore mourning, and her pale serene face was encircled with nun-like bands of white. Goujet was a colossus of twenty-three with a clear fresh complexion, and honest eyes. At the manufactory he went by the name of the Gucule-d'Or, on account of his beautiful blonde beard.

Gervaise took a great fancy to these people, and when she first entered their apartment was charmed with the exquisite cleanliness of all she saw. Madame Goujet opened the door into her son's room to show it to her. It was as pretty and white as the chamber of a young girl. A narrow iron bed, white curtains and quilt, a dressing-table and book-shelves, made up the furniture. A few colored engravings were pinned against the wall and Madame Goujet said that her son was a good deal of a boy still —he liked to look at pictures rather than read. Gervaise sat for an hour with her neighbor, watching her at work with her cushion, its numberless pins and the pretty lace.

The more she saw of her new friends the better Gervaise liked them. They were frugal but not parsimonious. They were the admiration of the neighborhood. Goujet was never seen with a hole or a spot on his garments. He was very polite to all, but a little diffident, in spite of his height and broad shoulders. The girls in the street were much amused to see him look away when they met him—he did not fancy their ways—their forward boldness and loud laughs. One day he came home tipsy. His mother uttered no word of reproach, but brought out a picture of his father which was piously preserved in her wardrobe. And after that lesson Goujet drank no more liquor, though he conceived no hatred for wine.

On Sunday he went out with his mother who was his idol. He went to her with all his troubles and with all his joys as he had done when little.

At first he took no interest in Gervaise, but after a while he began to like her, and treated her like a sister with abrupt familiarity.

Cadet-Cassis—who was a thorough Parisian—thought Gucule-d'Or very stupid. What was the sense of turning away from all the pretty girls he met in the street? But this did not prevent the two young fellows from liking each other very heartily.

For three years the lives of these people flowed tranquilly on, without an event. Gervaise had been elevated in the laundry where she worked, had higher wages, and decided to place Etienne at school. Notwithstanding all her expenses of the household, they were able to save twenty and thirty francs each month. When these savings amounted to six hundred francs, Gervaise could not rest, so tormented was she by ambitious dreams. She wished to open a small establishment herself, and hire apprentices in her turn. She hesitated naturally to take the definite steps, and said they would look around for a shop that would answer their purpose; their money in the savings bank was quietly rolling up. She had bought her clock, the object of her ambition; it was to be paid for in a year—so much each month. It was a wonderful clock, rosewood with fluted columns, and gilt mouldings and pendulum. She kept her bank book under the glass shade, and often when she was thinking of her shop, she stood with her eyes fixed on the clock, as if she were waiting for some especial and solemn moment.

The Coupeaus and the Goujets now went out on Sundays together. It was an orderly party with a dinner at some quiet restaurant. The men drank a glass or two of wine, and came home with the ladies and counted up and settled the expenditures of the day before they separated. The Lorilleux were bitterly jealous of these new friends of their brother's. They declared it had a very queer look to see him and his wife always with strangers rather than with his own family, and Madame Lorilleux began to say hateful things again of Gervaise. Madame Lerat on the contrary, took her part, while mamma Coupeau tried to please every one.

The day that Nana—which was the pet name given to the little girl—was three years old, Coupeau on coming in found his wife in a state of great excitement. She refused to give any explanation, saying in fact there really was nothing the matter, but she finally became so abstracted that she stood still with the plates in her hand, as she laid the table for dinner, and her husband insisted on an explanation.

"If you must know," she said, "that little shop in *la Rue de la Goutte d'Or* is vacant. I heard so only an hour ago and it struck me all of a heap!"

It was a very nice shop in the very house of which they had so often thought. There was the shop itself—a back room—and two others. They were small, to be sure, but convenient and well arranged—only she thought it dear—five hundred francs.

"You asked the price then?"

"Yes, I asked it just out of curiosity," she answered, with an air of indifference, "but it is too dear, decidedly too dear. It would be unwise I think, to take it."

But she could talk of nothing else the whole evening. She drew the plan of the rooms on the margin of a newspaper, and

217

as she talked, she measured the furniture, as if they were to move the next day. Then Coupeau, seeing her great desire to have the place, declared he would see the owner the next morning, for it was possible he would take less than five hundred francs; but how would she like to live so near his sister, whom she detested?

Gervaise was displeased at this, and said she detested no one, and even defended the Lorilleux, declaring they were not so bad, after all. And when Coupeau was asleep, her busy brain was at work arranging the rooms, which as yet they had not decided to hire.

The next day, when she was alone, she lifted the shade from the clock and opened her bank book. Just to think, that her shop and future prosperity lay between those dirty leaves!

Before going to her work she consulted Madame Goujet, who approved of the plan. With a husband like hers, who never drank, she could not fail of success. At noon she called on her sister-in-law to ask her advice, for she did not wish to have the air of concealing anything from the family.

Madame Lorilleux was confounded. What! did Wooden-Legs think of having an establishment of her own! and with an envious heart she stammered out that it would be very well certainly; but when she had recovered herself a little she began to talk of the dampness of the courtyard, and of the darkness of the rez-de-chaussée. Oh! yes, it was a capital place for rheumatism; but of course, if her mind was made up, anything she could say would make no difference.

That night Gervaise told her husband that if he had thrown any obstacles in the way of her taking the shop, she believed she should have fallen sick and died, so great was her longing. But before they came to any decision, they must see if no diminution of the rent could be obtained.

"We can go to-morrow if you say so," was her husband's reply; "you can call for me at six o'clock."

Coupeau was then completing the roof of a three-storied house, and was laying the very last sheets of zinc. It was May, and a cloudless evening. The sun was low in the horizon, and against the blue sky the figure of Coupeau was clearly defined, as he cut his zinc, as quietly as a tailor might have cut out a pair of breeches in his workshop. His assistant, a lad of seventeen, was blowing up the furnace with a pair of bellows, and at each puff a great cloud of sparks arose.

"Put in the irons, Zidore!" shouted Coupeau.

Coupeau took up his last sheet of zinc. It was to be placed on the edge of the roof, near the gutter. Just at that spot the roof was very steep. The man walked along in his list slippers much as if he had been at home, whistling a popular melody. He allowed himself to slip a little, and caught at the chimney, calling to Zidore as he did so:

"Why in thunder don't you bring the irons? What are you staring at?"

Coupeau began to solder the zinc, supporting himself on the point of one foot, or by one finger, not rashly, but with calm deliberation and perfect coolness. He knew what he could do, and never lost his head. His pipe was in his mouth, and he would occasionally turn to spit down into the street below.

"Hallo! Madame Boche!" he cried, as he suddenly caught sight of his old friend crossing the street.

She looked up, laughed, and a brisk conversation ensued between the roof and the street.

They raised their voices, because a carriage was passing, and this brought to a neighboring window a little old woman, who stood in breathless horror, expecting to see the man fall from the roof in another minute.

"Well, good-night!" cried Madame Boche, "I must not detain you from your work."

Coupeau turned and took the iron Zidore held out to him. At the same moment Madame Boche saw Gervaise coming toward her, with little Nana trotting at her side. She looked up to the roof to tell Coupeau, but Gervaise closed her lips with an energetic signal, and then as she reached the old Concierge, she said in a low voice, that she was always in deadly terror that her husband would fall. She never dared look at him when he was in such places.

"It is not very agreeable, I admit," answered Madame Boche. "My man is a tailor, and I am spared all this."

"At first," continued Gervaise, "I had not a moment's peace. I saw him in my dreams on a litter; but now I have got accustomed to it somewhat."

She looked up, keeping Nana behind her skirts, lest the child should call out, and startle her father, who was at that moment on the extreme edge. She saw the soldering iron, and the tiny flame that rose as he carefully passed it along the edges of the zinc. Gervaise, pale with suspense and fear, raised her hands mechanically with a gesture of supplication. Coupeau ascended the steep roof with a slow step; then glancing down, he beheld his wife.

"You are watching me, are you?" he cried, gayly. "Ah, Madame Boche, is she not a silly one? She was afraid to speak to me. Wait ten minutes, will you?"

The two women stood on the sidewalk, having as much as they could do to restrain Nana, who insisted on fishing in the gutter.

The old woman still stood at the window, looking up at the roof, and waiting.

"Just see her," said Madame Boche. "What is she looking at?"

Coupeau was heard lustily singing; with the aid of a pair of compasses, he had drawn some lines, and now proceeded to cut a large fan, this he adroitly, with his tools, folded into the shape of a pointed mushroom. Zidore was again heating the irons. The sun was setting just behind the house, and the whole western sky was flushed with rose fading to a soft violet, and against this sky, the figures of the two men, immeasurably exaggerated, stood clearly out, as well as the strange form of the zinc which Coupeau was then manipulating.

"Zidore! the irons!"

The irons hissed as he applied them, and he called to Gervaise:

"I am coming!"

The chimney to which he had fitted this cap was in the centre of the roof. Gervaise stood watching him, soothed by his calm self-possession. Nana clapped her little hands.

"Papa! Papa!" she cried. "Look!"

The father turned—his foot slipped—he rolled down the roof slowly, unable to catch at anything.

"Good God!" he said, in a choked voice, and he fell—his body turned over twice and crashed into the middle of the street with the dull thud of a bundle of wet linen.

Gervaise stood still. A shriek was frozen on her lips. Madame Boche snatched Nana in her arms, and hid her head that she might not see—and the little old woman opposite, who seemed to have waited for this scene in the drama, quietly closed her windows.

For a week Coupeau's life hung on a thread. His family and his friends expected to see him die from one hour to another. The physician, an experienced physician, whose every visit cost five francs, talked of a lesion, and that word was in itself very terrifying to all but Gervaise, who pale from her vigils, but calm and resolute, shrugged her shoulders, and would not allow herself to be discouraged. Her man's leg was broken, that she knew very well—"but he need not die for that!"—and she watched at his side night and day—forgetting her children, and her home, and everything but him.

On the ninth day, when the physician told her he would recover, she dropped, half fainting, on a chair—and at night she slept for a couple of hours with her head on the foot of his bed.

When she saw Coupeau out of danger, Gervaise allowed his family to approach him as they saw fit. His convalescence would be a matter of months. This was a ground of indignation for Madame Lorilleux.

"What nonsense it was," she said, "for Gervaise to take him home! had he gone to the Hospital he would have recovered as quickly again."

And then she made a calculation of what these four months would cost:—First, there was the time lost, then the physician, the medicines, the wines, and finally the meat for beef-tea. "Yes, it would be a pretty sum to be sure! If they got through it on their savings they would do well; but she believed that the end would be, that they would find themselves head over heels in debt, and they need expect no assistance from his family, for none of them were rich enough to pay for sickness at home!"

One evening Madame Lorilleux was malicious enough to say:

"And your shop, when do you take it? The Concierge is waiting to know what you mean to do."

Gervaise gasped. She had utterly forgotten the shop. She saw the delight of these people when they believed that this plan was given up, and from that day they never lost an occasion of twitting her, on her dream that had toppled over like a house of cards, and she grew morbid, and fancied they were pleased at the accident to their brother which had prevented the realization of their plans.

She tried to laugh, and to show them she did not grudge the money that had been expended in the restoration of her husband's health. She did not withdraw all her savings from the bank at once, for she had a vague hope that some miracle would intervene which would render the sacrifice unnecessary.

Madame Goujet never went out without coming to inquire if there was anything she could do, any commission she could execute. She brought innumerable bowls of soup, and even when Gervaise was particularly busy, washed her dishes for her. Goujet filled her buckets every morning with fresh water, and this was an economy of at least two sous, and in the evening came to sit with Coupeau. He did not say much but his companionship cheered and comforted the invalid. He was tender and compassionate, and was thrilled by the sweetness of Gervaise's voice when she spoke to her husband. Never had he seen such a brave good woman; he did not believe she sat in her chair fifteen minutes in the whole day—she was never tired—never out of temper, and the young man grew very fond of the poor woman as he watched her.

His mother had found a wife for him. A girl whose trade was the same as her own, a lace mender, and as he did not wish to go contrary to her desires he consented that the marriage should take place in September.

But when Gervaise spoke of his future he shook his head.

"All women are not like you, Madame Coupeau," he said, "if they were I should like ten wives."

At the end of two months Coupeau was on his feet again, and could move—with difficulty of course—as far as the window, where he sat with his leg on a chair. The poor fellow was sadly shaken by his accident. He was no philosopher, and he swore from morning until night. His accident was a cursed shame. If his head had been disturbed by drink it would have been different, but he was always sober and this was the result. He saw no sense in the whole thing!

"My father," he said, "broke his neck. I don't say he deserved it, but I do say there was a reason for it. But I had not drunk a drop, and yet over I went, just because I spoke to my child! If there be a Father in Heaven as they say, who watches over us all, I must say He manages things strangely enough sometimes!"

For two months more Coupeau walked with a crutch, and after a while was able to get into the street and then to the outer Boulevard, where he sat on a bench in the sun. His gayety returned, he laughed again and enjoyed doing nothing. For the first time in his life he felt thoroughly lazy, and indolence seemed to have taken possession of his whole being. When he got rid of his crutches he sauntered about and watched the buildings which were in the process of construction in the vicinity, and he jested with the men and indulged himself in a general abuse of work. Of course he intended to begin again as soon as he was quite well, but at present the mere thought made him feel ill, he said.

In the afternoons Coupeau often went to his sister's apartment; she expressed a great deal of compassion for him and showed every attention. When he was first married, he had escaped from her influence, thanks to his affection for his wife, and her's for him. Now he fell under her thumb again; they brought him back by declaring that he lived in mortal terror of his wife.

The first quarrel in their home arose on the subject of Etienne. Coupeau had been with his sister. He came in late and found the children fretting for their dinner. He cuffed Etienne's ears, bade him hold his tongue, and scolded for an hour. He was sure he did not know why he let that boy stay in the house, he was none of his; until that day, he had accepted the child as a matter of course.

Three days after this, he gave the boy a kick, and it was not long before the child, when he heard him coming, ran into the Goujets', where there was always a corner at the table for him.

Gervaise had long since resumed her work. She no longer lifted the globe of her clock to take out her bank book, her savings were all gone, and it was necessary to count the sous pretty closely, for there were four mouths to feed, and they were all dependent on the work of her two hands. When any one found fault with Coupeau and blamed him, she always took his part.

"Think how much he has suffered," she said, with tears in her eyes. "Think of the shock to his nerves! Who can wonder that he is a little sour? Wait awhile though until he is perfectly well, and you will see that his temper will be as sweet as it ever was."

And if any one ventured to observe that he seemed quite well, and that he ought to go to work, she would exclaim:

"No indeed, not yet. It would never do." She did not want him down in his bed again. She knew what the doctor had said, and she every day, begged him to take his own time. She even slipped a little silver into his vest pocket. All this Coupeau accepted as a matter of course. He complained of all sorts of pains and aches to gain a little longer period of indolence, and at the end of six months had begun to look upon himself as a confirmed invalid.

He almost daily dropped into a wine shop with a friend—it was a place where he could chat a little, and where was the harm? Besides, who ever heard of a glass of wine killing a man. But he swore to himself that he would never touch anything but wine—not a drop of brandy should pass his lips. Wine was good for one—prolonged one's life, aided digestion—but brandy was a very different matter. Notwithstanding all these wise resolutions, it came to pass more than once that he came in, after visiting a dozen different cabarets, decidedly tipsy. On these occasions, Gervaise locked her doors and declared she was ill, to prevent the Goujets from seeing her husband.

The poor woman was growing very sad. Every night and morning she passed the shop for which she had so ardently longed. She made her calculations over and over again, until her brain was dizzy. Two hundred and fifty francs rent—one hundred and fifty for moving and the apparatus she needed—one hundred francs to keep things going until business began to come in. No, it could not be done under five hundred francs.

She said nothing of this to any one, deterred only by the fear of seeming to regret the money she had spent for her husband during his illness. She was pale and dispirited at the thought that she must work five years at least before she could save that much money.

One evening, Gervaise was alone. Goujet entered—took a chair in silence, and looked at her as he smoked his pipe. He seemed to be revolving something in his mind. Suddenly he took his pipe from his mouth.

"Madame Gervaise," he said, "will you allow me to lend you the money you require?"

She was kneeling at a drawer, laying some towels in a neat pile. She started up, red with surprise. He had seen her standing that very morning for a good ten minutes, looking at the shop; so absorbed that she had not seen him pass.

She refused his offer, however. No, she could never borrow money when she did not know how she could return it, and when he insisted, she replied:

"But your marriage? This is the money you have saved for that."

"Don't worry on that account," he said with a heightened color. "I shall not marry. It was an idea of my mother's, and I prefer to lend you the money."

They looked away from each other. Their friendship had a certain element of tenderness which each silently recognized.

Gervaise accepted finally, and went with Goujet to see his mother, whom he had informed of his intentions. They found her somewhat sad, with her serene, pale face bent over her work. She did not wish to thwart her son, but she no longer approved of the plan, and she told Gervaise why. With kind frankness, she pointed out to her that Coupeau had fallen into evil habits and was living on her labors, and would in all probability continue to do so.

Finally it was agreed she should have five hundred francs, and should return the money by paying each month, twenty francs on account.

"Well, well!" cried Coupeau, as he heard of this financial transaction; "we are in luck. There is no danger with us to be sure, but if he were dealing with knaves, he might never see hide or hair of his cash again!"

The next day the shop was taken, and Gervaise ran about with such a light heart, that there was a rumor that she had been cured of her lameness by an operation.

┤ CHAPTER V ├

Ambitious Dreams

THE BOCHE COUPLE, on the first of April, moved also, and took the lôge of the great house in La Rue de la Goutte d'Or. Things had turned out very nicely for Gervaise who, having always got on very comfortably with the Concierge in the house in Rue Neuve, dreaded lest she should fall into the power of some tyrant who would quarrel over every drop of water that was spilled, and a thousand other trifles like that. But with Madame Boche, all would go smoothly.

The day the lease was to be signed, and Gervaise stood in her new home, her heart swelled with joy. She was finally to live in that house, like a small town, with its intersecting corridors, instead of streets.

She felt a strange timidity—a dread of failure—when she found herself face to face with her enterprise. The struggle for bread was a terrible and an increasing one, and it seemed to her for a moment that she had been guilty of a wild, foolhardy act— like throwing herself into the jaws of a machine.

In four days the shop should have been ready for them; but the repairs hung on for three weeks. At first they intended simply to have the paint scrubbed but it was so shabby and worn, that Gervaise repainted at her own expense. Coupeau went every morning, not to work, but to inspect operations; and Boche dropped the vest or pantaloons on which he was working, and gave the benefit of his advice, and the two men spent the whole day smoking and spitting, and arguing over each stroke of the brush. Some days the painters did not appear at all; on others they came and walked off in an hour's time, not to return again.

Poor Gervaise wrung her hands in despair. But finally after

two days of energetic labor, the whole thing was done, and the men walked off with their ladders, singing lustily.

Then came the moving, and finally Gervaise called herself settled in her new home and was pleased as a child. As she came up the street she could see her sign afar off.

CLEAR STARCHER.

LACES AND EMBROIDERIES

DONE UP WITH ESPECIAL CARE.

The two first words were painted in large yellow letters on a pale blue ground.

In the recessed window, shut in at the back by muslin curtains, lay men's shirts, delicate handkerchiefs and cuffs—all these were on blue paper and Gervaise was charmed.

Gervaise seated herself and looked round, happy in the cleanliness of all about her.

Behind the shop was her bedroom and her kitchen from which a door opened into the court. Nana's bed stood in a little room at the right, and Etienne was compelled to share his with the baskets of soiled clothes.

The new shop created a great excitement in the neighborhood. Some people declared that the Coupeaus were on the road to ruin, they had in fact spent the whole five hundred francs, and were penniless contrary to their intentions. The morning that Gervaise first took down her shutters, she had only six francs in the world, but she was not troubled, and at the end of a week she told her husband after two hours of abstruse calculations, that they had taken in enough to cover their expenses.

The Lorilleux were in a state of rage, and one morning when the apprentice was emptying on the sly a bowl of starch which she had burned in making, just as Madame Lorilleux was passing, she rushed in and accused her sister-in-law of insulting her. After this all friendly relations were at an end.

"It all looks very strange to me," sniffed Madame Lorilleux; "I can't tell where the money comes from, but I have my suspicions," and she went on to intimate that Gervaise and Goujet were altogether too intimate. This was the groundwork of many fables, she said Wooden Legs was so mild and sweet that she had deceived her to the extent that she had consented to become Nana's god-mother, which had been no small expense; but now things were very different. If Gervaise were dying and asked her for a glass of water she would not give it.

Gervaise lived a busy life, and took no notice of all this foolish gossip and strife. She greeted her friends with a smile from the door of her shop, where she went for a breath of fresh air. All the people in the neighborhood liked her. When people called her good she laughed. Why should she not be good? She had seen all her dreams realized. She remembered what she once said—that she wanted to work hard, have plenty to eat—a home to herself, where she could bring up her children—not be beaten, and die in her bed! As to dying in her bed, she added—she wanted that still, but she would put it off as long as possible, "if you please!" It was to Coupeau himself that Gervaise was especially sweet. He had finally resumed his trade, and as the shop where he worked was at the other end of Paris, she gave him every morning forty sous for his breakfast, his wine and tobacco. Two days out of six, however, Coupeau would meet a friend, drink up his forty sous, and return to breakfast. Once, indeed, he sent a note, saying that his account at the cabaret exceeded his forty sous—he was in pledge, as it were—would his wife send the money? She laughed and shrugged her shoulders. Where was the harm in her husband's amusing himself a little? A woman must give a man a long rope if she wished to live in peace and comfort. It was not far from words to blows—she knew that very well.

The hot weather had come. One afternoon in June the ten irons were heating on the stove, the door was open into the street, but not a breath of air came in.

"What a melting day!" said Gervaise, who was stooping over a great bowl of starch. She had rolled up her sleeves and taken off her smock, and stood in her chemise and white skirt; the soft hair in her neck was curling on her white throat. She dipped each cuff in the starch, the fronts of the shirts and the whole of the skirts. Then she rolled up the pieces tightly and placed them neatly in a square basket, after having sprinkled with clear water all those portions which were not starched.

"This basket is for you, Madame Putois," she said; "and you will have to hurry, for they dry so fast in this weather."

Madame Putois was a thin little woman, who looked cool and comfortable in her tightly-buttoned dress. She had not taken her cap off, but stood at the table, moving her irons to and fro with the regularity of an automaton. Suddenly she exclaimed:

"Put on your smock, Clémence; there are three men looking in, and I don't like such things."

Clémence grumbled and growled. What did she care what she liked? She could not and would not roast to suit anybody.

"Clémence, put on your smock," said Gervaise; "Madame Putois is right—it is not proper."

Clémence muttered, but obeyed, and consoled herself by giving the apprentice, who was ironing hose and towels by her side, a little push. Gervaise had a cap belonging to Madame Boche in her hand, and was ironing the crown with a round ball, when a tall bony woman came in. She was a laundress.

"You have come too soon, Madame Bijard!" cried Gervaise; "I said tonight. It is very inconvenient for me to attend to you at this hour." At the same time, however, Gervaise amiably laid down her work and went for the dirty clothes, which she piled up in the back shop. It took the two women nearly an hour to sort them and mark them with a stitch of colored cotton.

At this moment Coupeau entered.

"By Jove!" he said; "the sun beats down on one's head like a hammer." He caught at the table to sustain himself; he had been drinking—a spider's web had caught in his dark hair, where many a white thread was apparent. His under jaw dropped a little, and his smile was good-natured but silly.

Gervaise asked her husband if he had seen the Lorilleux, in rather a severe tone; when he said no, she smiled at him without a word of reproach.

"You had best go and lie down," she said pleasantly, "we are very busy and you are in our way. Did I say thirty-two handkerchiefs, Madame Bijard? Here are two more, that makes thirty-four."

But Coupeau was not sleepy and he preferred to remain where he was. Gervaise called Clémence and bade her to count the linen while she made out the list. She glanced at each piece as she wrote. She knew many of them by the color. That pillow-slip belonged to Madame Boche because it was stained with the pomade she always used, and so on through the whole. Gervaise was seated with these piles of soiled linen about her. Augustine, whose great delight was to fill up the stove had done so now, and it was red hot. Coupeau leaned towards Gervaise.

"Kiss me," he said. "You are a good woman."

As he spoke he gave a sudden lurch and fell among the skirts.

"Do take care," said Gervaise impatiently, "you will get them all mixed again," and she gave him a little push with her foot whereat all the other women cried out.

"He is not like most men," said Madame Putois, "they generally wish to beat you when they come in like this."

Gervaise already regretted her momentary vexation and assisted her husband to his feet and then turned her cheek to him with a smile, but he put his arm round her and kissed her neck. She pushed him aside with a laugh.

"You ought to be ashamed!" she said, but yielded to his embrace, and the long kiss they exchanged before these people, amid the sickening odor of the soiled linen, and the alcoholic fumes of his breath, was the first downward step in the slow descent of their degradation.

Gervaise quietly pushed him toward his room. He struggled a little, and with a silly laugh asked if Clémence was not coming too.

Gervaise undressed her husband and tucked him up in bed as if he had been a child, and then returned to her fluting irons in time to still a grand dispute that was going on about an iron that had not been properly cleaned.

The day after all this, Coupeau had a frightful headache, and did not rise until late—too late to go to his work. About noon he began to feel better, and toward evening was quite himself. His wife gave him some silver, and told him to go out and take the air, which meant, with him, taking some wine.

One glass washed down another, but he came home as gay as a lark, and quite disgusted with the men he had seen who were drinking themselves to death.

"Where is your lover?" he said to his wife, as he entered the shop. This was his favorite joke. "I never see him nowadays, and must hunt him up."

He meant Goujet, who came but rarely, lest the gossips in the neighborhood should take it upon themselves to gabble. Once in about ten days he made his appearance in the evening, and installed himself in a corner in the back shop, with his pipe. He rarely spoke, but laughed at all Gervaise said.

On Saturday evenings the establishment was kept open half the night. A lamp hung from the ceiling, with the light thrown down by a shade. The shutters were put up at the usual time, but as the nights were very warm, the door was left open; and as the hours wore on, the women pulled their jackets open a little more at the throat, and he sat in his corner and looked on as if he were at a theatre.

The silence of the street was broken by a passing carriage. Two o'clock struck—no longer a sound from outside. At half-past two a man hurried past the door, carrying with him a vision of flying arms, piles of white linen, and a glow of yellow light.

Goujet, wishing to save Etienne from Coupeau's rough treatment, had taken him to the place where he was employed, to blow the bellows, with the prospect of becoming an apprentice as soon as he was old enough; and Etienne thus became another tie between the clear-starcher and the blacksmith.

All their little world laughed, and told Gervaise that her friend worshipped the very ground she trod upon. She colored and looked like a girl of sixteen.

"Dear boy," she said to herself, "I know he loves me; but never has he said, or will he say, a word of the kind to me!" And she was proud of being loved in this way. When she was disturbed about anything, her first thought was to go to him. When by chance they were left alone together, they were never disturbed by wondering if their friendship verged on love. There was no harm in such affection.

Nana was now six years old and a most troublesome little sprite. Her mother took her every morning to a school in la Rue Polonçeau, to a certain Mademoiselle Josse. Here she did all manner of mischief. She put ashes into the teacher's snuff box, pinned the skirts of her companions together. Twice the young lady was sent home in disgrace, and then taken back again for the sake of the six francs each month. As soon as school hours were over, Nana revenged herself for the hours of enforced quiet she had passed, by making the most frightful din in the courtyard and the shop.

She found able allies in Pauline and Victor Boche. The whole great house resounded with the most extraordinary noises. The thumps of children falling down stairs, little feet tearing up one stair-case and down another, and bursting out on the sidewalk like a band of pilfering, impudent sparrows.

Madame Gaudron alone had nine—dirty, unwashed and unkempt—their stockings hanging over their shoes and the slits in their garments showing the white skin beneath. Another woman on the fifth floor had seven, and they came out in twos and threes from all the rooms. Nana reigned over this band, among which there were some half-grown and others mere infants. Her prime ministers were Pauline and Victor; to them she delegated a little of her authority, while she played mamma— undressed the youngest only to dress them again—cuffed them and punished them at her own sweet will, and with the most fantastic disposition. The band pranced and waded through the gutter that ran from the dye-house and emerged with blue or green legs. Nana decorated herself and the others with shavings from the cabinet makers, which they stole from under the very noses of the workmen.

One day there was a terrible scene. Nana had invented a beautiful game. She had stolen a wooden shoe belonging to Madame Boche; she bored a hole in it and put in a string, by which she could draw it like a cart. Victor filled it with apple-parings, and they started forth in a procession, Nana drawing the shoe in front, followed by the whole flock, little and big, an imp about the height of a cigar box at the end. They all sang a melancholy ditty full of "ah's" and "oh's." Nana declared this to be always the custom at funerals.

"What on earth are they doing now?" murmured Madame Boche suspiciously, and then she came to the door and peered out.

"Good heavens!" she cried; "it is my shoe they have got."

She slapped Nana, cuffed Pauline and shook Victor. Gervaise

was filling a bucket at the fountain, and when she saw Nana with her nose bleeding, she rushed toward the Concierge, and asked how she dared strike her child.

The Concierge replied that any one who had a child like that, had best keep her under lock and key. The end of this was, of course, a complete break between the old friends.

It was not long before Gervaise realized she had made a mistake—for when she was one day late with her October rent, Madame Boche complained to the proprietor, who came blustering to her shop with his hat on. Of course, too, the Lorilleux extended the right hand of fellowship at once to the Boche people.

There came a day, however, when Gervaise found it necessary to call on the Lorilleux. It was on Mamma Coupeau's account, who was sixty-seven years old, nearly blind and helpless. They must all unite in doing something for her now. Gervaise thought it a burning shame that a woman of her age, with three well-to-do children, should be allowed for a moment to regard herself as friendless and forsaken. And as her husband refused to speak to his sister, Gervaise said she would.

She entered the room like a whirlwind, without knocking. Everything was just as it was on that night when she had been received by them in a fashion which she had never forgotten nor forgiven. "I have come," cried Gervaise, "and I dare say you wish to know why, particularly as we are at daggers-drawn. Well! then, I have come on Mamma Coupeau's account. I have come to ask if we are to allow her to beg her bread from door to door—"

"Indeed!" said Madame Lorilleux, with a sneer, and she turned away.

But Lorilleux lifted his pale face.

"What do you mean?" he asked, and as he had understood perfectly, he went on.

"What is this cry of poverty about? The old lady ate her dinner with us yesterday. We do all we can for her, I am sure. We have not the mines of Peru within our reach, but if she thinks she is to run to and fro between our houses, she is much mistaken. I, for one, have no liking for spies." He then added, as he took up his microscope, "When the rest of you agree to give five francs per month toward her support, we will do the same." Gervaise was calmer now—these people always chilled the very marrow in her bones—and she went on to explain her views. Five francs were not enough for each of the old lady's children to pay. She could not live on fifteen francs per month.

"And why not?" cried Lorilleux, "she ought to do so. She can see well enough to find the best bits in a dish before her, and she can do something toward her own maintenance." If he had the means to indulge such laziness he should not consider it his duty to do so, he added.

Then Gervaise grew angry again. She looked at her sister-in-law, and saw her face set in vindictive firmness.

"Keep your money," she cried. "I will take care of your mother. I found a starving cat in the street the other night and took it in. I can take in your mother too. She shall want for nothing. Good heavens, what people!"

Gervaise shut the door with a bang.

On the very next day, Madame Coupeau came to her. A large bed was put in the room where Nana slept. The moving did not take long, for the old lady had only this bed, a wardrobe, table, and two chairs. The table was sold, and the chairs new-seated, and the old lady the evening of her arrival washed the dishes and swept up the room, glad to make herself useful.

Three years passed away. There were reconciliations and new quarrels. Gervaise continued to be liked by her neighbors; she paid her bills regularly, and was a good customer. When she went out she received cordial greeting on all sides, and she was more fond of going out in these days than of yore. She liked to stand at the corners and chat. She liked to loiter with her arms full of bundles at a neighbor's window and hear a little gossip.

CHAPTER VI

Goujet at His Forge

ONE AUTUMNAL AFTERNOON Gervaise, who had been to carry a basket of clothes home to a customer who lived a good way off, found herself in La Rue des Poissonnièrs just as it was growing dark. It had rained in the morning, and the air was close and warm. She was tired with her walk, and felt a great desire for something good to eat. Just then she lifted her eyes and seeing the name of the street, she took it into her head that she would call on Goujet at his forge. But she would ask for Etienne, she said to herself. But she did not know the number, but she could find it, she thought. She wandered along and stood bewildered, looking toward Montmartre; all at once she heard the measured click of hammers—and concluded that she had stumbled on the place at last. She did not know where the entrance to the building was, but she caught a gleam of a red light in the distance; she walked toward it and was met by a workman.

"Is it here, sir," she said, timidly, "that my child—a little boy, that is to say—works? A little boy by the name of Etienne?"

"Etienne! Etienne!" repeated the man, swaying from side to side. The wind brought from him to her an intolerable smell of brandy, which caused Gervaise to draw back, and say timidly:

"Is it here that Monsieur Goujet works?"

"Ah! Goujet, yes. If it is Goujet you wish to see, go to the left."

Gervaise obeyed his instructions and found herself in a large room with the forge at the further end. She spoke to the first man she saw, when suddenly the whole room was one blaze of light. The bellows had sent up leaping flames which lighted every crevice and corner of the dusty old building, and Gervaise recognized Goujet before the forge, with two other men. She went toward him.

"Madame Gervaise!" he exclaimed in surprise, his face radiant with joy, and then seeing his companions laugh and wink, he pushed Etienne toward his mother. "You came to see your boy," he said; "he does his duty like a hero."

"I am glad of it," she answered; "but what an awful place this is to get at!"

And she described her journey as she called it, and then asked why no one seemed to know Etienne there.

"Because," said the blacksmith, "he is called Zou Zou here, as his hair is cut as short as a Zouave's."

This visit paid by Gervaise to the Forge was only the first of many others. She often went on Saturdays when she carried the clean linen to Madame Goujet, who still resided in the same house as before. The first year Gervaise had paid them twenty francs each month, or rather the difference between the amount of their washing, seven or eight francs, and the twenty which she agreed upon. In this way she had paid half the money she had borrowed, when one quarter-day, not knowing to whom to turn, as she had not been able to collect her bills punctually, she ran to the Goujets and borrowed the amount of her rent from them. Twice since she had asked a similar favor, so that the amount of her indebtedness now stood at four hundred and twenty-five francs.

Now she no longer paid any cash, but did their washing.

The Saturday after the first visit paid by Gervaise to the Forge was also the first of the month. When she reached Madame Goujet's, her basket was so heavy that she panted for two good minutes before she could speak.

"Have you brought everything?" asked Madame Goujet, who was very exacting on this point.

"Everything is here," answered Gervaise, with a smile. "You know I never leave anything behind."

"That is true," replied the elder woman. "You have many faults, my dear; but not that one yet."

And while the laundress emptied her basket, laying the linen on the bed, Madame Goujet paid her many compliments. She never burned her clothes, nor ironed off the buttons, nor tore them; but she did use a trifle too much blueing, and made her shirts too stiff.

"I have no intention of disparaging your work," answered Madame Goujet. "I never saw any one who did up laces and embroideries as you do, and the fluting is simply perfect: the only trouble is a little too much starch, my dear. Goujet does not care to look like a fine gentleman."

She took up her book and drew a pen through the pieces as she spoke. Everything was there. She brought out the bundle of soiled clothes. Gervaise put them in her basket, and hesitated.

"Madame Goujet," she said, at last, "if you do not mind, I should like to have the money for this week's wash."

The account this month was larger than usual, ten francs and over. Madame Goujet looked at her gravely.

"My child," she said, slowly, "it shall be as you wish. I do not refuse to give you the money if you desire it; only this is not the way to get out of debt. I say this with no unkindness, you understand. Only you must take care."

Gervaise, with downcast eyes, received the lesson meekly. "I need the ten francs to complete the amount due the coal merchant," she said.

But her friend heard this with a stern countenance, and told her she should reduce her expenses; but she did not add, that she too, intended to do the same, and that in future she should do her washing herself, as she had formerly done, if she were to be out of pocket thus.

When Gervaise was on the staircase her heart was light, for she cared little for the reproof now that she had the ten francs in her hand; she was becoming accustomed to paying one debt by contracting another.

Midway on the stairs she met a tall woman coming up with a fresh mackerel in her hand, and behold! it was Virginie, the girl whom she had whipped in the Lavatory. The two looked each other full in the face. Gervaise instinctively closed her eyes, for she thought the girl would slap her in the face with the mackerel. But no; Virginie gave a constrained smile. Then the laundress, whose huge basket filled up the stairway, and who did not choose to be outdone in politeness, said:

"I beg your pardon—"

"Pray don't apologize," answered Virginie, in a stately fashion.

And they stood and talked for a few minutes with not the smallest allusion, however, to the past.

Virginie, then about twenty-nine, was really a magnificent-looking woman; head well-set on her shoulders, and a long, oval face crowned by bands of glossy black hair. She told her history in a few brief words. She was married. Had married the previous spring a cabinet-maker who had given up his trade, and was hoping to obtain a position on the police force. She had just been out to buy this mackerel for him.

"He adores them," she said, "and we women spoil our husbands, I think. But come up. We are standing in a draught here."

When Gervaise had in her turn told her story, and added that Virginie was living in the very rooms where she had lived, and where her child was born, Virginie became still more urgent that she should go up. "It is always pleasant to see a place where one has been happy," she said. She herself had been living on the other side of the water, but had got tired of it, and had moved into these rooms only two weeks ago. She was not settled yet. Her name was Madame Poisson.

"And mine," said Gervaise, "is Coupeau."

Gervaise was a little suspicious of all this courtesy. Might not some terrible revenge be hidden under it all? and she determined to be well on her guard. But as Virginie was so polite just now, she must be polite in her turn.

Poisson, the husband, was a man of thirty-five, with a moustache and imperial; he was seated at a table near the window, making little boxes. His only tools were a pen-knife, a tiny saw, and a glue pot; he was executing the most wonderful and delicate carving, however. He never sold his work, but made presents of it to his friends. It amused him while he was awaiting his appointment.

Poisson rose, and bowed politely to Gervaise, whom his wife called an old friend. But he did not speak—his conversational powers not being his strong point. He cast a plaintive glance at the mackerel, however, from time to time. Gervaise looked around the room, and described her furniture, and where it had stood. How strange it was, after losing sight of each other so long, that they should occupy the same apartment! Virginie entered into new details. He had a small inheritance from his aunt, and she herself sewed a little—made a dress now and then. At the end of a half hour Gervaise rose to depart; Virginie went to the head of the stairs with her, and there both hesitated. Gervaise fancied that Virginie wished to say something about Lantier and Adèle, but they separated without touching on these disagreeable topics.

This was the beginning of a great friendship. In another week Virginie could not pass the shop without going in, and sometimes she remained for two or three hours. At first, Gervaise was very uncomfortable; she thought every time Virginie opened her lips that she should hear Lantier's name. Lantier was in her mind all the time she was with Madame Poisson. It was a stupid thing to do after all, for what on earth did she care what had become of Lantier or of Adèle? but she was none the less curious to know something about them.

Winter had come—the fourth winter that the Coupeaus had spent in La Rue de la Goutte d'Or. This year December and January were especially severe, and after New Year's the snow lay three weeks in the street without melting. There was plenty of work for Gervaise, and her shop was delightfully warm and singularly quiet, for the carriages made no noise in the snow-covered streets.

Gervaise took especial pleasure in her coffee at noon. Her apprentices had no reason to complain, for it was hot and strong and unadulterated by chicory. On the morning of Twelfth Day the clock had struck twelve and then half-past, and the coffee was not ready. Gervaise was ironing some muslin curtains. Clémence, with a frightful cold, was as usual at work on a man's shirt. Madame Putois was ironing a skirt on a board, with a cloth laid on the floor to prevent the skirt from being soiled. Mamma Coupeau brought in the coffee, and as each one of the women took a cup with a sigh of enjoyment, the street door opened, and Virginie came in with a rush of cold air.

"Heavens!" she cried, "it is awful! my ears are cut off!"

"You have come just in time for a cup of hot coffee," said Gervaise, cordially.

"And I shall be only too glad to have it!" answered Virginie, with a shiver. She had been waiting at the grocer's, she said, until she was chilled through and through. The heat of that room was delicious, and then she stirred her coffee, and said she liked the damp, sweet smell of the freshly ironed linen. She and Mamma Coupeau were the only ones who had chairs; the others sat on wooden footstools, so low that they seemed to be on the floor. Virginie suddenly stooped down to her hostess, and said, with a smile:

"Do you remember that day at the Lavatory?"

Gervaise colored; she could not answer. This was just what she had been dreading. In a moment she felt sure she should hear Lantier's name. She knew it was coming, Virginie drew nearer to her. The apprentices lingered over their coffee, and told each other, as they looked stupidly into the street, what they would do if they had an income of ten thousand francs. Virginie changed her seat and took a footstool by the side of Gervaise, who felt weak and cowardly, and helpless to change the conversation, or to stave off what was coming. She breathlessly awaited the next words, her heart big with an emotion which she would not acknowledge to herself.

"I do not wish to give you any pain," said Virginie, blandly. "Twenty times the words have been on my lips, but I hesitated. Pray don't think I bear you any malice."

She tipped up her cup and drank the last drop of her coffee. Gervaise, with her heart in her mouth, waited in a dull agony of suspense, asking herself if Virginie could have forgiven the insult in the Lavatory. There was a glitter in the woman's eyes she did not like.

"You had an excuse," Virginie added, as she placed her cup on the table. "You had been abominably treated. I should have killed some one," and then dropping her little affected tone, she continued more rapidly—

"They were not happy, I assure you, not at all happy. They lived in a dirty street, where the mud was up to their knees. I went to breakfast with them two days after he left you, and found them in the height of a quarrel. You know that Adèle is a wretch. She is my sister, to be sure, but she is a wretch all the same. As to Lantier—well, you know him, so I need not describe him. But for a 'yes' or a 'no,' he would not hesitate to thrash any woman that lives. Oh, they had a beautiful time! their quarrels were heard all over the neighborhood. One day the police were sent for, they made such a hubbub."

She talked on and on, telling things that were enough to make the hair stand up on one's head. Gervaise listened, as pale as death, with a nervous trembling of her lips which might have been taken for a smile. For seven years she had never heard Lantier's name, and she would not have believed that she could have felt any such overwhelming agitation. She could no longer be jealous of Adèle, but she smiled grimly as she thought of the blows she had received in her turn from Lantier, and she would have listened for hours to all that Virginie had to tell; but she did not ask a question for some time. Finally she said:

"And do they still live in that same place?"

"No, indeed! but I have not told you all yet. They separated a week ago."

"Separated!" exclaimed the clear-starcher.

"Who is separated?" asked Clémence, interrupting her conversation with Mamma Coupeau.

"No one," said Virginie, "or at least no one whom you know."

As she spoke she looked at Gervaise, and seemed to take a positive delight in disturbing her still more. She suddenly asked her, what she would do or say if Lantier should suddenly make his appearance, for men were so strange, no one could ever tell what they would do—Lantier was quite capable of returning to his old love. Then Gervaise interrupted her and rose to the occasion. She answered with grave dignity that she was married now, and that if Lantier should appear she should ask him to leave. There could never be anything more between them, not even the most distant acquaintance.

"Madame Poisson, he shall never touch my little finger again! It is finished."

As she uttered these last words she traced a cross in the air to seal her oath; and as if desirous to put an end to the conversation, she called out to her women—

"Do you think the ironing will be done to-day, if you sit still? To work! to work!"

The women did not move; they were lulled to apathy by the heat and Gervaise herself found it very difficult to resume her labors. Her curtains had dried in all this time, and some coffee had been spilled on them, and she must wash out the spots.

"Au revoir!" said Virginie. "I came out to buy a half-pound of cheese. Poisson will think I am frozen to death!"

The better part of the day was now gone, and it was this way every day—for the shop was the refuge and haunt of all the chilly people in the neighborhood. Gervaise liked the reputation of having the most comfortable room in the Quartier, and she held her receptions—as the Lorilleux and Boche clique said, with a sniff of disdain. She would, in fact, have liked to bring in the very poor whom she saw shivering outside. She became very friendly toward a journeyman painter, an old man of seventy, who lived in a loft of the house, where he shivered with cold and hunger. He had lost his three sons in the Crimea, and for two years his hand had been so cramped by rheumatism that he could not hold a brush.

Whenever Gervaise saw Father Bru she called him in, made a place for him near the stove, and give him some bread and cheese. Father Bru, with his white beard, and his face wrinkled like an old apple, sat in silent content, for hours at a time, enjoying the warmth and the crackling of the coke.

"What are you thinking about?" Gervaise would say, gayly.

"Of nothing—of all sorts of things," he would reply, with a dazed air.

The workwomen laughed, and thought it a good joke to ask if he were in love. He paid little heed to them, but relapsed into silent thought.

From this time Virginie often spoke to Gervaise of Lantier, and one day she said she had just met him. But as the clear-starcher made no reply, Virginie then said no more. But on the next day she returned to the subject, and told her that he had talked long and tenderly of her. Gervaise was much troubled by these whispered conversations in the corner of her shop. The name of Lantier made her faint and sick at heart. She believed herself to be an honest woman. She meant, in every way, to do right and to shun the wrong, because she felt that only in doing so could she be happy. She did not think much of Coupeau, because she was conscious of no short-comings towards him. But she thought of her friend at the Forge, and it seemed to her that this return of her interest in Lantier, faint and undecided as it was, was an infidelity to Goujet, and to that tender friendship which had become so very precious to her. Her heart was much troubled in these days. She dwelt on that time when her first lover left her. She imagined another day, when, quitting Adèle, he might return to her with that old familiar trunk.

When she went into the street, it was with a spasm of terror. She fancied that every step behind her was Lantier's. She dared not look around, lest his hand should glide about her waist. He might be watching for her at any time. He might come to her door in the afternoon, and this idea brought a cold sweat to her forehead, because he would certainly kiss her on her ear, as he had often teased her by doing in the years gone by. It was this kiss she dreaded. Its dull reverberation deafened her to all out-side sounds, and she could hear only the beatings of her own heart. When these terrors assailed her, the Forge was her only asylum, from whence she returned smiling and serene, feeling that Goujet—whose sonorous hammer had put all her bad dreams to flight—would protect her always.

By degrees her unreasonable fears of Lantier were conquered. Coupeau was behaving very badly at this time, and one evening, as she passed the Assommoir, she was certain she saw him drink-ing with Mes-Bottes. She hurried on lest she should seem to be watching him. But as she hastened she looked over her shoulder. Yes, it was Coupeau who was tossing down a glass of liquor with an air as if it were no new thing. He had lied to her, then; he did drink brandy. She was in utter despair, and all her old horror of brandy returned. Wine she could have forgiven—wine was good for a working man; liquor, on the contrary, was his ruin, and took from him all desire for the food that nourished, and gave him strength for his daily toil. Why did not the government interfere and prevent the manufacture of such pernicious things?

When she reached her home she found the whole house in confusion. Her employées had left their work and were in the court-yard. She asked what the matter was.

"It is Father Bijard beating his wife; he is as drunk as a fool, and he drove her up the stairs to her room, where he is murder-ing her. Just listen!"

Gervaise flew up the stairs. She was very fond of Madame Bijard, who was her laundress and whose courage and industry she greatly admired. On the sixth floor a little crowd was assem-bled. Madame Boche stood at an open door.

"Have done!" she cried; "have done! or the police will be summoned."

No one dared enter the room, because Bijard was well known to be like a madman when he was tipsy. He was rarely thor-oughly sober; and on the occasional days when he condescended to work, he always had a bottle of brandy at his side. He rarely ate anything, and if a match had been touched to his mouth, he would have taken fire like a torch.

"Would you let her be killed!" exclaimed Gervaise, trembling from head to foot, and she entered the attic room, which was very clean and very bare, for the man had sold the very sheets off the bed to satisfy his mad passion for drink. In this terrible struggle for life, the table had been thrown over, and the two chairs also. On the floor lay the poor woman, with her skirts drenched as she had come from the wash-tub, her hair streaming over her bloody face, uttering low groans at each kick the brute gave her.

The neighbors whispered to each other that she had refused to give him the money she had earned that day. Boche called up the staircase to his wife:

"Come down, I say; let him kill her if he will: it will only make one fool the less in the world!"

Father Bru followed Gervaise into the room, and the two expostulated with the madman. But he turned toward them pale and threatening; a white foam glistened on his lips, and in his faded eyes there was a murderous expression. He grasped Father Bru by the shoulder and threw him over the table, and shook Gervaise until her teeth chattered, and then returned to his wife, who lay motionless, with her mouth wide open and her eyes closed; and during this frightful scene little Lalie, four years old, was in the corner looking on at the murder of her mother. The child's arms were round her sister Henriette, a baby who had just been weaned. She stood with a sad, solemn face, and serious melancholy eyes, but shed no tears.

When Bijard slipped and fell, Gervaise and Father Bru helped the poor creature to her feet, who then burst into sobs. Lalie went to her side, but she did not cry, for the child was already habituated to such scenes. And as Gervaise went down the stairs, she was haunted by the strange look of resignation and courage in Lalie's eyes—it was an expression belonging to maturity and experience, rather than to childhood.

"Your husband is on the other side of the street," said Clémence, as soon as she saw Gervaise; "he is as tipsy as possible!"

Coupeau reeled in, breaking a square of glass with his shoulder as he missed the doorway. He was not tipsy, but drunk, with his teeth set firmly together, and a pinched expression about the nose. And Gervaise instantly knew that it was the liquor of the Assommoir which had vitiated his blood. She tried to smile, and coaxed him to go to bed. But he shook her off and as he passed her gave her a blow.

He was just like the other—the beast up-stairs who was now snoring, tired out by beating his wife. She was chilled to the heart and desperate. Were all men alike? She thought of Lantier and of her husband, and wondered if there were no happiness in the world.

-{ *CHAPTER VII* }-

A Birthday Fête

T HE 19TH OF JUNE was the clear-starcher's birthday. There was always an excuse for a fête in the Coupeau mansion. And Gervaise accepted this excuse.

Gervaise was much troubled as to whom she should invite. She wanted exactly twelve at table, not one more nor one less. She, her husband, her mother-in-law, and Madame Lerat were four. The Goujets and Poissons were four more. At first she thought she would not ask her two women, Madame Putois and Clémence, lest it should make them too familiar; but as the entertainment was constantly under discussion before them, she ended by inviting them too. Thus there were ten: she must have too more; she decided on a reconciliation with the Lorilleux, who had extended the olive-branch several times lately. "Family quarrels were bad things," she said. When the Boche people heard of this, they showed several little courtesies to Gervaise, who felt obliged to urge them to come also. This made fourteen without counting the children. She had never had a dinner like this, and she was both triumphant and terrified.

The 19th fell on a Monday, and Gervaise thought it very fortunate, as she could begin her cooking on Sunday afternoon. On Saturday, while the women hurried through their work, there was an endless discussion as to what the dishes should be. In the last three weeks only one thing had been definitely decided upon—a roast goose stuffed with onions. The goose had been purchased, and Madame Coupeau brought it in that

Madame Putois might guess its weight. The thing looked enormous, and the fat seemed to burst from its yellow skin.

"Soup before that, of course," said Gervaise, "and we must have another dish."

Gervaise proposed a spare-rib of pork and potatoes, which brightened all their faces, just as Virginie came in like a whirlwind.

"You are just in season. Mamma Coupeau, show her the goose," cried Gervaise.

Virginie admired it, guessed the weight, and laid it down on the ironing-table between an embroidered skirt and a pile of shirts. She was evidently thinking of something else. She soon led Gervaise into the back shop.

"I have come to warn you," she said quickly. "I just met Lantier at the very end of this street, and I am sure he followed me, and I naturally felt alarmed on your account, my dear."

Gervaise turned very pale. What did he want of her? and why on earth should he worry her now amid all the busy preparations for the fête?

But Virginie declared that she would look out for her. If Lantier followed her she would certainly give him over to the police. Her husband had been in office now for a month, and Virginie was very dictatorial and aggressive, and talked of arresting every one who displeased her. She raised her voice as she spoke but Gervaise implored her to be cautious, because her women could hear every word.

The next day at three, Mamma Coupeau lighted the two furnaces belonging to the house, and a third one borrowed from Madame Boche; and at half-past three the soup was gently simmering in a large pot lent by the restaurant at the corner. The back shop was ruddy with the glow from the three furnaces—sauces were bubbling with a strong smell of browned flour. Mamma Coupeau and Gervaise, each with large, white aprons were washing celery, and running hither and thither with pepper and salt. The smell of the cooking found its way out into the street and up through the house and the neighbors, impelled by curiosity, came down on all sorts of pretexts, merely to discover what was going on.

About five Virginie made her appearance. She had seen

Lantier twice. Indeed, it was impossible nowadays to enter the street and not see him. Madame Boche, too, had spoken to him on the corner below. Then Gervaise, who was on the point of going for a sou's worth of fried onions to season her soup, shuddered from head to foot, and said she would not go out ever again.

Virginie said she would go for the onions. When she returned, she reported that Lantier was no longer there. The conversation around the stove that evening never once drifted from that subject. Madame Boche said that she, under similar circumstances, should tell her husband: but Gervaise was horror-struck at this, and begged her never to breathe one single word about it. She knew Coupeau so well, that she had long since discovered that he was still jealous of Lantier; and while the four women discussed the imminent danger of a terrible tragedy, the sauces and the meats hissed and simmered on the furnaces, and they ended by each taking a cup of soup to discover what improvement was desirable.

Monday arrived. Now that Gervaise had invited fourteen to dine, she began to be afraid there would not be room, and finally decided to lay the table in the shop.

Mamma Coupeau and Gervaise began to lay their table at three o'clock. They had hung curtains before the window, but as the day was warm, the door into the street was open. The two women did not put on a plate or salt-spoon without the avowed intention of worrying the Lorilleux. They had given them seats where the table could be seen to the best advantage, and they placed before them the real china plates.

"No, no, mamma," cried Gervaise, "not those napkins. I have two which are real damask."

"Well! well! I declare!" murmured the old woman. "What will they say to all this?"

And they smiled as they stood at opposite sides of this long table with its glossy white cloth, and its places for fourteen carefully laid. They worshipped there as if it had been a chapel erected in the middle of the shop.

At four o'clock the goose was roasting, and Augustine, seated on a little footstool, was given a long-handled spoon, and bidden to watch and baste it every few minutes. Gervaise was busy with the peas, and Mamma Coupeau, with her head a little confused, was waiting until it was time to heat the veal and the pork. At five the guests began to arrive. Clémence and Madame Putois, gorgeous to behold in their Sunday rig, were the first.

After them came Virginie in scarf and hat, though she had only to cross the street; she wore a printed muslin, and was as imposing as any lady in the land. She brought a pot of red carnations, and put both her arms around her friend and kissed her.

The offering brought by Boche was a pot of pansies, and his wife's was mignonette; Madame Lerat's a lemon verbena. The three furnaces filled the room with an overpowering heat, and the frying potatoes drowned their voices. Gervaise was very sweet and smiling, thanking every one for the flowers, at the same time making the dressing for the salad.

The ladies covered the bed with their shawls and bonnets, and then went into the shop that they might be out of the way, and talked through the open door with much noise and loud laughing.

At this moment Goujet appeared, and stood timidly on the threshold with a tall white rose-bush in his arms whose flowers brushed against his yellow beard. Gervaise ran toward him with her cheeks reddened by her furnaces. She took the plant, crying:

"How beautiful!"

He dared not kiss her, and she was compelled to offer her cheek to him; and both were embarrassed. He told her, in a confused way, that his mother was ill with sciatica and could not come. Gervaise was greatly disappointed, but she had no time to say much just then: she was beginning to be anxious about Coupeau—he ought to be in—then, too, where were the Lorilleux? She called Madame Lerat, who had arranged the reconciliation, and bade her go and see.

Madame Lerat put on her hat and shawl with excessive care and departed. A solemn hush of expectation pervaded the room.

Madame Lerat presently reappeared. She had come round by the street to give a more ceremonious aspect to the affair. She held the door open, while Madame Lorilleux, in a silk dress, stood on the threshold. All the guests rose, and Gervaise went forward to meet her sister and kissed her, as had been agreed upon.

"Come in! come in!" she said. "We are friends again."

"And I hope for always," answered her sister-in-law, severely.

After she was ushered in, the same programme had to be followed out with her husband. Neither of the two brought any flowers. They had refused to do so, saying that it would look as if they were bowing down to Wooden Leg. Gervaise summoned Augustine, and bade her bring some wine, and then filled glasses for all the party, and each drank the health of the family.

"It is a good thing before soup," muttered Boche.

Mamma Coupeau drew Gervaise into the next room.

"Did you see her?" she said, eagerly. "I was watching her, and when she saw the table, her face was as long as my arm, and now she is gnawing her lips, she is so mad!"

It was true the Lorilleux could not stand that table, with its white linen, its shining glass, and square piece of bread at each place. It was like a restaurant on the Boulevard, and Madame Lorilleux felt of the cloth stealthily to ascertain if it were new.

"We are all ready," cried Gervaise, reappearing, and pulling down her sleeves over her white arms.

"Where can Coupeau be?" she continued.

"He is always late! he always forgets!" muttered his sister. Gervaise was in despair. Everything would be spoiled. She proposed that some one should go out and look for him. Goujet offered to go, and she said she would accompany him. Virginie followed, all three bare headed. Every one looked at them, so gay and fresh on a week day. Virginie, in her pink muslin, and Gervaise in a white cambric with blue spots, and a gray silk handkerchief knotted round her throat. They went to one wine-shop after another, but no Coupeau. Suddenly, as they went toward the Boulevard, Gervaise uttered an exclamation.

"What is the matter?" asked Goujet. The clear-starcher was very pale, and so much agitated that she could hardly stand. Virginie knew at once, and leaning over her, looked in at the restaurant and saw Lantier quietly dining.

"I turned my foot," said Gervaise, when she could speak.

Finally, at the Assommoir they found Coupeau and Poisson. They were standing in the centre of an excited crowd. Coupeau, in a gray blouse, was quarrelling with some one, and Poisson, who was not on duty that day, was listening quietly—his red moustache and imperial giving him, however, quite a formidable aspect.

Goujet left the women outside, and going in placed his hand on Coupeau's shoulder, who, when he saw his wife and Virginie, fell into a great rage.

No, he would not move! He would not stand being followed about by women in this way! They might go home and eat their rubbishy dinner themselves! He did not want any of it!

To appease him, Goujet was compelled to drink with him, and finally he persuaded him to go with him.

Gervaise was trembling from head to foot. She had been speaking of Lantier to Virginie, and begged the other to go on in front, while the two women walked on either side of Coupeau to prevent him from seeing Lantier as they passed the open window where he sat eating his dinner.

But Coupeau knew that Lantier was there, for he said:

"There's a fellow I know, and you know him, too!"

He then went on to accuse her, with many a coarse word, of coming out to look—not for him—but for her old lover, and then all at once he poured out a torrent of abuse upon Lantier, who, however, never looked up or appeared to hear it.

Virginie at last coaxed Coupeau on, whose rage disappeared when they turned the corner of the street. They returned to the shop, however, in a very different mood from the one in which they had left it, and found the guests, with very long faces, awaiting them.

Coupeau shook hands with the ladies in succession, with difficulty keeping his feet as he did so, and Gervaise, in a choked voice, begged them to take their seats. But suddenly she perceived that Madame Goujet not having come, there was an empty seat next to Madame Lorilleux.

"We are thirteen," she said, much disturbed, as she fancied this to be an additional proof of the misfortune which, for some time, she had felt to be hanging over them.

The ladies, who were seated, started up. Madame Putoi

offered to leave, because, she said, no one should fly in the face of Destiny; besides, she was not hungry. As to Boche, he laughed, and said it was all nonsense.

"Wait!" cried Gervaise, "I will arrange it."

And rushing out on the sidewalk, she called to Father Bru, who was crossing the street, and the old man followed her into the room.

"Sit there," said the clear-starcher. "You are willing to dine with us, are you not?"

He nodded acquiescence.

"He will do as well as another," she continued, in a low voice. "He rarely, if ever, had as much as he wanted to eat, and it will be a pleasure to us to see him enjoy his dinner."

Goujet's eyes were damp, so much was he touched by the kind way in which Gervaise spoke, and the others felt that it would bring them good luck. Madame Lorilleux was the only one who seemed displeased. She drew her skirts away and looked down with disgusted mien upon the patched blouse at her side.

Gervaise served the soup, and the guests were just lifting their spoons to their mouths, when Virginie noticed that Coupeau had disappeared. He had probably returned to the more congenial society at the Assommoir, and some one said he might stay in the street—certainly no one would go after him; but just as they had swallowed the soup Coupeau appeared bearing two pots, one under each arm—a balsam and a wallflower. All the guests clapped their hands. He placed them on either side of Gervaise, and, kissing her, he said:

"I forgot you, my dear; but all the same I loved you very much."

This little act on the part of the host brought back the smiles to the faces around the table. The wine began to circulate, and the voices of the children were heard in the next room. Etienne, Nana, Pauline, and little Victor Fauconnier were installed at a small table, and were told to be very good.

When the blanquette du veau was served, the guests were moved to enthusiasm. It was now half-past seven. The door of the shop was shut to keep out inquisitive eyes, and curtains hung before the windows. The veal was a great success; the sauce was delicious, and the mushrooms extraordinarily good. Then came the spare-ribs of pork. Of course all these good things demanded a large amount of wine.

In the next room, at the children's table, Nana was playing the mistress of the household. She was seated at the head of the table, and for a while was quite dignified, but her natural gluttony made her forget her good manners when she saw Augustine stealing the peas from the plate, and she slapped the girl vehemently.

"Take care, Mademoiselle," said Augustine, sulkily, "or I will tell your mother that I heard you ask Victor to kiss you."

Now was the time for the goose. Gervaise left the table, to reappear presently bearing the goose in triumph. Lorilleux and his wife exchanged a look of dismay.

"Who will cut it?" said the clear-starcher. "No, not I: it is too big for me to manage!"

Coupeau said he could do it. After all it was a simple thing enough—he should just tear it to pieces.

There was a cry of dismay.

Madame Lerat had an inspiration.

"Monsieur Poisson is the man," she said, "of course he understands the use of arms," and she handed the sergeant the carving-knife. Poisson made a stiff inclination of his whole body and drew the dish toward him, and went to work in a slow, methodical fashion. As he thrust his knife into the breast, Lorilleux was seized with momentary patriotism, and he exclaimed:

"If it were only a Cossack!"

At last the goose was carved and distributed, and the whole party ate as if they were just beginning their dinner. Presently there was a grand outcry about the heat, and Coupeau opened the door into the street. Gervaise devoured large slices of the breast, hardly speaking, but a little ashamed of her own gluttony in the presence of Goujet. She never forgot old Bru, however, and gave him the choicest morsels, which he swallowed unconsciously, his palate having long since lost the power of distinguishing flavors. Mamma Coupeau picked a bone with her two remaining teeth.

And the wine! Good heavens! how much they drank! A pile

of empty bottles stood in the corner. When Madame Putois asked for water, Coupeau himself removed the carafes from the table. No one should drink water, he declared, in his house— did she want to swallow frogs and live things? and he filled up all the glasses.

Suddenly Gervaise remembered the six bottles of sealed wine she had omitted to serve with the goose as she had intended. She produced them amid much applause. The glasses were filled anew, and Poisson rose and proposed the health of their hostess.

"And fifty more birthdays!" cried Virginie.

"No, no," answered Gervaise, with a smile that had a touch of sadness in it. "I do not care to live to be very old. There comes a time when one is glad to go!"

A little crowd had collected outside, and smiled at the scene, and the smell of the goose pervaded the whole street. The clerks in the grocery opposite licked their lips, and said it was good, and curiously estimated the amount of wine that had been consumed.

None of the guests were annoyed by being the subjects of observation, although they were fully aware of it, and in fact rather enjoyed it. Coupeau catching sight of a familiar face, held up a bottle, which, being accepted with a nod, he sent it out with a glass. This established a sort of fraternity with the street.

In the next room the children were unmanageable. They had taken possession of a saucepan and were drumming on it with spoons.

None of the guests were dismayed at the dessert, although they had eaten so enormously. They had the night before them, too; there was no need of haste. The men lighted their pipes and drank more wine while they watched Gervaise cut the cake. Poisson, who prided himself on his knowledge of the habits of good society, rose and took the rose from the top, and presented it to the hostess amid the loud applause of the whole party. She fastened it just over her heart. A song was then proposed—comic songs were a specialty with Boche—and the whole party joined in the chorus. The men kept time with their heels, and the women with their knives on their glasses. The windows of the shop jarred with the noise. Virginie had disappeared twice, and the third time, when she came back, she said to Gervaise:

"My dear, he is still at the restaurant, and pretends to be reading his paper. I fear he is meditating some mischief."

She spoke of Lantier. She had been out to see if he were anywhere in the vicinity. Gervaise became very grave.

"Is he tipsy?" she asked.

"No, indeed; and that is what troubled me. Why on earth should he stay there so long if he is not drinking? My heart is in my mouth, I am so afraid something will happen."

The clear-starcher begged her to say no more. Madame Putois started up and began a fierce piratical song—standing stiff and erect in her black dress, her pale face surrounded by her black lace cap, and gesticulating violently. Poisson nodded approval. He had been to sea, and he knew all about it.

Gervaise, assisted by her mother-in-law, now poured out the coffee. Her guests insisted on a song from her, declaring that it was her turn. She refused. Her face was disturbed and pale, so much so that she was asked if the goose disagreed with her.

Finally she began to sing a plaintive melody, all about dreams and rest. Her eyelids half closed as she ended, and she peered out into the darkness. Then followed a barcarolle from Madame Boche, and a romance from Lorilleux, in which figured perfumes of Araby—ivory throats—ebony hair—kisses—moonlight and guitars! Clémence followed with a song, which recalled the country with its descriptions of birds and flowers. Virginie brought down the house with her imitation of a vivandière, standing with her hand on her hip, and a wine glass in her hand, which she emptied down her throat as she finished.

Virginie whispered to Gervaise:

"I have just seen Lantier pass the door. Good heavens! There he is again, standing still and looking in."

Gervaise caught her breath and timidly turned around. The crowd had increased, attracted by the songs. There were soldiers and shop-keepers, and three little girls, five or six years old, holding each other by the hand, grave and silent, struck with wonder and admiration.

Lantier was directly in front of the door. Gervaise met his

eyes, and felt the very marrow of her bones chilled, she could not move hand or foot.

Coupeau called for more wine, and Clémence helped herself to more strawberries. The singing ceased, and the conversation turned upon a woman, who had hung herself the day before in the next street.

Gervaise and Virginie watched the shadows outside. Madame Boche in her turn now caught a glimpse of Lantier, and uttered an exclamation as she wiped away her fast falling tears. The three women exchanged terrified, anxious glances.

"Good heavens!" muttered Virginie. "Suppose Coupeau should turn around. There would be a murder, I am convinced." And the earnestness of their fixed eyes became so apparent that finally he said:

"What are you staring at?"

And leaning forward he too saw Lantier.

"This is too much," he muttered, "the dirty ruffian! It is too much, and I won't have it!"

As he started to his feet with an oath, Gervaise put her hand on his arm imploringly.

"Put down that knife," she said, "and do not go out, I entreat of you."

Virginie took away the knife that Coupeau had snatched from the table, but she could not prevent him from going into the street. The other guests saw nothing, so entirely absorbed were they in the touching song which Madame Lerat had begun to sing.

Gervaise sat with her hands clasped convulsively, breathless with fear, expecting to hear a cry of rage from the street and see one of the two men fall to the ground. Virginie and Madame Boche had something of the same feeling. Coupeau had been so overcome by the fresh air that when he rushed forward to take Lantier by the collar he missed his footing and found himself seated quietly in the gutter.

Lantier moved aside a little, without taking his hands from his pocket.

Coupeau staggered to his feet again, and a violent quarrel commenced. Gervaise pressed her hands over her eyes; suddenly all was quiet, and she opened her eyes again and looked out.

To her intense astonishment she saw Lantier and her husband talking in a quiet, friendly manner.

Gervaise exchanged a look with Madame Boche and Virginie. What did this mean?

As the women watched them, the two men began to walk up and down in front of the shop. They were talking earnestly. Coupeau seemed to be urging something, and Lantier refusing. Finally Coupeau took Lantier's arm and almost dragged him toward the shop.

"I tell you, you must!" he cried. "You shall drink a glass of wine with us. Men will be men all the world over. My wife and I know that perfectly well."

Madame Lerat had finished her song and seated herself with the air of being utterly exhausted. She asked for a glass of wine. When she sang that song, she said, she was always torn to pieces, and it left her nerves in a terrible state.

Lantier had been placed at the table by Coupeau, and was eating a piece of cake, leisurely dipping it into his glass of wine. With the exception of Madame Boche and Virginie, no one knew him.

The Lorilleux looked at him with some suspicion, which, however, was very far from the mark. An awkward silence followed, broken by Coupeau, who said simply:

"He is a friend of ours!"

And turning to his wife, he added:

"Can't you move round a little? Perhaps there is a cup of hot coffee!"

Gervaise looked from one to the other. She was literally dazed. When her husband first appeared with her former lover, she had clasped her hands over her forehead, with that instinctive gesture with which in a great storm one waits for the approach of the thunder-clap.

Then, seeing the two men calmly seated together, it all at once seemed perfectly natural to her. She was tired of thinking about it, and preferred to accept it. Why after all should she worry? No one else did. Every one seemed to be satisfied; why should not she be also?

She would not disturb the serenity of matters now, so she brought in the coffee-pot and poured out a cup for Lantier, who received it without even looking up at her, as he murmured his thanks.

"Now it is my turn to sing!" shouted Coupeau.

His song was one familiar to them all, and even to the street, for the little crowd at the door joined in the chorus. The guests within were all more or less tipsy, and there was so much noise that the policemen ran to quell a riot; but when they saw Poisson they bowed respectfully and passed on.

No one of the party ever knew how or what hour the festivities terminated. It must have been very late, for there was not a human being in the street when they departed. They vaguely remembered having joined hands and danced around the table. Gervaise remembered that Lantier was the last to leave—that he passed her as she stood in the doorway. She felt a breath on her cheek, but whether it was his or the night air she could not tell.

Madame Lerat had refused to return to Batignolles so late, and a mattress was laid on the floor in the shop near the table. She slept there amid the debris of the feast, and a neighbor's cat profited by an open window to establish herself by her side, where she crunched the bones of the goose all night between her fine, sharp teeth.

-[CHAPTER VIII]-

An Old Acquaintance

THE FOLLOWING SATURDAY Coupeau, who had not been home to dinner, came in with Lantier about ten o'clock. They had been eating pig's feet at a restaurant at Montmarte.

"Don't scold, wife," said Coupeau, "we have not been drinking, you see; we can walk perfectly straight;" and he went on to say, how they had met each other quite by accident in the street.

Nana and Mamma Coupeau were in bed, and Gervaise, who was just closing her shutters when her husband appeared, brought out some glasses and the remains of a bottle of brandy. Lantier did not sit down, and avoided addressing her directly. When she served him, however, he exclaimed:

"A drop, Madame; a mere drop!"

Coupeau looked at them for a moment, and then expressed his mind fully. They were no fools, he said, nor were they children. The Past was the Past. If people kept up their enmities for nine or ten years, no one would have a soul to speak to soon. As for himself, he was made differently. He knew they were honest people, and he was sure he could trust them.

"Of course," murmured Gervaise, hardly knowing what she said, "of course."

"I regard her as a sister," said Lantier, "only as a sister."

"Give us your hand on that," cried Coupeau, "and let us be good friends in the Future. After all a good heart is better than gold, and I estimate Friendship as above all price."

And he gave himself a little tap on his breast, and looked about for applause, as if he had uttered rather a noble sentiment.

Then the three silently drank their brandy. Gervaise looked at Lantier, and saw him for the first time, for on the night of the fête she had seen him, as it were, through a glass, darkly.

He had grown very stout, and his arms and legs very heavy. But his face was still handsome, although somewhat bloated by liquor and good living. He was dressed with care, and did not look any older than his years. He was thirty-five.

"I must go," he said, presently.

He was at the door, when Coupeau recalled him to say that he must never pass without coming in to say, "How do you do?"

Meanwhile, Gervaise, who had disappeared, returned, pushing Etienne before her. The boy was half asleep, but smiled as he rubbed his eyes. When he saw Lantier he stared, and looked uneasily from him to Coupeau.

"Do you know this gentleman?" said his mother.

The child looked away, and did not answer, but when his mother repeated the question he made a little sign that he remembered him. Lantier, grave and silent, stood still. When Etienne went toward him, he stooped and kissed the child, who did not look at him but burst into tears, and when he was violently reproached by Coupeau, he rushed away.

"It is excitement," said his mother, who was herself very pale.

"He is usually very good and very obedient," said Coupeau.

"I have brought him up well, as you will find out. He will soon get used to you. He must learn something of life, you see, and will understand, one of these days, that people must forget and forgive; and I would cut off my head sooner than prevent a father from seeing his child!"

He then proposed to finish the bottle of brandy. They all three drank together again. Lantier was quite undisturbed, and before he left, he insisted on aiding Coupeau to shut up the shop. Then, as he dusted his hands with his handkerchief, he wished them a careless good-night.

Lantier was seen from that time very often in the shop. He came only when Coupeau was home, and asked for him before he crossed the threshold. Then seated near the window, always wearing a frock coat, fresh linen, and carefully shaved, he kept up a conversation like a man who had seen something of the world. By degrees Coupeau learned something of his life. For the last eight years he had been at the head of a hat manufactory, and when he was asked why he had given it up, he said, vaguely, that he was not satisfied with his partner; he was a rascal, and so on.

But his former position still imparted to him a certain air of importance. He said, also, that he was on the point of concluding an important matter—that certain business houses were in process of establishing themselves, the management of which would be virtually in his hands. In the meantime he had absolutely not one thing to do, but to walk about with his hands in his pocket.

The truth was that Lantier, excessively talkative in regard to other people's affairs, was very reticent about his own. He lied quite as often as he spoke the truth, and would never tell where he resided. He said he was never at home, so it was of no use for any one to come and see him.

It was now November. Lantier occasionally brought a bunch of violets to Gervaise. By degrees his visits became more frequent. He seemed determined to fascinate the whole house, even the Quartier, and he began by ingratiating himself with Clémence and Madame Putois, showing them both the greatest possible attention.

These two women adored him at the end of a month.

Madame Boche, whom he flattered by calling on her in her lôge, had all sorts of pleasant things to say about him.

As to the Lorilleux they were furious when they found out who he was, and declared that it was a sin and a disgrace for Gervaise to bring him into her house. But one fine day Lantier bearded them in their den, and ordered a chain made for a lady of his acquaintance, and made himself so agreeable that they begged him to sit down, and kept him an hour. After this visit they expressed their astonishment that a man so distinguished could ever have seen anything in Wooden Legs to admire. By degrees therefore people had become accustomed to seeing him, and no longer expressed their horror or amazement. Goujet was the only one who was disturbed. If Lantier came in while he was there he at once departed, and avoided all intercourse with him.

Gervaise was very unhappy. She was conscious of a returning inclination for Lantier, and she was afraid of herself and of him. She thought of him constantly; he had taken entire possession of her imagination. But she grew calmer as days passed on, finding that he never tried to see her alone, and that he rarely looked at her, and never laid the tip of his finger on her.

Virginie, who seemed to read her through and through, asked her what she feared. Was there ever a man more respectful?

But out of mischief or worse, the woman contrived to get the two into a corner one day, and then led the conversation into a most dangerous direction. Lantier, in reply to some question, said in measured tones that his heart was dead, that he lived now only for his son. He never thought of Claude who was away. He embraced Etienne every night, but soon forgot he was in the room, and amused himself with Clémence.

Then Gervaise began to realize that the Past was dead. Lantier had brought back to her the memory of Plassans and the Hotel Boncœur. But this faded away again, and seeing him constantly, the Past was absorbed in the Present. She shook off these memories almost with disgust. Yes, it was all over, and should he ever dare to allude to former years she would complain to her husband.

She began again to think of Goujet, almost unconsciously.

One morning Clémence said that the night before she had seen Lantier walking with a woman who had his arm. Yes, he was coming up La Rue Notre-Dame de Lorette; the woman was a blonde, and no better than she should be. Clémence added that she had followed them until the woman reached a house where she went in. Lantier waited in the street, until there was a window opened, which was evidently a signal, for he went into the house at once.

Gervaise was ironing a white dress; she smiled slightly, and said that she believed a Provençal was always crazy after women, and at night when Lantier appeared, she was quite amused at Clémence who at once attacked him. He seemed to be on the whole rather pleased that he had been seen. The person was an old friend, he said, one whom he had not seen for some time—a very stylish woman, in fact; and he told Clémence to smell of his handkerchief on which his friend had put some of the perfume she used. Just then Etienne came in, and his father became very grave and said that he was in jest—that his heart was dead.

Gervaise nodded approval of this sentiment, but she did not speak.

When spring came Lantier began to talk of moving into that neighborhood. He wanted a furnished, clean room. Madame Boche and Gervaise tried to find one for him. But they did not meet with any success. He was altogether too fastidious in his requirement. Every evening at the Coupeaus' he wished he could find people like themselves who would take a lodger.

"You are very comfortable here, I am sure," he would say regularly.

Finally, one night when he had uttered this phrase as usual, Coupeau cried out:

"If you like this place so much, why don't you stay here? We can make room for you."

He explained that the linen-room could be so arranged that it would be very comfortable, and Etienne could sleep on a mattress in the corner.

"No, no," said Lantier, "it would trouble you too much. I know that you have the most generous heart in the world, but

I cannot impose upon you. Your room would be a passageway to mine, and that would not be agreeable to any of us."

"Nonsense," said Coupeau. "Have we no invention? There are two windows: can't one be cut down to the floor and used as a door? In that case you would enter from the court and not through the shop. You would be by yourself, and we by ourselves."

There was a long silence, broken finally by Lantier.

"If this could be done," he said, "I should like it, but I am afraid you would find yourselves too crowded."

He did not look at Gervaise as he spoke, but it was clear that he was only waiting for a word from her. She did not like the plan at all; not that the thought of Lantier living under their roof disturbed her, but she had no idea where she could put the linen as it came in to be washed and again when it was rough-dry.

But Coupeau was enchanted with the plan. The rent, he said, had always been heavy to carry, and now they should gain twenty francs per month. It was not dear for him, and it would help them decidedly. He told his wife that she could have two great boxes made in which all the linen of the Quartier could be piled.

Gervaise still hesitated, questioning Mamma Coupeau with her eyes. Lantier had long since propitiated the old lady by bringing her gum-drops for her cough.

"If we could arrange it, I am sure—" said Gervaise, hesitatingly.

"You are too kind," remonstrated Lantier. "I really feel that it would be an intrusion."

Coupeau flamed out, "Why do you not speak up, I should like to know, instead of stammering and behaving like a fool?"

"Etienne! Etienne!" he shouted.

The boy was asleep with his head on the table. He started up.

"Listen to me. Say to this gentleman, 'I wish it.' Say just those words and nothing more."

"I wish it!" stammered Etienne, half asleep.

Everybody laughed. But Lantier almost instantly resumed his solemn air. He pressed Coupeau's hand cordially.

"I accept your proposition," he said. "It is a most friendly one, and I thank you in my name and in that of my child."

It was early in June that Lantier took possession of his new quarters. Coupeau had offered the night before to help him with his trunk in order to avoid the thirty sous for a *fiacre*. But the other seemed embarrassed, and said his trunk was heavy, and it seemed as if he preferred to keep it a secret even now where he resided.

He came about three o'clock. Coupeau was not there, and Gervaise, standing at her shop-door, turned white, as she recognized the trunk on the *fiacre*. It was their old one with which they had travelled from Plassans. Now it was banged and battered, and strapped with cords.

She saw it brought in as she had often seen it in her dreams, and she vaguely wondered if it were the same *fiacre* which had taken him and Adèle away. Boche welcomed Lantier cordially. Gervaise stood by in silent bewilderment, watching them place the trunk in her lodger's room. Then, hardly knowing what she said, she murmured:

"We must take a glass of wine together—"

Lantier, who was busy untying the cords on his trunk, did not look up, and she added:

"You will join us, Monsieur Boche!"

And she went for some wine and glasses. At that moment she caught sight of Poisson passing the door. She gave him a nod and a wink which he perfectly understood: it meant, when he was on duty, that he was offered a glass of wine; he went round by the court-yard in order not to be seen.

Gervaise had filled three glasses on the table. She did not care for any wine; she was sick at heart, as she stood looking at Lantier kneeling on the floor by the side of the trunk. She was wild to know what it contained. She remembered that in one corner was a pile of stockings, a shirt or two, and an old hat. Were those things still there? Was she to be confronted with those tattered relics of the Past?

Lantier did not lift the lid however; he rose, and going to the table held his glass high in his hands.

"To your health, Madame!" he said.

And Poisson and Boche drank with him.

Gervaise filled their glasses again. The three men wiped their lips with the backs of their hands.

Then Lantier opened his trunk. It was filled with a hodge-podge of papers, books, old clothes, and bundles of linen. He pulled out a saucepan, then a pair of boots followed by an embroidered shirt and a pair of ragged pantaloons, and Gervaise perceived a mingled and odious smell of tobacco, leather and dust.

No, the old hat was not in the left corner; in its place was a pin-cushion, the gift of some woman. All at once the strange anxiety with which she had watched the opening of this trunk disappeared, and in its place came an intense sadness as she followed each article with her eyes as Lantier took them out, and wondered which belonged to her time, and which to the days when another woman filled his life.

From the very first Lantier was made thoroughly at home. Lantier had his separate room, private entrance and key. But he went through the shop almost always. The accumulation of linen disturbed Gervaise, for her husband never arranged the boxes he had promised, and she was obliged to stow it away in all sorts of places, under the bed and in the corner. She did not like making up Etienne's mattress late at night either.

Goujet had spoken of sending the child to Lille to his own old master, who wanted apprentices. The plan pleased her, particularly as the boy, who was not very happy at home, was impatient to become his own master. But she dared not ask Lantier, who had come there to live, ostensibly to be near his son. She felt, therefore, that it was hardly a good plan to send the boy away within a couple of weeks after his father's arrival.

When, however, she did make up her mind to approach the subject, he expressed warm approval of the idea, saying that youths were far better in the country than in Paris.

Finally it was decided that Etienne should go, and, when the morning of his departure arrived, Lantier read his son a long lecture and then sent him off, and the house settled down into new habits.

Gervaise became accustomed to seeing the dirty linen lying

about, and to seeing Lantier coming in and going out. He still talked with an important air, of his business operations. He went out daily, dressed with the utmost care, and came home declaring that he was worn out with the discussions in which he had been engaged, and which involved the gravest and most important interests.

He rose about ten o'clock, took a walk if the day pleased him, and if it rained he sat in the shop and read his paper. He liked to be there. It was his delight to live surrounded by a circle of worshipping women, and he basked indolently in the warmth and atmosphere of ease and comfort, which characterized the place.

At first Lantier took his meals at the restaurant at the corner. But after a while he dined three or four times a week with the Coupeaus, and finally requested permission to board with them, and agreed to pay them fifteen francs each Saturday. Thus he was regularly installed and was one of the family. He was seen in his shirt sleeves in the shop every morning attending to any little matters, or receiving orders from the customers. He induced Gervaise to leave her own wine merchant and go to a friend of his own. Then he found fault with the bread, and sent Augustine to the Vienna bakery in a distant faubourg. He changed the grocer, but kept the butcher on account of his political opinions.

At the end of a month he had instituted a change in the cuisine. Everything was cooked in oil: being a Provençal, that was what he adored. He made the omelettes himself, which were as tough as leather. He superintended Mamma Coupeau, and insisted that the beefsteaks should be thoroughly cooked, until they were like the soles of an old shoe. He watched the salad to see that nothing went in which he did not like. His favorite dish was vermicelli, into which he poured half a bottle of oil. This he and Gervaise ate together, for the others being Parisians, could not be induced to taste it.

By degrees Lantier attended to all those affairs which fall to the share of the master of the house, and to various details of their business in addition. He insisted that if the five francs which the Lorilleux people had agreed to pay toward the support of Mamma Coupeau was not forthcoming, that they should go to law about it. In fact, ten francs was what they ought to pay. He himself would go and see if he could not make them agree to that. He went up at once and asked them in such a way that he returned in triumph with the ten francs.

He expressed his mind freely in regard to Nana also. In his opinion she was brought up very badly, and here he was quite right; for when her father cuffed her, her mother upheld her, and when in her turn the mother reproved, the father made a scene.

Nana was delighted at this, and felt herself free to do much as she pleased.

She had started a new game at the Farriery opposite. She spent entire days swinging on the shafts of the wagons. She concealed herself, with her troop of followers, at the back of the dark court, redly lighted by the forge, and then would make sudden rushes, with screams and whoops, followed by every child in the neighborhood, reminding one of a flock of martins or sparrows.

Lantier was the only one whose scoldings had any effect. She listened to him graciously. This child of ten years of age, precocious and vicious, coquetted with him as if she had been a grown woman. He finally assumed the care of her education. He taught her to dance and talk slang!

Thus a year passed away. The whole neighborhood supposed Lantier to be a man of means—otherwise, how did the Coupeaus live as they did? Gervaise, to be sure, still made money; but she supported two men who did nothing, and the shop, of course, did not make enough for that. The truth was that Lantier had never paid one sou, either for board or lodging. He said he would let it run on, and when it amounted to a good sum, he would pay it all at once.

After that Gervaise never dared to ask him for a centime. She got bread, wine and meat on credit; bills were running up everywhere, for their expenditures amounted to three and four francs every day. She had never paid anything, even a trifle on account, to the man of whom she had bought her furniture, nor to Coupeau's three friends who had done the work in Lantier's room. The trades-people were beginning to grumble, and treated her with less politeness.

About the middle of summer Clémence departed, for there was not enough work for two women; she had waited for her money for some weeks. Lantier and Coupeau were quite undisturbed, however. They were in the best of spirits, and seemed to be growing fat over the ruined business.

In the Quartier there was a vast deal of gossip. Everybody wondered as to the terms on which Lantier and Gervaise now stood. The Lorilleux viciously declared that Gervaise would be glad enough to resume her old relations with Lantier, but that he would have nothing to do with her, for she had grown old and ugly. The Boche people took a different view; but while every one declared that the whole arrangement was a most improper one, they finally accepted it as quite a matter of course, and altogether natural.

It is quite possible there were other homes which were quite as open to invidious remarks, within a stone's throw, but these Coupeaus as their neighbors said, were good, kind people. Lantier was especially ingratiating. It was decided, therefore, to let things go their own way undisturbed.

Gervaise lived quietly indifferent to, and possibly entirely unsuspicious of, all these scandals. By-and-by it came to pass that her husband's own people looked on her as utterly heartless. Madame Lerat made her appearance every evening, and she treated Lantier as if he were utterly irresistible, into whose arms any and every woman would be only too glad to fall. An actual league seemed to be forming against Gervaise: all the women insisted on giving her a lover.

She could not understand what others saw in him to admire. And she said so one day to Virginie. Then Madame Lerat and Virginie vied with each other in the stories they told of Clémence and himself—what they did and said whenever her back was turned—and now they were sure, since she had left the establishment, that he went regularly to see her.

"Well, what of it?" asked Gervaise, her voice trembling. "What have I to do with that?"

And she looked into Virginie's dark brown eyes, which were specked with gold, and emitted sparks as do those of cats. But the woman put on a stupid look as she answered:

"Why, nothing, of course; only I should think you would advise him not to have anything to do with such a person."

Lantier was gradually changing his manner to Gervaise. Now, when he shook hands with her, he held her fingers longer than was necessary. He watched her incessantly, and fixed his bold eyes upon her. He leaned over her so closely that she felt his breath on her cheek. But one evening, being alone with her, he caught her in both arms. At that moment Goujet entered. Gervaise wrenched herself free, and the three exchanged a few words as if nothing had happened. Goujet was very pale and seemed embarrassed, supposing that he had intruded upon them, and that she had pushed Lantier aside only because she did not choose to be embraced in public.

The next day Gervaise was miserable, unhappy and restless. She could not iron a handkerchief. She wanted to see Goujet, and tell him just what had happened, but ever since Etienne had gone to Lille, she had given up going to the Forge, as she was quite unable to face the knowing winks with which his comrades received her. But this day she determined to go; and taking an empty basket on her arms she started off, pretending that she was going with skirts to some customers in La Rue des Portes-Blanches.

Goujet seemed to be expecting her, for she met him loitering on the corner.

"Ah," he said, with a wan smile, "you are going home, I presume?"

He hardly knew what he was saying, and they both turned toward Montmartre without another word. They merely wished to go away from the Forge. They passed several manufactories and soon found themselves with an open field before them. A goat was tethered near by and bleating as it browsed, and a dead tree was crumbling away in the hot sun.

"One might almost think one's self in the country," murmured Gervaise.

They took a seat under the dead tree. The clear-starcher set the basket down at her feet. Before them stretched the heights of Montmartre, with its rows of yellow and gray houses amid clumps of trees, and when they threw back their heads a little they saw the whole sky above, clear and cloudless; but the sunlight dazzled them, and they looked over to the misty outlines of the faubourg, and watched the smoke rising from tall chimneys in regular puffs, indicating the machinery which impelled it. These great sighs seemed to relieve their own oppressed breasts.

"Yes," said Gervaise, after a long silence. "I have been on a long walk, and I came out—"

She stopped: after having been so eager for an explanation she found herself unable to speak, and overwhelmed with shame. She knew that he as well as herself had come to that place with the wish and intention of speaking on one especial subject, and yet neither of them dared to allude to it. The occurrence of the previous evening weighed on both their souls.

Then with a heart torn with anguish, and with tears in her eyes, she told him of the death of Madame Bijard, who had breathed her last that morning after suffering unheard-of agonies.

"It was caused by a kick of Bijard's," she said, in her low, soft voice; "some internal injury. For three days she has suffered frightfully. Why are not such men punished? I suppose, though, if the law undertook to punish all the wretches who kill their wives that it would have too much to do. After all, one kick more or less: what does it matter in the end? And this poor creature in her desire to save her husband from the scaffold, declared she had fallen over a tub."

Goujet did not speak. He sat pulling up the tufts of grass.

"It is not a fortnight," continued Gervaise, "since she weaned her last baby; and here is that child Lalie, left to take care of two mites. She is not eight years old, but as quiet and sensible as if she were a grown woman; and her father kicks and strikes her too. Poor little soul! There are some persons in this world who seem born to suffer."

Goujet looked at her, and then said suddenly, with trembling lips:

"You made me suffer yesterday."

Gervaise clasped her hands imploringly, and he continued:

"I knew of course how it must end: only you should not have allowed me to think—"

He could not finish. She started up, seeing what his convictions were. She cried out:

"You are wrong! I swear to you that you are wrong! He was going to kiss me, but his lips did not touch me, and it is the very first time that he made the attempt. Believe me, for I swear—on all that I hold most sacred—that I am telling you the truth."

But the blacksmith shook his head. He knew that women did not always tell the truth on such points. Gervaise then became very grave.

"You know me well," she said; "you know that I am no liar. I again repeat that Lantier and I are friends. We shall never be anything more, for if that should ever come to pass, I should regard myself as the vilest of the vile, and should be unworthy of the friendship of a man like yourself." Her face was so honest, her eyes were so clear and frank, that he could do no less than believe her. Once more he breathed freely. He held her hand for the first time. Both were silent. White clouds sailed slowly above their heads with the majesty of swans. The goat looked at them and bleated piteously, eager to be released, and they stood hand in hand on that bleak slope with tears in their eyes.

"Your mother likes me no longer," said Gervaise, in a low voice. "Do not say no;—how can it be otherwise? We owe you so much money."

He roughly shook her arm in his eagerness to check the words on her lips—he would not hear her. He tried to speak, but his throat was too dry; he choked a little, and then he burst out:

"Listen to me," he cried, "I have long wished to say something to you. You are not happy. My mother says things are all going wrong with you, and"—he hesitated; "we must go away together and at once."

She looked at him, not understanding him, but impressed by this abrupt declaration of a love from him, who had never before opened his lips in regard to it.

"What do you mean?" she said.

"I mean," he answered, without looking in her face, "that we two can go away and live in Belgium. It is almost the same to me as home, and both of us could get work and live comfortably."

The color came to her face, which she would have hidden on his shoulder to hide her shame and confusion.

"Ah, Monsieur Goujet!" she murmured; but she could say no more.

"Yes," he said; "we two would live all by ourselves."

But as her self-possession returned, she refused with firmness.

"It is impossible," she said; "and it would be very wrong. I am married, and I have children. I know that you are fond of me, and I love you too much to allow you to commit any such folly as you are talking of, and this would be an enormous folly. No; we must live on as we are. We respect each other now. Let us continue to do so. That is a great deal, and will help us over many a roughness in our paths. And when we try to do right, we are sure of a reward."

He shook his head as he listened to her, but he felt she was right. Suddenly, he snatched her in his arms and kissed her furiously once, and then dropped her and turned abruptly away. She was not angry, but the blacksmith trembled from head to foot. He began to gather some of the wild daisies, not knowing what to do with his hands, and tossed them into her empty basket. This occupation amused him and tranquillized him. He broke off the heads of the flowers, and when he missed his mark and they fell short of the basket, laughed aloud.

Gervaise sat with her back against the tree, happy and calm. And when she set forth on her walk home, her basket was full of daisies, and she was talking of Etienne.

In reality, Gervaise was more afraid of Lantier than she was willing to admit even to herself. She was fully determined never to allow the smallest familiarity; but she was afraid that she might yield to his persuasions, for she well knew the weakness and amiability of her nature, and how hard it was for her to persist in any opposition to any one.

Lantier, however, did not put this determination on her part to the test. He was often alone with her now, and was always quiet and respectful. Coupeau declared to every one that Lantier was a true friend. There was no nonsense about him; he could be relied upon always and in all emergencies. And he trusted him thoroughly, he declared. When they went out together—the three, on Sundays—he bade his wife and Lantier walk arm-in-arm, while he mounted guard behind, ready to cuff the ears of any one who ventured on a disrespectful glance, a sneer or a wink.

He laughed good-naturedly before Lantier's face, told him he put on a great many airs with his coats and his books, but he liked him in spite of them. They understood each other, he said, and a man's liking for another man is more solid and enduring than his love for a woman.

Coupeau and Lantier made the money fly. Lantier was continually borrowing money from Gervaise; ten francs, twenty francs, whenever he knew there was money in the house. It was always because he was in pressing need for some business matter. But still on those same days he took Coupeau off with him, and at some distant restaurant ordered and devoured such dishes as they could not obtain at home, and these dishes were washed down by bottle after bottle of wine.

They never alluded to these dinners the next morning at their simple breakfast with Gervaise. Naturally, people cannot frolic and work too, and since Lantier had become a member of this household, Coupeau had never lifted a tool. He knew every drinking-shop for miles around, and would sit and guzzle, deep into the night, not always pleased to find himself deserted by Lantier, who never was known to be overcome by liquor.

About the first of November, Coupeau turned over a new leaf; he declared he was going to work the next day, and Lantier thereupon preached a little sermon, declaring that labor ennobled man, and in the morning arose before it was light, to accompany his friend to the shop, as a mark of the respect he felt. But when they reached a wineshop on the corner, they entered to take a glass merely to cement good resolutions.

Near the counter they beheld Bibi-la-Grillade smoking his pipe with a sulky air.

"What is the matter, Bibi?" cried Coupeau.

"Nothing!" answered his comrade, "except that I got my walking-ticket, yesterday. Perdition seize all masters!" he added, fiercely.

And Bibi accepted a glass of liquor. Lantier defended the

masters. They were not so bad after all: then, too, how were the men to get along without them? "To be sure," continued Lantier, "I manage pretty well, for I don't have much to do with them myself!"

"Come, my boy," he added, turning to Coupeau, "we shall be late if we don't look out."

Bibi went out with them. Day was just breaking, gray and cloudy. It had rained the night before, and was damp and warm. The street-lamps had just been extinguished. There was one continued tramp of men going to their work.

Coupeau, with his bag of tools on his shoulder, shuffled along: his footsteps had long since lost their ring.

"Bibi," he said, "come with me; the master told me to bring a comrade if I pleased."

"It won't be me, then," answered Bibi. "I wash my hands of them all. No more masters for me, I tell you! But I dare say Mes-Bottes would be glad of the offer."

And as they reached the Assommoir, they saw Mes-Bottes within. Notwithstanding the fact that it was daylight, the gas was blazing in the Assommoir. Lantier remained outside, and told Coupeau to make haste, as they had only ten minutes.

"Do you think I will work for your master?" cried Mes-Bottes. "He is the greatest tyrant in the kingdom. No, I should rather suck my thumbs for a year. You won't stay there, old man! No, you won't stay there three days, now I tell you!"

"Are you in earnest?" asked Coupeau, uneasily.

"Yes, I am in earnest. You can't speak—you can't move. Your nose is held close to the grindstone all the time. He watches you every moment. If you drink a drop, he says you are tipsy, and makes no end of a row!"

"Thanks for the warning. I will try this one day, and if the master bothers me, I will just tell him what I think of him, and turn on my heel and walk out."

Coupeau shook his comrade's hand and turned to depart, much to the disgust of Mes-Bottes, who angrily asked if the master could not wait five minutes. He could not go until he had taken a drink. Lantier entered to join in, and Mes-Bottes stood there with his hat on the back of his head—shabby, dirty and staggering, ordering Father Colombe to pour out the glasses, and not to cheat.

At that moment Goujet and Lorilleux were seen going by. Mes-Bottes shouted to them to come in, but they both refused—Goujet saying he wanted nothing, and the other—as he hugged a little box of gold chains close to his heart—that he was in a hurry.

"Milksops!" muttered Mes-Bottes; "they had best pass their lives in the corner by the fire!"

Returning to the counter, he renewed his attack on Father Colombe, whom he accused of adulterating his liquors.

It was now bright daylight, and the proprietor of the Assommoir began to extinguish the lights. Coupeau made excuses for his brother-in-law, who he said could never drink; it was not his fault, poor fellow! He approved, too, of Goujet, declaring that it was a good thing never to be thirsty. Again he made a move to depart and go to his work, when Lantier, with his dictatorial air, reminded him that he had not paid his score, and that he could not go off in that way, even if it were to his duty.

"I am sick of the words 'work' and 'duty,'" muttered Mes-Bottes.

They all paid for their drinks with the exception of Bibi-la-Grillade, who stooped toward the ear of Father Colombe and whispered a few words. The latter shook his head, whereupon Mes-Bottes burst into a torrent of invective; but Colombe stood in impassive silence, and when there was a lull in the storm, he said:

"Let your friends pay for you, then—that is a very simple thing to do."

By this time Mes-Bottes was what is properly called howling drunk, and as he staggered away from the counter, he struck the bag of tools which Coupeau had over his shoulder.

"You look like a peddler with his pack, or a humpback. Put it down!"

Coupeau hesitated a moment; and then slowly and deliberately, as if he had arrived at a decision after mature deliberation, he laid his bag on the ground.

"It is too late to go this morning. I will wait until after breakfast now. I will tell him my wife was sick. Listen, Father

Colombe: I will leave my bag of tools under this bench and come for them this afternoon."

Lantier assented to this arrangement. Of course work was a good thing, but friends and good company were better; and the four men stood, first on one foot and then on the other, for more than an hour, and then they had another drink all round. After that a game of billiards was proposed, and they went noisily down the street to the nearest billiard-room, which did not happen to please the fastidious Lantier; who, however, soon recovered his good humor under the effect of the admiration excited in the minds of his friends by his play, which was really very extraordinary.

When the hour arrived for breakfast Coupeau had an idea.

"Let us go and find Bec Sali. I know where he works. We will make him breakfast with us."

The idea was received with applause. The party started forth. A fine drizzling rain was now falling, but they were too warm within to mind this light sprinkling on their shoulders.

Coupeau took them to a factory where his friend worked, and at the door gave two sous to a small boy to go up and find Bec Sali, and to tell him that his wife was very sick and had sent for him.

Bec Sali quickly appeared, not in the least disturbed, as he suspected a joke.

"Ah! ha!" he said, as he saw his friend. "I knew it!" They went to a restaurant and ordered a famous repast of pigs' feet and they sat and sucked the bones and talked about their various employers.

"Will you believe," said Bec Sali, "that mine has had the brass to hang up a bell! Does he think we are slaves to run when he rings it? Never was he so mistaken—"

"I am obliged to leave you!" said Coupeau, rising at last with an important air. "I promised my wife to go to work to-day, and I leave you with the greatest reluctance."

The others protested and entreated, but he seemed so decided that they all accompanied him to the Assommoir to get his tools. He pulled out the bag from under the bench and laid it at his feet, while they all took another drink. The clock struck one and Coupeau kicked his bag under the bench again. He would go to-morrow to the factory; one day really did not make much difference.

The rain had ceased, and one of the men proposed a little walk on the Boulevards to stretch their legs. The air seemed to stupefy them, and they loitered along with their arms swinging at their sides, without exchanging a word. When they reached the wineshop on the corner of La Rue des Poissonnièrs, they turned in mechanically. Lantier led the way into a small room divided from the public one by windows only. This room was much affected by Lantier, who thought it more stylish by far than the public one. He called for a newspaper, spread it out, and examined it with a heavy frown. Coupeau and Mes-Bottes played a game of cards, while wine and glasses occupied the centre of the table.

"What is the news?" asked Bibi.

Lantier did not reply instantly; but presently, as the others emptied their glasses, he began to read aloud an account of a frightful murder, to which they listened with eager interest. Then ensued a hot discussion, and argument as to the probable motives for the murder.

By this time the wine was exhausted, and they called for more. About five, all except Lantier were in a state of beastly intoxication, and he found them so disgusting, that as usual, he made his escape without his comrades noticing his defection.

Lantier walked about a little, and then, when he felt all right, went home, and told Gervaise that her husband was with his friends. Coupeau did not make his appearance for two days. Rumors were brought in that he had been seen in one place and then in another, and always alone. His comrades had apparently deserted him. Gervaise shrugged her shoulders with a resigned air.

"Good heavens!" she said, "what a way to live!" She never thought of hunting him up. Indeed, on the afternoon of the third day, when she saw him through the window of a wine-shop, she turned back and would not pass the door. She sat up for him, however, and listened for his step or the sound of his hand fumbling at the lock.

The next morning he came in, only to begin the same thing at night again. This went on for a week; and at last Gervaise went to the Assommoir to make inquiries. Yes, he had been there a number of times, but no one knew where he was just then. Gervaise picked up the bag of tools and carried them home.

Lantier, seeing that Gervaise was out of spirits, proposed that she should go with him to a Café concert. She refused at first, being in no mood for laughing, otherwise she would have consented, for Lantier's proposal seemed to be prompted by the purest friendliness. He seemed really sorry for her trouble, and indeed assumed an absolutely paternal air.

Coupeau had never stayed away like this before, and she continually found herself going to the door, and looking up and down the street. She could not keep to her work, but wandered restlessly from place to place. Had Coupeau broken a limb? Had he fallen into the water? She did not think she could care so very much if he were killed, if this uncertainty were over—if she only knew what she had to expect. But it was very trying to live in this suspense.

Finally, when the gas was lighted, and Lantier renewed his proposition of the café, she consented. After all, why should she not go? Why should she refuse all pleasures because her husband chose to behave in this disgraceful way? If he would not come in, she should go out.

They hurried through their dinner, and as she went out with Lantier at eight o'clock, Gervaise begged Nana and Mamma Coupeau to go to bed early. The shop was closed and she gave the key to Madame Boche, telling her that if Coupeau came in, it would be as well to look out for the lights.

Lantier stood whistling while she gave these directions. Gervaise wore her silk dress, and she smiled as they walked down the street, in alternate shadow and light from the shop windows.

The Café concert was on the Boulevard de Rochechoumart. It had once been a café, and had had a concert-room built on of rough planks.

Over the door was a row of glass globes brilliantly illuminated. Long placards, nailed on wood, were standing quite out in the street by the side of the gutter.

"Here we are!" said Lantier. "Mademoiselle Amanda makes her début tonight."

Bibi-la-Grillade was reading the placard. Bibi had a black eye, as if he had been fighting.

"Hallo!" cried Lantier. "How are you? Where is Coupeau? Have you lost him?"

"Yes, since yesterday. We had a little fight with a waiter at Baquets. He wanted us to pay twice for what we had, and somehow Coupeau and I got separated, and I have not seen him since."

And Bibi gave a great yawn. He was in a disgraceful state of intoxication. He looked as if he had been rolling in the gutter.

"And you know nothing of my husband?" asked Gervaise.

"No, nothing. I think, though, he went off with a coachman."

Lantier and Gervaise passed a very agreeable evening at the Café concert, and when the doors were closed at eleven, they went home in a sauntering sort of fashion. They were in no hurry, and the night was fair, though a little cool. Lantier hummed the air which Amanda had sung, and Gervaise added the chorus. The room had been excessively warm, and she had drank several glasses of wine.

"Everybody is asleep," said Gervaise, after she had rung the bell three times.

She knocked at the door of the Boche quarters, and asked for her key.

The sleepy Concierge muttered some unintelligible words, from which Gervaise finally gathered that Coupeau had been brought in by Poisson, and that the key was in the door.

Gervaise stood aghast at the disgusting sight that met her eyes as she entered the room where Coupeau lay wallowing on the floor.

She shuddered and turned away. This sight annihilated every ray of sentiment remaining in her heart.

"What am I to do?" she said, piteously. "I can't stay here!"

Lantier snatched her hand.

"Gervaise," he said, "listen to me."

But she understood him, and drew hastily back.

"No, no! Leave me, Auguste. I can manage."

But Lantier would not obey her. He put his arm around her waist, and pointed to her husband as he lay snoring, with his mouth wide open.

"Leave me!" said Gervaise, imploringly; and she pointed to the room where her mother-in-law and Nana slept.

"You will wake them!" she said. "You would not shame me before my child? Pray go!"

He said no more, but slowly and softly kissed her on her ear, as he had so often teased her by doing in those old days. Gervaise shivered, and her blood was stirred to madness in her veins.

"What does that beast care?" she thought. "It is his fault," she murmured; "all his fault. He sends me from his room!"

And as Lantier drew her toward his door, Nana's face appeared for a moment at the window which lighted her little cabinet.

The mother did not see the child, who stood in her night-dress, pale with sleep. She looked at her father as he lay, and then watched her mother disappear in Lantier's room. She was perfectly grave, but in her eyes burned the sensual curiosity of premature vice.

⦗ CHAPTER IX ⦘

Clouds in the Horizon

T HAT WINTER MAMMA COUPEAU was very ill with an asthmatic attack, which she always expected in the month of December.

The poor woman suffered much, and the depression of her spirits was naturally very great. When left alone during the day, she moaned incessantly, rolling her head about on her pillow.

"Ah!" she said, "how unhappy I am! It is the same as a prison. I wish I were dead!"

And as soon as a visitor came in—Virginie or Madame Boche —she poured out her grievances. "I should not suffer so much among strangers. I should like, some times, a cup of tisane, but I can't get it; and Nana—that child whom I have raised from the cradle, disappears in the morning and never shows her face until night, when she sleeps right through and never once asks me how I am, or if she can do anything for me. It will soon be over, and I really believe this clear-starcher would smother me herself—if she were not afraid of the law!"

Gervaise, it is true, was not as gentle and sweet as she had been. Everything seemed to be going wrong with her, and she had lost heart and patience together. Mamma Coupeau had overheard her saying that she was really a great burden. This naturally cut her to the heart, and when she saw her eldest daughter, Madame Lerat, she wept piteously, and declared that she was being starved to death.

She told the most preposterous tales to Madame Lerat about Gervaise—of her new finery, and of cakes and delicacies eaten in the corner, and many other things of infinitely more consequence. Then in a little while she turned against the Lorilleux, and talked of them in the most bitter manner. At the height of her illness it so happened that her two daughters met one afternoon at her bedside. Their mother made a motion to them to come closer. Then she went on to tell them, between paroxysms of coughing, that her son came home dead-drunk the night before, and that she was absolutely certain that Gervaise spent the night in Lantier's room. "It is all the more disgusting," she added, "because I am certain that Nana heard what was going on quite as well as I did."

The two women did not appear either shocked or surprised.

"It is none of our business," said Madame Lorilleux. "If Coupeau does not choose to take any notice of her conduct, it is not for us to do so."

All the neighborhood were soon informed of the condition of things by her two sisters-in-law, who declared they entered her doors only on their mother's account, who poor thing, was compelled to live amid these abominations.

Every one accused Gervaise now of having perverted poor Lantier. "Men will be men," they said; "surely you can't expect them to turn a cold shoulder to women who throw themselves at their heads. She has no possible excuse; she is a disgrace to the whole street!"

Amid this sudden and fierce indignation, Gervaise lived—indifferent, dull and stupid. At first she loathed herself, and if Coupeau laid his hand on her she shivered, and ran away from him. But, by degrees, she became accustomed to it. Her indolence had become excessive, and she only wished to be quiet and comfortable.

After all, she asked herself, why should she care? If her lover and her husband were satisfied, why should she not be, too? So the household went on much as usual to all appearance. In reality, whenever Coupeau came in tipsy, she left and went to Lantier's room to sleep. She was not led there by passion or affection; it was simply that it was more comfortable. She was very like a cat in her choice of soft, clean places.

Mamma Coupeau never dared to speak out openly to the clear-starcher, but after a dispute she was unsparing in her hints and allusions. The first time, Gervaise fixed her eyes on her, and heard all she had to say in profound silence. Then without seeming to speak of herself, she took occasion to say not long afterward that when a woman was married to a man who was drinking himself to death, that a woman was very much to be pitied, and by no means to blame if she looked for consolation elsewhere.

Another time, when taunted by the old woman, she went still further, and declared that Lantier was as much her husband as was Coupeau—that he was the father of two of her children. She talked a little twaddle about the laws of nature, and a shrewd observer would have seen that she—parrot-like—was repeating the words that some other person had put into her mouth. Besides, what were her neighbors doing all about her? They were not so extremely respectable that they had the right to attack her. And then she took house after house, and showed her mother-in-law that while apparently so deaf to gossip, she yet knew all that was going on about her. Yes, she knew—and now seemed to gloat over that, which once had shocked and revolted her.

"It is none of my business, I admit," she cried; "let each person live as he pleases, according to his own light, and let everybody else alone."

One day when Mamma Coupeau spoke out more clearly, she said with compressed lips:

"Now look here: you are flat on your back, and you take advantage of that fact. I have never said a word to you about your own life, but I know it all the same—and it was atrocious! That is all! I am not going into particulars, but remember, you had best not sit in judgment on me!"

The old woman was nearly suffocated with rage and her cough.

The next day Goujet came for his mother's wash while Gervaise was out. Mamma Coupeau called him into her room and kept him for an hour. She read the young man's heart; she knew that his suspicions made him miserable. And in revenge for something that had displeased her, she told him the truth with many sighs and tears, as if her daughter-in-law's infamous conduct was a bitter blow to her.

When Goujet left her room, he was deadly pale, and looked ten years older than when he went in. The old woman had, too, the additional pleasure of telling Gervaise on her return that Madame Goujet had sent word that her linen must be returned to her at once, ironed or unironed. And she was so animated and comparatively amiable that Gervaise scented the truth, and knew instinctively what she had done, and what she was to expect with Goujet. Pale and trembling, she piled the linen neatly in a basket, and set forth to see Madame Goujet. Years had passed since she had paid her friends one penny. The debt still stood at four hundred and twenty-five francs. Each time she took the money for her washing she spoke of being pressed just at that time. It was a great mortification for her.

Coupeau was, however, less scrupulous, and said with a laugh, that if she kissed her friend occasionally in the corner, it would keep things straight and pay him well. Then Gervaise, with eyes blazing with indignation, would ask if he really meant that. Had he fallen so low? Neither should he speak of Goujet in that way in her presence.

Every time she took home the linen of these former friends she ascended the stairs with a sick heart.

Gervaise soon grew to care for nothing but her three meals per day. The shop ran itself; one by one her customers left her. Gervaise shrugged her shoulders half indifferently, half insolently; everybody could leave her, she said: she could always get work. But she was mistaken; and soon it became necessary for her to dismiss Madame Putois, keeping no assistant except Augustine, who seemed to grow more and more stupid as time went on. Ruin was fast approaching for Gervaise.

Her debts were increasing, but they had ceased to give her

any uneasiness. She was no longer honest or straightforward. She did not care whether she ever paid or not, so long as she got what she wanted. When one shop refused her more credit, she opened an account next door. She owed something in every shop in the whole Quartier. She dared not pass the grocer nor the baker in her own street, and was compelled to make a lengthy circuit each time she went out. The tradespeople muttered and grumbled, and some went so far as to call her a thief and a swindler.

It was very stupid of these people, after all, she said to Lantier. How could she pay them if she had no money? and where could she get money? She closed her eyes to the inevitable, and would not think of the Future. Mamma Coupeau was well again, but the household had been disorganized for more than a year. In summer there was more work brought to the shop—white skirts and cambric dresses. There were ups and downs, therefore: days when there was nothing in the house for supper, and others when the table was loaded.

Mamma Coupeau was seen almost daily, going out with a bundle under her apron, and returning without it and with a radiant face, for the old woman liked the excitement of going to the Mont-de-Piété.

Gervaise was gradually emptying the house—linen and clothes—tools and furniture. In the beginning she took advantage of a good week, to take out what she had pawned the week before, but after a while she ceased to do that, and sold her tickets. There was only one thing which cost her a pang, and that was selling her clock. She had sworn she would not touch it; not unless she was dying of hunger, and when at last she saw her mother-in-law carry it away, she dropped into a chair and wept like a baby. But when the old woman came back with twenty-five francs, and she found she had five francs more than was demanded by the pressing debt, which had caused her to make the sacrifice, she was consoled, and sent out at once for four sous worth of brandy. When these two women were on good terms, they often drank a glass together sitting at the corner of the ironing-table.

Mamma Coupeau had a wonderful talent for bringing a glass in the pocket of her apron without spilling a drop. She did not care to have the neighbors know, but, in good truth, the neighbors knew very well, and laughed and sneered as the old woman went in and out.

This, as was natural and right, increased the prejudice against Gervaise. Every one said that things could not go on much longer, the end was near.

Amid all this ruin Coupeau thrived surprisingly. Bad liquor seemed to affect him agreeably. His appetite was good in spite of the amount he drank, and he was growing stout. Lantier, however, shook his head, declaring that it was not honest flesh, and that he was bloated. But Coupeau drank all the more after this statement, and was rarely or ever sober. There began to be a strange blueish tone in his complexion.

He was ignorant of his wife's infidelity; at least, so all his friends declared. They believed, moreover, that were he to discover it there would be great trouble. But Madame Lerat, his own sister shook her head doubtfully, averring that she was not so sure of his ignorance.

Lantier was also in good health and spirits, neither too stout nor too thin. He wished to remain just where he was, for he was thoroughly well satisfied with himself, and this made him critical in regard to his food, as he had made a study of the things he should eat and those he should avoid, for the preservation of his figure. Even when there was not a cent he asked for eggs and cutlets; nourishing and light things were what he required, he said. He ruled Gervaise with a rod of iron, grumbled and found fault far more than Coupeau ever did. It was a house with two masters, one of whom, cleverer by far than the other, took the best of everything. He skimmed the Coupeaus, as it were, and kept all the cream for himself. He was fond of Nana because he liked girls better than boys. He troubled himself little about Etienne.

When people came and asked for Coupeau, it was Lantier who appeared in his shirt-sleeves with the air of the man of the house who is needlessly disturbed. He answered for Coupeau; said it was one and the same thing.

Gervaise did not find this life always smooth and agreeable. She had no reason to complain of her health. She had become very stout. But it was hard work to provide for and please these two men. When they came in, furious and out of temper, it was on her that they wrecked their rage. Coupeau abused her frightfully, and called her by the coarsest epithets. Lantier, on the contrary, was more select in his phraseology, but his words cut her quite as deeply.

One night she dreamed she was at the bottom of a well. Coupeau was pushing her down with his fists, and Lantier was tickling her to make her jump out quicker. And this she thought was a very fair picture of her life!

The utter deterioration of her nature was shown by the fact that she detested neither her husband nor Lantier. In a play at Gaïté, she had seen a woman hate her husband, and poison him for the sake of her lover. This she thought very strange and unnatural. Why could the three not have lived together peaceably? It would have been much more reasonable!

Toward autumn Lantier became more and more disgusted; declared he had nothing to live on but potato-parings, and that his health was suffering. He was enraged at seeing the house so thoroughly cleared out, and he felt that the day was not far off when he must take his hat and depart.

One day it came to pass that there was not a mouthful in the house, not even a radish. Lantier sat by the stove in sombre discontent. Finally he started up and went to call on the Poissons, to whom he suddenly became friendly to a degree. He showed himself especially civil to Virginie, whom he considered a clever woman, and well able to steer her bark through stormy seas.

Virginie one day happened to say in his presence that she should like to establish herself in some business. He approved the plan, and paid her a succession of adroit compliments on her capabilities, and cited the example of several women he knew, who had made or were making their fortunes in this way.

Virginie had the money, an inheritance from an aunt; but she hesitated, for she did not wish to leave the Quartier, and she did not know of any shop she could have. Then Lantier led her into a corner and whispered to her for ten minutes: he seemed to be persuading her to something. They continued to talk together in this way at intervals for several days, seeming to have some secret understanding.

Lantier all this time was fretting and scolding at the Coupeaus, asking Gervaise what on earth she intended to do, begging her to look things fairly in the face. She owed five or six hundred francs to the trades-people about her. She was behind-hand with her rent, and Marescot, the landlord, threatened to turn her out if they did not pay before the first of January.

The Mont-de-Piété had taken everything; there was literally nothing but the nails in the walls left. What did she mean to do?

Gervaise listened to all this at first listlessly, but she grew angry at last and cried out:

"Look here! I will go away to-morrow and leave the key in the door. I had rather sleep in the gutter than live in this way!"

"And I can't say that it would not be a wise thing for you to do!" answered Lantier insidiously. "I might possibly assist you to find some one to take the lease off your hands whenever you really conclude to leave the shop."

"I am ready to leave it at once!" cried Gervaise, violently. "I am sick and tired of it."

Then Lantier became serious and business-like. He spoke openly of Virginie, who, he said, was looking for a shop; in fact he now remembered having heard her say that she would like just such a one as this.

But Gervaise shrank back, and grew strangely calm at this name of Virginie.

"She would see," she said; "on the whole she must have time to think. People said a great many things when they were angry, which on reflection were found not to be advisable."

Lantier rang the changes on this subject for a week; but Gervaise said she had decided to employ some woman and go to work again, and if she were not able to get back her old customers she could try for new ones. She said this merely to show Lantier that she was not so utterly downcast and crushed as he had seemed to take for granted was the case.

He was reckless enough to drop the name of Virginie once more, and she turned upon him in a rage.

"No, no, never!" She had always distrusted Virginie, and if she wanted the shop it was only to humiliate her. Any other woman might have it, but not this hypocrite, who had been waiting for years to gloat over her downfall. No, she understood now only too well the meaning of the yellow sparks in her cat's-eyes. It was clear to her that Virginie had never forgotten the scene in the Lavatory, and if she did not look out there would be a repetition of it.

Lantier stood aghast at this anger, and this torrent of words, but presently he plucked up courage and bade her hold her tongue, and told her she should not talk of his friends in that way. As for himself he was sick and tired of other people's affairs; in future he should let them all take care of themselves, without a word of counsel from him.

January arrived, cold and damp. Mamma Coupeau took to her bed with a violent cold which she expected each year at this time. But those about her said she would never leave the house again, except feet first.

Her children had learned to look forward to her death as a happy deliverance for all. The physician who came once was not sent for again. A little tisane was given her from time to time, that she might not feel herself utterly neglected. She was just alive, that was all. It now became a mere question of time with her; but her brain was clear still, and in the expression of her eyes there were many things to be read—sorrow at seeing no sorrow in those she left behind her, and anger against Nana, who was utterly indifferent to her.

One Monday evening Coupeau came in, as tipsy as usual, and threw himself on the bed, all dressed. Gervaise intended to remain with her mother-in-law part of the night, but Nana was very brave, and said she should hear if her grandmother moved and wanted anything.

About half-past three Gervaise woke with a start; it seemed to her that a cold blast had swept through the room. Her candle had burned down, and she hastily wrapped a shawl around her with trembling hands, and hurried into the next room. Nana was sleeping quietly, and her grandmother was dead in the bed at her side.

Gervaise went to Lantier and waked him.

"She is dead," she said.

"Well! what of it?" he muttered, half asleep. "Why don't you go to sleep?"

She turned away in silence, while he grumbled at her coming to disturb him, by the intelligence of a death in the house.

Gervaise dressed herself, not without tears, for she really loved the cross old woman whose son lay in the heavy slumbers of intoxication.

When she went back to the room, she found Nana sitting up and rubbing her eyes. The child realized what had come to pass, and trembled nervously in the face of this death of which she had thought much in the last two days, as of something which was hidden from children.

"Get up!" said her mother, in a low voice. "I do not wish you to stay here."

The child slipped from her bed slowly and regretfully, with her eyes fixed on the dead body of her grandmother.

Gervaise did not know what to do with her, nor where to send her. At this moment Lantier appeared at the door. He had dressed himself, impelled by a little shame at his own conduct.

"Let the child go into my room," he said, "and I will help you."

Nana looked first at her mother and then at Lantier, and then trotted with her little bare feet into the next room and slipped into the bed that was still warm.

She lay there wide awake, with blazing cheeks and eyes, and seemed to be absorbed in thought.

While Lantier and Gervaise were silently occupied with the dead, Coupeau lay and snored.

Gervaise hunted in a bureau to find a little crucifix which she had brought from Plassans, when she suddenly remembered that Mamma Coupeau had sold it. They each took a glass of wine, and sat by the stove until daybreak.

About seven o'clock Coupeau woke. When he heard what had happened, he declared they were jesting. But when he saw the body he fell on his knees and wept like a baby. Gervaise was touched by these tears, and found her heart softer toward her husband than it had been for many a long year.

By nine o'clock the family were assembled in the shop, whose shutters had not been taken down. Lorilleux only remained for a few moments, and then went back to his shop. Madame

Lorilleux shed a few tears, and then sent Nana to buy a pound of candles.

"How like Gervaise!" she murmured. "She can do nothing in a proper way!"

Madame Lerat went about among the neighbors to borrow a crucifix. She brought one so large that when it was laid on the breast of Mamma Coupeau the weight seemed to crush her.

Then some one said something about holy water, so Nana was sent to the church with a bottle. The room assumed a new aspect. On a small table burned a candle, near it a glass of holy water in which was a branch of box.

"Everything is in order," murmured the sisters; "people can come now as soon as they please."

Lantier made his appearance about eleven. He had been to make inquiries in regard to funeral expenses.

"The coffin," he said, "is twelve francs, and if you want a mass, ten francs more. A hearse is paid for according to its ornaments."

"And who will pay for it?" asked Madame Lorilleux. "We can't, for we lost much money last week, and I am quite sure you would find it hard work!"

Coupeau, when he was consulted, shrugged his shoulders with a gesture of profound indifference. Madame Lerat said she would pay her share.

"There are three of us," said Gervaise, after a long calculation; "if we each pay thirty francs we can do it with decency."

But Madame Lorilleux burst out furiously:

"I will never consent to such folly. It is not that I care for the money, but I disapprove of the ostentation. You can do as you please."

"Very well," replied Gervaise, "I will. I have taken care of your mother while she was living, I can bury her now that she is dead."

Then Madame Lorilleux fell to crying, and Lantier had great trouble in preventing her from going away at once, and the quarrel grew so violent, that Madame Lerat hastily closed the door of the room where the dead woman lay, as if she feared the noise would waken her. The children's voices rose shrill in the air with Nana's perpetual "Tra-la-la" above all the rest.

"Heavens! how wearisome those children are with their songs," said Lantier. "Tell them to be quiet, and make Nana come in and sit down."

Gervaise obeyed these dictatorial orders, while her sisters-in-law went home to breakfast, while the Coupeaus tried to eat, but they were made uncomfortable by the presence of Death in their crowded quarters. The details of their daily life were disarranged.

Gervaise went to Goujet and borrowed sixty francs, which, added to thirty from Madame Lerat, would pay the expenses of the funeral.

By evening the Coupeaus felt it was more than they could bear. It was a mistake to keep a body so long. One has, after all, only so many tears to shed, and that done, grief turns to worry. Mamma Coupeau—stiff and cold—was a terrible weight on them all. They gradually lost the sense of oppression however, and spoke louder.

After a while Monsieur Marescot appeared. He went to the inner room and knelt at the side of the corpse. He was very religious, they saw. He made a sign of the cross in the air and dipped the branch into the holy water and sprinkled the body. Monsieur Marescot, having finished his devotions, passed out into the shop and said to Coupeau:

"I came for the two quarters that are due. Have you got the money for me?"

"No, sir; not entirely," said Gervaise, coming forward, excessively annoyed at this scene taking place in the presence of her sisters-in-law. "You see, this trouble came upon us—"

"Undoubtedly," answered her landlord; "but we all of us have our troubles. I cannot wait any longer. I really must have the money. If I am not paid by to-morrow I shall most assuredly take immediate measures to turn you out."

Gervaise clasped her hands imploringly, but he shook his head, saying that discussion was useless; besides, just then it would be a disrespect to the dead.

"A thousand pardons!" he said, as he went out. "But remember that I must have the money to-morrow."

And as he passed the open door of the lighted room, he saluted the corpse with another genuflection.

After he had gone, the ladies gathered around the stove, where a great pot of coffee stood, enough to keep them all awake, for the whole night. The Poissons arrived about eight o'clock; then Lantier, carefully watching Gervaise, began to speak of the disgraceful act committed by the landlord in coming to a house to collect money at such a time.

"He is a thorough hypocrite," continued Lantier; "and were I in Madame Coupeau's place, I would walk off and leave his house on his hands."

Gervaise heard, but did not seem to heed.

The Lorilleux, delighted at the idea that she would lose her shop, declared that Lantier's idea was an excellent one. They gave Coupeau a push and repeated it to him.

Gervaise seemed to be disposed to yield; and then Virginie spoke in the blandest of tones.

"I will take the lease off your hands," she said, "and will arrange the back rent with your landlord."

"No! no! thank you," cried Gervaise, shaking off the lethargy in which she had been wrapped. "I can manage this matter, and I can work. No, no, I say."

Lantier interposed and said, soothingly:

"Never mind! we will talk of it another time—to-morrow, possibly."

The family were to sit up all night. Nana cried vociferously when she was sent into the Boche quarters to sleep; the Poissons remained until midnight. Virginie began to talk of the country: she would like to be buried under a tree, with flowers and grass on her grave. Madame Lerat said, that in her wardrobe—folded up in lavender—was the linen sheet in which her body was to be wrapped.

When the Poissons went away Lantier accompanied them, in order, he said, to leave his bed for the ladies, who could take turns in sleeping there. But the ladies preferred to remain together about the stove.

The night seemed endless. They drank coffee, and went by turns to look at the body, lying silent and calm under the flickering light of the candle.

The interment was to take place at half-past ten, but Gervaise would gladly have given a hundred francs, if she had had them, to any one who would have taken Mamma Coupeau away three hours before the time fixed.

"Ah!" she said to herself, "it is no use to disguise the fact: people are very much in the way after they are dead, no matter how much you have loved them!"

Father Bazouge, who was never known to be sober, appeared with the coffin and the pall. When he saw Gervaise he stood with his eyes starting from his head.

"I beg your pardon," he said, "but I thought it was for you"; and he was turning to go away.

"Leave the coffin!" cried Gervaise, growing very pale. Bazouge began to apologize:

"I heard them talking yesterday, but I did not pay much attention. I congratulate you that you are still alive. Though why I do, I do not know, for life is not such a very agreeable thing."

Gervaise listened with a shiver of horror, and a morbid dread that he would take her away and shut her up in his box and bury her. She had once heard him say that he knew a woman who would be only too thankful if he would do exactly that.

"He is horribly drunk," she murmured, in a tone of mingled disgust and terror.

"It will come for you another time," he said, with a laugh; "you have only to make me a little sign. I am a great consolation to women sometimes; and you need not sneer at poor Father Bazouge, for he has held many a fine lady in his arms, and they made no complaint when he laid them down to sleep in the shade of the evergreens."

"Do hold your tongue," said Lorilleux; "this is no time for such talk. Be off with you!"

The clock struck ten. The friends and neighbors had assembled in the shop, while the family were in the back room nervous and feverish with suspense.

Four men appeared—the undertaker, Bazouge, and his three assistants placed the body in the coffin. Bazouge held the screws in his mouth and waited for the family to take their last farewell.

Then Coupeau, his two sisters and Gervaise kissed their mother, and their tears fell fast on her cold face. The lid was put on and fastened down.

The hearse was at the door, to the great edification of the

trades-people of the neighborhood, who said under their breath that the Coupeaus had best pay their debts.

Coupeau and Lorilleux, with their hats in their hands, walked at the head of the procession of men. After them followed the ladies, headed by Madame Lorilleux, in her black skirt—wrenched from the dead—her sister trying to cover a purple dress with a large black shawl.

Gervaise had lingered behind to close the shop and give Nana into the charge of Madame Boche, and then ran to overtake the procession, while the little girl stood with the Concierge, profoundly interested in seeing her grandmother carried in that beautiful carriage.

Just as Gervaise joined the procession, Goujet came up a side street and saluted her with a slight bow and with a faint sweet smile. The tears rushed to her eyes. She did not weep for Mamma Coupeau, but rather for herself; but her sisters-in-law looked at her as if she were the greatest hypocrite in the world.

At the church the ceremony was of short duration. The Mass dragged a little because the priest was very old.

The cemetery was not far off, and the cortège soon reached it. A priest came out of a house near by, and shivered as he saw his breath rise with each De Profundis he uttered.

The coffin was lowered, and as the frozen earth fell upon it, more tears were shed, accompanied, however, by sighs of relief.

The procession dispersed outside the gates of the cemetery, and at the very first cabaret Coupeau turned in, leaving Gervaise alone on the sidewalk. She beckoned to Goujet, who was turning the corner.

"I want to speak to you," she said, timidly. "I want to tell you how ashamed I am for coming to you again to borrow money, but I was at my wit's end."

"I am always glad to be of use to you," answered the blacksmith. "But pray never allude to the matter before my mother, for I do not wish to trouble her. She and I think differently on many subjects."

She looked at him sadly and earnestly. Through her mind flitted a vague regret that she had not done as he desired, that she had not gone away with him somewhere. Then a vile temptation assailed her. She trembled.

"You are not angry now?" she said, entreatingly.

"No, not angry, but still heart-sick. All is over between us now and forever." And he walked off with long strides, leaving Gervaise stunned by his words.

"All is over between us!" she kept saying to herself, "and what more is there for me then in life!"

She sat down in her empty, desolate room, and drank a large tumbler of wine. When the others came in, she looked up suddenly, and said to Virginie, gently:

"If you want the shop, take it!"

Virginie and her husband jumped at this, and sent for the Concierge, who consented to the arrangement on condition that the new tenants would become security for the two quarters then due.

This was agreed upon. The Coupeaus would take a room on the sixth floor, near the Lorilleux. Lantier said politely, that if it would not be disagreeable to the Poissons, he should like much to retain his present quarters.

The policeman bowed stiffly, but with every intention of being cordial—and said he decidedly approved of the idea.

Then Lantier withdrew from the discussion entirely, watching Gervaise and Virginie out of the corners of his eye.

That evening when Gervaise was alone again, she felt utterly exhausted. The place looked twice its usual size. It seemed to her that in leaving Mamma Coupeau in the quiet cemetery, she had also left much that was precious to her, a portion of her own life, her pride in her shop, her hopes and her energy. These were not all either that she had buried that day. Her heart was as bare and empty as her walls and her home. She was too weary to try and analyze her sensations, but moved about as if in a dream.

At ten o'clock, when Nana was undressed, she wept, begging that she might be allowed to sleep in her grandmother's bed. Her mother vaguely wondered that the child was not afraid, and allowed her to do as she pleased.

Nana was not timid by nature, and only her curiosity, not her fears, had been excited by the events of the last three days, and she curled herself up with delight in the soft, warm, feather bed.

⊰[*CHAPTER X*]⊱

Disasters and Changes

THE NEW LODGING of the Coupeaus was next that of the Bijards. Almost opposite their door was a closet under the stairs which went up to the roof—a mere hole without light or ventilation, where Father Bru slept.

A chamber and a small room, about as large as one's hand, were all the Coupeaus had now. Nana's little bed stood in the small room, the door of which had to be left open at night, lest the child should stifle.

The first few days she spent in tears. She felt smothered and cramped; after having had so much room to move about in, it seemed to her that she was smothering. It was only at the window she could breathe. The courtyard was not a place calculated to inspire cheerful thoughts. Opposite her was the window which years before had elicited her admiration, where every successive summer, scarlet beans had grown to a fabulous height on slender strings. Her room was on the shady side, and a pot of mignonette would die in a week on her sill.

Nevertheless, when Gervaise became accustomed to her new surroundings, she grew more content. The pieces of furniture she had sold to Virginie had facilitated her installation. When the fine weather came, Coupeau had an opportunity of going into the country to work. He went and lived three months without drinking—cured for the time being, by the fresh, pure air. It does a man sometimes an infinite deal of good to be taken away from all his old haunts, and from Parisian streets, which always seem to exhale a smell of brandy and of wine.

He came back as fresh as a rose, and he brought four hundred francs, with which he paid the Poissons the amount for which they had become security, as well as several other small but pressing debts. Gervaise had now two or three streets open to her again, which for some time she had not dared to enter.

She now went out to iron by the day, and had gone back to her old mistress, Madame Fauconnier, who was a kind-hearted creature, and ready to do anything for any one who flattered her adroitly.

With diligence and economy Gervaise could have managed to live comfortably and pay all her debts; but this prospect did not charm her particularly. She suffered acutely in seeing the Poissons in her old shop. She was by no means of a jealous or envious disposition, but it was not agreeable to her to hear the admiration expressed for her successors by her husband's sisters. To hear them, one would suppose that never had so beautiful a shop been seen before. They spoke of the filthy condition of the place when Virginie moved in—who had paid, they declared, thirty francs for cleaning it.

Virginie, after some hesitation, had decided on a small stock of groceries—sugar, tea, and coffee; also bonbons and chocolate. Lantier had advised these because he said the profit on them was immense. The shop was repainted, and shelves and cases were put in, and a counter with scales such as are seen at confectioners'. The little inheritance that Poisson held in reserve was seriously encroached upon. But Virginie was triumphant, for she had her way, and the Lorilleux did not spare Gervaise the description of a case or a jar.

It was said in the street that Lantier had deserted Gervaise—that she gave him no peace running after him; but this was not true, for he went and came to her apartment as he pleased. Scandal was connecting his name and Virginie's. They said Virginie had taken the clear-starcher's lover as well as her shop! The Lorilleux talked of nothing when Gervaise was present but Lantier, Virginie and the shop. Fortunately, Gervaise was not inclined to jealousy, and Lantier's infidelities had hitherto left her undisturbed; but she did not accept this new affair with equal tranquillity. She colored or turned pale as she heard these allusions, but she would not allow a word to pass her lips, as she was fully determined never to gratify her enemies by allowing them to see her discomfiture; but a dispute was heard by the neighbors about this time between herself and Lantier, who went angrily away, and was not seen by any one in the Coupeau quarters for more than a fortnight.

Coupeau behaved very oddly. This blind and complacent husband, who had closed his eyes to all that was going on at home, was filled with virtuous indignation at Lantier's indifference. Then Coupeau went so far as to tease Gervaise in regard to this desertion of her lovers. She had had bad luck, he said, with hatters and blacksmiths—why did she not try a mason?

He said this as if it were a joke, but Gervaise had a firm conviction that he was in deadly earnest. A man who was tipsy from one year's end to the next is not apt to be fastidious; and there are husbands who at twenty are very jealous, and at thirty have grown very complacent, under the influence of constant tippling.

Lantier preserved an attitude of calm indifference. He kept the peace between the Poissons and the Coupeaus. Thanks to him, Virginie and Gervaise affected for each other the most tender regard. He ruled the brunette as he had ruled the blonde, and he would swallow her shop as he had that of Gervaise.

It was in June of this year that Nana partook of her first communion. She was about thirteen, slender and tall as an asparagus plant; and her air and manner was the height of impertinence and audacity.

She had been sent away from the catechism class the year before on account of her bad conduct. And if the Curé did not make a similar objection this year, it was because he feared she would never come again, and that his refusal would launch on the Parisian pavé another castaway.

Nana danced with joy at the mere thought of what the Lorilleux—as her god-parents—had promised, while Madame Lerat gave the veil and cup, Virginie the purse, and Lantier a prayer-book; so that the Coupeaus looked forward to the day without anxiety.

The Poissons—probably through Lantier's advice—selected this occasion for their house-warming. They invited the Coupeau and the Boche family, as Pauline made her first communion on that day, as well as Nana.

The evening before, while Nana stood in an ecstasy of delight before her presents, her father came in, in an abominable condition. His virtuous resolutions had yielded to the air of Paris, he had fallen into evil ways again, and he now assailed his wife and child with the vilest epithets, which did not seem to shock Nana, for they could fall from her tongue on occasion with facile glibness.

"Mother and daughter!" he cried, "a nice pair they make. I understand very well what all this row is for: it is merely to show yourself in a new gown. I will put you in a bag and tie it close round your throat, and you will see if the Curé likes that!"

Nana looked her father full in the face, and, forgetting the lessons taught her by her priest, she said, in a low, concentrated voice:

"Beast!" That was all.

After Coupeau had eaten his soup he fell asleep, and in the morning woke quite amiable. He admired his daughter, and said she looked quite like a young lady in her white robe. Then he added, with a sentimental air, that a father on such days was naturally proud of his child. When they were ready to go to the church, and Nana met Pauline in the corridor, she examined the latter from head to foot, and smiled condescendingly on seeing that Pauline had not a particle of *chic*.

At the church Coupeau wept all the time. He was not the only person who wept, he was glad to see, and when the ceremony was over, he left the church feeling that it was the happiest day of his life. But an hour later he quarrelled with Lorilleux in a wine-shop because the latter was so hard-hearted.

The house-warming at the Poissons that night was very gay. Lantier sat between Gervaise and Virginie, and was equally civil and attentive to both. Opposite was Poisson with his calm, impassive face, a look he had cultivated since he began his career as a police officer.

But the Queens of the Fête were the two little girls, Nana and Pauline, who sat very erect lest they should crush and deface their pretty white dresses. At dessert there was a serious discussion in regard to the Future of the children. Madame Boche said that Pauline would at once enter a certain manufactory, where she would receive five or six francs per week. Gervaise had not decided yet, for Nana had shown no especial leaning in any direction. She had a good deal of taste, but she was butter-fingered and careless.

"I should make a florist of her," said Madame Lerat. "It is clean work, and pretty work, too."

"I have no objection to your trade," interrupted Gervaise. "If Nana likes to make flowers let her do so. Say, Nana, would you like it?"

The little girl did not look up from her plate, into which she was dipping a crust of bread. She smiled faintly as she replied:

"Yes, mamma; if you desire it, I have no objection."

The decision was instantly made, and Coupeau wished his sister to take her the very next day to the place where she herself worked—Rue du Caire; and the circle talked gravely of the duties of life. Boche said that Pauline and Nana were now women, since they had been to Communion, and they ought to be serious, and learn to cook and to mend. They alluded to their future marriages, their homes and their children, and the girls touched each other under the table, giggled and grew very red. Lantier asked them if they did not have little husbands already, and Nana blushingly confessed that she loved Victor Fauconnier, and never meant to marry any one else.

Madame Lorilleux said to Madame Boche on their way home:

"Nana is our goddaughter now, but if she goes into that flower business, in six months she will be on the pavé, and we will have nothing to do with her."

Gervaise told Boche that she thought the shop admirably arranged. She had looked forward to an evening of torture, and was surprised that she had not experienced a pang.

But this was the last bright day in that household. Two years passed away, and their prospects grew darker and their demoralization and degradation more evident. They went without food and without fire, but never without brandy.

They found it almost impossible to meet their rent, and a certain January came when they had not a penny, and Father Boche ordered them to leave.

It was frightfully cold, with a sharp wind blowing from the north.

Monsieur Marescot appeared in a warm overcoat, and his hands encased in warm woollen gloves, and told them they must go even if they slept in the gutter. The whole house was oppressed with woe, and a dreary sound of lamentation arose from most of the rooms, for half the tenants were behind-hand. Gervaise sold her bed and paid the rent. Nana made nothing as yet, and Gervaise had so fallen off in her work that Madame Fauconnier had reduced her wages. She was irregular in her hours, and often absented herself from the shop for several days together, but was none the less vexed to discover that her old employée, Madame Putois, had been placed above her. Naturally, at the end of the week, Gervaise had little money coming to her.

As to Coupeau, if he worked, he brought no money home, and his wife had ceased to count upon it. Sometimes he declared he had lost it, through a hole in his pocket, or it had been stolen; but after a while he ceased to make any excuses.

Gervaise now quarrelled with her husband incessantly. The warmth of affection of husband and wife, of parents for their children, and children for their parents had fled, and left them all shivering, each apart from the other.

Gervaise did not shudder when she saw her husband lying drunk in the gutter. She would not have pushed him in, to be sure; but if he were out of the way it would be a good thing for everybody. She even went so far as to say one day, in a fit of rage, that she should be glad to see him brought home on a shutter. Of what good was he to any human being? He ate, and he drank, and he slept. His child learned to hate him, and she read the accidents in the papers with the feelings of an unnatural daughter. What a pity it was that her father had not been the man who was killed when that omnibus tipped over!

In addition to her own sorrows and privations, Gervaise, whose heart was not yet altogether hard, was condemned to hear now of the sufferings of others. The corner of the house in which she lived seemed to be consecrated to those who were as poor as herself. No smell of cooking filled the air, which, on the contrary, was laden with the shrill cries of hungry children—heavy with the sighs of weary, heart-broken mothers, and with the oaths of drunken husbands and fathers.

Gervaise pitied Father Bru from the bottom of her heart; he lay the greater part of the time rolled up in the straw in his den under the staircase leading to the roof. When two or three days elapsed without his showing himself, some one opened the door and looked in, to see if he were still alive.

Yes, he was living; that is, he was not dead. When Gervaise had bread she always remembered him. If she had learned to

hate men because of her husband, her heart was still tender toward animals, and Father Bru seemed like one to her. She regarded him as a faithful old dog.

Gervaise was also troubled by the vicinity of the undertaker Bazouge—a wooden partition alone separated their rooms. When he came in at night she could hear him throw down his glazed hat, which fell, with a dull thud like a shovelful of clay, on the table. The black cloak hung against the wall rustled like the wings of some huge bird of prey. She could hear his every movement, and she spent most of her time listening to him with morbid horror, while he—all unconscious—hummed his vulgar songs and tipsily staggered to his bed, under which the poor woman's sick fancy pictured a dead body concealed.

She would as lief have resided at Père La Chaise and watched the moles at their work. The man terrified her; his incessant laughter dismayed her. She talked of moving, but at the same time was reluctant to do so, for there was a strange fascination about Bazouge after all. Had he not told her once that he would come for her and lay her down to sleep in the shadow of waving branches, where she would know neither hunger nor toil?

She wished she could try it for a month. And she thought how delicious it would be in midwinter, just at the time her quarter's rent was due. But alas! this was not possible. The rest and the sleep must be Eternal; this thought chilled her, and her longing for Death faded away before the unrelenting severity of the bonds exacted by Mother Earth.

One night she was sick and feverish, and instead of throwing herself out of the window as she was tempted to do, she rapped on the partition and called loudly—

"Father Bazouge! Father Bazouge!"

The undertaker was kicking off his slippers, singing a vulgar song as he did so.

"What is the matter?" he answered.

But at his voice Gervaise awoke as from a nightmare. What had she done? Had she really tapped? she asked herself, and she recoiled from his side of the wall in chill horror. It seemed to her that she felt the undertaker's hands on her head. No! No! She was not ready. She told herself that she had not intended to call him. It was her elbow that had knocked the wall accidentally,

301

and she shivered from head to foot at the idea of being carried away in this man's arms.

"What is the matter?" repeated Bazouge. "Can I serve you in any way, Madame?"

"No! No! It is nothing!" answered the laundress, in a choked voice. "I am very much obliged."

While the undertaker slept she lay wide awake, holding her breath and not daring to move, lest he should think she called him again.

She said to herself that under no circumstances would she ever appeal to him for assistance, and she said this over and over again with the vain hope of reassuring herself, for she was by no means at ease in her mind.

Gervaise had before her a noble example of courage and fortitude in the Bijard family. Little Lalie, that tiny child—about as big as a pinch of salt—swept and kept her room like wax; she watched over the two younger children with all the care and patience of a mother. This she had done since her father had kicked her mother to death. She had entirely assumed that mother's place, even to receiving the blows which had fallen formerly on that poor woman. It seemed to be a necessity of his nature that when he came home drunk he must have some woman to abuse. Lalie was too small, he grumbled; one blow of his fist covered her whole face, and her skin was so delicate that the marks of his five fingers would remain on her cheek for days!

He would fly at her like a wolf at a poor little kitten, for the merest trifle. Lalie never answered, never rebelled, and never complained. She merely tried to shield her face, and suppressed all shrieks, lest the neighbors should come; her pride could not endure that.

Gervaise had conceived a strong affection for this little neighbor. She treated her like a woman who knew something of life.

One day she was altering a dress of Nana's for her, and when the child tried it on, Gervaise was chilled with horror at seeing her whole back purple and bruised—the tiny arm bleeding—all the innocent flesh of childhood martyrized by the brute—her father.

Bazouge might get the coffin ready, she thought, for the little girl could not bear this long. But Lalie entreated her friend to say nothing, telling her that her father did not know what he was doing; that he had been drinking. She forgave him with her whole heart—for madmen must not be held accountable for their deeds. After that, Gervaise was on the watch whenever she heard Bijard coming up the stairs. But she never caught him in any act of absolute brutality.

One afternoon Lalie completed her day's labors, was kneeling and playing with the children. The window was open, and the air shook the door so that it sounded like gentle raps.

"It is Mr. Wind," said Lalie; "come in, Mr. Wind—how are you today?"

And she made a low curtsy to Mr. Wind. The children did the same in high glee, and she was quite radiant with happiness, which was not often the case.

"Come in, Mr. Wind!" she repeated; but the door was pushed open by a rough hand, and Bijard entered. Then a sudden change came over the scene. The two children crouched in a corner, while Lalie stood in the centre of the floor frozen stiff with terror, for Bijard held in his hand a new whip, with a long and wicked-looking lash. He laid this whip on the bed, and did not kick either one of the children, but smiled in the most vicious way, showing his two lines of blackened, irregular teeth. He was very drunk and very noisy.

He lay down without undressing, and watched the child as she moved about the room. Troubled by this strange conduct, the child ended by breaking a cup. Then, without disturbing himself, he took up the whip and showed it to her.

"Look here, fool," he said, grimly: "I bought this for you, and it cost me fifty sous; but I expect to get a good deal more than fifty sous' worth of good out of it. With this long lash I need not run about after you, for I can reach you in every corner of the room. You will break the cups, will you? Come, now, jump about a little, and say good-morning to Mr. Wind again!"

He did not even sit up in the bed, but with his head buried in the pillow, snapped the whip with a noise like that made by a postilion. The lash curled round Lalie's slender body—she

303

fell to the floor; but he lashed her again, and compelled her to rise.

A light foam was on his lips, and his suffused eyes were starting from their sockets. Poor little Lalie darted about the room like a terrified bird, but the lash tingled over her shoulders, coiled around her slender legs, and stung like a viper.

The door opened, and Gervaise entered. She had heard the noise. She stood aghast at the scene, and then was seized with noble rage.

"Let her be!" she cried. "I will go myself and summon the police."

Bijard growled like an animal who is disturbed over his prey.

"Why do you meddle?" he exclaimed. "What business is it of yours?"

And with another adroit movement he cut Lalie across the face. The blood gushed from her lip. Gervaise snatched a chair and flew at the brute, but the little girl held her skirts and said it did not hurt much, it would be over soon, and she washed the blood away, speaking gently to the frightened children.

When Gervaise thought of Lalie she was ashamed to complain. She wished she had the courage of this child. She knew that she had lived on dry bread for weeks, and that she was so weak she could hardly stand, and the tears came to the woman's eyes as she saw the precocious mite, who had known nothing of the innocent happiness of her years. And Gervaise took this slender creature for example, whose eyes alone told the story of her misery and hardships, for in the Coupeau family, the vitriol of the Assommoir was doing its work of destruction. Gervaise had seen a whip. Gervaise had learned to dread it, and this dread inspired her with tenderest pity for Lalie. Coupeau had lost the flesh and the bloated look which had been his, and he was thin and emaciated. His complexion was gradually acquiring a leaden hue. His appetite was utterly gone. It was with difficulty that he swallowed a mouthful of bread. His stomach turned against all solid food, but he took his brandy every day. This was his meat as well as his drink, and he touched nothing else.

When he crawled out of his bed in the morning he stood

for a good fifteen minutes, coughing and spitting out a bitter liquid that rose in his throat and choked him.

He did not feel any better until he had taken what he called "a good drink," and later in the day his strength returned. He felt strange prickings in the skin of his hands and feet. But lately his limbs had grown heavy. This pricking sensation gave place to the most excruciating cramps, which he did not find very amusing. He rarely laughed now, but often stopped short and stood still on the sidewalk, troubled by a strange buzzing in his ears, and by flashes of light before his eyes. Everything looked yellow to him; the houses seemed to be moving away from him. At other times when the sun was full on his back, he shivered as if a stream of ice-water had been poured down between his shoulders. But the thing he liked the least about himself, was a nervous trembling in his hands, the right hand especially.

"Have I become an old woman, then?" he asked himself, with sudden fury. He tried with all his strength to lift his glass and command his nerves enough to hold it steady. But the glass had a regular tremulous movement from right to left, and left to right again, in spite of all his efforts.

Then he emptied it down his throat, saying that when he had swallowed a dozen more, he should be all right and as steady as a monument. Gervaise told him on the contrary that he must leave off drinking, if he wished to leave off trembling.

In March Coupeau came in one night drenched to the skin. He had been caught out in a shower. That night he could not sleep for coughing. In the morning he had a high fever, and the physician who was sent for advised Gervaise to send him at once to the hospital.

And Gervaise made no objection; once she had refused to trust her husband to these people; but now she consigned him to their tender mercies without a regret, in fact she should regard it as a mercy.

Nevertheless, when the litter came, she turned very pale, and if she had had even ten francs in her pocket would have kept him at home. She walked to the hospital by the side of the litter, and went into the ward where he was placed. The room looked to her like a miniature Père La Chaise, with its rows of beds

305

on either side, and its path down the middle. She went slowly away, and in the street she turned and looked up. How well she remembered when Coupeau was at work on those gutters, cheerily singing in the morning air! He did not drink in those days, and she, at her window in the Hotel Boncœur, had watched his athletic form against the sky, and both had waved their handkerchiefs. Yes, Coupeau had worked more than a year on this hospital, little thinking that he was preparing a place for himself. Now he was no longer on the roof—he had built a dismal nest within. Good God! was she, and the once happy wife and mother, one and the same? How long ago those days seemed!

The next day when Gervaise went to make inquiries, she found the bed empty. A Sister explained that her husband had been taken to the asylum of Sainte-Anne, because the night before he had suddenly become unmanageable from delirium, and had uttered such terrible howls that it disturbed the inmates of all the beds in that ward.

The clear-starcher went home, but how or by what route she never knew. Her husband was mad—she heard these words reverberating through her brain. Life was growing very strange. Nana simply said that he must, of course, be left at the asylum, for he might murder them both.

On Sunday only could Gervaise go to Sainte-Anne. It was a long distance off. Fortunately there was an omnibus which went very near. She got out at La Rue Santé, and bought two oranges that she might not go quite empty-handed.

But when she went in, to her astonishment she found Coupeau sitting up. He welcomed her gayly.

"You are better!" she exclaimed.

"Yes, nearly well," he replied; and they talked together a while, and she gave him the oranges, which pleased and touched him, for he was a different man, now that he drank tisane instead of liquor. She did not dare allude to his delirium, but he spoke of it himself.

"Yes," he said, "I was in a pretty state! I saw rats running all over the floor and the walls, and you were calling me; and I saw all sorts of horrible things! But I am all right now. Once in a while I have a bad dream, but everybody does, I suppose

Gervaise remained with him until night. When the house surgeon made his rounds at six o'clock, he told him to hold out his hands. They scarcely trembled—an almost imperceptible motion of the tips of his fingers was all. But as the room grew darker, Coupeau became restless. Two or three times he sat up and peered into the remote corners.

Suddenly he stretched out his arms, and seemed to crush some creature on the wall.

"What is it?" asked Gervaise, terribly frightened.

"Rats!" he said, quietly; "only rats!"

After a long silence, he seemed to be dropping off to sleep, with disconnected sentences falling from his lips.

"Dirty beasts! Look out, one is under your skirts!" He pulled the covering hastily over his head, as if to protect himself against the creature he saw.

Then, starting up in mad terror, he screamed aloud. A nurse ran to the bed, and Gervaise was sent away mute with horror at this scene.

But when, on the following Sunday, she went again to the hospital, Coupeau was really well. All his dreams had vanished. He slept like a child, ten hours without lifting a finger. His wife, therefore, was allowed to take him away. The house surgeon gave him a few words of advice before he left, assuring him, if he continued to drink, he would be a dead man in three months. All depended on himself. He could live at home just as he had lived at Sainte-Anne's, and must forget that such things as wine and brandy existed.

"He is right," said Gervaise, as they took their seats in the omnibus.

"Of course he is right," answered her husband. But after a moment's silence he added:

"But then, you know, a drop of brandy now and then never hurts a man: it aids digestion."

That very evening he took a tiny drop, and for a week was very moderate; he had no desire, he said, to end his days at Bicêtre. But he was soon off his guard, and one day his little drop ended in a full glass—to be followed by a second, and so on. At the end of a fortnight he had fallen back in the old rut.

Gervaise did her best, but after all what can a wife do in such circumstances?

She had been so startled by the scene at the asylum, that she had fully determined to begin a regular life again, and hoped that he would assist her and do the same himself. But now she saw that there was no hope—that even the knowledge of the inevitable results could not restrain her husband now.

Then the Hell on earth began again; hopeless and intolerant, Nana asked indignantly why he had not remained in the asylum. All the money she made, she said, should be spent in brandy for her father, for the sooner it was ended, the better for them all.

Gervaise blazed out one day, when he lamented his marriage, and told him that it was for her to curse the day when she first saw him.

Gervaise, now utterly discouraged, grew more indolent every day. Her room was rarely swept. The Lorilleux said they could not enter it, it was so dirty. They talked all day long over their work of the downfall of Wooden Legs. They gloated over her poverty and her rags.

"Well! well!" they murmured. "A great change has indeed come to that beautiful blonde who was so fine in her blue shop."

One Saturday, Coupeau had told his wife he would take her to the circus; he had earned a little money and insisted on indulging himself. Nana was obliged to stay late at the place where she worked, and would sleep with her aunt, Madame Lerat.

Seven o'clock came, but no Coupeau. Her husband was drinking with his comrades probably. She had washed a cap and mended an old gown with the hope of being presentable. About nine o'clock, in a towering rage, she sallied forth on an empty stomach to find Coupeau.

"Are you looking for your husband?" said Madame Boche. "He is at the Assommoir. Boche has just seen him there."

Gervaise muttered her thanks and went with rapid steps to the Assommoir.

A fine rain was falling. The gas in the tavern was blazing brightly—lighting up the mirrors, the bottles and glasses. She stood at the window and looked in. He was sitting at a table with his comrades. The atmosphere was thick with smoke, and he looked stupefied and half asleep.

She shivered, and wondered why she should stay there, and so thinking turned away, only to come back twice to look again.

Finally, she determined on a bold step: she opened the door and deliberately walked up to her husband. After all, why should she not ask him why he had not kept his promise of taking her to the circus? At any rate she would not stay out there in the rain, and melt away like a cake of soap.

"She is crazy!" said Coupeau, when he saw her. "I tell you she is crazy!"

He and all his friends shrieked with laughter, but no one condescended to say what it was that was so very droll. Gervaise stood still, a little bewildered by this unexpected reception. Coupeau was so amiable that she said:

"Come, you know it is not too late to see something."

"Sit down a minute," said her husband, not moving from his seat.

Gervaise saw she could not stand there among all those men, so she accepted the offered chair. She looked at the glasses whose contents glittered like gold. She looked at these dirty, shabby men, and at the others crowding around the counter. She turned around and saw the still, the machine that created drunkards. That evening the copper was dull and glittered only in one round spot. The shadows of the apparatus on the wall behind were strange and weird—creatures with tails—monsters opening gigantic jaws as if to swallow the whole world.

"What will you take to drink?" said Coupeau.

"Nothing," answered his wife. "You know I have had no dinner!"

"You need it all the more, then! Have a drop of something!"

As she hesitated, Mes-Bottes said, gallantly:

"The lady would like something sweet like herself."

"I like men," she answered, angrily, "who do not get tipsy and talk like fools! I like men who keep their promises!"

Her husband laughed.

"You had better drink your share," he said; "for the devil a bit of a circus will you see to-night."

She looked at him fixedly. A heavy frown contracted her eyebrows. She answered slowly:

"You are right; it is a good idea. We can drink up the money together."

Bibi brought her a glass of anisette. As she sipped it, she remembered all at once the brandied fruit she had eaten in the same place with Coupeau, when he was courting her. That day she had left the brandy and took only the fruit; and now she was sitting there drinking liqueur.

But the anisette was good. When her glass was empty she refused another, and yet she was not satisfied.

She looked around at the infernal machine behind her—a machine that should have been buried ten fathoms deep in the sea. Nevertheless, it had for her a strange fascination, and she longed to quench her thirst with that liquid fire.

"What is that you have in your glasses?" she asked.

"That, my dear," answered her husband, "is Father Colombe's own especial brew. Taste it."

And when a glass of the vitriol was brought to her, Coupeau bade her swallow it down, saying it was good for her.

After she had drunk this glass, Gervaise was no longer conscious of the hunger that had tormented her. Coupeau told her they could go to the circus another time, and she felt she had best stay where she was. It did not rain in the Assommoir, and she had come to look upon the scene as rather amusing. She was comfortable and sleepy. She took a third glass, and then put her head on her folded arms, supporting them on the table, and listened to her husband and his friends as they talked.

Behind her the still was at work, with constant drip—drip—and she felt a mad desire to grapple with it as with some dangerous beast, and tear out its heart. She seemed to feel herself caught in those copper fangs, and fancied that those coils of pipe were wound around her own body—slowly but surely crushing out her life.

She vaguely heard a quarrel arise, and a crash of chairs and tables, and then Father Colombe promptly turned every one into the street.

It was still raining, and a cold sharp wind blowing. Gervaise lost Coupeau—found him—and then lost him again. She wanted to go home, but she could not find her way. At the corner of the street she took her seat by the side of the gutter, thinking herself at her wash-tub. Finally she got home and endeavored to walk straight past the door of the Concierge, within whose room she was vaguely conscious of the Poissons and Lorilleux holding up their hands in disgust at her condition.

She never knew how she got up those six flights of stairs. But when she turned into her own corridor little Lalie ran towards her with loving, extended arms.

"Dear Madame Gervaise," she cried, "papa has not come in; please come and see my children. They are sleeping so sweetly!"

But when she looked up in the face of the clear-starcher she recoiled, trembling from head to foot. She knew only too well that alcoholic smell—those wandering eyes, and convulsed lips.

Then as Gervaise staggered past her without speaking, the child's arms fell at her side, and she looked after her friend with sad and solemn eyes.

ᐊ CHAPTER XI ᐅ
Little Nana

NANA WAS GROWING fast—fair, fresh and dimpled—her skin, velvety like a peach, and eyes so bright that men often asked her if they might not light their pipes at them. Her mass of blonde hair—the color of ripe wheat—looked around her temples as if it were powdered with gold. She had a quaint little trick of sticking out the tip of her tongue between her white teeth, and this habit, for some reason, exasperated her mother.

She was very fond of finery and very coquettish. In this house, where bread was not always to be got, it was difficult for her to indulge her caprices in the matter of costume, but she did wonders. She brought home odds and ends of ribbons, from the shop where she worked, and made them up into bows and knots with which she ornamented her dirty dresses.

Summer was the season of her triumphs. In a calico dress that cost five or six francs, she was as fresh and sweet as a spring morning, and made the dull street radiant with her youth and her beauty. She went by the name of "The Little

Chicken." One gown in particular suited her to perfection. It was white, with rose-colored dots, without trimming of any kind. The skirt was short and showed her feet. The sleeves were very wide, and displayed her arms to the elbows. She turned the neck away and fastened it with pins—in a corner in the corridor, dreading her father's jests—to exhibit her pretty rounded throat. A rose-colored ribbon, knotted in the rippling masses of her hair, completed her toilet. She was a charming combination of child and woman.

Sundays at this period of her life were her days for coquetting with the public. She looked forward to them all the week through, with a longing for liberty and fresh air.

Early in the morning she began her preparations, and stood for hours in her chemise before the bit of broken mirror nailed by the window, and as every one could see her, her mother would be very much vexed, and ask how long she intended to show herself in that way.

But she, quite undisturbed, went on fastening down the little curls on her forehead with a little sugar and water, and then sewed the buttons on her boots, or took a stitch or two in her frock; bare-footed all this time, and with her chemise slipping off her rounded shoulders.

She was very lovely in this scanty costume, the color flushing her cheeks in her indignation at her father's sometimes coarse remarks. She did not dare answer him however, but bit off her thread in silent rage. After breakfast, she went down to the court-yard.

Five or six girls—Nana, Pauline and others—lingered in the court-yard for a time, and then took flight all together into the streets, and thence to the outer Boulevards. They walked in a line, filling up the whole sidewalk, with ribbons fluttering in their uncovered hair.

Nana walked in the centre and gave her arm to Pauline; and, as they were the oldest and tallest of the band, they gave the law to the others, and decided where they should go for the day, and what they should do.

Nana and Pauline were deep ones. They did nothing without premeditation. If they ran it was to show their slender ankles, and when they stopped and panted for breath it was sure to be at the side of some youths—young workmen of their acquaintance—who smoked in their faces as they talked. Nana had her favorite, whom she always saw at a great distance—Victor Fauconnier; and Pauline adored a young cabinet-maker, who gave her apples.

Toward sunset the great pleasure of the day began. A band of mountebanks would spread a well-worn carpet, and a circle was formed to look on. Nana and Pauline were always in the thickest of the crowd, their pretty fresh dresses crushed between dirty blouses, but insensible to the mingled odors of dust and alcohol, tobacco and dirt. They heard vile language; it did not disturb them; it was their own tongue—they heard little else. They listened to it with a smile, their delicate cheeks unflushed.

The only thing that disturbed them, was the appearance of their fathers, particularly if these fathers seemed to have been drinking. They kept a good lookout for this disaster.

"Look!" cried Pauline. "Your father is coming, Nana."

Then the girl would crouch on her knees and bid the others stand close around her, and when he had passed on after an inquiring look she would jump up, and they would all utter peals of laughter.

But one day Nana was kicked home by her father, and Boche dragged Pauline away by her ear.

The girls would ordinarily return to the court-yard in the twilight, and establish themselves there with the air of not having been away; and each invented a story with which to greet their questioning parents. Nana now received forty sous per day at the place where she had been apprenticed. The Coupeaus would not allow her to change, because she was there under the supervision of her aunt, Madame Lerat, who had been employed for many years in the same establishment.

The girl went off at an early hour in her little black dress, which was too short and too tight for her, and Madame Lerat was bidden, whenever she was after her time, to inform Gervaise, who allowed her just twenty minutes, which was quite long enough. But she was often seven or eight minutes late, and she spent her whole day coaxing her aunt not to tell her mother. Madame Lerat, who was fond of the girl and understood the follies of youth, did not tell; but, at the same time, she read Nana many a long sermon on her follies, and talked of her own responsibility, and of the dangers a young girl ran in Paris.

"You must tell me everything," she said. "I am too indulgent to you, and if evil should come of it I should throw myself into the Seine. Understand me, my little kitten; if a man should speak to you, you must promise to tell me every word he says. Will you swear to do this?"

Nana laughed an equivocal little laugh. Oh! yes, she would promise.

The place where the aunt and niece worked side by side was a large room, with a long table down the centre. Shelves against the wall were piled with boxes and bundles—all covered with a thick coating of dust. The gas had blackened the ceiling. The two windows were so large that the women, seated at the table, could see all that was going on in the street below.

Madame Lerat was the first to make her appearance in the morning, but in another fifteen minutes all the others were there. One morning in July Nana came in last, which, however, was the usual case.

"I shall be glad when I have a carriage!" she said, as she ran to the window without even taking off her hat—a shabby little straw.

"What are you looking at?" asked her aunt, suspiciously. "Did your father come with you?"

"No indeed," answered Nana, carelessly; "nor am I looking at anything. It is awfully warm, and of all things in the world I hate to be in a hurry."

The morning was indeed frightfully hot. The work-women had closed the blinds, leaving a crack, however, through which they could inspect the street, and they took their seats on each side of the table—Madame Lerat at the further end. There were eight girls, four on either side, each with her little pot of glue, her pincers and other tools; heaps of wires of different lengths and sizes lay on the table, spools of cotton, and of different-colored papers, petals and leaves cut out of silk, velvet and satin.

"Did you know," said Léonie, as she picked up a roseleaf

with her pincers, "how wretched poor Caroline is with that fellow who used to call for her regularly every night?"

Before any one could answer, Léonie added: "Hush! here comes Madame."

And in sailed Madame Titreville, a tall, thin woman, who usually remained below in the shop. Her employées stood in dead terror of her, as she was never known to smile. She went from one to another, finding fault with all: she ordered one woman to pull a marguerite to pieces and make it over, and then went out as stiffly and silently as she had come in.

"Houp! Houp!" said Nana, under her breath, and a giggle ran round the table.

"Really, young ladies," said Madame Lerat, "you will compel me to severe measures."

But no one was listening, and no one feared her. She was very tolerant. They could say what they pleased, provided they put it in decent language.

Nana was certainly in a good school! Her instincts, to be sure, were vicious; but these instincts were fostered and developed in this place, as is too often the case, when a crowd of girls are herded together. It was the story of a basket of apples, the good ones spoiled by those that were already rotten. If two girls were whispering in a corner, ten to one they were telling some story that could not be told aloud.

Nana was not yet thoroughly perverted; but the curiosity which had been her distinguishing characteristic as a child had not deserted her, and she scarcely took her eyes from a girl by the name of Lisa, about whom strange stories were told.

"How warm it is!" she exclaimed, suddenly rising and pushing open the blinds. Léonie saw a man standing on the sidewalk opposite.

"Who is that old fellow," she said. "He has been there a full quarter of an hour."

"Some fool who has nothing better to do, I suppose," said Madame Lerat. "Nana, will you come back to your work? I have told you that you should not go to that window."

Nana took up her violets, and they all began to watch this man. He was well dressed, about fifty, pale and grave. For a full hour he watched the windows.

"Look!" said Léonie, "he has an eyeglass. Oh! he is very *chic*. He is waiting for Augustine." But Augustine sharply answered that she did not like the old man.

"You make a great mistake then," said Madame Lerat, with her equivocal smile.

Nana listened to the conversation which followed—revelling in indecency—as much at home in it, as a fish is in water. All the time her fingers were busy at work. She wound her violet stems, and fastened in the leaves with a slender strip of green paper. A drop of gum—and then behold a bunch of delicate fresh verdure which would fascinate any lady. Her fingers were especially deft by Nature. No instruction could have imparted this quality.

The gentleman had gone away, and the workshop settled down into quiet once more. When the bell rang for twelve, Nana started up, and said she would go out and execute any commissions. Léonie sent for two sous worth of shrimp; Augustine for some fried potatoes; Sophie for a sausage; and Lisa for a bunch of radishes. As she was going out, her aunt said, quietly:

"I will go with you. I want something."

Lo! in the lane running up by the shop was the mysterious stranger. Nana turned very red, and her aunt drew her arm within her own, and hurried her along.

So, then, he had come for her! Was not this pretty behavior for a girl of her age? And Madame Lerat asked question after question; but Nana knew nothing of him, she declared, though he had followed her for five days.

Madame Lerat looked at the man out of the corners of her eyes. "You must tell me everything," she said.

While they talked, they went from shop to shop, and their arms grew full of small packages; but they hurried back, still talking of the gentleman.

"It may be a good thing," said Madame Lerat, "if his intentions are only honorable."

The work-women ate their breakfast on their knees; they were in no hurry, either, to return to their work; when, suddenly, Léonie uttered a low hiss, and, like magic, each girl was busy. Madame Titreville entered the room, and again made her rounds.

Madame Lerat did not allow her niece after this day to set foot on the street without her. Nana at first was inclined to rebel, but on the whole, it rather flattered her vanity to be guarded like a treasure. They had discovered that the man who followed her with such persistency was a manufacturer of buttons, and one night the aunt went directly up to him and told him that he was behaving in a most improper manner. He bowed, and turning on his heel, departed—not angrily by any means, and the next day he did as usual.

One day, however, he deliberately walked between the aunt and the niece, and said something to Nana in a low voice. This frightened Madame Lerat, who went at once to her brother and told him the whole story, whereupon he flew into a violent rage, shook the girl until her teeth chattered, and talked to her as if she were the vilest of the vile.

"Let her be!" said Gervaise, with all a woman's sense. "Let her be! Don't you see that you are putting all sorts of things into her head?"

And it was quite true he had put ideas into her head, and had taught her some things she did not know before, which was very astonishing. One morning, he saw her with something in a paper. It was poudre de riz, which, with a most perverted taste, she was plastering upon her delicate skin. He rubbed the whole of the powder into her hair until she looked like a miller's daughter. Another time she came in with red ribbons to retrim her old hat: he asked her furiously where she got them.

Whenever he saw her with a bit of finery, her father flew at her with insulting suspicions and angry violence. She defended herself and her small possessions with equal violence. One day he snatched from her a little cornelian heart, and ground it to dust under his heel.

She stood looking on, white and stern: for two years she had longed for this heart. She said to herself that she would not bear such treatment long. Coupeau occasionally realized that he had made a mistake; but the mischief was done.

He went every morning with Nana to the shop door, and

317

waited outside for five minutes to be sure that she had gone in. But one morning, having stopped to talk with a friend on the corner for some time, he saw her come out again, and vanish like a flash around the corner. She had gone up two flights higher than the room where she worked, and had sat down on the stairs until she thought him well out of the way.

When he went to Madame Lerat, she told him that she washed her hands of the whole business; she had done all she could, and now he must take care of his daughter himself. She advised him to marry the girl at once, or she would do worse.

All the people in the neighborhood knew Nana's admirer by sight. He had been in the court-yard several times, and once he had been seen on the stairs.

At first, Nana thought the whole thing a great joke, but at the end of a month she began to be afraid of him. Often when she stopped before the jeweller's he would suddenly appear at her side, and ask her what she wanted.

She did not care so much for jewelry or ornaments as she did for many other things. Sometimes as the mud was spattered over her from the wheels of a carriage, she grew faint and sick with envious longings to be better dressed—to go to the theatre—to have a pretty room all to herself. She longed to see another side of life—to know something of its pleasures. The stranger invariably appeared at these moments, but she always turned and fled, so great was her horror of him.

But when winter came, existence became well nigh intolerable. Each evening Nana was beaten, and when her father was tired of this amusement, her mother scolded. They rarely had anything to eat, and were always cold. If the girl bought some trifling article of dress, it was taken from her.

Gervaise went to the Assommoir nightly—for her husband, she said—and remained there. When Nana saw her mother sometimes, as she passed the window, seated among a crowd of men, she turned livid with rage, because youth has little patience with the vice of intemperance. It was dreary life for her—a comfortless home and a drunken father and mother. A saint on earth could not have remained there, that she knew very well; and she said she would make her escape some fine day, and then perhaps her parents would be sorry, and would admit that they had pushed her out of the nest.

One Saturday Nana, coming in, found her mother and father in a deplorable condition—Coupeau lying across the bed, and Gervaise sitting in a chair, swaying to and fro. She had forgotten the dinner, and one untrimmed candle lighted the dismal scene.

"Is that you, girl?" stammered Gervaise. "Well! your father will settle with you!"

Nana did not reply. She looked around the cheerless room, at the cold stove, at her parents. She did not step across the threshold. She turned and went away.

And she did not come back! The next day, when her father and mother were sober, they each reproached the other for Nana's flight.

This was really a terrible blow to Gervaise, who had no longer the smallest motive for self-control, and she abandoned herself at once to a wild orgie that lasted three days. Coupeau gave his daughter up, and smoked his pipe quietly. Occasionally, however, when eating his dinner, he would snatch up a knife and wave it wildly in the air, crying out that he was dishonored, and then laying it down as suddenly, resume his seat and his soup.

In this great house, whence each month a girl or two took flight, this incident astonished no one. The Lorilleux were rather triumphant at the success of their prophecy. Lantier defended Nana.

"Of course," he said, "she has done wrong; but bless my heart, what would you have? A girl as pretty as that could not live all her days in such poverty!"

"You know nothing about it!" cried Madame Lorilleux one evening when they were all assembled in the room of the Concierge. "Wooden Legs sold her daughter out and out. I know it! I have positive proof of what I say. The time that the old gentleman was seen on the stairs, he was going to pay the money. Nana and he were seen together at the Ambigu the other night! I tell you I know it!"

They finished their coffee. This tale might or might not be true; it was not improbable, at all events. And after this it was circulated and generally believed in the Quartier, that Gervaise had sold her daughter.

The clear-starcher, meanwhile, was going from bad to worse. She had been dismissed from Madame Fauconnier's, and in the last few weeks had worked for eight laundresses, one after the other—dismissed from all for her untidiness.

As she seemed to have lost all skill in ironing, she went out by the day to wash, and by degrees was intrusted with only the roughest work.

Her womanly pride and vanity had all departed. Lantier never seemed to see her when they met by chance, and she hardly noticed that the liaison which had stretched along for so many years, had ended in a mutual disenchantment.

Lantier had done wisely, so far as he was concerned, in counselling Virginie to open the kind of shop she had. He adored sweets, and could have lived on pralines and gumdrops, sugar-plums and chocolate.

Lantier suggested to Virginie that she should have Gervaise come in once each week, to wash the floors, shop and the rooms. This she did, and received thirty sous each time. Gervaise appeared on Saturday mornings, with her bucket and brush, without seeming to suffer a single pang at doing this menial work in the house where she had lived as mistress.

One Saturday Gervaise had hard work. It had rained for three days, and all the mud of the streets seemed to have been brought into the shop. Virginie stood behind the counter, with collar and cuffs trimmed with lace. Near her on a low chair lounged Lantier, and he was as usual eating candy.

"Really, Madame Coupeau!" cried Virginie, "can't you do better than that? You have left all the dirt in the corners. Don't you see? Oblige me by doing that over again."

Gervaise obeyed. She went back to the corner, and scrubbed it again. She was on her hands and knees, with her sleeves rolled up over her arms. Her old skirt clung close to her stout form, and the sweat poured down her face.

Madame Poisson enjoyed this, for her cat's eyes sparkled with malicious joy, and she glanced at Lantier with a smile. At last she was avenged for that mortification at the Lavatory, which had for years weighed heavy on her soul.

"By the way," said Lantier, addressing himself to Gervaise, "I saw Nana last night."

Gervaise started to her feet with her brush in her hand.

"Yes, I was coming down La Rue des Martyrs. In front of me was a young girl on the arm of an old gentleman. As I passed I glanced at her face, and assure you that it was Nana. She was well dressed, and looked happy."

"Ah!" said Gervaise, in a low, dull voice.

Lantier, who had finished one jar, now began another.

"What a girl that is!" he continued. "Imagine that she made me a sign to follow with the most perfect self-posesion. She got rid of her old gentleman in a café and beckoned me to the door. She asked me to tell her about everybody."

"Ah!" repeated Gervaise.

She stood waiting. Surely this was not all. Her daughter must have sent her some especial message. Lantier ate his sugar-plums.

"I would not have looked at her," said Virginie. "I sincerely trust, if I should meet her, that she would not speak to me, for really it would mortify me beyond expression. I am sorry for you, Madame Gervaise, but the truth is, that Poisson arrests every day a dozen just such girls."

Gervaise said nothing; her eyes were fixed on vacancy. With her two hands clasped around the handle of the brush she pushed the water before her toward the door. After this she had only to rinse the floor after sweeping the dirty water into the gutter.

When all was accomplished she stood before the counter waiting for her money. When Virginie tossed it toward her she did not take it up instantly.

"Then she said nothing else?" Gervaise asked.

"She!" Lantier exclaimed, "who is she? Ah! yes, I remember. Nana! No; she said nothing more."

And Gervaise went away with her thirty sous in her hand— her skirts dripping and her shoes leaving the mark of their broad soles on the sidewalk.

In the Quartier, all the women who drank like herself, took her part, and declared she had been driven to intemperance by her daughter's misconduct. She, too, began to believe this herself, and assumed at times a tragic air, and wished she were dead. Unquestionably she had suffered from Nana's departure. A mother does not like to feel that her daughter will leave her for the first person who asks her to do so.

But she was too thoroughly demoralized to care long, and soon she had but one idea: that Nana belonged to her. Had she not a right to her own property?

She roamed the streets day after day, night after night, hoping to see the girl. That year half the Quartier was being demolished. All one side of the Rue des Poissonnières lay flat on the ground. Lantier and Poisson disputed day after day on these demolitions. The one declared that the Emperor wanted to build palaces and drive the lower classes out of Paris, while Poisson, white with rage, said the Emperor would pull down the whole of Paris merely to give work to the people.

Gervaise did not like the improvements either, or the changes in the dingy Quartier, to which she was accustomed. It was, in fact, a little hard for her to see all these embellishments, just when she was going down hill so fast over the piles of brick and mortar, while she was wandering about in search of Nana.

She heard of her daughter several times. There are always plenty of people to tell you things you do not care to hear. She was told that Nana had left her elderly friend for the sake of some young fellow.

She heard too, that Nana had been seen at a ball in the *Grand Salon*—Rue de la Chapelle; and Coupeau and she began to frequent all these places, one after another, whenever they had the money to spend.

One November night they entered the *Grand Salon,* as much to get warm as anything else. Outside it was hailing, and the rooms were naturally crowded. They could not find a table, and they stood waiting until they could establish themselves. Coupeau was directly in the mouth of the passage, and a young man, in a frock coat, was thrown against him. The youth uttered an exclamation of disgust, as he began to dust off his coat with his handkerchief. The blouse worn by Coupeau was assuredly none of the cleanest.

"Look here, my good fellow!" cried Coupeau, angrily, "those

airs are very unnecessary. I would have you to know that the blouse of a working-man can do your coat no harm, if it has touched it!"

The young man turned around and looked at Coupeau from head to foot.

"Learn," continued the angry workman, "that the blouse is the only wear for a man!"

Gervaise endeavored to calm her husband, who, however, tapped his ragged breast, and repeated loudly—

"The only wear for a man, I tell you!"

The youth slipped away and was lost in the crowd.

Coupeau tried to find him, but it was quite impossible; the crowd was too great. The orchestra was playing a quadrille, and the dancers were bringing up the dust from the floor in great clouds, which obscured the gas.

"Look!" said Gervaise, suddenly.

"What is it?"

"Look at that velvet bonnet!"

Quite at the left there was a velvet bonnet, black with plumes, only too suggestive of a hearse. They watched these nodding plumes breathlessly.

"Do you not know that hair?" murmured Gervaise, hoarsely. "I am sure it is she!"

In one second Coupeau was in the centre of the crowd. Yes, it was Nana, and in what a costume! She wore a ragged silk dress, stained and torn. She had no shawl over her shoulders to conceal the fact that half the buttonholes on her dress were burst out. In spite of all her shabbiness the girl was pretty and fresh. Nana, of course, danced on unsuspiciously. Her airs and graces were beyond belief. She curtsied to the very ground, and then in a twinkling threw her foot over her partner's head. A circle was formed and she was applauded vociferously.

At this moment Coupeau fell on his daughter.

"Don't try and keep me back!" he said, "for have her I will!"

Nana turned and saw her father and mother.

Coupeau discovered that his daughter's partner was the young man for whom he had been looking. Gervaise pushed him aside and walked up to Nana and gave her two cuffs on her ears. One sent the plumed hat on the side, the other left five red marks on that pale cheek. The orchestra played on. Nana neither wept nor moved.

The dancers began to grow very angry. They ordered the Coupeau party to leave the room.

"Go!" said Gervaise, "and do not attempt to leave us; for so sure as you do, you will be given in charge of a policeman."

The young man had prudently disappeared.

Nana's old life now began again; for after the girl had slept for twelve hours on a stretch, she was very gentle and sweet for a week. She wore a plain gown and a simple hat, and declared she would like to work at home. She rose early and took a seat at her table by five o'clock the first morning, and tried to roll her violet stems; but her fingers had lost their cunning in the six months in which they had been idle.

Then the glue-pot dried up, the petals and the paper were dusty and spotted; the mistress of the establishment came for her tools and materials, and made more than one scene. Nana relapsed into utter indolence, quarrelling with her mother from morning until night. Of course an end must come to this; so one fine evening the girl disappeared.

The Lorilleux, who had been greatly amused by the repentance and return of their niece, now nearly died laughing. If she returned again they would advise the Coupeaus to put her in a cage like a canary.

The Coupeaus pretended to be rather pleased, but in their hearts they raged; particularly as they soon learned that Nana was frequently seen in the Quartier. Gervaise declared this was done by the girl to annoy them.

Nana adorned all the balls in the vicinity, and the Coupeaus knew that they could lay their hands on her at any time they chose; but they did not choose, and they avoided meeting her.

But, one night, just as they were going to bed, they heard a rap on the door. It was Nana, who came to ask, as coolly as possible, if she could sleep there. What a state she was in! all rags and dirt. She devoured a crust of dried bread, and fell asleep with a part of it in her hand. This continued for some time, the girl coming and going like a will-of-the-wisp. Weeks and months would elapse without a sign from her, and then she would reappear, without a word to say where she had been, sometimes in rags and sometimes well-dressed. Finally her parents began to take these proceedings as a matter of course. She might come in—they said—or stay out, just as she pleased, provided she kept the door shut. Only one thing exasperated Gervaise now, and that was when her daughter appeared with a bonnet and feathers, and a train. This she would not endure. When Nana came to her it must be as a simple working-woman! None of this dearly-bought finery should be exhibited there, for these trained dresses had created a great excitement in the house.

One day Gervaise reproached her daughter violently for the life she led, and finally, in her rage, took her by the shoulder and shook her.

"Let me be!" cried the girl. "You are the last person to talk to me in that way. You did as you pleased: why can't I do the same?"

"What do you mean?" stammered the mother.

"I have never said anything about it, because it was none of my business; but do you think I did not know where you were when my father lay snoring? Let me alone. It was you who set me the example."

Gervaise turned away pale and trembling, while Nana composed herself to sleep again.

Coupeau's life was a very regular one—that is to say, he did not drink for six months and then yielded to temptation, which brought him up with a round turn and sent him to Sainte-Anne's. When he came out he did the same thing, so that in three years he was seven times at Sainte-Anne's; and each time he came out, the fellow looked more broken and less able to stand another orgie.

He had grown very thin, his cheeks were hollow, and his eyes inflamed. Those who knew his age shuddered as they saw him pass, bent and decrepit as a man of eighty.

The last summer of his life was especially trying to Coupeau. His voice was entirely changed; he was deaf in one ear; and some days he could not see, and was obliged to feel his way up and down-stairs as if he were blind. One evening when his wife and daughter came in he was not in his bed; in his place lay the bolster carefully tucked in. They found him at last crouched on the floor under the bed, with his teeth chattering with cold and fear. He told them he had been attacked by assassins.

The two women coaxed him back to bed as if he had been a baby.

Coupeau knew but one remedy for all this, and that was a good stout morning dram. His memory had long since fled, his brain had softened. When Nana appeared after an absence of six weeks, he thought she had been on an errand around the corner. She met him in the street too, very often now, without fear, for he passed without recognizing her. One night in the autumn Nana went out, saying she wanted some baked pears from the fruiterer's. She felt the cold weather coming on and she did not care to sit before a cold stove. The winter before, she went out for two sous worth of tobacco and came back in a month's time; they thought she would do the same now, but they were mistaken. Winter came and went, as did the spring, and even when June arrived they had seen and heard nothing of her.

She was evidently comfortable somewhere; and the Coupeaus, feeling certain that she would never return, had sold her bed: it was very much in their way and they could drink up the six francs it brought.

One morning Virginie called to Gervaise as the latter passed the shop, and begged her to come in and help a little, as Lantier had had two friends to supper the night before; and Gervaise washed the dishes while Lantier sat in the shop smoking. Presently, he said:

"Oh! Gervaise, I saw Nana the other night."

Virginie, who was behind the counter, opening and shutting drawer after drawer, with a face that lengthened as she found each empty, shook her fist at him indignantly.

She had begun to think he saw Nana very often. She did not speak, but Madame Lerat, who had just come in, said, with a significant look:

"And where did you see her?"

"Oh! in a carriage," answered Lantier with a laugh. "And I was on the sidewalk." He turned toward Gervaise and went on:

"Yes, she was in a carriage, dressed beautifully. I did not recognize her at first, but she kissed her hand to me. Her friend this time must be a vicomte at the least. She looked as happy as a queen."

Gervaise wiped the plate in her hands, rubbing it long and carefully, though it had long since been dry. Virginie, with wrinkled brows, wondered how she could pay two notes which fell due the next day; while Lantier, fat and hearty from the sweets he had devoured, asked himself if these drawers and jars would be filled up again, or if the ruin he anticipated was so near at hand that he should be compelled to pull up stakes at once.

When Gervaise went back to her room she found Coupeau sitting on the side of the bed weeping and moaning. She took a chair near by and looked at him, without speaking.

"I have news for you," she said at last. "Your daughter has been seen. She is happy and comfortable. Would that I were in her place!"

Coupeau was looking down on the floor intently. He raised his head and said, with an idiotic laugh:

"Do as you please, my dear; don't let me be any hindrance to you. When you are dressed up, you are not so bad-looking after all."

CHAPTER XII

Poverty and Degradation

THE WEATHER WAS intensely cold about the middle of January. Gervaise had not been able to pay her rent, due on the first. She had little or no work, and consequently no food to speak of. The sky was dark and gloomy, and the air heavy with the coming of a storm. Gervaise thought it barely possible that her husband might come in with a little money. After all everything is possible, and he had said that he would work. Gervaise after a little, by dint of dwelling on this thought, had come to consider it a certainty. Yes, Coupeau would bring home some money, and they would have a good, hot, comfortable dinner. As to herself, she had given up trying to get work, for no one would have her. This did not much trouble her however, for she had arrived at that point when the mere exertion of moving had become intolerable to her. She now lay stretched on the bed, for she was warmer there.

Gervaise called it a bed. In reality it was only a pile of straw in the corner, for she had sold her bed and all her furniture. She occasionally swept the straw together with a broom, and after all it was neither dustier nor dirtier than everything else in the place. On this straw therefore, Gervaise now lay, with her eyes wide open. How long, she wondered, could people live without eating? She was not hungry, but there was a strange weight at the pit of her stomach. Her haggard eyes wandered about the room in search of anything she could sell. She vaguely wished some one would buy the spiderwebs which hung in all the corners. She knew them to be very good for cuts, but she doubted if they had any market value.

Tired of this contemplation, she got up and took her one chair to the window.

She sat at the window looking at the pale sky, and finally fell asleep. She dreamed that she was out in a snowstorm, and could not find her way home. She awoke with a start, and saw that night was coming on. How long the days are when one's stomach is empty! She waited for Coupeau, and the relief he would bring.

The clock struck in the next room. Could it be possible? Was it only three? Then she began to cry. How could she ever wait until seven! After another half hour of suspense, she started up. Yes, they might say what they pleased, but she, at least, would try if she could not borrow ten sous from the Lorilleux.

There was a continual borrowing of small sums in this corridor during the winter; but no matter what was the emergency, no one ever dreamed of applying to the Lorilleux. Gervaise summoned all her courage, and rapped at the door.

"Come in!" cried a sharp voice.

How good it was there! warm and bright with the glow of the forge. And Gervaise smelled the soup, too; and it made her feel faint and sick.

"Ah! it is you, is it?" said Madame Lorilleux. "What do you want?"

Gervaise hesitated. The application for ten sous stuck in her throat, because she saw Boche seated by the stove.

"What do you want?" asked Lorilleux, in his turn.

"Have you seen Coupeau?" stammered Gervaise. "I thought he was here."

His sister answered with a sneer, that they rarely saw Coupeau. They were not rich enough to offer him as many glasses of wine as he wanted in these days.

Gervaise stammered out a disconnected sentence. He had promised to come home. She needed food, she needed money.

A profound silence followed. Madame Lorilleux fanned her fire, and her husband bent more closely over his work, while Boche smiled with an expectant air.

"If I could have ten sous," murmured Gervaise.

The silence continued.

"If you would lend them to me," said Gervaise, "I would give them back in the morning."

Madame Lorilleux turned and looked her full in the face, thinking to herself that if she yielded once, that the next day it would be twenty sous, and who could tell where it would stop?

"But, my dear," she cried, "you know we have no money and no prospect of any; otherwise, of course, we would oblige you."

"Certainly," said Lorilleux, "the heart is willing, but the pockets are empty."

Gervaise bowed her head, but she did not leave instantly. She looked at the gold wire on which her sister-in-law was working, and at that in the hands of Lorilleux, and thought that it would take a mere scrap to give her a good dinner. On that day the room was very dirty and filled with charcoal dust, but she saw it resplendent with riches like the shop of a money-changer, and she said once more in a low, soft voice:

"I will bring back the ten sous. I will, indeed!" Tears were in her eyes, but she was determined not to say that she had eaten nothing for twenty-four hours.

"I can't tell you how much I need it," she continued.

The husband and wife exchanged a look. Wooden Legs begging at their door! Well! well! who would have thought it? Why had they not known it was she, when they rashly called out, "Come in"? Really, they could not allow such people to cross their threshold: there was too much that was valuable in the room. They had several times distrusted Gervaise, she looked about so queerly, and now they would not take their eyes off of her.

Gervaise went toward Lorilleux as she spoke.

"Take care!" he said, roughly. "You will carry off some of the particles of gold on the soles of your shoes. It looks really as if you had greased them!"

Gervaise drew back. She leaned against the étagère for a moment, and seeing that her sister-in-law's eyes were fixed on her hands she opened them and said in a gentle, weary voice—the voice of a woman who had ceased to struggle:

"I have taken nothing. You can look for yourself."

And she went away; the warmth of the place and the smell of the soup were unbearable.

Gervaise crawled down the corridor with slip-shod shoes and slouching shoulders, but at her door she hesitated: she could not go in: she was afraid. She would walk up and down a little—that would keep her warm. As she passed, she looked in at Father Bru, but to her surprise he was not there; and she asked herself, with a pang of jealousy, if any one could possibly have asked him out to dine. When she reached the Bijards, she heard a groan. She went in.

"What is the matter?" she said.

The room was very clean, and in perfect order. Lalie that very morning had swept and arranged everything. In vain did the cold blast of poverty blow through that chamber, and bring with it dirt and disorder. Lalie was always there; she cleaned, and scrubbed, and gave to everything a look of gentility. There was little money, but much cleanliness within those four walls.

The two children were cutting out pictures in a corner, but Lalie was in bed, lying very straight and pale, with the sheet pulled over her chin.

"What is the matter?" asked Gervaise, anxiously.

Lalie slowly lifted her white lids, and tried to speak.

"Nothing," she said faintly, "nothing, I assure you!"

But her face bore the traces of such frightful agony, that Gervaise fell on her knees by the side of the bed. She knew that the child had had a cough for a month, and she saw the blood trickling from the corners of her mouth.

"It is not my fault," Lalie murmured; "I thought I was strong enough, and I washed the floor; I could not finish the windows, though. Everything but those are clean. But I was so tired that I was obliged to lie down—"

She interrupted herself to say:

"Please see that my children are not cutting themselves with the scissors."

She started at the sound of a heavy step on the stairs; her father noisily pushed open the door. As usual he had drunk too much, and in his eyes blazed the lurid flames kindled by alcohol.

When he saw Lalie lying down, he walked to the corner and took up the long whip.

"This is a good joke!" he said. "The idea of your daring to go to bed at this hour. Come! up with you!"

He snapped the whip over the bed, and the child murmured, softly:

"I cannot, for I am dying."

Gervaise had snatched the whip from Bijard, who stood with his under jaw dropped, glaring at his daughter. What could the little fool mean? Who ever heard of a child dying like that when she had not even been sick? Oh! she was lying!

"You will see that I am telling you the truth," she replied. "I did not tell you as long as I could help it. Be kind to me now, papa, and say good-bye as if you loved me."

Bijard passed his hand over his eyes. She did look very strangely—her face was that of a grown woman. The presence of Death in that cramped room sobered him suddenly. He looked around with the air of a man who had been suddenly awakened from a dream. He saw the two little ones clean and happy, and the room neat and orderly.

He fell into a chair.

"Dear little mother!" he murmured; "dear little mother!"

This was all he said; but it was very sweet to Lalie, who had never been spoiled by over praise. She comforted him. She told him how grieved she was, to go away and leave him, before she had entirely brought up her children. He would watch over them, would he not? And in her dying voice she gave him some little details in regard to their clothes. He—the alcohol having regained its power—listened with round eyes of wonder.

After a long silence, Lalie spoke again:

"We owe four francs and seven sous to the baker. He must be paid. Madame Gaudron has an iron that belongs to us; you must not forget it. This evening I was not able to make the soup, but there are bread and cold potatoes."

Gervaise tried to keep back her tears. She held Lalie's hands, and as the bedclothes slipped away, she re-arranged them. In doing so, she caught a glimpse of the poor little figure. The sight might have drawn tears from a stone. Lalie wore only a tiny chemise over her bruised and bleeding flesh—marks of a lash striped her sides—a livid spot was on her right arm—and from head to foot she was one bruise.

Gervaise was paralyzed at the sight. She wondered if there was a God above, how He could have allowed the child to stagger under so heavy a cross.

"Madame Coupeau," murmured the child, trying to draw the sheet over her. She was ashamed—ashamed for her father.

Gervaise could not stay there. The child was fast sinking. Her eyes were fixed on her little ones, who sat in the corner still cutting out their pictures. The room was growing dark, and Gervaise fled from it.

Almost unconsciously Gervaise took her way to the shop where her husband worked, or rather pretended to work. She would wait for him and get the money before he had a chance to spend it.

It was a very cold corner where she stood. The sounds of the carriages and footsteps were strangely muffled by reason of the fast-falling snow. Gervaise stamped her feet to keep them from freezing. The people who passed offered few distractions, for they hurried by with their coat-collars turned up to their ears. But Gervaise saw several women watching the door of the

factory quite as anxiously as herself—they were wives who, like herself, probably wished to get hold of a portion of their husbands' wages. She did not know them, but it required no introduction to understand their business.

The door of the factory remained firmly shut for some time. Then it opened to allow the egress of one workman—then two—three followed, but these were probably those, who well behaved, took their wages home to their wives, for they neither retreated nor started when they saw the little crowd. One woman fell on a pale little fellow, and plunging her hand into his pocket, carried off every sou of her husband's earnings, while he, left without enough to pay for a pint of wine, went off down the street almost weeping.

Gervaise still stood watching the entrance. Where was Coupeau? She asked some of the men, who teased her by declaring that he had just gone by the back door. She saw by this time that Coupeau had lied to her; that he had not been at work that day. She also saw that there was no dinner for her. There was not a shadow of hope—nothing but hunger, and darkness, and cold.

She toiled up La Rue des Poissonnièrs, when she suddenly heard Coupeau's voice, and glancing in at the window of a wine-shop, she saw him drinking with Mes-Bottes, who had had the luck to marry the previous summer a woman with some money. He was now therefore, well clothed and fed, and altogether a happy mortal. Gervaise laid her hands on her husband's shoulders as he left the cabaret.

"I am hungry," she said softly.

"Hungry, are you? Well, then, eat your fist, and keep the other for tomorrow."

"Shall I steal a loaf of bread?" she asked, in a dull, dreary tone.

Mes-Bottes smoothed his chin, and said in a conciliatory voice:

"No, no! Don't do that: it is against the law. But if a woman manages—"

Coupeau interrupted him with a coarse laugh.

"Yes; a woman, if she has any sense, can always get along, and it is her own fault if she starves."

And the two men walked on toward the outer Boulevard. Gervaise followed them.

"Good God!" Coupeau exclaimed, turning upon her furiously. "What can I do? I have nothing. Be off with you, unless you want to be beaten."

He lifted his fist—she recoiled and said, with set teeth:

"Very well, then; I will go and find some man who has a sou."

Coupeau pretended to consider this an excellent joke. Yes, of course, she could make a conquest; by gaslight she was still passably good-looking. If she succeeded he advised her to dine at the Capucin, where there was very good eating.

Gervaise, with his infernal mirth ringing in her ears, hurried down the street. She was determined to take this desperate step. She had only a choice between that and theft, and she considered that she had a right to dispose of herself as she pleased. The question of right and wrong did not present itself very clearly to her eyes. She walked slowly up and down the Boulevard. This part of Paris was crowded now with new buildings, between whose sculptured façades ran narrow lanes leading to haunts of squalid misery, which were cheek-by-jowl with splendor and wealth.

It seemed strange to Gervaise, that among this crowd who elbowed her, there was not one good Christian to divine her situation, and slip some sous into her hand. Her head was dizzy, and her limbs would hardly bear her weight. At this hour ladies with hats, and well-dressed gentlemen, who lived in these fine new houses, were mingled with the people—with the men and women whose faces were pale and sickly from the vitiated air of the workshops in which they passed their lives.

Gervaise went with the crowd. No one looked at her, for the men were all hurrying home to their dinner. Suddenly she looked up and beheld the Hotel Boncœur. It was empty, the shutters and doors covered with placards, and the whole façade, weather-stained and decaying. It was there, in that hotel, that the seeds of her present life had been sown. She stood still and looked up at the window of the room she had occupied, and recalled her youth passed with Lantier, and the manner in which he had left her. But she was young then, and soon recovered from the blow. This was twenty years ago, and now what was she?

The sight of the place made her sick, and she turned toward Montmartre. She passed crowds of workwomen with little parcels in their hands, and children who had been sent to the baker's, carrying four-pound loaves of bread as tall as themselves, which looked like shining brown dolls.

By degrees the crowd dispersed, and Gervaise was almost alone. Every one was at dinner. She thought how delicious it would be, to lie down and never rise again—to feel that all toil was over. And this was the end of her life!

Again she looked up: she had reached the hospital with its high, gray walls, with two wings opening out like a huge fan. A door in the wall was the terror of the whole Quartier—the Door of the Dead it was called—through which all the bodies were carried.

She hurried past this solid oak door, and went down to the railroad-bridge, under which a train had just passed, leaving in its rear a floating cloud of smoke. She wished she were on that train, which would take her into the country, and she pictured to herself open spaces, and the fresh air, and expanse of blue sky; perhaps she could live a new life there.

As she thought this, her weary eyes began to puzzle out in the dim twilight the words on a printed hand-bill pasted on one of the pillars of the arch. She read one—an advertisement, offering fifty francs for a lost dog. Some one must have loved the creature very much.

Gervaise turned back again. The street-lamps were being lighted, and defined long lines of streets and avenues. The restaurants were all crowded, and people were eating and drinking. Before the Assommoir stood a crowd waiting their turn, and room within; and as a respectable tradesman passed he said, with a shake of the head, that many a man would be drunk that night in Paris. And over this scene hung the dark sky, low and clouded.

Gervaise wished she had a few sous: she would in that case have gone into this place, and drunk until she ceased to feel hungry; and through the window she watched the still, with an angry consciousness that all her misery and all her pain came from that. If she had never touched a drop of liquor all might have been so different.

She started from her reverie; this was the hour of which she must take advantage. Men had dined and were comparatively amiable. She looked around her, and toward the trees where —under the leafless branches—she saw more than one female figure. Gervaise watched them, determined to do what they did. Her heart was in her throat: it seemed to her that she was dreaming a bad dream.

She stood for some fifteen minutes; none of the men who passed looked at her. Finally she moved a little and spoke to one who, with his hands in his pockets, was whistling as he walked.

"Sir," she said, in a low voice, "please listen to me."

The man looked at her from head to foot, and went on whistling louder than before.

Gervaise grew bolder. She forgot everything except the pangs of hunger. The women under the trees walked up and down with the regularity of wild animals in a cage.

"Sir," she said again, "please listen."

But the man went on. She walked toward the Hotel de Boncœur again, past the hospital, which was now brilliantly lighted. There she turned and went back over the same ground —the dismal ground between the slaughterhouses and the place where the sick lay dying. With these two places she seemed to feel bound by some mysterious tie.

"Sir, please listen!"

It was growing late. Man after man, in a beastly state of intoxication, reeled past her; quarrels and disputes filled the air.

Gervaise walked on, half asleep. She was conscious of little except that she was starving. She wondered where her daughter was, and what she was eating, but it was too much trouble to think, and she shivered and crawled on. As she lifted her face she felt the cutting wind, accompanied by the snow, fine and dry like gravel. The storm had come.

She saw one man walking slowly. She went towards him.

"Sir, please listen!"

The man stopped. He did not seem to notice what she said, but extended his hand and murmured in a low voice—

"Charity, if you please!"

The two looked at each other. Merciful heavens! It was Father Bru begging, and Madame Coupeau doing worse. They stood looking at each other—equals in misery. The aged workman had been trying to make up his mind all the evening to beg, and the first person he stopped was a woman as poor as himself! They looked at each other once more, and without a word, each went his own way through the fast falling snow, which blinded Gervaise as she struggled on, the wind wrapping her thin skirts around her legs so that she could hardly walk.

Suddenly an absolute whirlwind struck her and bore her breathless and helpless along—she did not even know in what direction. When at last she was able to open her eyes, she could see nothing through the blinding snow, but she heard a step and the outlines of a man's figure. She snatched him by the blouse.

"Sir," she said, "please listen."

The man turned. It was Goujet.

Goujet looked at her, while the snow whitened his yellow beard.

"Come!" he said.

And he walked on, she following him. Neither spoke.

Poor Madame Goujet had died in October of acute rheumatism, and her son continued to reside in the same apartment. He had this night been sitting with a sick friend.

He entered, lighted a lamp, and turned toward Gervaise, who stood humbly on the threshold.

"Come in!" he said, in a low voice, as if his mother could have heard him.

Gervaise entered with the air of a woman who is startled at finding herself in a respectable place. He was pale and trembling. They crossed his mother's room softly, and when Gervaise stood within his own, he closed the door.

It was the same room in which he had lived ever since she knew him—small and almost virginal in its simplicity. Gervaise dared not move.

Goujet snatched her in his arms, but she pushed him away faintly.

The stove was still hot and a dish was on the top of it. Gervaise looked toward it. Goujet understood. He placed the dish on the table, poured her out some wine and cut a slice of bread.

"Thank you," she said. "How good you are!"

She trembled to that degree, that she could hardly hold her fork. Hunger gave her eyes the fierceness of a famished beast, and to her head the tremulous motion of senility. After eating a potato she burst into tears, but continued to eat, with the tears streaming down her cheeks and her chin quivering.

"Will you have some more bread?" he asked. She said "No"; she said "Yes"; she did not know what she said.

And he stood looking at her in the clear light of the lamp. How old and shabby she was! The heat was melting the snow on her hair and clothing, and water was dripping from all her garments. Her hair was very gray and roughened by the wind. Where was the pretty white throat he so well remembered? He recalled the days when he first knew her, when her skin was so delicate, and she stood at her table, briskly moving the hot irons to and fro. He thought of the time when she had come to the Forge, and of the joy with which he would have welcomed her then to his room.

She finished her bread amid great silent tears, and then rose to her feet.

Goujet took her hand.

"I love you, Madame Gervaise; I love you still," he cried.

"Do not say that," she exclaimed; "for it is impossible."

He leaned toward her.

"Will you allow me to kiss you?" he asked, respectfully.

He kissed her, gravely and solemnly and then pressed his lips upon her gray hair. He had never kissed any one since his mother's death, and Gervaise was all that remained to him of the Past.

He turned away, and throwing himself on his bed, sobbed aloud. Gervaise could not endure this. She exclaimed:

"I love you, Monsieur Goujet, and I understand. Farewell!"

And she rushed through Madame Goujet's room, and then

through the street to her home. The house was all dark, and the arched door into the court-yard looked like huge, gaping jaws.

She looked at the court-yard, and fancied it a Cemetery surrounded by high walls. The snow lay white within it. She stepped over the usual stream from the dyer's, but this time the stream was black, and opened for itself a path through the white snow. The stream was the color of her thoughts.

As she toiled up the six long flights in the darkness, she laughed aloud. She recalled her old dream—to work quietly—have plenty to eat—a little home to herself, where she could bring up her children—never to be beaten—and to die in her bed! It was droll how things had turned out. She worked no more; she had nothing to eat; she lived amid dirt and disorder. Her daughter had gone to the bad, and her husband beat her whenever he pleased. As for dying in her bed, she had none.

And then she laughed again, as she remembered that she had once said, that after she had worked for twenty years, she should retire into the country.

Yes, she would go into the country, for she should soon have her little green corner in Père La Chaise.

Her poor brain was disturbed. She had bidden an eternal farewell to Goujet. They would never see each other again.

As she passed the Bijards, she looked in and saw Lalie lying dead, happy and at peace. It was well with the child.

"She is lucky," muttered Gervaise.

At this moment she saw a gleam of light under the undertaker's door. She threw it wide open, with a wild desire that he should take her as well as Lalie. Bazouge had come in that night more tipsy than usual, and had thrown his hat and cloak in the corner, while he lay in the middle of the floor.

He started up, and called out:

"Shut that door! And don't stand there—it is too cold. What do you want?"

Then Gervaise, with arms outstretched, not knowing or caring what she said, began to entreat him with passionate vehemence:

"Oh! take me," she cried; "I can bear it no longer. Take me, I implore you!"

And she knelt before him, a lurid light blazing in her haggard eyes.

Father Bazouge, with garments stained by the dust of the Cemetery, seemed to her as glorious as the sun. But the old man, yet half asleep, rubbed his eyes and could not understand her.

"What are you talking about?" he muttered.

"Take me," repeated Gervaise, more earnestly than before. "Do you remember one night when I rapped on the partition? Afterwards I said I did not, but I was stupid then, and afraid. But I am not afraid now. Here, take my hands—they are not cold with terror. Take me, and put me to sleep, for I have but this one wish now."

Bazouge, feeling that it was not proper to argue with a lady, said:

"You are right. I have buried three women to-day, who would each have given me a jolly little sum out of gratitude, if they could have put their hands in their pockets. But you see, my dear woman, it is not such an easy thing you are asking of me."

"Take me!" cried Gervaise. "Take me! I want to go away!"

"But there is a certain little operation first, you know—" And he pretended to choke and rolled up his eyes.

Gervaise staggered to her feet. He too rejected her and would have nothing to do with her. She crawled into her room and threw herself on her straw. She was sorry she had eaten anything and delayed the work of starvation.

-[*CHAPTER XIII*]-

The Hospital

THE NEXT DAY Gervaise received ten francs from her son Etienne, who had steady work. He occasionally sent her a little money, knowing that there was none too much of that commodity in his poor mother's pocket.

She cooked her dinner and ate it alone, for Coupeau did not appear, nor did she hear a word of his whereabouts for nearly a week. Finally a printed paper was given her which frightened her at first, but she was soon relieved to find that it simply conveyed to her the information that her husband was at Sainte-Anne's again.

Gervaise was in no way disturbed. Coupeau knew the way back well enough; he would return in due season.

On Sunday, as Gervaise had a nice little repast ready for the evening, she decided that an excursion would give her an appetite. The letter from the asylum stared her in the face and worried her.

When she reached the hospital she heard a strange story. It seems that Coupeau, how no one could say, had escaped from the hospital, and had been found under the bridge. He had thrown himself over the parapet, declaring that armed men were driving him with the point of their bayonets.

One of the nurses took Gervaise up the stairs. At the head she heard terrific howls which froze the marrow in her bones.

"It is he!" said the nurse.

"He? Whom do you mean?"

"I mean your husband. He has gone on like that ever since day before yesterday; and he dances all the time, too. You will see!"

The cell was cushioned from the floor to the ceiling, and on the floor were mattresses on which Coupeau danced and howled in his ragged blouse. The sight was terrific. He threw himself wildly against the window and then to the other side of the cell, shaking his hands as if he wished to break them off, and fling them in defiance at the whole world.

"What is it? What is it?" gasped Gervaise.

A house-surgeon, a fair and rosy youth, was sitting, calmly taking notes.

"You can stay a while," he said, "but keep very quiet. He will not recognize you, however."

Coupeau, in fact, did not seem to notice his wife, who had not yet seen his face. She went nearer. Was that really he? She never would have known him, with his blood-shot eyes and distorted features. He was dancing, it is true, but as if on burning plow-shares; not a motion seemed to be voluntary.

Gervaise went to the young surgeon, who was beating a tune on the back of his chair.

"What is he saying? Hark! He is talking now."

"Just be quiet, will you?" said the young man, "I wish to listen."

Coupeau was speaking fast, and looking all about, as if he were examining the underbrush in the Bois de Vincennes.

"Where is it now?" he exclaimed; and then straightening himself, he looked off into the distance.

"It is a fair," he exclaimed, "and lanterns in the trees, and the water is running everywhere; fountains, cascades, and all sorts of things."

He drew a long breath, as if enjoying the delicious freshness of the air.

By degrees, however, his features contracted again with pain, and he ran quickly around the wall of his cell.

"More trickery," he howled. "I knew it!"

He started back with a hoarse cry; his teeth chattered with terror.

"No, I will not throw myself over! All that water would drown me! No, I will not!"

"I am going," said Gervaise to the surgeon. "I cannot stay another moment."

She was very pale. Coupeau kept up his infernal dance while she tottered down the stairs, followed by his hoarse voice.

How good it was to breathe the fresh air outside!

That evening every one in the huge house in which Coupeau had lived talked of his strange disease. The Concierge, crazy to hear the details, condescended to invite Gervaise to take a glass of cordial, forgetting that he had turned a cold shoulder upon her for many weeks.

Madame Lorilleux and Madame Poisson were both there also. Boche had heard of a cabinet-maker who had danced the polka until he died. He had drunk absinthe.

Gervaise finally, not being able to make them understand her description, asked for the table to be moved, and there, in the centre of the lodge, imitated her husband making frightful leaps and horrible contortions.

"Yes, that was what he did!"

The next day she said to herself when she rose that she would never go to the hospital again: she could do no good.

But as mid-day arrived, she could stay away no longer and started forth, without a thought of the length of the walk, so great were her mingled curiosity and anxiety.

She was not obliged to ask a question; she heard the frightful sounds at the very foot of the stairs. The keeper, who was carrying a cup of tisane across the corridor, stopped when he saw her.

"He keeps it up well!" he said.

She went in, but stood at the door, as she saw there were people there. The young surgeon had surrendered his chair to an elderly gentleman wearing several decorations. He was the chief physician of the hospital, and his eyes were like gimlets.

Gervaise tried to see Coupeau over the bald head of that gentleman. Her husband was leaping and dancing with undiminished strength. The perspiration poured more constantly from his brow now, that was all.

Gervaise asked herself why she had come back. She had been accused the evening before of exaggerating the picture, but she had not made it strong enough. The next time she imitated him she could do it better. She listened to what the physicians were saying: the house-surgeon was giving the details of the night, with many words which she did not understand; but she gathered that Coupeau had gone on in the same way all night. Finally, he said this was the wife of the patient. Whereupon the surgeon-in-chief turned and interrogated her with the air of a police judge.

"Did this man's father drink?"

"A little, sir. Just as everybody does. He fell from a roof, when he had been drinking, and was killed."

"Did his mother drink?"

"Yes, sir—that is, a little now and then. He had a brother who died in convulsions; but the others are very healthy."

The surgeon looked at her, and said, coldly:

"You drink, too?"

Gervaise attempted to defend herself and deny the accusation.

"You drink," he repeated, "and see to what it leads. Some day you will be here, and like this."

She leaned against the wall, utterly overcome. The physician turned away. He knelt on the mattress and carefully watched

343

Coupeau; he wished to see if his feet trembled as much as his hands. His extremities vibrated as if on wires. The disease was creeping on, and the peculiar shivering seemed to be under the skin—it would cease for a minute or two and then begin again. The belly and the shoulders trembled like water just on the point of boiling.

Coupeau seemed to suffer more than the evening before. His complaints were curious· and contradictory. A million pins were pricking him. There was a weight under the skin; a cold, wet animal was crawling over him. Then there were other creatures on his shoulder.

"I am thirsty," he groaned; "so thirsty."

The house-surgeon took a glass of lemonade from a tray and gave it to him. He seized the glass in both hands, drank one swallow, spilling the whole of it at the same time. He at once spat it out in digust.

"It is brandy!" he exclaimed.

Then the surgeon, on a sign from his chief, gave him some water, and Coupeau did the same thing.

"It is brandy!" he cried. "Brandy! Oh, my God!"

For twenty-four hours he had declared that everything he touched to his lips was brandy, and with tears begged for something else—for it burned his throat, he said. Beef-tea was brought to him; he refused it, saying it smelled of alcohol. He seemed to suffer intense and constant agony from the poison which he vowed was in the air. He asked why people were allowed to rub matches all the time under his nose, to choke him with their vile fumes.

The physicians watched Coupeau with care and interest. The surgeon-in-chief turned to the assistant.

"You keep the temperature at forty degrees?" he asked.

"Yes, sir."

A dead silence ensued. Then the surgeon shrugged his shoulders.

"Well, continue the same treatment—beef-tea, milk, lemonade, and quinine as directed. Do not leave him, and send for me if there is any change."

And he left the room, Gervaise following close at his heels, seeking an opportunity of asking him if there was no hope.

But he stalked down the corridor with so much dignity, that she dared not approach him.

She stood for a moment undecided whether she should go back to Coupeau or not, but hearing him begin again the lamentable cry for water—

"Water, not brandy!"

She hurried on, feeling that she could endure no more that day. In the streets the galloping horses made her start with a strange fear that all the inmates of Sainte-Anne's were at her heels. She remembered what the physician had said—with what terrors he had threatened her, and she wondered if she already had the disease.

When she reached the house the Concierge and all the others were waiting, and called her into the lodge.

"Was Coupeau still alive?" they asked.

Boche seemed quite disturbed at her answer, as he had made a bet that he would not live twenty-four hours. Every one was astonished. Madame Lorilleux made a mental calculation:

"Sixty hours," she said. "His strength was extraordinary."

Then Boche begged! Gervaise to show them once more what Coupeau did.

The demand became general, and it was pointed out to her that she ought not to refuse, for there were two neighbors there who had not seen her representation the night previous, and who had come in expressly to witness it.

They made a space in the centre of the room, and a shiver of expectation ran through the little crowd.

Gervaise was very reluctant. She was really afraid—afraid of making herself ill. She finally made the attempt, but drew back again hastily.

No, she could not; it was quite impossible. Every one was disappointed, and Virginie went away.

Then every one began to talk of the Poissons. A warrant had been served on them the night before. Poisson was to lose his place. As to Lantier he was hovering around a woman who thought of taking the shop and meant to sell hot tripe. Lantier was in luck as usual.

As they talked, some one caught sight of Gervaise, and pointed her out to the others. She was at the very back of the lodge, her feet and hands trembling, imitating Coupeau in fact. They spoke to her. She stared wildly about as if awaking from a dream, and then left the room.

The next day she left the house at noon, as she had done before. And as she entered Sainte-Anne's she heard the same terrific sounds.

When she reached the cell, she found Coupeau raving mad! He was fighting in the middle of the cell with invisible enemies. He tried to hide himself; he talked and he answered, as if there were twenty persons. Gervaise watched him with distended eyes. He fancied himself on a roof laying down the sheets of zinc. He blew the furnace with his mouth, and he went down on his knees, and made a motion as if he had soldering irons in his hand. He was troubled by his shoes: it seemed as if he thought they were dangerous. On the next roofs stood persons who insulted him by letting quantities of rats loose. He stamped here and there in his desire to kill them.

And he leaped at the wall, but the soft cushions threw him back.

"Whom do you see?" asked the young doctor.

"Lantier! Lantier!"

He fell back against the wall, with his hands wide open before him, as if he were repelling the approach of some frightful object. He uttered two long, low groans, and then fell flat on the mattress.

"He is dead! He is dead!" moaned Gervaise.

The keeper lifted Coupeau. No, he was not dead; his bare feet quivered with a regular motion. The surgeon-in-chief came in, bringing two colleagues. The three men stood in grave silence watching the man for some time. They uncovered him, and Gervaise saw his shoulders and back.

The tremulous motion had now taken complete possession of the body as well as the limbs; and a strange ripple ran just under the skin.

"He is asleep," said the surgeon-in-chief, turning to his colleagues.

Coupeau's eyes were closed, and his face twitched convulsively. Coupeau might sleep, but his feet did nothing of the kind.

Gervaise, seeing the doctors lay their hands on Coupeau's

body, wished to do the same. She approached softly, and placed her hand on his shoulder, and left it there for a minute.

What was going on there? A river seemed hurrying on under that skin. It was the liquor of the Assommoir, working like a mole through muscle, nerves, bone and marrow.

The doctors went away, and Gervaise, at the end of another hour, said to the young surgeon:

"He is dead, sir."

But the surgeon, looking at the feet, said: "No," for those poor feet were still dancing.

Another hour, and yet another passed. Suddenly the feet were stiff and motionless, and the young surgeon turned to Gervaise.

"He is dead," he said.

Death alone had stopped those feet.

When Gervaise went back she was met at the door by a crowd of people, who wished to ask her questions, she thought.

"He is dead," she said, quietly, as she moved on.

But no one heard her. They had their own tale to tell then. How Poisson had nearly murdered Lantier. Poisson was a tiger, and he ought to have seen what was going on long before. And Boche said the woman had taken the shop, and that Lantier was, as usual, in luck again, for he adored tripe.

In the meantime, Gervaise went directly to Madame Lerat and Madame Lorilleux, and said, faintly:

"He is dead—after four days of horror."

Then the two sisters were in duty bound to pull out their handkerchiefs. Their brother had lived a most dissolute life, but then he was their brother.

Boche shrugged his shoulders, and said in an audible voice:

"Pshaw! it is only one drunkard the less!"

After this day Gervaise was not always quite right in her mind, and it was one of the attractions of the house to see her act Coupeau.

But her representations were often involuntary. She trembled at times from head to foot, and uttered little spasmodic cries. She had taken the disease in a modified form at Sainte-Anne's from looking so long at her husband. But she never became altogether like him in the few remaining months of her existence.

She sank lower day by day. As soon as she got a little money from any source whatever, she drank it away at once. Her landlord decided to turn her out of the room she occupied; and as Father Bru was discovered dead one day in his den under the stairs, Monsieur Marescot allowed her to take possession of his quarters. It was there, therefore, on the old straw bed, that she lay waiting for Death to come. Apparently, even Mother Earth would have none of her. She tried several times to throw herself out of the window, but Death took her by bits, as it were. In fact, no one knew exactly when she died, nor exactly what she died of. They spoke of cold and hunger.

But the truth was she died of utter weariness of life, and Father Bazouge came the day she was found dead in her den.

Under his arm he carried a coffin, and he was very tipsy, and as gay as a lark.

"It is foolish to be in a hurry, because one always gets what one wants finally. I am ready to give you all your good pleasure when your time comes. Some want to go, and some want to stay. And here is one who wanted to go, and was kept waiting."

And when he lifted Gervaise in his great, coarse hands, he did it tenderly. And as he laid her gently in her coffin, he murmured, between two hiccoughs:

"It is I—my dear, it is I," said this rough consoler of women. "It is I. Be happy now, and sleep quietly, my dear!"

THE END

FOR A NIGHT OF LOVE

For a Night of Love

I

HE LITTLE TOWN is built on a hill. At the foot of the old ramparts runs a deep brook, the Chanteclair, doubtless so named from the crystalline sound of its limpid waters. When one arrives by the Versailles road, one crosses the Chanteclair at the south gate of the city, over a stone bridge with a single arch, of which the broad parapets, low and rounded, serve as benches for all the old people of the suburbs. Opposite, rises Beau-Soleil Street, at the end of which is a silent square, Quatre-Femmes, paved with huge cobbles and invaded by a thickset weed which makes it green as a meadow. The houses sleep. Every half hour, the dragging step of a passer-by starts a dog barking behind a stable-door, and the one excitement in the square is the regular appearance, twice a day, of officers who go to their table d'hote in Beau-Soleil Street.

In the house of a gardener, to the left, lived Julien Michon. The gardener had rented him a large room, on the first floor; and, as the landlord occupied the other side of the house, facing his garden, Julien was left to himself. Having his own private entrance and stairway, he already lived, although only twenty-five years of age, like a retired bourgeois of small means.

The young man had lost his father and his mother while very young. An uncle had sent the child to a boarding-school. Then, the uncle died, and Julien had been filling a position as clerk in the post-office for the past five years. His salary was fifteen hundred francs, without any hope of ever getting more. But he could economize on that, and he did not imagine a larger or a happier life than his.

Tall, strong, bony, Julien had large hands that seemed in his way.

He felt himself to be ugly, with his square head left in a sketchy state as if roughly modeled by an indifferent sculptor. And that made him timid, especially in the presence of young women. His awkwardness engendered a startled attitude of mind, and a morbid desire for mediocrity and seclusion. He seemed resigned to grow old thus, without a comrade, without a love affair, with his tastes of a cloistered monk.

And that life did not weigh heavily upon his broad shoulders. Julien was very happy. He had a calm, transparent soul. His daily existence, with its fixed rules, was serenity itself. In the morning, he went to his office, peacefully took up the work left off the preceding day; then lunched on a small loaf, and continued his work. Afterwards, he dined, he went to bed and slept. The next day, the sun brought with it the same routine.

On holidays, he would go off on a tramp all alone, happily reeling off the miles, and returning broken with fatigue.

He had never been seen in the company of a petticoat, in the evenings on the ramparts. The working girls of P...., sharp-tongued wantons, had ended by leaving him alone, after seeing him, on several occasions, stand before them almost suffocated from embarrassment, and taking their laughs of encouragement for mockery.

Julien's paradise, the one place where he breathed freely, was his room. There only, he felt sheltered from the world. There, he straightened up; he laughed to himself; and, when he caught sight of himself in the mirror, he was surprised to find himself so young.

His room was vast. He had furnished it with a large canopy bed, a round table, two chairs and an armchair. But there still remained plenty of room for walking about. The bed was lost in the depths of an immense alcove; a small chest of drawers, between the two windows, looked like a child's plaything. He walked about, stretched himself, and never seemed bored. He never wrote away from the bureau, and reading tired him. His only passion was music. He would spend entire evenings playing the flute. That was, above everything, his greatest recreation.

Julien had learned by himself to play the flute. For a long time, an old yellow flute at a bric-a-brac merchant's on the market square had aroused his covetousness. He had the money, but he did not dare enter and buy it, for fear of exciting ridicule. At last, one evening, he grew bold enough to get the flute and carry it away on the run, hidden under his coat. Then, doors and windows closed, he had studied for two years out of an old method that he had picked up at a bookseller's.

During the last six months only, he risked playing with the windows open. He knew nothing but ancient airs, slow and simple, romances of the last century, which acquired an infinite tenderness as he stumbled over them with the awkwardness of a pupil filled with emotion. In the warm evenings, when the quarter was asleep, and this light song floated from the large room lighted by a single candle it seemed like a voice of love confiding to the solitude of the night what it never would have uttered in broad daylight.

Julien feared that they might complain of him in the neighborhood, but they sleep soundly in the country towns. Besides, Quatre-Femmes Square was inhabited only by a notary, M. Savournin, and a retired gendarme, Captain Pidoux, very convenient neighbors who went to bed and to sleep at nine o'clock. Julien was more anxious in regard to the inmates of a noble mansion, the Marsanne residence, which reared itself on the other side of the square, directly in front of his windows. It had a sad, gray facade, of the severity of a monastery. A flight of five steps, invaded by weeds, led up to a round door that was studded with enormous nails. The only story had ten windows in a row, the shutters of which were opened and closed always at the same hours, without allowing a view of the rooms, behind their heavy drawn curtains. To the left, the large chestnut trees of the garden made a green mass that spread in a widening wave to the ramparts.

Throughout the countryside, the mansion was celebrated, and it was said that strangers came long distances to visit it. There were also legends afloat concerning the wealth of the Marsannes. But Julien, during all the hours that he had sat at his windows seeking to penetrate the mysteries of that enormous fortune, had never seen anything but the gray facade and the dark mass of the chestnut trees. Never had anyone mounted the steps, never had the moss-grown door opened. The Marsannes had ceased to use that door; they went in and out through an iron gate on Saint-Anne Street. There was, besides, at the end of a lane near the ramparts, a little gate opening into the garden, that Julien could not see. For him, the house remained dead, like a palace in a fairy story peopled by invisible inhabitants.

One Sunday, in the square before the church, one of the post-office employees pointed out to Julien a tall old man and an old lady, telling him that they were the Marquis and Marquise de Marsanne. Then his companion informed him that they had a daughter still in the convent, Mademoiselle Therese de Marsanne; and that little Colombel, M. Savournin's clerk, was her foster-brother. As the old couple were about to turn into Saint-Anne Street, little Colombel approached, and the marquis held out his hand,—an honor he had not accorded anyone else. Julien suffered from that handshake; for this Colombel, a youth of twenty years, with sharp eyes and a mean mouth, had long been his enemy. He made fun of Julien's timidity; he had stirred up the laundry-girls of Beau-Soleil Street against him; and one evening, the two youths had come to blows on the ramparts, with the result that the notary's clerk retired with two black eyes.

Julien had lived five years on Quatre-Femmes Square when, one July evening, an event upset his existence. The night was very warm. He was playing his flute without a light, but absent-mindedly, when, all of a sudden, opposite him, a window in the Marsanne mansion opened, showing a brilliant light in the somber facade. A young girl leaned upon the window-railing and she raised her head as if listening. Julien, trembling, had stopped playing. He could not distinguish the face of the young girl, he could only see the waving mass of her loosened hair. And a light voice reached him in the midst of the silence.

"Didst thou not hear, Francoise? It sounded like music."

"A nightingale, miss," answered a coarse voice from the room. "Close the blinds; look out for night-insects."

When the facade had grown dark again, Julien could not leave his armchair. An hour later, he began to play again very softly. He smiled at the thought that the young girl probably imagined that there was a nightingale in the chestnut trees.

II

THE NEXT DAY, at the post-office, the great news was that Mademoiselle Therese de Marsanne had left the convent. Julien did not relate that he had seen her, with bare throat, and loosened hair. He entertained an indefinable sentiment toward that young lady who was to derange his habits. How could he henceforth play his flute? He played too badly to be heard by a young lady who evidently knew music.

Julien returned home furtively that evening. He did not light a candle. The window opposite did not open, but, towards ten o'clock a pale light shone through the blades of the blinds. Then, the light was extinguished, and he was left contemplating the dark window. Every evening, in spite of himself, he began that spying. Nothing seemed changed in the house; the old mansion slept on as before. It required trained eyes and ears to detect the new life. Sometimes, a light ran behind the windows, a corner of a curtain was lifted, there was a glimpse of an immense room. At other times, a light step crossed the garden, the sound of a piano was faintly heard accompanying a voice. Julien explained his curiosity by pretending to be annoyed at the noises. How he regretted the time when the empty house sent back a soft echo of his flute!

One of his most ardent wishes, though he would not admit it, was to see Therese again. He imagined her with pink cheeks, a mocking air, and shining eyes. But, as he did not dare approach his window in the daytime, he saw her only at night, enveloped by a gray shadow. One morning, as he was about to close one of his shutters to keep out the sun, he saw Therese standing in the middle of her room. She seemed to be reflecting. She was tall, very pale, with beautiful, regular features. He was almost afraid of her,— she was so different from the gay image he had formed of her. She had a rather large mouth, of a vivid red, and deep-set eyes, black and without a sparkle, giving her the air of a cruel queen. She came slowly toward the window; but she did not appear to see Julien. She went away again, and the rhythmic movement of her neck had so strong a grace that he felt as weak as a child beside her, in spite of his broad shoulders.

Then began a miserable existence for the young man. That beautiful young woman, so serious and noble, living so near him, made him despair. She never looked at him; she ignored his existence. After a month had passed, he suffered from the disdain of the young girl. She came to the window, looked out on the deserted pavement, and retired without divining his proximity, as he watched, anxious, on the other side of the square.

On warm evenings, he began playing again. He left his shutters open, and played, in the obscurity, those airs of bygone days, naive as the roundels of little girls. He chose moonless nights; the square was dark; no one knew whence came that song so sweet, brushing the sleeping houses with the soft wing of a nocturnal bird. And, the first evening, he had the emotion of seeing Therese approach the window, all in white negligee. She leaned on her elbows, surprised to hear again the music that greeted her the evening of her arrival.

"Listen, Francoise," she said, in her serious voice, turning towards the room. "It is not a bird."

"Oh!" answered the old woman, of whom Julien could see only the shadow, "it is some comedian amusing himself, a long distance from here."

"Yes, a long distance," repeated the young girl, after a silence.

From then on, Julien played louder every evening. His fever passed into the old flute of yellow wood. And Therese, who listened, was astonished at that music, the vibrant phrases of which, flitting from roof to roof, awaited the night to make their way to her. One night, the song burst forth so near that she surmised that it came from one of the old houses in the square. Julien breathed into the flute all his passion; the instrument vibrated like crystal. The darkness lent him such audacity that he hoped to draw her to him by the force of his song. And, effectually, Therese bent forward, as if attracted and conquered.

"Come in," said the voice of the aged lady. "The night is stormy; you will have nightmare."

That night, Julien could not sleep. He imagined that Therese had guessed him to be the musician, had seen him perhaps. Yet, he decided that he would not show himself. He was in front of his window, at six o'clock the next morning, putting his flute into its case, when the blinds of Therese's window were suddenly thrown open.

The young girl, who never arose before eight o'clock, leaned upon the railing. Julien did not move; he looked her in the face, unable to turn away. Therese, in her turn, examined him with a steady and haughty regard. She seemed to study him in his large bones, in his enormous and badly formed body, in all the ugliness of this timid giant. When she had judged him, with the tranquil air with which she would have asked herself whether a dog in the street pleased her or not, she condemned him with a slight pout. Then turning her back, she closed the window with deliberation.

Julien, his legs giving way under him, fell into his armchair.

"Ah! mon Dieu!" he exclaimed, brokenly. "I am displeasing to her! And I love her, and I shall die!"

He bowed his head upon his hands and sobbed. Why had he shown himself? When one was so ugly, he should hide himself and not shock young girls. He cursed himself, furious with his looks. He should have remained for her a sweet music,—nothing but ancient airs descriptive of a mysterious love.

In effect, he vainly breathed forth the liquid tender melodies: Therese no longer listened. She came and went in her room, leaned out of the window, as if he had not been opposite, declaring his love in humble little notes. One day, even, she exclaimed:

"Mon Dieu! How annoying that flute is, with its false notes!"

So, in despair, he threw the flute into a drawer, and played no more.

Little Colombel, too, scoffed at Julien. One day, on his way to the office, he had seen Julien at his window practising, and, each time that he passed, he laughed his mean little laugh. Julien knew that the notary's clerk was received at the Marsanne's, and it broke his heart,—not that he was jealous of that shrimp, but because he would have given his life to be for one hour in his place.

Francoise, the mother of the young man, had been for years one of the Marsanne household, and now she took care of Therese. Long ago, the aristocratic young lady and the little peasant had grown up together, and it seemed natural that they should preserve some of their former comradeship. Julien suffered none the less when he met Colombel in the streets with his lips puckered into a thin smile. His repulsion increased when he realized that the shrimp was not bad looking. He had a round cat-like head, but very delicate, pretty, and diabolical, with green eyes and a light curly beard on his soft chin.

Julien did not relinquish his dream of love without a great struggle. He remained hidden for several weeks, ashamed of his ugliness. Then, he was shaken by rage. He felt the need to display his large limbs, to force on her sight his rough face, burning with fever. So, he remained for weeks at his window, he wearied her with his regard. Even, on two occasions, he had sent her ardent kisses, with the brutality shown by timid people when they are prompted to audacity. Therese exhibited no anger. When he was concealed from her view he saw her going about with her royal air; and, when he thrust himself upon her, she preserved that air and was even colder and haughtier.

During that first year, the days followed each other without a break. When the summer came around again, he experienced a peculiar sensation: Therese seemed to have acquired a different manner. The same little events took place, —the shutters were opened in the morning and closed at night, there were the same appearances at the accustomed hours; but a new breath seemed to emanate from her room. Therese was paler and taller. On a very feverish day, he dared for the third time to send her a kiss. She looked at him intently, with her disquieting seriousness. It was he who retired from the window, his face crimson.

A single occurrence, toward the end of the summer, upset him, although it was very simple. Nearly every day, at twilight, the casement opposite was closed violently. The noise made him shudder, without his knowing why. For a long time, he could not distinguish whose hand closed the window; but, one evening, he recognized the pale hands of Therese. It was she who turned the fastening with that furious movement. And when, an hour later, she reopened the window,—but without haste, rather with a dignified slowness,—she seemed weary.

One autumn evening, gray and soft, there was a terrible grinding of the window fastening. Julien shuddered and tears sprang to his eyes. He waited for the window to open again. It was thrown wide as violently as it had been closed. Therese appeared. She was very white, with distended eyes and hair falling over her shoulders. She put her ten fingers upon her lips and sent a kiss to Julien.

Distracted, he pressed his fists against his chest and asked if that kiss was for him. Then, Therese, thinking that he had shrunk back, leaned forward and sent him a second kiss. She followed it with a third. He stood rooted, thunderstruck. When she considered that he was vanquished, she glanced over the little square. Then in a muffled voice, she said simply,—

"Come!"

He went down and approached the mansion. As he raised his head, the door at the top of the steps opened slightly,— that rusty door that was almost sealed with moss. But he walked in a stupor,—nothing astonished him. As soon as he entered, the door closed, and a small icy hand led him upstairs. He went along a corridor, passed through a room, and, at last, found himself in a room that he knew. It was the dreamed-of paradise, the room with the rose silk curtains. He was tempted to sink to his knees. Therese stood before him very erect, her hands tightly clasped, and resolutely holding under control the tremor that had possession of her.

"You love me?" she asked in a low voice.

"Oh! yes, yes!" he stammered.

She made a gesture, as if to forestall any useless words. She continued, with a haughty manner that seemed to render her words natural and chaste.

"If I gave myself to you, you would do anything for me, —wouldn't you?"

He could not answer,—he clasped his hands. For a kiss from her, he would sell himself.

"Well! I have a service to exact of you. We must swear to keep the bargain. I swear to carry out my part of it. Now, swear, swear!"

"Oh, I swear,—anything you wish!" he cried, in absolute abandonment.

The pure odor of her room intoxicated him. The curtains of the alcove were drawn, and the thought of that virgin bed in the softened shadow of the rose silk, filled him with a religious ecstasy.

Then, with a brutal movement, she tore the curtains apart, revealing the alcove, into which the faint evening light penetrated. The bed was in disorder. The coverings trailed over the sides, a pillow on the floor was ripped open as if by teeth. And, in the midst of the rumpled laces, lay the body of a man, thrown across the bed.

"There!" she explained in a strangled voice. "That man was my lover. I pushed him and he fell. I know no more. Well, he is dead; and you must carry him away! You understand? That is all,—yes, that is all! There!"

III

WHEN VERY SMALL, Therese de Marsanne made Colombel her fag and butt. He was her elder by about six months, and Francoise, his mother, had weaned him in order to nurse Therese.

Therese was a terrible child. Not that she was a noisy tomboy. On the contrary, she had a singular seriousness that made her appear as a well bred child before visitors, for whom she made graceful curtseys. But she had very strange ways; she would burst into inarticulate cries, stamping madly about, when she was alone.

No ever knew her thoughts. Even as a child, instead of her eyes being clear mirrors revealing her soul, they were like dark cavities, of an inky blackness, in which it was impossible to read.

At six years of age, she began to torture Colombel. He was small and delicate. She would take him to the bottom of the garden, under the chestnut trees, and, jumping on his back, would make him carry her. He was the horse, she was the lady. When, dizzy, he seemed ready to fall, she would bite his ear, clinging to him with such fury that she would sink her nails into his flesh.

Later, in the presence of her parents, she would pinch him and forbid his crying out under pain of being thrown out into the street. They thus had a sort of secret existence, their attitude when alone together changing in company. When they were alone, she treated him like a plaything, with a desire to break him. And as she wearied of reigning over him only when they were alone, she added the pleasure of giving him a kick or pricking him with a pin while in company at the same time fixing him with her somber eyes and daring him to so much as twitch.

Colombel bore that martyr's existence with dumb revolts that left him trembling, his eyes lowered, with a desire to strangle his young mistress. But, he was of a sly and vindictive nature. It did not altogether displease him to be beaten; he immediately gloated in his rancor. He would avenge himself by falling on the stones, dragging Therese with him, so that he would escape injury and she would be scratched and bruised. If he did not cry out when she pinched or pricked him, it was because he wished no one to interfere between them. It was their own affair,—a quarrel from which he intended to issue the conqueror later on.

Meanwhile, the marquis was worried about the violent conduct of his daughter. He considered it his duty to submit her to a rigid education. So, he placed her in a convent, hoping that the discipline would soften her nature. She remained there until her eighteenth year.

When Therese returned home, she was very well-behaved and very tall. Her parents were pleased to note in her a profound piety. The marquis and the marquise, secluded for fifteen years in the big house, prepared to open the drawing-room again. They gave several dinners to the nobility of the neighborhood; they had dancing. Their design was to marry Therese. And, in spite of her coldness, she made herself very agreeable. She adorned herself and she waltzed, but always with a face so pale that the young men who thought of falling in love with her were uneasy.

Therese had never mentioned little Colombel. The marquis had taken an interest in him, and, after giving him a schooling, had placed him in M. Savournin's office. One day, Francoise led her son up to Therese and presented to the young girl her comrade of former days. Colombel was smiling, very calm, and without a sign of embarrassment. Therese looked at him calmly, said she remembered him, and turned her back.

But, a week later, Colombel returned; and he had soon resumed his former habits. He came every evening to the house, bringing music and books. He was treated as of no consequence,—he was sent on errands like a servant or a poor relation. So they left him alone with the young girl, without thinking of harm. As in the old days, the two shut themselves up in the vast rooms, or remained for hours in the shade of the garden. In verity, they no longer played the same games. Therese walked slowly, with her skirt brushing the grass. Colombel, dressed like the rich young men of the town, accompanied her, whipping the path with a supple cane that he invariably carried.

Yet, she was again the queen and he the slave. She tortured him with her fantastic humors, affectionate one moment and hard the next. He, when she turned her head, swept her with a glittering glance, sharp as a sword, and his whole vicious figure stretched and watched, dreaming a treachery.

One summer evening, they had strolled in the heavy shadow of the chestnut trees for some time in silence, when Therese suddenly remarked:

"I am tired, Colombel. Suppose you carry me as you used to."

He laughed lightly; then answered seriously:

"I am willing, Therese."

Without another word, Therese sprang upon his back with her old agility.

"Now go!" she cried.

She snatched his cane, lashed his legs with it, and almost choking him between the flesh of her mature thighs forced him into a gallop beneath the thick foliage. He said not a word but breathed hard and tried to stiffen his slender legs, as the warm weight of the voluptuous girl bore him down.

But, when she cried out "Enough!" he did not stop. He ran all the faster, as if carried on by the impetus of the start. In spite of lashings and the digging in of her nails, he made for a shed in which the gardener kept his tools. There, he threw her roughly upon a heap of straw, and, his vindictiveness lending strength to his puny body, he vanquished her. At last, it was his turn to be master!

Therese became even paler, while her eyes grew blacker than ever and her mouth a more vivid crimson. She continued her devotional life.

Several days after the first occurrence, Therese, still panting with the desire to subjugate little Colombel, again leaped upon his back and lashed him. But the scene had the same ending. Again, she was thrown upon the straw and he had his way with her.

Before the world, she maintained a sisterly attitude toward him. He, also, was of a smiling tranquillity. They were again, as at six years of age, a couple of unruly animals, amusing themselves in secret by biting each other. Only, to-day, the male was victorious.

Therese received Colombel in her room. She had given him a key to the little gate that opened on the lane at the ramparts. At night, he was obliged to pass through the first room, in which his mother slept. But the lovers showed such calm audacity that they were never surprised. They dared make appointments in the daytime. Colombel came before dinner, and Therese, expecting him, would close the window to escape the neighbors' eyes.

They felt the constant need to see each other,—not to exchange tender expressions of love, but to continue the combat for supremacy. Often, they would quarrel fiercely, in low voices, all the more shaken by anger as they dared not scream or fight.

One evening, Colombel arrived before dinner. As he was walking across the room, still with bare feet and in his shirt-sleeves, he suddenly seized Therese and tried to lift her up, as he had seen strong men do at the fairs. Therese tried to break away, saying:

"Leave me alone. You know I am stronger than you. I will hurt you."

Colombel laughed his little laugh.

"Well! Hurt me!" he murmured.

He shook her as a preliminary to throwing her down. She closed her arms about him. They often played this game. It was usually Colombel who went down on the carpet, breathless, with inert limbs. But, this day, Therese slipped to her knees, and Colombel, with a sudden thrust, threw her over backward. He triumphed.

"So, you see you are not the stronger," he said with an insulting laugh.

She was livid. She raised herself slowly, and dumb, she grasped him again, her whole form so shaken by anger that he shivered. For a minute, they struggled in silence; then, with a last and terrible effort, she threw him backward. He struck his temple against a corner of a chest and fell heavily to the floor.

Therese drew a deep breath. She gathered up her hair before the mirror, she smoothed out her petticoat, affecting to pay no attention to the conquered Colombel. He could pick himself up. Then, she touched him with her foot. She saw that his face was of the color of wax, his eyes glassy, and his mouth twisted. On his right temple there was a hole. Colombel was dead.

She straightened up, chilled with horror. She spoke aloud in the silence.

"Dead! Here he is dead now!"

A terror held her rigid above the corpse. She heard his mother passing along the corridor! Other noises arose,— steps, voices, preparations for an evening's entertainment. They might call her, come to look for her at any moment. And here was this dead body of her lover, whom she had killed and who had fallen back upon her shoulders, with the crushing weight of their sin.

Then, crazed by the clamor in her brain, she began walking back and forth. She sought a hole into which to cast this body that was threatening her future. She looked under all the furniture, in the corridors, trembling with an enraged realization of her impotence. No, there was no hole, the alcove was not deep enough, the wardrobes were too narrow, the whole room refused its aid. And it was in this room that they had hidden their kisses. He used to enter with his light, cat-like step, and went away as softly. Never should she have imagined that he could become so heavy.

She still roved about the room like a trapped animal.

366

Suddenly, she had an inspiration. Suppose she should throw the body out of the window? But it would be found, and it would be easy to guess where it had come from.

Meanwhile, she had raised the curtain to look out into the street; and there, opposite, was the imbecile who played the flute, leaning out of his window with his tame-dog expression. She well knew his sallow face, unceasingly turned toward her and wearying her with its avowal of timid tenderness. The sight of Julien, so humble and so loving, stopped her short. A smile flitted across her pale face. Here was her salvation! The imbecile opposite loved her with the devotion of a dog who would obey her even to the commission of a crime. Besides she would reward him with all her heart, with all her body. She had not loved him because he was too gentle; but she would love him, she would buy him with the gift of her body, if he would help her conceal her crime.

Then, quickly, she took up the body of Colombel as if it were a bundle of linen, and threw it on the bed. Immediately opening the window, she threw kisses to Julien.

IV

JULIEN WALKED AS IN A NIGHTMARE. When he recognized Colombel on the bed, he was not astonished,—it seemed quite natural. Yes, no one but Colombel could be in that alcove, his temple indented, his limbs spread out in an attitude of revolting lewdness.

Meanwhile, Therese was speaking to him. He did not hear at first; the words flowed through his stupor with a confused sound. Then, he understood that she was giving him orders and he listened. Now, he must not leave the room; he must remain until midnight,—until the house grew dark and quiet. The party that the marquis was giving would prevent their doing anything sooner. But, in a way, it acted in their favor, for it so occupied everybody's attention that no one would think of coming up to the young girl's room. At the proper time, Julien was to take the body on his back, carry it down and throw it into the Chanteclair, at the bottom of Beau-Soleil Street. Therese explained the whole plan.

She ceased talking, and, placing her hands on the young man's shoulders, she asked:—

"You understand,—is it agreed?"

He shuddered.

"Yes, yes; everything you wish. I am yours."

Then, very serious, she leaned forward. As he did not understand, she said:—

"Kiss me."

He kissed her on her icy brow. And then they became silent.

Therese had again drawn the curtains of the bed. She sank into an armchair, where she rested, lost in the darkness. Julien also sat down. Francoise was no longer in the next room; the house sent them only muffled sounds. The room seemed to be asleep, and gradually filling with shadows. For nearly an hour, neither moved. Julien felt within his head great throbs, like blows, which prevented his reasoning. He was with Therese, and that filled him with happiness. But when the thought flashed on him that there was the corpse of a man in that alcove, he felt as if he would swoon. Was it possible that she had loved that shrimp? He excused her for having killed him. What fired his blood was the bare feet of that man in the midst of the rumpled laces. With what joy he would throw him into the Chanteclair, at the end of the bridge, at a dark and deep spot that he knew well! They would both be well quit of him; they could then belong to each other. At the thought of that happiness that he had not dared dream of in the morning, he saw himself on the bed in the very place where the corpse now lay; and the place was cold and he felt a terrified repugnance.

The clock struck, in the midst of the great silence. Therese got up slowly and lighted the candles on her dressing-table. She appeared possessed of her accustomed calm, coming and going with the quiet step of a person who busies herself in the intimacy of her room. She seemed to have forgotten the sprawling body behind the rose silk hanging. As she uncoiled her hair, she said, without even turning her head:—

"I am going to dress for the party. If anyone comes, hide yourself in the end of the alcove."

He remained seated; he watched her. She already treated him like a lover. With raised arms, she dressed her hair. He watched her with a thrill, so desirable she appeared with her back uncovered, lazily moving her delicate elbows and her tapering hands. Was she displaying her seductions, showing him the lover he was to possess, in order to make him brave?

She had just put on her slippers, when a step was heard in the corridor.

"Hide in the alcove," she said, in a low voice.

And, with a quick movement, she threw upon the stiffened body of Colombel all the linen that she had taken off,—a linen still warm with the perfume of her body.

It was Francoise who entered, saying,—

"They are waiting for you, Mademoiselle."

"I am coming, my good woman," peacefully answered Therese. "You can help me put on my dress."

Julien, through a slit in the curtain, could see them both, and he trembled at the audacity of the young girl. His teeth chattered so loudly that he grasped his jaw and held it in his hand. Beside him, under a chemise, he saw one of the icy feet of Colombel. If Francoise, the mother, should draw the curtain and strike against the bare foot of her child!

"Be careful," said Therese. "You are pulling off the flowers."

Her voice betrayed no emotion. She smiled like a girl

pleased to go to a ball. The dress was of white silk, trimmed with sweet briar,—white flowers, with the hearts touched with red. And when she stood in the middle of the room, she was like a large bouquet of virginal whiteness. Her bare arms and her bare neck continued the whiteness of the silk.

"Oh! how beautiful you are! How beautiful you are!" repeated the old Francoise. "And your garland,—wait!"

She searched for it, and was about to put her hand on the curtains to look on the bed. Julien almost let out a cry of anguish. But Therese, without haste, always smiling before the mirror, said:—

"It is there, on the chest. Give it to me. And don't touch my bed. I put some things on it, and you would mix them all up."

Francoise helped her to arrange the branch of sweet briar like a crown, with its flexible end drooping to the back of her neck. Francoise stood admiring her. She was ready and putting on her gloves.

"Ah! well," cried Francoise, "there are no holy Virgins in the church as white as you."

This compliment caused the young girl to smile again. She gave a last glance into the mirror, and started for the door, saying,—

"Come along; let us go down. You can put out the candles."

In the sudden darkness, Julien heard the door close and Therese's gown rustle along the corridor. The deep night was a veil before his eyes, but he preserved the sensation of that bare foot near him. He remained there, unconscious of the lapse of time, weighed down by thoughts heavy as sleep, when the door opened. By the rustle of silk, he knew it was Therese. She did not come in; she simply put something on the chest of drawers, while she murmured:—

"Here; you have not dined. You must eat, you understand."

The gown rustled away again. Julien shook himself and got up. He suffocated in the alcove; he could no longer remain near that bed, beside Colombel. The clock struck eight,—he had four hours to wait! He walked about muffling his footsteps. A feeble light, from the starlit night, made it possible to distinguish the dark masses of furniture.

Three times, he thought he heard a sigh issue from the alcove. He stopped, terrified. Then, when he listened intently, he found it was sounds from the festivities below,—dance music, the laughing murmur of a crowd. He closed his eyes; and, suddenly, instead of the blackness of the room, he saw brilliant lights, a flaming drawing-room, in which was Therese, in her white silk, waltzing to an amorous air. The whole house vibrated to joyous music. He was alone, in this horrible corner, shaking with fear!

Ten o'clock struck. He listened. It seemed as if he had been there years. Then, he waited bewildered. Having found bread and fruit under his hand, he ate avidly, with a gnawing of the stomach that he could not assuage. When he had eaten, he was overcome by lassitude. The night seemed never-ending. The distant music grew clearer; the dancing at times shook the floor. Carriages began to rumble.

He was looking fixedly at the door, when he saw a light through the keyhole. He did not hide. So much the worse, if anyone came in.

"No; thank you, Francoise," said Therese, appearing with a candle, "I can undress quite well alone. Go to bed,—you must be tired."

She closed the door and slipped the bolt. Then, she stood for a moment motionless, with her finger on her lip. The dance had not brought color to her cheeks. She did not speak. She set down the candle, and sat down opposite Julien. During a half-hour, they waited, looking at each other.

The doors had banged; the mansion had gone to sleep. But what worried Therese was the proximity of Francoise.

Francoise walked about a few minutes, then her bed creaked. For some time, she turned from side to side, as if unable to sleep. At last, her strong and regular breathing was heard through the wall.

Therese looked at Julien gravely. She said only one word, —"Come."

They drew aside the curtains. They wished to clothe the corpse which already had the rigidity of a lugubrious puppet. When that task was finished, their brows were moist.

"Come," she said a second time.

Without hesitation, Julien took up the body and threw it across his shoulders, as butchers carry calves.

"I will go before you," murmured Therese rapidly, "I will hold your coat,—you have only to follow. And walk softly."

They had first to pass through Francoise's room. They had crossed it, when one of the feet of the corpse struck against a chair. At the sound, Francoise awoke. They heard her raise her head, mumbling to herself. They remained motionless,—she, pressed against the door; he, crushed under the weight of the body, with the horrible fear that the mother might surprise them carrying her son to the river. It was a moment of anguish. Then, Francoise went to sleep again, and they stealthily reached the corridor.

But, here, another fright awaited them. The marquise had not gone to bed,—a streak of light came through the partly opened door. So, they dared neither go forward, nor retreat. For a quarter of an hour, they did not move, and Therese had the astounding courage to support the body so that Julien should not get tired. At last, the streak of light was obliterated. They could go on to the ground floor. They were saved.

It was Therese who again opened the ancient door. And when Julien found himself in the middle of Quatre-Femmes Square with his burden, he saw her standing on the flight of steps, in her white ball gown. She was waiting for him.

JULIEN HAD THE STRENGTH OF A BULL. When very young, in the forest near his native village, he amused himself helping the woodcutters, carrying tree trunks on his young shoulders. So, he carried little Colombel as easily as a feather. It was a bird on his back, that corpse of a shrimp. He hardly felt it,—he experienced an unholy joy in finding it so light, so thin, so absolutely nothing. Little Colombel would never sneer at him again, passing under his windows while he played the flute. He would never again humiliate him with his witticisms in the town. With a movement of the shoulder, he hoisted the body higher up, and, with set teeth, hastened his steps.

The town was dark. Yet, there was light in Quatre-Femmes Square, in Captain Pidoux's window. Doubtless, the captain was not feeling well; his large profile could be seen passing back and forth behind the curtains. Julien, anxious, slunk in the shadow of the houses. Suddenly, a slight cough froze him. He hid in a doorway. He recognized the wife of M. Savournin taking the air at her window. It seemed like fatality. Ordinarily, at that hour, Quatre-Femmes Square slept soundly. Fortunately, Madame Savournin soon returned to the side of M. Savournin, whose snores could be heard on the pavement.

Julien quickly crossed the square and breathed more freely in the narrowness of Beau-Soleil Street. There, the houses were so near together that the light of the stars did not penetrate the shadowy depths. As soon as he found himself thus sheltered, an irresistible desire to run sent him forward in a furious gallop. It was dangerous and stupid,— he knew it; but he still felt behind him the clear and empty space of Quatre-Femmes Square, with the windows of Madame Savournin and the captain lighted like two great eyes that watched him. His shoes made such a noise on the stones that he thought himself followed. Suddenly, he halted. He had heard, thirty yards away, the voices of the officers who patronized the table d'hote of the blonde widow. They must have been making merry over a punch, in honor of the exchange of one of their comrades. The young man told himself that if they came up the street, he was lost. There was no side street for him to turn into, and he would not have time to go back. He listened to the tread of their boots and the jingling of their swords with an anxiety that almost strangled him. For a moment, he could not have told whether they were approaching or going in the other direction. But the noises gradually grew fainter. He waited, then went on softly. At last, he reached the city gate. He passed through, but the sudden widening out of the country terrified him. There was a blue haze over the earth; a fresh breeze stirred; and it seemed to him that an immense crowd awaited him and breathed in his face.

Yet, there was the bridge. He could see the white roadway, the two parapets, low and gray like granite benches; he could hear the crystal music of the Chanteclair in the tall grasses. So, he risked it. He bent over, avoiding open space as much as possible, fearing to be seen by the thousand mute witnesses that he felt around him. The most terrible ordeal would be on the bridge itself, where he would be exposed to the view of the whole town, which was built like an amphitheatre. He had one last wavering of the will,—and then he crossed the bridge.

He leaned over; he saw the surface with its ripples like smiles. That was the spot. He unloaded his burden on the parapet. Before throwing the body in, he had an irresistible impulse to look at little Colombel again. He remained for several seconds face to face with the corpse. A cart in the distance rumbled and creaked. So Julien made haste; and, to avoid a noisy plunge, he let the body down slowly, leaning over as far as possible. He did not know how it happened, but the arms of the corpse caught around his neck and he was dragged over. He saved himself from going down, by a miracle. Little Colombel wanted to take him with him.

When he found himself seated on the stone, he was taken with a fit of weakness. He remained there, broken, his spine curved, his legs hanging, in the relaxed attitude of a tired pedestrian. And he contemplated the sleeping surface, where the laughing ripples had reappeared. One thing was certain,—little Colombel had tried to drag him down with him.

Then, he recalled Therese. She was waiting for him. He could see her standing at the head of the ruined steps, in her white silk dress with its sweet briar blossoms, all white and their hearts touched with red. But perhaps, she had felt cold and had gone to her room to wait for him.

No woman had ever waited for him before. Just one minute more, and then he would be at the rendezvous! But his legs were numb, and he feared that he would fall asleep. Was he a coward, then? And, to rouse himself, he pictured Therese as he had seen her at her toilet. He saw again her arms raised, moving her delicate elbows and her pale hands. He recalled that room of terrible voluptuousness, where he had known a mad intoxication. Was he to renounce that passion offered him, a foretaste of which was burning his lips? No; he would sooner drag himself upon his knees, if his legs refused to carry him!

But it was already a lost battle, in which his vanquished love had just expired. The image of Therese paled; a black wall arose, separating him from her. He had but one irresistible desire,—to sleep, to sleep forever! He would not go to the office to-morrow,—it would be useless. He would never again play the flute; he would never again sit by his window. So, why not sleep forever? His existence was ended,—he could go to bed. And he looked again at the river, trying to see if little Colombel was still there.

The surface spread, dimpled by the rapid smiles of its currents. The Chanteclair sang musically, while the country softened under the shadow of a sovereign peace. Julien murmured the name of "Therese." Then, he let himself go, and, rolling over, he fell like a bundle into the water, sending up great splashes of foam. And the Chanteclair continued its song among the grasses.

When the two bodies were found, it was thought there had been a combat, and a story was invented forthwith. Julien must have lain in wait for little Colombel to avenge his mocking; and he must have jumped into the river after killing his enemy with a blow on the temple.

Three months later, Mademoiselle Therese de Marsanne married the young Count de Veteuil. She wore a white dress, and her face was beautiful in its haughty purity.

LOVE POTIONS

Love Potions

I

*T*HE ONE great grief of Monsieur Chabre was that he had no children. He had married a Mademoiselle Catinot, the fair Estelle, a tall and beautiful girl of eighteen years. And for four years, he had been waiting, anxious, dismayed, hurt that his wishes should be unrealized.

M. Chabre was a retired grain merchant, with a big fortune. Although he had led the virtuous life of a bourgeois absorbed in the one idea of becoming a millionaire, he found himself at forty-five years of age with the heavy dragging steps of an old man. His pale face, lined by money cares, was flat and common-place as a pavement. And he despaired, for a man who has made a fortune that yields an annual income of fifty thousand francs certainly has a right to be astonished that it is more difficult to become a father than to become rich.

The beautiful Madame Chabre was then twenty-two years old. She was adorable with her peachy complexion and her golden hair. Her eyes of a greenish blue were like still water, beneath which it was difficult to read. When her husband complained of the sterility of their union, she drew up her supple figure, displaying the fullness of her hips and of her throat; and the smile that puckered the corners of her mouth said clearly, "Is it my fault?"

Among her acquaintances, Madame Chabre was considered a woman of perfect education incapable of giving grounds for scandal, sufficiently devout; in a word, nurtured in the good bourgeois traditions by a strict mother. Only, the delicate nostrils of her little white nose dilated nervously at times, which would have worried any other husband than a retired grain merchant.

Meanwhile, the family physician, Doctor Guiraud, a stout man, shrewd and smiling, had had several important conversations with Monsieur Chabre. He explained how backward science was still. Ah! no,—a child was not planted like an oak. However, not wishing to discourage anyone, he promised to think over M. Chabre's case. And, one morning in July he called to say to him,—

"You should go to the seaside, dear sir. Yes, it is excellent. And above all, eat a great quantity of shell-fish. Eat nothing but shell-fish."

M. Chabre, with rising hope, asked quickly,—

"Shell-fish, doctor? You think that shell-fish . . . ?"

"Exactly. The treatment has been known to succeed. You understand, every day, eat oysters, mussels, shrimps, sea-urchins, winkles, and even lobsters."

Then, as he was leaving, he added carelessly, on the threshold,—

"Don't bury yourself. Madame Chabre is young and needs amusement. Go to Tronville. The air there is very good."

Three days later, the Chabre household took its departure. But the former grain merchant had thought it unnecessary to go to Tronville where they would spend a large sum of money. One can be just as comfortable anywhere else while eating shell-fish; and, in a secluded place, the shell-fish should be more abundant and cheaper. As for amusements, there would always be more than enough of them. Besides, they were not going on a pleasure trip.

A friend had told M. Chabre of the little beach of Pouliguen, near Saint-Nazaire. Madame Chabre, after a journey of twelve hours, found the day passed at Saint-Nazaire very wearisome. They went to visit the port, they strolled about the streets where the shops hesitate between the dark little grocery shops of the villages and the large luxurious shops of the cities. At Pouliguen, there was not a single villa vacant. The little houses of boards and plaster, that seem to surround the bay with the brightly painted booths from a fair, were already occupied by English people and rich merchants from Nantes. Besides, Estelle pouted at those architectures, in which bourgeois artists had given reign to their imaginations.

The travelers were advised to go on to Guéraude for the night. It was Sunday. When they arrived, towards noon, M. Chabre experienced a sensation, although he was not of a poetic temperament. The sight of Guéraude, this feudal gem so well preserved, with its fortified walls and its deep-set gates, astonished him. Estelle gazed upon the silent city, surrounded by the great trees of its promenades; and, in the sleeping waters of her eyes, a revery smiled. But the carriage rolled along, the horse trotted under a gate, and the wheels danced upon the pointed stones of the narrow streets. The Chabres had not exchanged a word.

"A veritable hole!" at last murmured the former grain merchant. "The villages around Paris are better built."

As the couple left the carriage in front of the Hotel du Commerce, situated in the center of the city, the congregation of a near-by church began filing out from mass. While her husband looked after the baggage, Estelle sauntered up very much interested in the procession of the faithful, of whom a large number wore curious costumes. There were men who live on the salt marshes, dressed in white blouses and full breeches. There were farmers, a distinct race, who wore the short cloth vest and a large round hat. But Estelle was delighted, above all, with the rich costume of a young girl. The cap fitted in at the temples and terminated in a point. On her red bodice were embroidered showy flowers, and a belt embroidered in gold and silver clasped at the waist her three skirts of blue cloth, one over the other, pleated in tight pleats; while a long apron of orange silk was not long enough to hide her red woolen stockings and her little yellow slippers.

"Well, I declare!" said M. Chabre who had just come up behind his wife. "You have to be in Brittany to see such a carnival."

Estelle did not answer. A tall young man of twenty years issued from the church, offering his arm to an old lady. He had very white skin, a proud face, and hair of a tawny blond. He was almost a giant, with broad shoulders and members already knotted with muscles. And he was so tender, so delicate withal that that he had the pink face of a young girl without a hair on his cheeks. As Estelle looked at him intently, surprised by his great beauty, he turned his head, looked at her for a second, and blushed.

"Well!" murmured M. Chabre, "there at least is one with the face of a human being. He would make a handsome carabineer."

"It is Monsieur Hector," said the servant from the hotel. "He accompanies his mother, Madame de Plougastel. Oh! a child very gentle, very good!"

During the afternoon the Chabres went out upon the Mall, a vast raised promenade, forming a quarter of a circle, from the east gate to the south gate. Estelle remained thoughtful, gazing upon the admirable horizon that extended for miles beyond the roofs of the suburbs.

"Here is the young man of this morning," said M. Chabre suddenly. "Don't you think he resembles the Larivieres' little one? If he had a hump, the resemblance would be perfect."

Estelle had turned slowly. But Hector, on the edge of the Mall, absorbed by the distant view, appeared unconscious of their regard. Then the young woman resumed the walk slowly. She leaned upon the long stick of her sunshade. After a few steps, the bow on the sunshade became detached. And the Chabres heard a voice behind them.

"Madame, Madame. . . ."

It was Hector who had picked up the bow.

"A thousand thanks, sir," said Estelle with her calm smile.

He was very gentle, very good, this boy. He pleased M. Chabre right away. M. Chabre confided to him his perplexity in regard to a choice of a seaside resort. Hector, very timid, stammered,—

"I do not believe that you will find what you are looking for either at Croisic or at Batz," he said, pointing out the steeples of those little towns on the horizon. "I advise you to go to Piriac."

And he furnished details. Piriac was about nine miles away. He had an uncle in the neighborhood. Finally, upon a question from M. Chabre, he assured him that shell-fish were found there in abundance.

The young woman prodded the short grass with the tip of her sunshade. The young man did not raise his eyes to her, seemingly embarrassed by her presence.

"Guéraude is a very pretty town," said Estelle in her flute-like voice.

"Oh! very pretty," stammered Hector, suddenly devouring her with his eyes.

II

One morning, three days after the arrival of the couple at Piriac, M. Chabre, standing upon the pier that protects the little port, placidly watched Estelle as she swam and floated. The sun was already warm; and, correctly dressed in frock-coat and felt hat, he shielded himself with a tourist umbrella lined with green.

"Is it good?" he asked, to appear interested in his wife's bathing.

"Very good!" answered Estelle.

M. Chabre never bathed. He was in terror of the water, but he dissimulated this fear by saying that the doctors had strictly forbidden him sea-bathing. When a wave on the sands rolled up to the soles of his shoes, he drew back with a shudder, as if before a vicious beast that bared its teeth. Besides, the water would have disordered his habitual primness. He found it untidy and inconvenient.

"So it is good?" he repeated, dizzy from the heat, taken with an uneasy somnolence on the end of the pier.

Estelle did not answer, striking the water with her arms, swimming dog-fashion. With boyish daring, she bathed for hours, which greatly dismayed her husband who felt that the proprieties obliged him to wait for her on the shore. At Piriac Estelle found the baths she loved. She disdained the sloping beach; she went to the end of the pier, wrapped in her white fleece gown and, letting it slip off her shoulders, she calmly took a dive. Her bathing-suit, made in one piece without a skirt, outlined her tall form; and the wide blue girdle in compressing the waist rounded out the hips that balanced with a rhythmic movement. In the clear water, her hair imprisoned beneath a rubber cap, from which stray locks escaped, she had the suppleness of a blue fish, with a woman's head disquieting and pink.

M. Chabre had been for a quarter of an hour in the hot sun. Three times already, he had consulted his watch. He finally hazarded the timid remark,—

"You are staying in a long time, my dear. You should come out. Such long baths tire you."

"But I have only just gone in!" cried the young woman. "It is like being in milk."

Then, turning on her back,—

"If you are weary, you can go . . . I do not need you."

He shook his head; he declared that accidents happen so suddenly. And Estelle smiled in the thinking of what great help her husband would be if she were seized with a cramp. But, abruptly, she peered at the other side of the jetty, in the bay that curves to the left of the village.

384

"Hello!" she said. "What is that over there? I am going to see."

And she swam rapidly, with long, regular strokes.

"Estelle! Estelle!" cried M. Chabre. "Will you not go so far out? You know how I hate impudence!"

But Estelle did not listen to him; he had to resign himself. Standing on tiptoe to follow the white speck that his wife's hat made on the water, he was fain to content himself with passing the umbrella from one hand to the other, while he suffocated more and more in the overheated air.

"What did she see?" he murmured. "Ah! yes, that thing that is floating over there. Some dirty thing,—a bunch of seaweed, no doubt. Or a barrel. . . . No, it moves!"

And all of a sudden, he recognized the object.

"Why, it is a man swimming!"

Estelle, in the meanwhile, after a few strokes had also seen that it was a man. So she stopped swimming straight for him; but out of coquetry, pleased to show her daring, she did not return to the pier; she continued to swim for the open sea. She advanced quietly, pretending not to see the other swimmer. The latter, as if a current had borne him along, drew nearer and nearer to her. Then, when she turned to start back, there was a meeting which appeared quite accidental.

"Madame, how-do-you-do?" said the gentleman.

"Well! it is you, sir!" said Estelle gaily.

And she added with a light laugh,—

"How we meet again after all!"

It was the young Hector de Plougastel. He was still very timid, very strong, and very pink in the water. They swam without speaking, with a decent distance between them. They were obliged to raise their voices to be heard. Nevertheless, Estelle considered it her duty to be polite.

"We thank you for having recommended Piriac. . . . My husband is delighted."

"That is your husband,—is it not—all alone on the jetty?" asked Hector.

"Yes, sir," she answered.

And they were again silent. They looked at the husband, large as a black insect, above the water. M. Chabre, very puzzled, stretched upon his toes, asking himself what acquaintance his wife could have picked up on the open sea. It was unquestionable that his wife was talking to the gentleman. He could see them turn their heads towards each other. It must be one of their friends from Paris. But he searched in vain,—he could think of no one who would have dared venture so far out. And he waited, twirling his umbrella like a top.

"Yes," explained Hector to the beautiful Madame Chabre, "I came to spend a few days with my uncle, whose chateau you can see over there. Every day, for my bath, I leave that point opposite the terrace and swim to the pier. Then I return. Altogether, it is about a mile and a quarter. It is splendid exercise. But you, Madame, you are very brave,—I have never seen a lady so brave."

"Oh!" said Estelle, "when I was very small, I splashed about in the water. It is no stranger to me. We are old friends."

Little by little, they drew closer to avoid shouting. The conversation became more intimate. Hector pointed out several spots of interest on the coast.

"How beautiful!" she murmured. "How beautiful!"

She turned upon her back to rest.

"So, you were born at Guéraude?" she asked.

In order to talk more comfortably, Hector also turned over on his back.

"Yes, Madame; and I have been but once to Nantes."

He told her in detail of his education. He had been brought up near his mother, who was of a narrow piety, and who cherished intact the tradition of the ancient nobility. His preceptor, a priest, had taught him what is learned at

386

college, adding a great deal of catechism and heraldry. He could ride, fence,—in fact, was trained in bodily exercise. And still, with that, he seemed to have the innocence of a virgin. He went to communion every week, never read novels, and was engaged to marry, when he should come of age, a cousin who was very plain.

"What! You are only twenty years old!" cried Estelle, glancing at this colossal child.

Her manner became maternal. That flower of the strong Breton race interested her. As they floated, gazing into the transparence of the sky, they were wafted towards each other and he struck against her lightly.

"Oh! pardon!" he said blushing.

He dived, and reappeared some distance away. She began to swim again, laughing heartily.

"Your husband appears to be impatient," he said in an attempt to pick up the conversation.

"Oh, no," she replied calmly. "He is accustomed to waiting for me while I take my bath."

In reality, Monsieur Chabre fidgeted. He took four steps forward, returned, then started again, the while rotating his umbrella swiftly, evidently hoping to give himself more air. The conversation between his wife and the unknown swimmer began to surprise him.

Estelle suddenly surmised that he had not recognized Hector.

"I am going to call out to him that it's you," she said.

And, as soon as she could make herself heard from the pier, she raised her voice.

"You know, my dear, it is the gentleman from Guéraude who was so kind."

"Ah! very good! very good!" cried Monsieur Chabre.

He lifted his hat.

"Is the water good?" he inquired politely.

"Very good, sir," answered Hector.

The bathing continued under the husband's eyes, and he

did not dare complain although his feet were blistered by the burning stones. The young man and the young woman swam about. They advanced with short strokes, making the water foam about them. Then, they glided slowly in, making large circles that heaved and vanished. It was like a discreet and sensual intimacy thus to glide through the same wave. As the water closed up behind the fleeing form of Estelle, Hector sought to follow in the furrow, to place himself where her warm limbs had been.

"My dear, you are going to catch cold," murmured M. Chabre who was dripping with perspiration.

"I am coming out," she answered.

And she ran up the slope of the pier and was on the platform enveloped in her bathing-gown by the time Hector raised his head at the sound of the water dripping from her suit. He looked so surprised and vexed that she smiled, while she shivered slightly. She shivered because she knew that she was charming thus shaken, as her tall draped silhouette was thrown up against the sky.

The young man was obliged to take his leave.

"We shall look forward to seeing you again," said the husband.

III

THE CHABRES had rented at Piriac the first floor of a large house, with the window looking out upon the sea. As the inns were very second-rate, the Chabres had been obliged to a take a woman of the country to do the cooking. It was strange cooking,—roasts reduced to charcoal, and sauces of so disturbing a color that Estelle preferred to dine on bread. But, as M. Chabre said, they had not made the trip for the purpose of gormandizing. He rarely tasted either roast or gravy. He filled up on shell-fish, morning and evening, with the conviction of a man who takes medicine. The worst of it was that he detested those creatures of the sea, with their bizarre shapes; for, having been raised on bourgeois cooking, insipid and light, he had a child's taste for sweet things. The shell-fish, salted and peppered, so surprised his mouth with their strong and unexpected savors, that he could not prevent grimaces on swallowing them. But he would have swallowed the shells, too, if it had been necessary, so determined was he to become a father.

"My dear, you are not eating," he often cried to Estelle.

He insisted that she eat as many as he. It was necessary for the result, he said. Discussions arose. Estelle maintained that Dr. Guiraud had not spoken of her. But he answered that it was only logical for both of them to follow the treatment. Then the young woman puckered her lips, threw a glance at the sallow obesity of her husband, and a slight smile deepened the dimple in her chin. She said nothing more, not liking to wound anyone. Ever after, discovering a bed of oysters, she ate a dozen at each meal. Not that she, personally, needed them, but she adored oysters.

The life at Piriac was of a somnolent monotony. There were only three families that went into the water,—a wholesale grocer of Nantes, an old notary of Guéraude, who was deaf and unsophisticated, and a couple from Angers who fished all day long with the water to their waists. This little world made no noise. They bowed when then met, and their relations ended there. On the deserted wharf, the greatest event was to see two dogs fighting in the distance.

Estelle, accustomed to the noise of Paris, would have been bored to death if Hector had not come to see them every day. He became the great friend of M. Chabre after a walk they took together along the shore. M. Chabre, in a moment of expansion, confided to the young man the object of their journey, choosing for his narrative the chastest terms so as not to offend the purity of the big boy. When he had explained scientifically why he ate so many shell-fish, Hector, stupefied, forgetting to blush, looked him over from head to foot, without attempting to hide his wonder that a man should be obliged to follow such a diet. Yet, the following day, he presented himself carrying a small basket of prawns, which the retired grain merchant accepted with an air of gratitude. And, from that day, as he was a skilful fisherman and knew every rock in the bay, he never appeared without an offering of shell-fish. M. Chabre, delighted, no longer obliged to spend a cent, overwhelmed him with thanks.

Now, Hector always had an excuse to call. Each time that he arrived with his little basket, on meeting Estelle, he would say the same thing,—

"I bring some shell-fish for M. Chabre."

And the two smiled, their eyes crinkled up and shining. The shell-fish of M. Chabre amused them.

From then on, Estelle found Piriac charming. Every day, after the bath, she went for a walk with Hector. Her husband followed at a distance, for his legs were heavy and the young people walked too fast for him.

At high tide, for a diversion, they went to meet the sardine boats. When a sail came in sight, Hector signaled to the couple. But the husband, after the sixth boat, had declared that it was always the same thing. Estelle, on the contrary, appeared never to tire but to find renewed pleasure in running down to the wharf. Yet, little by little, Estelle and her companion neglected the sardines. They still went to see them, but they no longer looked at them. They started on a run and came back slowly as if weary, the while gazing at the sea in silence.

"Is there a good catch of sardines?" M. Chabre asked each time upon their return.

"Yes, fine," they answered.

Sunday evening, there was a ball in the open air at Piriac. The youths and the girls, with joined hands, whirled for hours, repeating the same verse to the same deep tone strongly accented. Those heavy voices, sounding out of the dusk, gradually acquired a barbaric charm. Estelle, seated on the beach, with Hector at her feet, listened, finally losing herself in a revery. The sea rose with a noise of caresses. One might have imagined a voice of passion, when the waves beat upon the sand; then, the voice softened suddenly, and the cry died away, with the water that receded, into a plaintive murmur of conquered love. The young woman dreamed of being thus loved, by a giant of whom she would have made a little boy.

"You must be weary of Piriac," M. Chabre sometimes suggested to his wife.

And she hastened to reply,—

"Why, no, my dear; I assure you I am not."

She enjoyed herself, in this secluded hole. The geese, the pigs, the sardines took on an extreme importance. At the end of two weeks, M. Chabre, who was bored to death, wished to return to Paris. The shell-fish must have taken effect by that time, he said. But she cried out,—

"Oh! my dear, you have not eaten nearly enough. I know you need a lot more."

IV

ONE EVENING, Hector said to the husband and wife,—

"To-morrow, we shall have a high-tide. We can fish for shrimps."

The proposition seemed to enchant Estelle. Yes, yes, they must go and fish for shrimps! M. Chabre raised objections. To begin with, one never caught anything. Secondly, it was much simpler to buy the shrimps from some woman of the place for a franc piece, and avoid wetting one's self to the waist and skinning one's feet. But he had to give in to the enthusiasm of his wife.

There was considerable preparation. Hector volunteered to furnish the nets. M. Chabre, in spite of his fear of cold water, had declared that he would be of the party. And from the moment that he consented to fish, he intended to fish seriously. In the morning, he had a pair of boots greased. Then, he dressed in light linen; but his wife could not prevail upon him to leave off his cravat, which he tied with loose ends as if he were going to a wedding. That knot was the protestation of a gentlemanly man against the rowdyism of the ocean. As for Estelle, she wore a short loose gown over her bathing suit. Hector, also, wore his bathing suit.

They started out at about two o'clock, each carrying a net over the shoulder. They had a mile and a half to walk over the sand and shingle to reach a rock where Hector claimed were veritable banks of shrimps. He led the party, calm, crossing the puddles, going straight ahead without thinking of the dangers of the path. Estelle followed him boldly, pleased with the freshness of the wet earth in which her little feet paddled. M. Chabre, who came last, did not see any necessity of wetting his boots before arriving at the scene of the fishing. He conscientiously went around the pools, jumped the little streams that the ebbing water left in the sand, chose the dry places with the careful manner of a Parisian who would seek the points of the paving-stones in the rue Vivienne on a muddy day. He was panting already, and he asked every few moments,—

"Is it still far, Monsieur Hector? Look! Why don't we fish here? I see some shrimps, I assure you. Besides, they are everywhere in the sea,—aren't they? I'll wager that it is only necessary to thrust in your net."

"Thrust it in, sir," answered Hector.

And M. Chabre, stopping to catch his breath, dipped his net into a pool as large as his hand. He drew out nothing, not even a weed. Then, he continued the tramp with a dignified air, his lips puckered. But losing the way in an endeavor to prove that there were shrimps everywhere, he found himself considerably behind the others.

The sea was ebbing fast, and was more than a mile from shore. The bottom of shingle and rocks was exposed, spread out like a moist desert, rugged, sadly magnificent, as if devastated by a storm.

Estelle gazed upon that naked immensity.

"Oh! how vast it is!" she murmured.

Hector pointed out certain rocks, green boulders, forming bars, worn by the tide.

"Those," he explained, "are uncovered only twice a month; then mussels are gathered from them. Do you see that brown speck over there? That is the 'Red Cow,' the best spot for lobsters. It is seen during only two tides of the year. But let us hurry. We are going to those rocks of which the tops are beginning to appear."

When Estelle entered the water, she lifted her feet high and splashed about, laughing as the foam spurted up. When the water was up to her knees, she had to struggle against the current.

"Don't be afraid," said Hector. "The water will be up to your waist, but the oceanbed rises immediately. We shall soon be there."

Little by little, they toiled upward, and found themselves upon a group of rocks that the receding water uncovered.

Estelle and Hector were ready for the first dip of their nets when a lamentable voice was heard. M. Chabre, planted in the middle of the small arm of the sea, inquired his way.

"Which way do you go? Straight ahead?" he cried.

He was in up to his waist; he dared not take a step, terrified by the thought that he might fall into a hole and disappear.

"To the left," cried Hector.

He went to the left, but as he sank deeper, he stopped again. He lamented.

"Come and give me a hand. I assure you there are holes,—I feel them!"

"To the right, sir; to the right!" cried Hector.

And the poor man was so ludicrous in the middle of the water, with his net over his shoulder and his beautiful knotted scarf that Estelle and Hector could not suppress a little laugh.

"I can't swim,—I can't!"

What worried him now was the return. When the young man had explained that they must not allow themselves to be overtaken by the tide, he became more worried.

"You will warn me,—won't you?"

"Have no fear; I'll look after you."

So they all began to fish. With their narrow nets, they rummaged in fissures. Estelle put into her quest all the ardor of a woman. It was she who caught the first shrimps, three large red ones that jumped about violently in the bottom of the net.

"It is curious," said M. Chabre, "I can't catch one."

As he didn't dare risk himself in the clefts, very much bothered besides by his heavy boots filled with water, he dragged his net over the sand and caught nothing but crabs, —five, eight, ten crabs at a time. He was scared to death of them and fought with them to drive them out of his net. Momentarily, he turned and looked anxiously at the sea.

"Are you sure it is still going out?" he asked Hector.

The young man contented himself with a nod. He was fishing boldly like one who knows the best places, and he was catching handfuls of shrimps.

When he raised his net beside Estelle, he put its contents into her little basket. For two hours, they fished.

"I assure you, the tide is coming in!" cried M. Chabre, agonizingly. "Look! A short time ago, that rock was uncovered."

"Without a doubt, it is coming in," said Hector, impatiently. "It is while it is coming in that one finds the most shrimps."

But M. Chabre lost his head. In his last fling with the net, he had brought up a strange fish, a devil of the sea, which terrified him. He had had enough.

"Come along. Let us go," he repeated. "It is stupid to be rash."

"When you are told that fishing is better when the tide turns. . . ." said Estelle.

"And it is coming in strong," murmured Hector with a mischievous gleam in his eye.

Effectually, the waves were coming in long swells, breaking against the docks with a loud clamor.

"I am going!" cried M. Chabre, with tears in his voice.

He started, despairingly sounding for holes with the handle of his net. When he had gone a few hundred feet, Hector persuaded Estelle to follow him.

"We are going to have the water to our shoulders," he said, smiling. "A real bath for M. Chabre. See how deep in he is already! You will have to get on my back and I will carry you. Otherwise, you would be soaked. Quick! Climb up!"

He held his back to her. She refused, embarrassed, blushing. But he insisted,—he was responsible for her safety. So she got up, placing her hands upon his shoulders. He, solid as a rock, straightened up as if he had no more than a bird upon his back.

"To the right,—isn't it?" cried M. Chabre in a lamentable voice, as the waves broke against his back.

"Yes; to the right, always to the right."

Then, as the husband went forward, shivering as he felt the water rising to his armpits, Hector dared to kiss one of the little hands resting on his shoulders. Estelle tried to withdraw them, but he warned her not to move or he would not answer for the consequences. And he forthwith began covering her hands with kisses.

"I beg of you, don't do that," pleaded Estelle, affecting anger. "You take a strange advantage. I shall jump into the water."

He began again, and she did not jump. He clasped her ankles firmly and devoured her hands with kisses, while he kept an eye on what could be seen of M. Chabre's back, —a tragic remnant of a back that threatened to disappear at every step.

"Did you say to the right?" implored the husband.

"To the left, if you wish."

M. Chabre took a step to the left and gave a cry. He sank to the neck, submerging his knotted scarf. Hector seized the opportunity to avow himself.

"I love you."

"Be still, sir, I command you!"

"I love you. I adore you. 'Til now, respect has kept me quiet. . . ."

He continued his long strides, with the water risen to his chest. She could not refrain from laughing, the situation appeared so ridiculous.

"Now, be quiet," she said, maternally, giving him a pat on the shoulder. "Be sensible; and above all, don't stumble."

That little pat filled Hector with enchantment; it was a promising sign. And, as the husband stood still in distress, the young man called out gaily,—

"Turn to the right now."

When they reached the shore, M. Chabre wanted to explain things.

"I came near staying out there," he stammered. "It was my boots. . . ."

But Estelle opened her basket and showed it to him filled with shrimps.

"What! You caught all those?" he cried astonished. "Why, you know how to fish!"

"Oh!" she said, smiling and looking at Hector, "Monsieur showed me how."

V

THE CHABRES were to leave Piriac in two days. Hector seemed dismayed, furious, and yet humble. As for M. Chabre, he questioned his health every morning and remained perplexed.

"You cannot leave here without having seen the rocks of the Castelle," said Hector. "We must arrange a tramp for to-morrow."

The rocks were barely a mile out. They would follow the shore, with its caves hollowed out by the waves, for about a mile and a half.

"Well, we'll go to-morrow," Estelle said finally. "Is the walking difficult?"

"No; there are two or three places where you will get your feet wet,—that is all."

But M. Chabre did not wish to wet his feet. Since his bath during the shrimp-fishing, he bore the ocean ill-will. So he showed himself hostile to this excursion.

Hector, to persuade him, had a sudden inspiration.

"Listen," he said. "You will pass the semaphore of the Castelle. The telegraph operators always have a quantity of superb shell-fish that they will sell you for almost nothing."

"Ah! that's a good idea!" said the grain merchant. "I will carry a little basket, and I'll have one more good fill."

The next day, they waited for low tide. The way was rough. They walked along a beach of dry sand into which their feet sank. The retired merchant puffed like a steer.

"Well! I am going to leave you and walk along the bank," he said finally.

"That is better. Follow the path," said Hector.

They watched him climb to the top of the cliff. Once there, he opened his umbrella and waved his basket, crying,—

"This is much better! Now, don't be rash! Besides, I am watching you."

Hector and Estelle climbed over huge rocks. The young man, in high boots, went before, springing from boulder to boulder with the grace and skill of a mountain hunter.

Estelle chose the same rocks, and when he turned to ask, "Shall I give you a hand?" she answered,—

"Why, no! I am not a grandmother!"

As they issued from a narrow passage, M. Chabre cried out from the cliff,—

"Ah! there you are! I was uneasy . . . Those chasms are terrifying."

He was six feet from the edge, shaded by his umbrella, his basket on his arm. He added,—

"The tide comes in rapidly. Take care!"

"We have plenty of time. Don't worry," replied Hector.

"Is that the semaphore,—the house with the mast?" asked M. Chabre. "I am going after the shell-fish. I will catch up with you."

Estelle ran over the rocks like a child. She leaped the pools, she approached the sea, seized with a caprice to climb to the summit of a mass of boulders which formed an island at high tide. And, after a laborious climb, she hoisted herself upon the top stone and surveyed the tragic devastation of the coast. She lost herself in revery, as if she had looked into a mysterious country.

When she returned to the base of the cliff, she found Hector with his handkerchief filled with limpets.

"They are for M. Chabre," he said. "I'll take them to him."

At that moment, M. Chabre returned disappointed.

"They have not so much as a mussel at the semaphore. I didn't want to come,—I was quite right."

But, when the young man showed him the limpets, he calmed down. And he was astounded at the agility displayed by the young fellow as he climbed up the face of the cliff by a way known only to himself. His descent was even more audacious.

"That's nothing," he said. "It is a veritable stairway,— you only need to know where the steps are."

M. Chabre wanted to start back. The sea was growing restless. The young man laughed and declared that they

398

would have to go on to the end. They had not seen the caves. So, M. Chabre had to resume his walk on the crest of the bluff. As the sun sank, he closed his umbrella and used it as a cane. In the other hand, he carried his basket of limpets.

"Are you tired?" Hector asked softly.

"Yes; a little," answered Estelle.

She accepted his offered arm. She was not tired, but a delicious abandonment invaded her more and more. They looked at each other, silent and smiling. The sea arose in short choppy waves, but they did not hear it. M. Chabre, above them, called out and they did not hear him, either.

"But this is crazy!" cried the merchant, shaking his umbrella and his basket of limpets. "Estelle, Monsieur Hector! You are going to be caught! You are walking in the water!"

They had not felt the freshness of the little waves.

"What is it?" murmured the young woman.

"Ah! it is you, M. Chabre! This is nothing,—don't be afraid. We have only 'Madame's Grotto' to see."

M. Chabre gesticulated despairing.y, adding,—

"It is madness! You are going to be drowned!"

They no longer listened to him. To escape the incoming tide, they went over the rocks and finally reached "Madame's Grotto." It was an excavation in a block of granite that formed a promontory. The roof rounded into a dome. During tempests, the water had polished the walls till they gleamed like agate. The gravel on the floor, still wet, retained a transparence that made it resemble a bed of precious stones. At the back, there was a bank of sand, soft and dry, of a pale yellow, almost white.

Estelle seated herself upon the sand and examined the cave.

"One could live here," she murmured.

But Hector, who appeared to be watching the sea, said suddenly,—

"My God! we are caught! The tide has cut us off. We will have to wait here two hours."

He went out and sought M. Chabre. That gentleman was on the cliff just above the grotto. When the young man announced their predicament, he cried triumphantly,—

"What did I tell you? But you wouldn't listen to me! Is there any danger?"

"None," answered Hector. "The sea enters the grotto only five or six yards. Only don't worry,—we can't get out for two hours."

M. Chabre became angry. Then, they were not to have dinner! He was already hungry. This was a nice excursion, he must say! Then, grumbling, he sat down on the short grass, placing his umbrella to his left and the basket of limpets to his right.

"I'll wait, there's nothing else to do. Go back to my wife. See that she doesn't take cold."

In the grotto, Hector seated himself beside Estelle. After a silence, he took her hand, and she did not withdraw it. She looked into the distance. The dusk fell. Little by little, the water entered the cave, rolling the gravel with a soft caressing sound. It brought with it the voluptuousness of space, a crooning voice, and irritating odor, charged with desire.

"Estelle, I love you," repeated Hector, covering her hands with kisses.

She did not answer; she was suffocated, as if lifted by that sea that rose. On the soft sand, half lying, she resembled a daughter of the sea, surprised and defenseless.

And, suddenly, the voice of M. Chabre reached them, thin, aerial.

"Aren't you hungry? I am famished! Fortunately I have my knife. I am eating my limpets."

"I love you, Estelle," repeated Hector, who held her clasped in his arms.

The night was black, the white sea lighted the sky. At the

entrance to the cave, the sea uttered a low complaint, while beneath the roof, a last remnant of light was extinguished. Then, Estelle let her head droop upon Hector's shoulder. And the evening breeze bore away their sighs.

Above, by the light of the stars, M. Chabre ate his shell-fish methodically. He gave himself indigestion eating so many without bread.

VI

NINE MONTHS after her return to Paris, the beautiful Madame Chabre gave birth to a boy.

M. Chabre, in ecstasies, took aside Dr. Guiraud, and confided to him with pride,—

"It was the limpets, I'll take my oath on it! Yes, a whole basket of limpets that I ate one evening under the most curious circumstances. Just the same, Doctor, I never should have believed that shell-fish possessed such properties!"

SHAKESPEARE HOUSE

These exquisite examples of bookbinders' and printers' arts are for you who appreciate the luxury of fine books. The decorative touch of 24 carat gold edged paper and many other elements add beauty and dignity to any library. The quality of the paper is high, the type modern and legible and, although individual volumes may contain more than 600 pages, they are designed to balance easily in the reader's hand. The varied contents are especially selected to insure reading enjoyment for the entire family. This book-lover's dream can be realized by anyone seeking to add really fine volumes, handsomely bound, to their own home libraries.

ASHENDEN or THE BRITISH AGENT

by W. Somerset Maugham

A thrilling story based on the eminent author's own experiences as a war-time secret government agent. Go with him (as Ashenden) on his perilous adventures into Italy, Germany, and Russia—where a slip means death.

PIPING HOT AND OTHER STORIES

by Emile Zola

Two of the greatest novels written by a world master of realism are presented here, along with two of his most applauded novellas. The books are PIPING HOT, a penetrating picture of Paris middle-class life, and NANA'S MOTHER, an equally vivid study of that city's lower class. The novellas are FOR A NIGHT OF LOVE and LOVE POTIONS, two piquant and pleasing romantic episodes.

SONNETS FROM THE PORTUGUESE

by Elizabeth Barrett Browning

These classical verses are probably the most intense love poems ever to be written in the English language. They bear simple eloquent testimony to a great love whose spell has enchanted all those who have read them.

RUBAIYAT OF OMAR KHAYYAM

Translated by Edward Fitzgerald

Here is the complete and unexpurgated Fitzgerald translation of tender, passionate verses by Omar, the Tentmaker—fully illustrated. It is poetry, the beauty of which has survived nearly 1,000 years!

COLLECTED WORKS OF PIERRE LOUYS

The immortal masterpieces of the great French student of pre-Christian manners and pagan moralities, in a single beautiful volume. Includes, in unabridged form, APHRODITE, THE ADVENTURES OF KING PAUSOLE, THE SONGS OF BILITIS, and SANGUINES. The volume is prefaced with a biographical and literary account of the author, and critical commentaries of the past and present.

THE FIRST LADY CHATTERLEY

by D. H. Lawrence

The D. H. Lawrence who achieved fame for his monumental portrayals of modern men and women in love, his profoundly searching examinations of the most intimate relationships between women and men, has written in THE FIRST LADY CHATTERLEY what is perhaps his most compassionate and revealing document, a novel of overwhelming candor and beauty. This edition also carries a biographical and literary appreciation on the author by his widow.

GILBERT AND SULLIVAN OPERAS

(Words and Music)

Here is the complete text of the three most popular comic operas of Gilbert and Sullivan: THE MIKADO, H.M.S. PINAFORE, THE PIRATES OF PENZANCE. The full librettos and words of the most popular songs, and thirty-eight pages of the musical score to enable the reader to hum, sing, or play them at will. Dotted throughout with Gilbert's amusing pen-and-ink sketches of the characters, and with a special introduction by Alan Pitt Robbins, this is a book that every music-lover and radio listener will value.

THE MODERN IMPROVED COOKBOOK

by Pearl V. Metzelthin

An up-to-the-minute housewife's and gastronomer's dream-book; provides 570 recipes and variations for every food from ice-cream to venison; gives more than 100 cooking hints that will delight the fledgling cook and grandma as well; has an entire section devoted to pressure cooking. Prepared by an internationally famous dietician.

BUTTERFIELD 8

by John O'Hara

Gloria Wandrous fell in love with one man—and had love affairs with many! She was a beautiful woman with a past—at an age when most girls are completely wrapped in their future. In BUTTERFIELD 8—a tragic wanton woman travels far—down the loneliest road!

ILL WIND

by James Hilton

An unforgettable tale of three women and six men—some of whom have no direct contact with the others; yet each is bound to the rest by an almost incredible series of adventures and exotic loves! From the pen of the author of "Goodbye Mr. Chips" and "Lost Horizon."

GLADIATOR

by Philip Wylie

Scientists were amazed by Hugo Danner's almost peerless mentality. Athletes envied his seemingly superhuman speed and strength. And women found in Hugo a lover such as had never been known before! The story of Hugo's remarkable powers began when his father had a tadpole, and—but that's Hugo's secret!

EASTERN LOVE STORIES

Here is a new and different reading experience. In this volume are assembled some of the best of the classic tales of China and the East. Written in a graceful and beautiful style, each story is redolent of the exotic excitement and unusual pleasures of the Orient. Here are charming and unusual tales such as "The Counterfeit Old Woman," "Eastern Shame Girl," "A Complicated Marriage," and a selection of stories from the Arabian Nights as well. Illustrated.

BUBU OF MONTPARNASSE

By Charles-Louis Philippe

The brilliant novel that gives the last unanswerable word on the shame of the streets—girls forced into the world's oldest profession by poverty, circumstances, and the predatory will of greedy men, and by romance conceived in trickery and flowered in vileness. A story of great emotional impact. Prefaced by T. S. Eliot, Nobel Prize winning poet.

A SHROPSHIRE LAD

by A. E. Housman

Bitter but sweet; emotional but calm—the verses of this unabridged collection are a source of stirring pleasure and comfort to lovers of lyric poetry everywhere. They are illustrated by Elinore Blaisdell.

A WOMAN'S HEART AND OTHER STORIES

by Guy de Maupassant

Here is the story of a young woman on the threshold o. life. A world-famous writer takes her through the passions, conflicts and intimacies, of romance, engagements, marriage, and finally disillusionment, in a novel remarkable for the depth of its understanding of the feminine psyche. A selected group of the Author's outstanding short stories are also included in this fine edition.